P9-DGV-848

REMEMBER THE ALIBI

LT-M Squire
Squire, Elizabeth Daniels
Remember the alibi /
G.K. Hall & Co.,
2000, c1994.

DATE DUE

MYNDERSE LIBRARY

Seneca Falls, N.Y.

Also by Elizabeth Daniels Squire
in Large Print:

Who Killed What's-Her-Name?

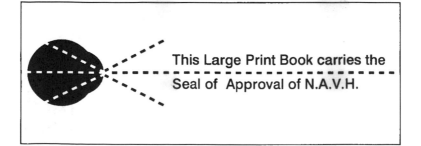

This Large Print Book carries the
Seal of Approval of N.A.V.H.

REMEMBER THE ALIBI

ELIZABETH DANIELS SQUIRE

G.K. Hall & Co. • Thorndike, Maine

WYNOERSE LIBRARY
31 FALL STREET
SENECA FALLS, NEW YORK 13140

Copyright © 1994 by Elizabeth Daniels Squire.

All rights reserved.

Published in 2000 by arrangement with Luna Carne-Ross.

G.K. Hall Large Print Paperback Series.

The text of this Large Print edition is unabridged.
Other aspects of the book may vary from the original edition.

Set in 16 pt. Plantin.

Printed in the United States on permanent paper.

Library of Congress Cataloging-in-Publication Data

Squire, Elizabeth Daniels.
    Remember the alibi / Elizabeth Daniels Squire.
       p.   cm.
    ISBN 0-7838-8858-9 (lg. print : sc : alk. paper)
    1. Dann, Peaches (Fictitious character) — Fiction. 2. Women
detectives — North Carolina — Fiction. 3. Large type books.
I. Title.
PS3569.Q43 R46 2000
  813'.54—dc21
                                              99-050004

LT-M

MYNDERSE LIBRARY
31 FALL STREET
SENECA FALLS, NEW YORK 13148

THANKS A MILLION

I'd like to thank the geography of western North Carolina for its unique beauty, and for allowing me the license to add a few roads that do not exist, especially near Boone in Watauga County, and at the high point of Maney Branch Road in Buncombe County.

I would like to thank all those wonderful people who have contributed information, expertise, and family jokes to this book. Thanks to:

— Joe Swofford of the Weaverville Pharmacy, who gave me valuable advice about prescription drugs that can be misused to kill.

— The incredible computer team at *The News & Observer* in Raleigh for showing me how stored information that has appeared in newspapers and information in the public domain, such as coroners' reports, can be combined by reporters to produce amazing discoveries. I want to specially thank Lany McDonald, who first piqued my interest, Dan Woods, one of the pioneers in exploring the possibilities in this field; Pat Stith another pioneer, and Mary E. Miller, the reporter whose interesting story about most likely dates of death contributed elements to the plot.

— *The Citizen-Times* in Asheville for allowing me to set a scene in its library, and Librarian Holly MacKenzie for being so helpful therein.

— *The Watauga Democrat* in Boone, and especially Rachel Rivers-Coffey, for use of the paper's bound volumes and for her expertise.

— Dr. Daniel L. Alcon, chief of the Neural Systems Lab at the National Institutes of Health and senior scientist at the Marine Biological Laboratory at Woods Hole, Massachusetts, for allowing me to use his fascinating book, *Memory's Voice: Deciphering the Mind-Brain Code*, almost as a character in this book.

— Bill Wright of Wright's Coin Shop in Asheville, for arranging an intriguing coin collection for Pop.

— Elizabeth Silver Cheshire for great suggestions on classic ways to forget, and Cleves Smith for continuing use of her house, with a few modifications, for Mary's.

— Elizabeth Benson Booz, Patricia Houck Sprinkle, Worth Squire, Bettie Parker, Gerry Koontz, and Jo Osborne for anecdotes, song lyrics, and jokes.

— My wonderful indispensable writing group: P. B. Parris, Geraldine Powell, Dershie McDevitt, Virginia Sampson, and Florence Wallin.

— Luna Came-Ross, my agent, without whom . . .

— Melinda Metz, my editor, and all those other great folks at Berkley.

— And most of all, thanks to my husband, C. B. Squire, who has been helpful in so many ways that this book would never have seen the light of day without him.

CHAPTER 1

I couldn't really blame my Swiss-cheese memory with the holes in it for landing me with a gun at my head. All I forgot was how suspicious I would look in a graveyard with a shovel in my hands.

I couldn't blame Ted, though he was the one who was writing an article about old Southern gravestones. He doesn't know the mountains like I do.

I couldn't even blame reckless youth: I, Peaches Dann, am fifty-five and Ted is sixty-four. We may be newlyweds, but we're both well-seasoned.

So are our cars. They both broke down at once. So we set out for the cemetery in the old truck my first husband, Roger, had used to haul things for the craft shop. Somehow after Roger died I couldn't get rid of the truck, even after I sold my interest in the shop. The truck was part of my history. And it comes in handy. I leave a shovel right to-hand in the back because I like to collect wildflowers for the end of the garden.

We set out on a beautiful fall day, the leaves

7

beginning to turn, green with gold and just a few accents of rosy red, all in flecks of color. The trees shimmered. The air smelled good. The old truck jounced along the back roads from the winding hardtop onto gravel and finally to dirt. The springs squeaked on the bumps. We passed a small white house that made up for needing paint with a row of large, perfect dahlias in front. Then we passed several trailers that could have used dahlias. One trailer had a car up on blocks in the yard. We turned into a trail half-hidden by grass. We knew about the trail from a booklet somebody had left at my father's house. Maybe for Ted. Pop couldn't remember. The graveyard was on our left, up a hill, with a faint path leading in. We jumped out of the truck and took stock.

Not enough people came there to make the path plain. But we followed it in among the trees. Birds flew up in alarm as if they didn't expect us. Because the place belonged to them. They only lent it to us humans.

Ted carried his camera and notebook. I had the bag of stuff to make grave rubbings. Ted always looks like he knows exactly what he's doing, striding ahead, shoulders back. He'd look like a hero except for his hair, which is always mildly comic. No matter how he combs it, his hair does what it pleases and soon stands out in all directions. Like antennae, I always think, to catch all the news. Kind of nice. I look at him and think: Thank you, God.

"You have the extra film, don't you?" he asked.

I reached in among the rolls of paper and crayons we'd brought to make rubbings of unusual stones. I felt for the roll of film that I'd said I'd be sure to put in beside them. And a picture came to me of the yellow box of film on the front hall table. I'd been about to put it in the bag when the phone rang. Damn. No film.

Ted saw the horror on my face and laughed. "You'll have to put something in your book about how to remember to take film to photograph gravestones," he said. "You seem to be covering every other possible contingency."

"I need a chapter," I said, "called 'Do It Now. Before the Phone Rings.'"

You see, Ted's even helpful with the book I'm writing. It's called *How to Survive Without a Memory*. I began to write it because some of my friends are getting older and finding it harder to remember and it upsets them terribly. But I have never had a memory, so I've had to learn to get around that problem. And since I actually solved a murder with the help of memory tricks that I've collected for my book, some people treat me like a celebrity. It's downright embarrassing. But kind of fun to be an expert.

"And another good idea to mention in my book," I said, "is to marry someone who can make a useful suggestion when you forget. I know a gal whose husband has a tantrum. That doesn't help."

Ted looked rather pleased with himself, which is how he should have looked. "I have half a roll of film left in the camera. So we'll be O.K."

We tramped on into beauty.

A few shafts of sunlight filtered into the green area full of graves, not more than fifteen real stones, and a section of those flattish field stones that poor people used to use to mark their loved ones' final resting place. A small graveyard. No one had mowed, but the under-growth was low. Probably because of the shade from the trees and the dead leaves. Leaves were drifting down, joining debris from years past. A few wild asters and black-eyed Susans grew among the gravestones — some stones so old they were weathered black.

I had been close to death — violent death — in the last year, and at first I had thought that looking at old tombstones with Ted would rub that hurt. Instead, the peace of old graveyards helped me accept it.

And I could even look forward to today's amusing surprise. We always found one. Like the two-fer headstone that Ted found in the eastern part of the state: for husband and wife. The husband had died first and the stone said: Here lies Colonel Whatever-it-was, and then a Bible verse: "He rests from his labors." And nobody had thought how it would sound when his wife died and they added her name to the tombstone:

Here lies Colonel Whatever-it-was.
He rests from his labors
and his wife Mary Elizabeth

Since she died way back in 1895, it seemed O.K. to laugh. Near us, in this graveyard in the North Carolina mountains, were an assortment of carved stones, some flat, some small obelisks with flat sides.

I was standing in front of a large flat marker: *Peggy Albert, 1855-1905. Beloved Wife of John Albert. I Lay Me Down in Green Pastures.* A hand, carved in stone, held a few flowers. I was five years older than Peggy had been, but not at all ready for green pastures. Ted was fourteen years older than Peggy was when she died.

I went over and gave him a little hug from behind: Ted, beloved husband of Peaches. Still thoroughly alive. My grandmother used to say, "Love while you can." And then she'd sing an old song about how we might not be in this world too long, how we were only traveling through.

And I thought how Ted and I are too old to take life for granted. But young enough to enjoy it. I felt rich.

And I made up my mind to enjoy all the people close to me who may only be here for a little while. Like Pop. He's eighty-three and sometimes he is totally illogical. He can't bear to be bored, so he stirs up trouble. Which I need like a hole in the head. At least I told

11

myself, my father isn't dull. And I'm very fond of the old stinker. I must enjoy him while I can. Even if it kills me. A falling leaf drifted by me, autumn yellow.

"Here's an interesting stone," Ted said. *"Martha Jones, Much-loved Wife of Arthur Jones, Ezekiel Brown, Lawrence Carpenter. 1851-1930. Love Will Find a Way."*

Wow. We had never seen a triple-header before. The kids of all three husbands must have sprung for the stone together. (I assumed successive husbands. Country graveyards were not much on bigamy. And this would be bigamy, wouldn't it, if it was three in a row?) I unrolled a large piece of paper from my bag, held it against the stone, and began to make a rubbing of it. And as I ran the black crayon across the stone, making the indented letters show up white, I thought about my own first cousin Mary, who hadn't been able to keep love. Not even once. Mary was newly divorced, bringing her new boyfriends by to see us, and to see Pop, as if we could somehow help. I said a little prayer for her.

I finished the rubbing and walked around to the area where the field stones were. Now I saw the larger stones from the back. I was amazed. On the back of one that was blackened with age, someone had painted a swastika in light green Day-Glo paint. Vandalism was even here. In this out of the way, peaceful place. I shivered. And then, worse yet, at the edge of the woods I saw a small stone angel knocked flat. I showed Ted. He grimaced and shook his head. We found the base from which it had obviously been knocked loose, a small girl's marker. We lay the angel gently by the stone base and then left the grave quickly. Not wanting to spoil the afternoon.

"Here's an interesting thing," Ted said. I followed him back into the main graveyard to look. He pointed to a cement marker flush with the ground. As if someone had made a square hole in the ground, poured in cement and then, before it hardened, written in the name and dates with one finger: *Mary Lou Jones Klonk, 1942-1977. Wife of William Klonk. Deliver Us From Evil.* "I think that's one of the most unusual stones I've ever seen," said Ted.

"Klonk," I said. "What an odd name. It sounds like the noise you'd make if you hit somebody over the head."

"A family with ingenuity," Ted said. "They made their own gravestones. Here's another." It said: *Baby Klonk, Daughter of William and Mary Lou Klonk, 1975-1976. She Sleeps in Jesus.* The lettering was unsteady, like a child had written the words. But someone had cared. So many graves of children in these old cemeteries. Though most babies' stones were from the nineteenth century. Not recent like Baby Klonk. I made a rubbing. The sun had gone behind a cloud. The woods around us were dark. I began to shiver.

"Here's another Klonk," Ted called. *"Robert Bourk Klonk, 1920-1972. Beloved Father of William Klonk.* He has a much fancier stone than the poured ones. But he must have been the grandfather of your Baby Klonk."

"The family must have fallen on hard times. I feel like there's a sad story in those three stones." I shivered.

Then off to the side of the graveyard, I saw a pretty fern. And I wanted something live to take from this graveyard with me. I could put it in the wildflower bed at the shady end of the garden. I wouldn't have thought to take the fern if it had been the only one in the woods or if it had been near a grave. It sat off by itself under a maple tree, as if it wanted to belong to me.

"I'm going to the truck to get the shovel and dig up that fern over there," I told Ted. He was absorbed in a rubbing. He merely nodded. I came back with my shovel and stopped by to see what message he was lifting. He was just finishing so I could read it: *Greater Love Hath No Man Than This, That He Give His Life For a Friend.*

"So many interesting stories just hinted at on gravestones," I said, leaning on my shovel.

Instead of Ted's answer, I heard a raspy voice.

"You don't belong to be here," the voice said. "Here to disturb the dead."

My head bobbed up. 1 turned round. And there in the edge of the wood was a small man

14

in high shoes, overalls, and a black felt hat. He had the most determined eyes I ever saw in my life, glittering, slitted, steady. And he was looking at us down the barrel of a long ugly gun.

I shivered more, because I saw how I looked to him. Shovel in hand, standing near a grave in his graveyard. But he couldn't think I was a grave robber. He couldn't possibly, could he?

All of him was stringy and strong. The hands on the gun were gnarled and firm. His mouth was a thin, compressed line. He must have been old but the hair that showed from under his hat was still as black as tar. A clump of black-eyed Susans bloomed around him as if to color round the menace. His hat was battered. His overalls faded pale. A man used to hardship I thought. Used to making do. Was he a Klonk?

"Hello," I made myself say to the man, as pleasantly as I could, "this is a beautiful place, isn't it?" He couldn't possibly think that we were the ones who had painted the Day-Glo swastika, could he? Or knocked down the angel? That we were back to do more damage?

He didn't return my greeting. He eyed my shovel angrily. His eyes were the dark blue of a storm sky. I opened my mouth to protest. He looked at Ted and waited. To him, Ted was in charge. Black Hat was a down-home male chauvinist.

"We came to study this interesting graveyard," Ted said, hearty and cheerful as if the gun weren't there. "My name is Ted Holleran. I write about history. Perhaps you'd be willing to tell us the history of this place."

Black Hat did not lower his gun. He kept his stare fastened hard to my shovel. If I said I only meant to dig up his fern he might shoot. "My name is Matt Jones," he growled, "and I protect my own."

I felt as if we were caught in a time warp. Back in feuding days. Feuding used to be a way of life in some mountain back coves. But not now. I hoped. The gun was pointed at us *now.*

I can lie better than Ted can. I don't tell serious, mean lies. Only white lies, to save a situation. The kind where if you get caught, at least the person knows you care enough about missing their birthday party to make up a good excuse. And brother, did we need a good excuse for why we weren't grave robbers or vandals or God knows what!

I pointed at Ted's camera. "We only wanted to take photographs of each other pretending to dig," I said. "They're to illustrate a story we wrote. We're only writers."

What I took to be a look of respect crossed the man's face. A kind of crinkling at the corners of the eyes. Mountain people respect a first-rate storyteller. But the respect probably meant he knew I was lying. His eyes stayed hard with anger.

He rasped, "You folks get out of here, and if

16

you ever come back, I'll shoot. I'll know, and I'll shoot."

He motioned with his thumb for us to follow him. Then he turned and walked ahead of us down the path, leading the way toward our truck. Light and silent in those heavy, high-topped work shoes. Showing us the back of his plaid shirt. He couldn't be too afraid of us. Perhaps his back meant contempt.

Just as he got to the truck, he turned and glared at Ted. "And you folks were lucky," he said. "This here is a copperhead den. I wouldn't come here lest I had a gun."

Damn, I thought. I could have said the shovel was to kill copperheads. He might even have believed me.

Or was he lying about the snakes, just to keep us from coming back in case he wasn't looking? That gleam in his eyes: Was it just anger? Or was he laughing at us inside?

Ted tripped on a root, and Black Hat raised his gun as if to shoot. I screamed. He aimed at me. But he wasn't quite mean enough to shoot.

He stood by the side of the road in the goldenrod with his gun pointed at us, waiting for us to get in the truck and leave. He watched without expression as I threw the shovel in the back. With a loud *klonk.* Klonk — how appropriate! The sun was still under a cloud and the goldenrod had turned from gold to dirty yellow. I wished I had never come to that place. We left fast.

But by the time we got home to our square log house with the stone terrace at the side, I felt grandly relieved. We had been in danger, but we were just fine.

We would get a bite to eat and go on to see my father. I smiled to myself. My father, bound to his wheelchair, would relish our adventure. "Live life to the hilt," Pop liked to say. "The only true waste is to be bored."

So we walked into our sunshine-yellow kitchen feeling good. The phone on the kitchen table rang. Ted picked it up.

"What?" he said. His face went sharp. He jerked the pen from his pocket and wrote "Pop" on the pad by the phone. Then he listened a long time, frowning, with only an occasional "Yes" or "No." My stomach knotted. Something was wrong.

"A list?" he said. And then, "But we need to know sooner than tomorrow. Listen, damn it, you can't scare us to death and then put us off like this." And then, "O.K., O.K., tomorrow, then."

He hung up the phone and turned to me. And I was sure I must have heard him wrong.

He said: "Your father seems to be on a serial killer's hit list."

And I thought: What? Do serial killers actually make lists?

CHAPTER 2

ABOUT NOON, FRIDAY

"So how did you like your trip to the grave-yard?" Pop asked.

There he sat in his wheelchair, to the left of the double glass doors that look out on his garden and the mountains beyond. His nose was sharper than our Appalachian peaks. His hair was as white as snow on their heights. His eyes roved around like an eagle's. His clothes hung, because he was thin as a bunch of twigs, but as he sat at his favorite round table, bookshelves at his back, he still looked positively regal.

"Sit down." He waved his hand at the chairs on his left and on his right. "You and Ted look like you need to sit." He was right. We hadn't even decided what to tell him yet. Except to play the thing by ear. We hadn't even decided what we could believe yet.

You see, because Ted's an ex-newspaper man, teaching part-time now, he has all these contacts and sources all over the place. Including the world memory. That's what I call the international network of newspaper library computer files.

Ted's friend Millie, head honcho of a newspaper library in the central part of the state, was the one who had called us up about Pop. She'd helped us find out who killed my aunt Nancy, so we paid attention to her. But what she told Ted was wild.

She said one of the reporters who specialized in computer assisted reporting had turned up a series of killings that seemed to be related. Somebody was defrauding old people and then killing them. And Millie didn't exactly explain how a list of names in a library book fit in, but she said Pop's name was on the list. She said we had to come down east and hear it all from the reporter in person. Or we wouldn't believe it, the way the police didn't believe it. And the reporter was out of town and wouldn't be back until the next day. That's what Ted told me. We didn't even know how scared we ought to be.

But Pop in his innocence was chipper. "Personally," he said, as we sat down on either side of him, "I wouldn't dare go to the cemetery. I might discover I didn't have a round-trip ticket."

He was having one of his good days, when he thought he could afford to joke about the graveyard, even if he *was* eighty-three and crippled with arthritis, and couldn't see well enough to read. (Other than that, he never seemed to miss a thing.) He could outlive us all out of wild curiosity and bull determination. Unless fate intervened. He might get a little vague now and then. And on a bad day, he was scared of things that weren't there at all. Like burglars breaking in. Or going broke. But on good days, like I say, his whole effort was to find a way, no matter what, to bring more plot into his life.

And now, I thought, it's as if his fairy god-mother had a mean, wild sense of humor, and had given him too much of what he asked for.

Ted and I did the easy thing. We told Pop about Black Hat and his big long gun. Pop's eyes shone like Christmas. He asked for every detail.

Then he made a pronouncement: "I salute you! You're good at having adventures, Peaches. Why, once, by forgetting your pocket-book, you actually solved a crime. Which is why I have nicknamed you the Absent-Minded Detective!" He grinned, like that made him very important: Franklin D. Roosevelt without cigarette holder. "By using all your silly memory tricks, Peaches," he crowed, "you found the killer. And when you can do that, nobody can ever complain about how you forget things, can they?"

That was a nice thought.

But then he added, "I wish the absent-minded detective would ride again!"

Stop that, you old fool! I wanted to yell. That would not have been polite. Or useful.

"I don't want to be any kind of a detective, if you want the truth," I fumed. "What I'd really like," I said, "is to stay home quietly and concentrate on writing my book on how to survive without a memory."

Pop shrugged scornfully.

"And," I added, "I'd like a new nickname. You might call me the absent-minded match-maker. I'd like to see my cousin Mary find the right man."

Ted reached over and took my hand and looked me straight in the eyes. He did that when he meant: Please listen well. "You must not worry about that *now*," he said. He emphasized "now" so that I knew he meant with all this other stuff on our minds, all this worry about Pop.

"I know how it is," Ted said. "Because Mary lost her mother and her brother, and her husband left her, you feel guilty about her" — he said that gently — "when you have absolutely no reason to feel that way."

At least he didn't add what I knew he thought: that Mary was going overboard with so many new boyfriends, picked up God-knows-where. Mary kept bringing friends over to meet Pop. And we didn't really know who they were. And now it could be dangerous for Pop to meet new people.

But I couldn't keep my mouth shut. I just naturally want to see the people I love live one hundred percent. "I want everybody to be as happy as I am," I said. "I guess I do feel guilty when I don't help. And Mary's working hard to cheer herself up," I added, taking my hand back. "She has this new plaque on her refrigerator that says 'You have to kiss an awful lot of frogs before you find a prince.' "

The doorbell rang. I opened the door myself. I was closest, and Lily, Pop's sitter on duty, was out in the kitchen.

There was Mary with a frog, so to speak. It was her friend Harry, the one we'd met the other day. The one Pop liked because he listened so well.

Good, I'd have a chance to talk to Mary about the Pop problem.

Meanwhile I could remember Harry because he was un*hairy*. He had this smooth round face. Like one of the cherubs on the tombstones Ted was studying. And the hair on his head was such a pale blond it almost vanished. Unhairy Harry. I held onto that because it was a little bit funny. I can remember things better that are funny. I'd put that in Chapter One of *H.T. S.W.A.M.*

Unhairy Harry sure did want us to like him, I'll say that. He smiled like we were wonderful, and his eyes immediately sought out mine and then Pop's and then Ted's. He shook my hand and then stepped over to shake hands with Ted and Pop. It wasn't just that he had good manners. He had urgent good manners, as if we mattered to him a lot.

"You remember Harry August," Mary said. "He helped the kids make chocolate chip cookies, and they've sent you some, Pop." She put a plate of cookies on the table. That pleased Pop to death.

And the matchmaker in me was pleased to see this Harry was back. He seemed the nicest of Mary's boyfriends so far, at least the nicest that she would put up with at all. About thirty. Just a year or two younger than Mary. That's what she said. He was downright boyish, to tell the truth.

And I wanted someone to care for Mary with her Dutch-boy brown hair and slightly snubbed nose. She's not beautiful, but she's perky. Like a pixie. She moves quickly the way that somehow I imagine a pixie would. Oddly enough, her eyes can twinkle and be vulnerable at the same time. I didn't used to notice that. Men seem to like that combination. Constant good cheer and please-don't-hurt-me eyes. Her cheeks are pink. And no matter how bad things get, she always smiles.

Mary gave Pop a big hug, and asked if he was still reading the life of Attila the Hun. He liked biography, and he liked one sexy sitter who read it to him. Mary was wearing a cheerful red skirt and blouse. A red that matched Pop's Persian rug. Mary loved lively colors. She never wore anything else. She gave Ted a kiss on the cheek and sat down next to him. Hairy sat next to her, across Pop's round table from me.

I was glad Mary was reaching out, I told myself: Yes, it's true that whatever doesn't kill us makes us stronger. Sure, she'd met some

24

men in strange places, like that racing-car driver who was picking out vitamins at the health food store and asked her advice. Or the builder on vacation from New Jersey she took up with in a doughnut shop in the mall. I didn't like his roving-around eyes. O.K., I admit it. I thought she was being a little careless about where she met men. A little hysterically post-divorce lonely, maybe. But she'd said she met Harry on a Sierra Club hike. That wasn't too bad. And he'd told us he was a poet. Not husband material, alas. He worked at any job that came to hand. But pleasant company until husband material came along. And when Mary brought her boyfriends by, it really pleased Pop. And thereby got him off my back.

"Glad to see you, Harry," Pop said cordially. "You're just in time to hear how Peaches and Ted nearly got shot."

Harry stared across the table at me, eyes wide. His eyes were a dark blue. He turned to Ted in amazement. "Today?" he asked nervously, as if that put us all in danger. "How on earth did that happen?" He was such a gently rounded person all over, as if he still had baby fat under his jeans and plaid shirt. He made me feel maternal. Silly, but true. He made me feel like telling the whole graveyard story.

"The first thing that happened," I said, "was that we found a booklet on the floor by this table several days ago. Right about where you're sitting, Mary. You've still got it in your

25

jacket pocket, haven't you, Ted?"

Ted reached into the inside pocket of his tan corduroy jacket and pulled the booklet out. The cover was shiny with a picture of trees and a path and a large title in black letters: *Quiet Walks Near Asheville*. "We like to walk," he said.

"And I don't," Pop announced, patting the arm of his wheelchair. "So I told them I had no idea where the booklet came from, but they should take it, and they did. So, I suppose," he said, turning to me, "you could accuse me of getting you shot at." I ignored that. Ted's mouth twitched, as if he knew he shouldn't laugh. Could something as simple as a booklet that we couldn't trace be dangerous? Oh, come on!

"I'm collecting material for an article about old Southern tombstones," Ted said, "and the strange thing is that there was one walk that passed near an old graveyard, and somebody had turned down the corner of the page about that walk. Almost as if they'd left the booklet for me."

"In fact," I said, "we wondered if somebody hadn't done that and told Pop and he forgot."

"I had never seen the booklet before," Pop said firmly. "But someone could have left it for me. I used to hunt over near that graveyard when I was young. I once *was* young."

Harry began to smile, but he didn't say a word. He just looked pleased with himself. The cheerful cherub. And I thought maybe it was because he saw a good story coming.

Mary said, "What does a booklet have to do with getting shot?"

"We decided," I explained, "to drive to the graveyard that was on the map of the walk, and look at the tombstones."

"When I'm casing an old graveyard, we tend to make that a whole day's project," Ted said, "and so we drove."

"And we drove in my old truck which always has a shovel in the back." I could see Mary beginning to squirm. She likes people to get right to the point of stories. Preambles bore her.

Ted winked at me. He'd noticed too. And we plunged on into the adventure with Matt Jones, otherwise known as Black Hat. About how he pointed his gun at us because he must have thought we sprayed a stone green and knocked an angel flat. And because I had that damn shovel in my hand in his family graveyard, like I was up to no good. Pop was enjoying the whole story almost as much the second time.

But I shivered. I could feel that gun pointed right at my head again.

Pop laughed. "You're O.K. now, Peaches, and a little danger is a good thing. Keeps you lively."

"Speak for yourself, Pop," I told him.

I noticed that Harry was smiling broadly. He reached way over in front of Mary and picked up *Quiet Walks Near Asheville* in front of Ted.

"Maybe I can solve a part of the mystery for you," Harry said, obviously pleased with himself. "This book of walks was written by one of Mary's other friends." He turned to Mary. "Isn't that right?" Was there just a little resentment in his voice? Was he jealous?

Mary reached over and snatched the booklet. "By Aloysius Haven," she read, her voice rising in surprise. "But he teaches history! He teaches at the university. I didn't know he wrote anything. He never said so. And I only brought him here once just for a minute. He couldn't have given that book to Pop. I'd have noticed." Another visitor that I knew very little about.

"You must know him, Ted," I said. But Ted shook his head. "I only teach journalism part-time, and he's in another department. I've heard his name. The kids say they never know what he'll do next. They like that."

"And I don't remember him," Pop said. "Peaches, I expect you to figure this out."

Mary handed the booklet back to Ted, and turned to me. "That silly book isn't worth worrying about," she said. "I've found another joke to put in your book about how to survive without a memory." Mary can't bear for anyone to worry. Her way to show love is to keep you cheered up.

My way is to act grateful. I pulled out a pen and paper from the pocketbook that always hangs over my shoulder so it can't get away.

"Good," I said to Mary. "Tell me the joke. Because I have a whole chapter about how if you can't remember, you might as well laugh."

And Mary launched her story: "These two girls who were best friends in high school happened to meet about seventy years later and decided to have lunch together." Mary likes to dress a story up when *she* tells it. She said they had lunch at the Magnolia Grill and ordered oysters. "About halfway through lunch, one of them said, 'You know, I'm terribly embarrassed to admit this, but my memory just isn't what it used to be, and I know we're best friends and all that, but I hope you won't mind telling me your name.' The other one kind of frowned and squirmed and then she asked: 'How soon do you need to know?' "

We all laughed except Pop, who said he thought that was silly. "You're making fun of old people," he said, sad-eyed like a hound. How he can look like an old eagle and a young hound all at once I've never understood, but he can. "I'm only eighty-three," he said, "and that's not old anymore. But I don't like you making fun of old folks."

Mary just went on smiling and didn't seem to mind. Harry raised an eyebrow at her, at an angle where Pop couldn't see.

Yep, she was going to be a survivor. With our help. She had to be because she has those two kids. Who were home, I guessed, with a baby-sitter.

I thought how innocent Mary's poet looked in his jeans and running shoes and plaid shirt. Almost naive. Mary, too, with her shy-deer eyes and her pixie smile and bright colors and jokes. And Pop was innocent in his way. Almost like a child. And if it really was true that he was on some kind of a hit list, that childlike innocence could be dangerous.

Pop kept staring at Harry, as if he wanted to be sure the man would do for Mary to go out with. Like Pop was in charge of that. "What was your name again?" he asked.

Harry turned and winked at Mary as he asked Pop: "How soon did you need to know?" We all laughed, even Pop.

Mary stood. "We have to go. We just wanted to drop off the cookies."

"Wait, I wanted to show you something before you go," I said. I led her into Pop's bedroom, out of earshot. We stood by Pop's little bedside chest with the marble top. My mother's picture with the kind eyes looked at me over Mary's shoulder.

"Look," I said, "I don't exactly know how to put this, but our friend Millie Lyon who works on the newspaper down east, called and told us that a man who defrauds old people may be moving up this way." I decided not to tell her more than that until we knew it was true. Mary has a hard time keeping secrets. "Will you help me see that nobody suspicious gets a chance to meet Pop?"

Mary got the point and flushed red. "I only bring my friends by because I know he likes it," she said.

I threw my arms around her. She was stiff. "Oh, Mary, we want to meet your friends. We love you a lot. You know that. You're like a daughter to me. But we should all be careful — me, too." She relaxed a little, but not entirely. I felt bad. Mary needed to feel trusted.

She stepped back and smiled. Mary always smiled. "I'll let you meet my friends first and then decide which ones are X-rated, and which ones have your seal of approval."

After Mary and Harry left, I let Ted tell Pop to be careful. Pop does respect Ted's worldly savvy.

"Pop," he said, "you remember about my friend Millie Lyon, who runs the newspaper library."

"Of course," Pop said. "She helped you find out about all the people who might have killed Nancy, and sort out the right one." A wave of sadness passed over his face as he mentioned his sister. We were still recuperating in our hearts.

But Pop keeps his mind on the future, not the past.

"Millie called us," Ted said, "and warned us that there's someone who is stealing money from wealthy older people, and he may be moving into the Asheville area. She wants Peaches and me to look into this."

Pop burst into a pleased smile. "That's a good idea."

"But in the meantime," Ted said firmly, "while we find out more about this, I hope you'll be careful, especially of anyone who says that he can make you rich."

"But I am rich!" Pop cried, waving his arms at the antiques and Persian rugs. "All by my own smartness. Nobody will ever get the best of me!"

I prayed he was right.

CHAPTER 3

SATURDAY MORNING, OCTOBER 3

Before we actually took off for the newspaper in Raleigh, I put my coffee cup down on the kitchen table, where Ted and I were finishing breakfast, and picked up the phone to check on Pop. A large bluejay was splashing in the birdbath out the kitchen window. Cocky as my father. And the bird was just as vulnerable if my neighbor's cat outwitted him. The cat sat almost still, half-hidden by a clump of mint about twelve feet from the birdbath. A calico cat with one notched ear. Ginger. I punched the button for my father's number, which made a seven-note tune; then I listened to three rings with my eyes still on the cat. The mint was her favorite place for watching birds. If she went closer to the birdbath, I'd rap on the window and scare the jay away. I wished it were as simple to protect my father.

Pop answered. He kept a phone right by him at his favorite table. "What did you say the name of that man in the graveyard was?" he asked as soon as he recognized my voice. He sounded totally cheerful. Not worried about a thing.

"He told us his name," I said. "Now what was it? Why do you want to know?" A second bluejay arrived to fight with the first. I watched them swoop at each other and splash the water mean as could be. Pop was mean about his money. So he would be O.K., I told myself, even if this computer stuff were true.

"Never mind why I want to know his name," Pop said. "Ask Ted."

And unfortunately I asked Ted before I stopped to notice the tone in his voice. Pop has that dreamy tone when he's about to do something he knows I won't like.

"Matt Jones," Ted said, still sipping his coffee and reading the paper. He has to read every word first thing in the morning, no matter what.

Matt Jones. Somehow, even with my mind on seemingly more important things, I knew I was going to need to remember that name. So I tried a way that I'd been reading about in books on memory. Convert a word into a visual image and it'll stick better. Experiments actually proved that was so. So I pictured Black Hat pointing his gun at me. Then I pictured him rolled flat as a mat by a big bulldozer. Matt. I pictured him, flat as a mat, on a bed of bones, which rhymes with Jones. Also appropriate, since I met him in a graveyard. It couldn't happen to a nicer man. Matt Jones.

"You know, we are related to some Joneses," Pop said. "I think we are distantly related to a Matt Jones through my great-grandfather's brother Jeeter. Was he the one whose daughter married a Jones from Buncombe County?" He paused. "You know, that man was only trying to protect the family graveyard. I have to admire him for that."

"Admire him?" I gasped. My heart sank. Pop may be mean about money, but he can be dumb about people. Ted looked up from his newspaper and raised both eyebrows as if to say, What gives?

"That man pointed a gun at me," I said. "That's not something *I* admire."

"Oh, you always exaggerate," Pop said. "I think I'll ask him over and find out exactly how we're related. I've lost track of that side of the family. Family is important."

"Pop," I said, gripping the phone hard in one hand and clenching my other fist, "you need to be careful about who you invite into your house. Ted warned you about that. Someone might rob you."

"Pooh," he said. "I can take care of myself. And you're going off right now to see that Millie, aren't you? That's why you called."

"Pop," I said, "promise me you'll behave until we get back. Promise me you will not even call this Matt Jones while we're out of town. Because if you do, I'm not going to tell you one word about what we find out."

With the dignity of a Justice of the Supreme Court, Pop said, "I always take care of myself."

I hung up, gritted my teeth, and made up my

mind not to worry.

"Perhaps," I said to Ted, "I can find him a biography of a Supreme Court justice and bring it back for a present. He sure as heck needs a better role model than Attila the Hun." We both laughed. This was all so wild, we might as well laugh.

"I'll have to stop along the way and get some cash," Ted said as he sorted through his wallet. "We can use plastic, but it's always good to have some folding money."

"I've got some," I said. "I'll get it." Good. Something useful I could do to take my mind off Pop. "If you don't mind laundered money," I said.

Ted's eyebrows went up. "Don't tell me you've joined the Mafia. Even your father has never done that."

"No," I said as I cleared away the breakfast dishes, "I just got fifty dollars to have on hand in case we needed it and I forgot and left it in the pocket of my shirt when I washed it. I was keeping it separate from the money in my pocketbook because I wanted to stick it in a book in the bookcase for emergencies."

"I suppose you're writing a chapter on laundered money?" he asked dryly, stuffing his wallet in the back pocket of his khaki pants.

"Well, that's a thought," I said. "I could write a whole chapter on financial management for the absent-minded. And I happen to know a lot of tips. For example, Uncle Sam makes pretty durable stuff. Unless you use a lot of bleach, it comes out fine to use. But checks are totally ruined. And travelers checks end up almost blank. Whoever said that travelers checks were safer than money never put one through the washing machine."

Ted was grinning at me, as if the idea of laundered money delighted him.

"Why, you're trying to divert me!" I said. "And it worked. And of course, you're right. There's no point in worrying about Pop. It won't help. We simply have to find out the facts."

I poured myself another gulp of coffee and warmed my throat. One for the road. Then off to research serial killing. Or, God willing, something less.

Out the window, the cat was inching closer to the jays on her belly. And as I watched, she sprang for the birdbath. "No!" I screamed, and rapped the window. A wild flap of wings. The cat was left with tail feathers from one unlucky bird, but the jays flew away.

The birds depressed me. They'd be back. Ginger was not often successful in catching a bird. But now and then, my feline friend left me a dead bird on the lawn. To prove that guile can overcome wings? Or just to prove that predators are a part of nature? If Ginger didn't catch a bird in my sight, she'd catch a bird out of my sight. Which was all the same to the bird. But at least, I thought, cats did not kill their own kind. They left that to humans.

CHAPTER 4

LATE SATURDAY MORNING

We started the four-hour trip down to Millie's newspaper just an hour after I told Pop to behave, and just a day after Black Hat Matt Jones, which rhymes with bones, chased us from the graveyard.

I wore my most becoming green blouse and print skirt. If she was going to play up to Ted, per usual, at least I'd be armed. Ted swore Millie meant nothing by it. I knew he was just her old friend, right? In which case it could never hurt me to look my best anyway, right?

We drove up to the newspaper building and parked where a sign said "Reserved for Visitors." Since it was Saturday morning not too many cars were in the spaces. A spotted dog meandered in front of us and up the cement walk toward the building, not seeming sure where he was going. I wished him luck lost in the city.

We found our way past flower beds mulched with some gray fluffy stuff — by gosh, it was shredded newspapers: how appropriate! — and in to the big front desk where a young woman with long green earrings and curly eyelashes asked where we would like to go. She buzzed Millie as soon as we told her, and announced us. "Go to the third floor," she said.

Ted remembered the way we'd come months before: down a corridor and beyond a bank of desks. Millie came out to meet us, beaming. She was done up as sexily as ever in a red mini-skirt and sweater. Me in my green and Millie in red, and Millie all bangly with charm bracelets and gold earrings. We reminded me of Christmas. Though I certainly lacked the spirit.

"Thank you for coming," she said, and she reached out and took hold of our hands in welcome, but I knew whose hand she held tighter and enjoyed most. And was it just manners that made Ted say how good it was to see her again? She led us back into the library with its rows of shelves filled with books, tapes, files, and goodness knows what. We threaded our way back to her desk in a small clearing.

"Perhaps the best thing is just to introduce you to Watt Jenks right away, and let him explain what he's discovered," she said. "He can find out so much so fast with his computer that it makes our heads spin. But never anything like this before."

We followed her around several desks to a corner where a young man sat in front of a computer. He had black curly hair that looked impossible to comb, and piercing black eyes. He also looked about sixteen years old. Most people do to someone my age, but it always shocks me to find an expert who looks so young.

The time my computer disk crashed, a friend sent me a clipping from the *Shoe* comic strip, and the editor owl was saying, "If your computer won't work, there are only three things to do: Kick it, turn it off and back on, or ask the advice of somebody twelve years old." This boy almost qualified.

Anyway, Millie said, "This is Watt Jenks," and this Watt stood up from where he'd been at work in front of his computer terminal and shook hands. He was all angles: elbows, knees, nose, and more. If he ever hugged me, I'd expect to say Ouch. But there was no reason he ever would.

"I never dreamed I could use my computer to prevent murders," he cried. He ran around, captured three small chairs as angular as he was, waved us to sit down, and said, "Let's get to work. I'm going to start at the beginning and show you what I discovered step by step. Otherwise you won't believe it."

I wanted to say, But please hurry and tell us the part about my father. But I could see he was a one-step-at-a-time person, not the jump-to-the-end type.

He waved his hand at the computer screen, which had nothing on it but columns of numbers, and he said, "A pattern of murder. Waiting to happen again. And I only came across it by chance." His eyes were feverish. I thought, I'm glad he's the mad reporter and not the mad villain. I'd hate to have him after me.

Millie turned to us, pleased with herself. "This did not originate from any of the *ordinary* ways of computer reporting, although the usual ways have been a help, too."

Watt was off. He began to talk like lightning. And I thought, Yes, I can remember his name. Watt, short for kilowatt. Because when he gets on his subject he's downright electrified. And he wants to find out about killing. Kilowatt. Watt.

He had on faded jeans and a funky black T-shirt, but he seemed to shine with hope and fear. Gradually I was able to digest what he was saying.

Near his elbow a large reel — not unlike the thing one of my cousins used to put her knitting yarn on to wind it off into balls — had thin brown recording-type tape looped around it. The tape seemed to proceed into a personal computer. Watt sat in front of it. He had his elbow on the desk, half facing us.

"Now, on that reel," he said, "is a tape from one of the state government's mainframe computers. The tape is full of information that's in the public domain. A newspaper is entitled to see that information if we want to. Motor Vehicle Department records, for example, or Occupational Safety and Health Administration reports — or, in this case, county coroners' reports. These coroners' reports include all sorts of information about each person who dies. What county he died in, his age, the cause, the result of the autopsy, what his occupation was, whether he died in the hospital, and so forth. Only the names are not included. We actually have those reports covering the last twenty years."

I got busy taking notes. Ted did, too. Two heads are better than one. So are two notebooks.

I wondered how on earth you could start matching unsolved murders out of all that information. Wouldn't it be easier just to get them from police files?

Watt didn't give me long enough to ask. "Now, the wonderful thing is that software has been designed that will take that mainframe computer information and put it into a personal computer program," he continued. "One coroner's report won't tell us much, unless it's related to a story we are doing about a particular person. But if you get twenty years' worth of those reports, the computer can sort that information in all sorts of useful ways."

Watt acted as excited as if he were telling about exploring for buried treasure, even though except for an occasional wave of those big angular hands, he sat perfectly still. It was all in the eyes. They were like bomb fuses. I felt that if he got excited enough he would detonate. Millie seemed excited, too. She stood behind Ted with her hand on his shoulder. Those long fingers, tipped in red nail polish that matched her short skirt, were curling round my Ted. And when would we get to the list that included Pop?

"For example," said Watt, "if I had information for several counties, I could find out how common each kind of death was in each county. And if there were a huge spike of one kind of death in our county versus the others, I'd know that might be a problem worth looking into, right?

"In other words, there are ways of cutting all this raw material up into chunks that make sense and that a nontechnical person can understand."

Well, that was me, all right: about as nontechnical as it's possible to be.

"I got fascinated by the fact that there are certain days of the year when more people die than on any others," Watt continued. "Take February eleventh. On average, more people in our county die on that day than on any other day in the year. The next most common time to die is around Christmas."

"My grandmother died on Christmas," I said. "My mother said she thought Granny had deliberately held on in order not to miss it. She said with old people that seemed to happen a lot." But this was October. I was getting impatient.

"At any rate," Watt went on, "while I was

43

looking into this, I asked for all the individual death reports in our city for February eleventh for the last two years, and since our newspaper library computer has all the stories available, I also pulled up all the actual obituaries, and news stories about deaths for the same days. A few real cases make the statistics more concrete.

"And, because my uncle had once been the victim of a scam, I especially noticed one news story. This happened right here in our city and no one guessed what it meant. I've printed out copies for each of you," he said, handing us printouts.

The first story was dated February 12, nearly two years back:

Mary Anne Allison, 65, of 35 Winslow Road, was found dead in her living room Tuesday afternoon. Police said Mrs. Allison, a widow, was found near a glass with her fingerprints on it and an empty pill bottle. A neighbor had alerted the police that newspapers and mail were piling up for Mrs. Allison, who never traveled, and that she did not answer her door. The police department is continuing to investigate.

Mrs. Allison is survived by a son, Brian. Her husband, the late Arthur Allison, was a member of the state legislature in the 1970s.

The second printout said an autopsy confirmed that she died of an overdose of sleeping pills. Investigation showed that she had had at least $30,000 in her bank account a month before. On February 11 it contained only $75. Securities worth at least $100,000 had been liquidated, and that money was gone, too. Her broker told police that, beginning about two months before, she had said she was making other investments.

Well, Pop hadn't lost anything like $130,000. His broker knows Pop can be a little vague and he would have told us.

"Even though the investigation ended with a finding of suicide, that story brought me from statistics to here and now with a jolt," Mr. Kilowatt said. "I discovered it matched another story.

"I was in Winston-Salem visiting my brother John two weeks ago," he continued, "and I told him about the deadliness of February eleventh. And then I told him about poor Mary Anne Allison. And John said there was a story just like this one in the *Winston-Salem Journal* about six weeks ago." Watt pointed at the stories in our hands.

"So I pulled up sleeping-pill deaths in Winston for July and August, and by damn, he was right!"

He handed each of us another computer printout:

George and Anna Davis, 78 and 72, were found sitting together in their living room dead on Wednesday, July 28. Their only son, Martin Davis of Dallas, arrived on a visit to find them dead with two glasses and an empty bottle of sleeping pills between them, police said.

On the table near the pills was their bank statement, which showed their account was virtually empty. Their son reported that George Davis' valuable stamp collection had disappeared. A note found near the couple in George Davis' handwriting said, "We give ourselves unto the mercy of the Lord."

Police said crimes of fraud that victimize the elderly are on the rise, and these apparent suicides highlight the tragedy when old people are left destitute. Police are continuing to investigate.

"But, you see, the investigators in that case, and in the earlier one, believed they were dealing with fraud that resulted in suicide. They didn't look beyond that." Watt shook his head like he knew better.

And I thought with a jolt: Good grief, we must really watch Pop.

"Now, the recent case happened in the city of Winston-Salem," Watt said. "The other case was here, so of course there were different investigators. So I tracked down the man who had handled the case here, and I found out there had been a suicide note for Mary Anne Allison, too, and the amazing thing was the language was almost identical: *'I throw myself on the mercy of the Lord.'* "

Ted whistled softly. I got goose bumps. How eerie to use the same suicide words. How careless or crazy of the killer. And how had someone forced the victims to write that same note?

"So I got excited," Watt said. "I pulled up all the coroners' reports for the last ten years, and for a wide area, where death resulted from an overdose of sleeping pills. Five of those were between Christmas and February eleventh, though many others were not. More fell between Christmas and February eleventh than at any other time. I suspected some sort of pattern. So, through our regular newspaper computer database, I pulled up the obituaries or news stories about deaths at that time of year. And I've even researched newspapers that weren't part of the computer network, where I had friends on that paper who would look up sleeping-pill deaths for me in their files. All but one case involved fraud."

"But the recent case you found — the one that made you suspect murder — wasn't at that time of year," Ted said. "It was on July twenty-eighth." Count on Ted for logic.

Watt nodded strongly, like Ted was a genius. "Yes. Exactly. I wondered about that. So after I discovered the case in Winston in July, I then pulled up *all* the news stories that mentioned death by an overdose of sleeping pills in the Southeast in the last ten years. That is, cases at *any* time of year. And over the last six years, I found several more deaths that fit the pattern, even one in Atlanta with a nearly identical suicide note. So our killer prefers midwinter — but he doesn't always stick to it."

He handed Ted a large map of the Southeastern U.S. Also a highlighter. "You trace these," he said. "You'll see what I mean. We'll start with Miami six years ago. The regular computer network turned up a case there even before the first in this state. An elderly woman. Miami, February fifth. Now the next one was in Atlanta, January twenty-first of the following year, also an elderly woman. Next July the same year, an eighty-year-old man. He lived in Columbia, South Carolina. Our killer skipped around at first. And may have skipped around more than we know. I wasn't able to check some newspapers which weren't on-line." He scowled in disapproval of such papers.

"In January the next year," Watt continued, "an AIDS victim from Smithfield, North Carolina, fit the pattern more or less. His friends claimed money had vanished, but that wasn't proved. He was an eccentric who kept his money in cash. Then the lady here on February eleventh two years ago. Then, Durham in August of the same year. Next, a case in Greensboro just up Interstate Forty, back to February again. Now Winston-Salem on July twenty-eighth, just thirty miles farther up I-40. The killer seems to have angled up

48

I-40 in your direction."

A chilling thought.

Watt frowned. He began to crack his bony knuckles one by one. "And the frustrating thing is that I can't get the law excited. This is too scattered. On this case here in town two years back, I think I've persuaded them it was probably murder. But I'm not sure."

"What does the time of year have to do with it?" I asked. "Why so often at one time of year? But then not always. I gather you figure they were all murders, summer or winter?"

"I have a friend who is a forensic psychologist." Watt stopped cracking his knuckles and smiled a kind of lopsided smile. I could see he was pleased with himself. "So, of course I talked to her about this. She says that the time of year or time of the month or even the time of day can be part of the pattern that is the signature of a particular killer.

"My friend says that the time of a killing can either be related to some strong feeling invoked in the killer by that particular time, or simply by how often the pressure to kill builds up, or both."

"So, perhaps," said Ted, "some other circumstance or opportunity, in addition to time, sometimes builds up that pressure to kill. Is that what you're saying?" I could see he was hooked on finding out. But now, so was I. This did relate to Pop. If he was in danger, he was less in danger in October than in February. But that didn't mean he was safe.

Watt handed us another printout. "Now, there's another element that's showing up in some of these stories. This is the one from Durham, December a year and a half ago. A nurse, Ellen Eates, fifty-nine, was found dead on her terrace by some neighborhood kids. With an empty pill bottle, of course. The autopsy showed death was due to sleeping pills like the ones from the empty bottle. So I went over there and talked to the neighbors, who were still upset a year later about what happened. The kids knew her best. She'd been a great friend to the kids. The grown-ups and the kids both said she'd seemed happy. They'd seen a nice-looking young man take her out. The kids said he was fun. The grown-ups said he wore expensive-looking clothes. Had a red Jaguar convertible. Sent her flowers. No one could remember the young man's last name. They just knew he had black curly hair and was called Bill. A damn shame not to get the name, but I doubt that he used his real last name anyway."

Watt was downright radioactive. He glowed. He leaned towards us. "I talked to the police, and they said the woman's brother from Canada had showed up and told them she'd recently inherited money. Just a few weeks before she died, the estate had finally been settled. But, of course, he found the money from the estate had vanished from her bank account.

"Now, wherever I've been able to go back to the scene of the death and talk to people, there's been a young man who befriended the victims several months before they died and then disappeared about the time of their death. In each case, the young man has been dramatically different: a flashy dresser in Durham, a dowdy opera buff in Winston. But that may simply mean he likes to play roles. In two cases I found his name. Harvey Redding in Winston, and Orvil Cornwall here. So, of course, I traced those names, and I found just one story about each. Each one had opened an office as an investment counselor about three months before those people had died from an overdose of sleeping pills. I looked through the ads, and each of these men had also placed an ad for his new business." Watt was so excited, he almost rose in the air and floated. "And part of this killer's signature is that he repeats himself. He used almost the same phrase in both ads: One says 'You'll be pleased at our results.' The other says 'You'll be delighted at our results.' I don't believe this is chance, and I think we're dealing with the same man here."

"And you think he's after my father?" I couldn't stand the suspense anymore.

He scowled and sighed. "I think he may be. But it's all so scattered. I can't get the police to get as actively involved as they ought to be. I guess they have more than they can do, and this *is* kind of a long shot."

He turned the whole force of his excitement on Ted and me. His eyes were thousand-volt lamps. Sunlamps. I felt as if I might get burned. "But you can help!" he exclaimed. "Someone is killing. I can see you believe me. Killing mostly old folks," he added. "He's killing more than one a year; his pace is getting faster. And I think he's moving up your way."

I shivered involuntarily. I was also annoyed. Was what he wanted simply extra help on the case? Had he asked us down just to get us to volunteer to help unearth the story? If so, why didn't he just ask?

There was a certain looseness in all this. I could see that. It could almost have been co-incidence. Except for the similarity of two suicide notes. And the words so much alike in those two ads.

"But what on earth makes you think this man is a threat to my father?" I couldn't stand it any longer. I mean, starting in at the beginning did make some sense. But now I needed to know exactly how this threatened Pop.

"This the shaky part," he said apologetically. I sensed he'd been putting off this part because he wasn't on such firm ground. "But I'm just as sure as I can be of what happened."

"Then tell me," I demanded.

"I went to Winston-Salem," he continued, "because that was the most recent case, just two months ago, and I talked to anyone I could find who might have known this Harry

Redding who befriended the Davis couple. He had vanished suddenly, his landlord said. The office was re-rented to a man who did massage. The police were looking for Redding. They thought he was involved in a scam."

"But Millie said you found a list," I said.

"Yes, I'm coming to that," he said "Because Redding's office was near a branch library, it suddenly occurred to me the second time I went to Winston, to ask the librarian. You see, I couldn't stay in Winston. I have to fit this in around my other work. My editor is not positive it will come to anything." Watt cracked his knuckles again unhappily.

"Anyway," he went on, perking up, "this nice young librarian said she remembered Harvey Redding because he was so pleasant and his hair was so red and his name was *Red*-ding and he was the only person who ever took out *South East* magazine's book called *Venture Capitalists of the Southeast*."

And I thought Watt should thank God that memory tricks work even when it's not on purpose.

"Then this nice little librarian gasped and covered her mouth with her hand and said, 'Oh, dear, I shouldn't have said that! Please just forget I said it. I'm not supposed to tell what books anyone takes out, and I never do!' And then she said, 'But he didn't look like he'd be impressed with financial things. He was kind of old-fashioned looking and always humming

53

arias from operas.' It seemed the librarian loved operas." Watt was smiling like the cat that swallowed the canary. "I said, 'Of course,' very casually, and in a little bit she went out to lunch and I went over and looked at the book."

And this was supposed to lead to some list found in a library book? That's what Ted had said they found. But this was so farfetched, so long-arm-of-coincidence, I could hardly believe it.

"I didn't really expect to find anything," Watt said smugly, "but I believe in being thorough, and this book was about the only kind of lead I had. I hoped for a page marker left in it, maybe, which might or might not prove anything. I mean, the book had been sitting on the shelf for two months since Redding returned it."

Frankly, I was beginning to think this would never lead anywhere.

"I went through the book page by page looking for any underlining or notes in the margin or anything. And you won't believe this. Among the back pages I found a list of names."

Whether that was farfetched or not, my heart began to drum.

"The list was typewritten," he said. "There were names only — no addresses, no phone numbers. No way to tell even what state the people lived in. I copied the list. The police have it now and are trying to find the typewriter it was written on, and to track down the names. They still don't believe there was a murder, but they admit there is a slight possibility these could be prospective fraud victims."

"And my father's name was on the list," I burst out.

"Yes. When I showed the list to Millie, she recognized your father's name."

Ted reached over and took my hand and held it tight.

"It was at the top of the list," Millie said.

I felt sick.

"But remember," Ted said, "someone else could have put that list in the book. It must have been available in the library for nearly two months if he returned it before he vanished the end of July.

"And," Ted said firmly, "nothing connects that list to suspects in the Allison or Davis murders — which are, so far, only presumed murders — except the fact that this Harvey Redding was apparently the only person to check that book out. He would have been a fool to leave that list in the book. And since he has evidently been able to hide what he was doing for so many years, he can hardly be a fool."

I love logic.

But then Ted took the other tack: "Is there anything we can do to help track this man down if he is up our way? I agree he seems to exist as a killer even if he didn't draw up that list. How can we help?"

I realized Ted was right. We'd have to help.

"My problem," Watt said, "is that up in your

end of the state the papers still file back news stories in envelopes."

"As lots of smaller papers still do," Ted said.

"I see," I said. "Your world memory has holes in it. Just like mine."

"What I need you to do," Watt explained, "is to go to the papers in your area and look in the back issues, and find out whether there have been deaths there with this same pattern. After all, our man has sometimes skipped around. And also look for stories about young investment counselors, or advertisements. The man apparently left Winston two months ago. He could have been in Asheville ever since. Just look around and use your intuition. If we can spot this man before he kills again, that will be a break."

And if Pop was at the top of his list, we needed to work fast. Of course, I told myself, Ted was right — it was possible that was not the killer's list.

But, dear God, suppose it was?

CHAPTER
5

SATURDAY AFTERNOON AND SUNDAY

"Aside from everything in general, there's something in particular that's bothering me, and I can't think what," I said as we got in the car to start home. I was tired and discouraged and carrying a stack of computer printouts of all the various sleeping-pill-death stories.

Ted took the printouts and put them on the back seat. "It'll come to you," he said.

"That's the title of a chapter in my book," I said tartly, "but it's not coming to me."

The light outside was beginning to dim, everything still clear but faded. I had been listening and thinking so hard, my brains were faded too.

"Let's go by the Forty-Second Street Oyster Bar and have supper," Ted suggested. "The noise level of fish lovers enjoying themselves is so high that we can sit in a booth and say what we please, and nobody will hear us."

Oddly enough, that kind of a general hum of noise sounded restful. Like the ocean, only not exactly. We slipped into a booth and a waitress brought us a nice crispy dish of hush puppies and took my order for steamed clams and Ted's

57

for soft-shell crabs.

"Wait — what's bothering me has to do with that list of names," I said. "That's it! I have a feeling that Pop did something to get on that list! And I almost know what. Not quite. The harder I try, the less I can remember."

"Stop trying," he said, passing me a hush puppy. "Relax and remember your rule — I've seen it work — *Stop chasing it, and it'll come to you.*"

"But I can't stop," I said. "It's like trying not to think of a pink elephant. You can't think that you shouldn't, without thinking about what you shouldn't think about."

"Think about your book," he said firmly, crunching into a hush puppy. "That always distracts you. That will clear your mind."

"I need to improve the way it's organized," I said, latching onto that. I pulled out my notebook, which I keep handy for jotting down ideas.

"I have this outline," I said, "but it keeps changing." I opened the notebook. At the top in bold letters I'd written. "How to Survive Without a Memory" as if I knew exactly where I was going with it.

"The first chapter is fine," I said. "About how to get to know your own mind and use what you can remember to get around what you can't remember. About how I can remember jokes and things that rhyme and silly sayings. And I think it's interesting how lots of folks have used those as memory aids since way back in history. I think that chapter is a good start."

He nodded. He's read that one.

I hadn't thought of Pop or a pink elephant for at least thirty seconds. I rewarded myself with a hush puppy. I began to read the rest of the outline:

Chapter 2: Outfoxing yourself. By arranging things so that it doesn't matter if you don't remember, you can save your energy for the things that can't be outfoxed. Strategies: hang-one, trip-overs, etc.

I patted my pocketbook, which always hangs over my shoulder on its nice solid strap, except when it hangs on a special hook at home. And so I only lose it once in a great while, under special stress. "Should that stuff be Chapter Two?" I asked out loud. "Or should I go right into remembering names, which is what bothers people the most? I ought to give what bothers people most my first attention."

I stopped. "Attention! The thing I can't remember now," I said, "has to do with the way Pop likes attention." I paused. "But you're right. I mustn't chase it." I read on.

Chapter 3: Calendars, backup reminders, alarms.

"I have a lot of nice examples of the kind of

abbreviations I do well *not* to use on a write-in calendar," I said, "since I can forget what they mean. Like 'take chair,' which I once wrote for the meeting of my book club. So I took a folding chair, but the note meant I had promised a ride to the chairman who lived on the other side of town!"

Chapter 4: Names. First-degree, second-degree, and third-degree strategies to remember them, and how to fudge it when you can't.

Chapter 5: Helping others to help you. Labels and name tapes. String around your finger (which triggers others to ask why it's there). Rewards.

"Rewards!" I sat up straight. "The worry about Pop had to do with a reward," I said. "He felt he should get one, I think. Oh, why can't I remember!" I read on.

Chapter 6: On not losing things to begin with — red file folders, special hooks, and making absolutely sure never, for goodness' sake, to put something "in a safe place."

Chapter 7: Tools for a bad memory, or be prepared A list of emergency aids to carry in your pocketbook or pockets, from a pencil to write things down, to quarters for phone calls, to a pocket knife that can turn a trash bag into a raincoat, etc., and including a notebook with your book ideas in it.

Or why people ask me, "What do you carry in your pocketbook? Lead bricks?"

Chapter 8: Tips from the famous.

"Yes!" I cried out. "What Pop did that worried me had something to do with being famous! But what? I don't think I want to remember," I said. "I think that's the trouble. Oh, dear. That's the hardest kind to get around."

Last Chapter (whatever number that turns out to be): The advantages of a bad memory.

"I'll end with this to cheer my readers up."

"And where will you put that chapter you thought of yesterday?" Ted asked. " 'Money Management for the Absent-Minded.' I know there's a need for that. You could stick it in after the chapters on names."

"Money!" I cried. "That's it! That's what Pop was talking about that I was sure would get him in trouble. Of course! It was when the gal came and interviewed me for the feature about my talk at the library — the talk about memory systems and the book I'm working on." I reached across the table and grabbed Ted's hand. A passing waitress stared. I didn't care. "Yes! That's it! Pop told that girl she ought to be writing about *him* and how any poor boy who is smart enough can be rewarded by becoming rich. And he said he couldn't see why I should be more famous than him, when nobody has even offered me an advance on my book yet."

"At the time," Ted said, "it seemed like a good idea to do that interview at Pop's house, since the reporter lives next door. But I guess it wasn't."

Our food arrived: Ted's sautéed crabs and my steaming clams, my baked potato and his fries. Plus slaw and nice, tinkling glasses of iced tea.

As soon as the waitress left, I said "Unfortunately that reporter came back and did that story about Pop. You remember. With pictures. It's not a good thing to advertise that you're old and almost balmy and very rich."

"He sounded eccentric, not really balmy," Ted said, "when he talked about how anybody who puts his mind to it can be rich. I figured people who knew him would chuckle. People who didn't know him wouldn't care."

"Whereas," I said, going cold, "I felt as if he was tempting evil. We know there are evil people out there. Why attract them? I wish I had thought of a way to prevent him from doing that story."

Ted sipped his iced tea and considered. "I gather he's always been willful," he said.

"He has always been willful, but he used to have common sense." I took a gulp of my tea to comfort myself. "And I know it's not entirely his fault that he's like he is now. Dr. Spicewood says that sometimes old people lose the censor that tells us what *not* to say and do. It just goes. Perhaps he had a mild stroke. The doctor doesn't know what happened." I tried a few clams dipped in butter. They were delicious.

"He doesn't behave," Ted said. "But most of his antics are harmless."

"Harmless!" I almost choked. "You underestimate Pop. Because he's wealthy, he still has power. He can hire people to help him do what he wants to do. Without benefit of any internal censor to tell him what won't do. I hope to God he's not up to anything right now."

I enjoyed a few more clams and tried to be calm. "Pop can be so stubborn about having his way," I said, "that he absolutely drives me crazy. Like the way he kept his rare-coin collection in his bedside table and didn't even lock the drawer no matter how I worried about it." I mopped up clam juice with my roll. "He said he liked to look at the coins when he couldn't sleep. And I tell you, I thanked God I got those coins into the bank. All it took was for us to be robbed and almost killed."

"You're tired and upset," Ted said.

"Yes," I agreed, "but do me a favor. Call Watt. Ask him to work it out for us to check things out in Winston-Salem on our way home. We need to find out what newspapers the man with the list read. I bet you five dollars he read the Asheville paper. He read that feature about Pop. He saw his chance."

I could see Ted thought that was a long shot. But on our way out of the restaurant we stopped at a phone booth. I called Pop and he said he was absolutely fine and for us to take our time. Everything was quiet in the mountains. He didn't even ask what we'd found out. But then it was seven-thirty and Pop's often a little vaguer in the evening.

Then Ted called Watt, who worked it out for us to talk to the suspect's ex-landlord on Sunday. So we drove on to Winston and spent the night in a Comfort Inn there.

We weren't so lucky in the morning. When Ted called, Mr. Landlord said his mother-in-law was there and we couldn't come over. Anything to do with crime scared her sick. But he did talk to Ted. "What was this vanished tenant like?" Ted asked, "and what did he do that was unusual?"

Ted kind of fidgeted and didn't take many notes. He said "So he wasn't in the office much?" Then he fidgeted some more. "Well, thank you," he said finally. I held up the newspaper.

"Oh, yes," Ted said into the phone, "do you know what newspapers he read?" And suddenly Ted perked up and began to take notes like crazy. Finally he hung up and said, "Well, I'll be damned!"

"You owe me five dollars," I said.

'This Redding had stacks of newspapers," he said. "They were out for somebody to haul away when he vanished. The landlord says they were from cities all over North and South Carolina and Georgia. Mostly Sunday papers. He wondered how the man had time to read them all. And he specially noticed the Asheville paper. His mother-in-law is from Asheville. I think you're psychic."

"Whatever I am," I said, "I think we better get home quick."

We drove into our own driveway at two-thirty in the afternoon. Mighty glad to be back in the arms of the mountains. We'd been gone the better part of two days. Inside, we found the light was blinking on our telephone answering machine. I let Ted activate the thing. As if he could make it say something nice. No such luck.

The thing tells the time of each call. The first call had come at 11:15 A.M. from a Sandy Lyon saying that he had found a book that he thought would be useful to me in writing mine, and he'd get back in touch. Sandy who? Was he related to Millie? He must have read the newspaper feature which said I'd like to swap memory tricks. I'd worry about that later.

The second call had come in at 2 P.M., just half an hour ago.

It was Pop's sitter — the new one, Lily, sounding frantic. Pop was throwing up, had stomach cramps. Sweating like a pig. (Lily doesn't mince words.) "And something very strange," she gasped. "He says everything looks yellow, even me." She said the ambulance was rushing Pop "and the other man" to Memorial Mission Hospital. That bad. What other man? What in God's name was going on? She said she'd try to get Mary, since she couldn't get us.

We jumped back in the car and drove as fast as Ted dared (with Ted, that's like a jet airplane) straight to the hospital. Straight to Emergency.

Pop was on a table in a cubicle behind a curtain. He looked dreadful. His face was gray. Mary stood near him, pale face scared, in her kelly-green Sunday dress. I felt sick that we hadn't hurried back faster, that we hadn't somehow prevented this. Pop's eyes were strange, kind of out of focus. But he did evidently see me, and smiled faintly when I squeezed his hand. "I'm dying," he whispered importantly. That was a good sign. If he felt important, there was hope. He was hooked up to all sorts of plastic bags solutions with tubes fastened into his arm. Definitely not an upset stomach. And where was the other man? *Who* was the other man?

I asked Mary, but she had just arrived at the hospital herself. She didn't know. She managed to smile and say she was mighty glad I'd come, and hug me, but she also seemed on the point of tears. "And Lily will know who, but she's gone to the waiting room, to be out of the way."

A young man appeared, looking terribly official. He said the doctor had sent him, so he wasn't one. He took us a little distance from Pop and asked if Pop took heart medicine. If Pop "and his guest" could have taken an overdose of that heart medicine by mistake. Where did we keep it?

"But my father doesn't have trouble with his heart!" I cried out. "Whatever else is wrong, his heart's as strong as an ox. Where is Dr. Spicewood? He's Pop's doctor and he knows." Wouldn't you know, Dr. Spicewood had picked this moment to go out of town.

"And if you're not the doctor," I said, "where is the doctor?"

"I'm a medical student working with the doctor," he said sternly. "The doctor is trying to save the other man."

"Something is terribly wrong with my father," I said.

"Both patients have all the symptoms of digitoxin poisoning," he said, disapprovingly, as if my denial of heart medicine had put him on the spot. "We get results of tests as soon as possible, but I don't doubt what they'll say. Your father says he sees yellow, and that's a symptom. The EKG pattern is almost diagnostic. The other man has had a heart attack. They're moving him up to the cardiac care unit."

"Digitoxin poisoning?" I echoed. I felt confused and scared silly.

"A derivative of digitalis."

"I know about digitalis," I said. "It was why my mother told me never to eat the foxgloves when I was a little girl and made rose-petal tea." I was rambling. Thinking out loud. Trying to get unconfused. Trying to reach back to something safe. "Because she said foxglove blossoms could kill. Except for people with weak hearts. Then something in the blossoms called digitalis was medicine instead of poison." The young man listened politely.

"But, dear God," I said, pulling myself back to the present, "how could my father get poisoned?" I turned to Ted. "We knew he was in danger, but he hasn't even been robbed yet, and why wasn't it sleeping pills?"

I noticed Mary staring at me like I'd lost my mind.

I turned back to the doctor's helper. "Who is the other man?"

The young man looked down at a clipboard: "His name is Matt Jones."

CHAPTER 6

We thanked Mary for rushing down to the hospital when nobody could get hold of us. We each gave her a hug. Another family catastrophe upped her hug need. That's what I thought. She threw Pop a kiss and went on back to see about the kids who she'd dropped off with a neighbor.

Then, while an aide wheeled Pop off to the intensive care unit, Ted and I found a little empty cubicle and we conferred. "Do you think the doctor is going to call the police?" I asked him. "Do you think *we* ought to call the police? And, damn it, why did Pop have that Matt Jones over, when we told him not to do it? But if that man had poisoned Pop, he wouldn't have poisoned himself too. I'm so confused."

Ted ran his fingers through that hair of his that stands out like he's been in a high wind whether there's wind or not. His hair is like antennae, out to get the facts. He frowned. That meant he thought the answer wasn't simple.

"The doctor suspects something is wrong here," Ted said. "He ought to see that somebody investigates. He probably has or will. But bureaucracies do things slowly. A hospital is a bureaucracy." Then he nodded to himself, and smiled. "But if you call Lieutenant Wilson, who knows you and knows Pop, maybe he'll be more likely to get on the case."

"You mean Mustache!" Ted was right. John Wilson, whom I called Mustache in my mind because he had a luxuriant you-know-what, was more like a friend. We knew him because he was the investigating police detective in-volved in the recent hair-raising unpleasantness after Aunt Nancy's death. Mustache liked Pop. And he had even given me a few suggestions for my book. Like the word that's the key to all the deadly temptations he has to look for in his line of work: PWELGAS (pride, wrath, envy, lust, gluttony, avarice, sloth).

"Call him." Ted winked. "He'll come quicker for a damsel in distress. Of course, he may not be there on Sunday, but you tend to be lucky."

And, in fact, I actually reached Mustache himself, gravelly voice and all, and he said he'd be over to the hospital shortly and connect with us in the intensive-care waiting room. Either I'd had the luck to catch him when he wasn't busy, or he knew the potential for mayhem in our family and decided to take preventive measures right away at all costs. I was grateful.

The large gray waiting-room was filled with nervous or sleepy friends and relatives of the patients. We checked in at the desk and then went to look for two empty seats in a corner.

70

We almost passed Lily, Pop's sitter. I guess I was in shock. I hadn't really seen her. She stood up and folded me in a motherly hug, and cried out, "They told me you'd come here. Oh, I'm just so worried. And I feel so bad that this is somehow my fault." She was large and soft and warm as a feather bed and perspiring on top of that. Her voice throbbed with comfort. She let go of me and squeezed Ted's hand.

I was glad she was there. She was my favorite of Pop's three regular sitters. That's how many he needed for help around the clock. Plus occasional pinch hitters, plus Anna, his part-time housekeeper.

There was something solid about Lily, from her sensible laced shoes up to her watchful blue eyes. I had only known her three weeks, but if I had to pick one person besides Ted to be stranded on a desert island with, it might be Lily. I was sure she'd figure out how to catch fish and cook seaweed. If she had a fault, it was that she liked to talk. And now I wanted her to talk.

We led her with us to an empty corner. I sat down next to her. Ted put his coat on the chair next to me and said he was going over to the coffee machine and get us all coffee. We needed picking up.

I told Lily what the people down in Emergency had told me. She caught her breath and cried, "Oh, those poor men! And I gave them the last thing they ate or drank!"

71

I held her large moist hand tight. "You bring Pop practically half of what he eats, Lily," I said. "You bring him a present nearly every day. If someone was going to slip poison in his food, there'd be a good chance it would be in something you brought him."

So I was assuming he was poisoned on purpose. Though it didn't fit Watt's warning. It didn't make sense.

"God knows I wish I hadn't brought that tea," Lily wailed. "He must have drunk the poison with the tea. I ate the same dinner and I'm fine. But I didn't drink the tea, although I had some earlier. Another batch."

Ted handed us each a hot container of coffee. He looked at his watch. "Since you've got Lily to keep you company," he said, "let me go call the sitter service and Anna. She deserves to hear about this from a member of the family."

"And call Cousin Gloria in Madison County," I said. "She'll be upset if she hears secondhand that Pop is in the hospital. And she may be related to Matt Jones. This is all so ghastly. But she likes you. She won't mind if you call instead of me. She'll call the other cousins. And here," I added, "here are some quarters. Naturally I have lots."

Ted leaned down and kissed me on the lips. Then he said, "Your father's going to be all right." Ted has such a wise and gentle voice. It gives me goose bumps. "Back soon," he said.

I was glad Lily and I were sitting a little bit apart from the other people in the waiting room. My mind was jumping with questions. It jumped to that extra man, Matt Jones, Black Hat from the graveyard, who managed to get himself poisoned with Pop.

"That Mr. Jones," I said. "Was he there long before . . . ?" I got out my little black electronic organizer that Pop gave me, to put in the names and times. It's as small as a notebook. Pop called it a portable memory device and gave it to me for a wedding present. He and Sherrie, his favorite sitter, found it in a catalogue. It's called a Wizard.

"Mr. Jones came for dinner about noon," Lily said. "Your father invited him, and that was fine." She seemed pleased to be able to help me out with facts. "Anna's usually off Sundays, but your father asked if she'd come today instead of Monday, and since tomorrow is Anna's daughter's birthday, she was glad to come until about noon today. She really didn't have to, because you know I love to cook." She ran her hand across her mouth. "But, oh dear, that's not what you asked about!"

I patted her hand.

"Mr. Jones came, all dressed up in Sunday clothes, and while they ate my meatballs and Anna's slaw and rice and biscuits, they talked about ancestors — at least when I came in, that's what they were talking about." She narrowed her round blue eyes and I knew she was

73

visualizing the scene. "Mostly I left them alone."

"And you ate the same food, but not the tea?"

"Yes," she wheezed, eyes stricken. "I made a big batch of tea at home by mixing herbs. Then I made myself a pot from part of that batch earlier. And I was fine. Then I brought your father some yesterday as a present. I realized I was bringing him too many sweets. And your father does love sweets. He would eat the brownies I made and leave the rest of his lunch. So I brought him some herb tea mix instead."

In the distance a baby began to cry. I turned my head and saw the mother headed toward the hall. A ripple of heads turned to watch her go. I was reminded we were not alone. We should keep our voices down.

Tears began to run down Lily's face. "I love your father," she said. "I wouldn't hurt him for anything. He's the most interesting person I ever worked for."

"Try to remember," I said, "exactly what happened. Did you make the hot tea yourself? And bring out clean cups and saucers and spoons yourself?"

"Yes," she said, wiping her eyes with a tissue, "all myself."

"And did they put anything into the tea?"

Her eyes went narrow again. "Sugar," she said. "Your father put three spoons like he always does, and Mr. Jones was a real sugar lover. He put in about six." I wrote down the amount of sugar Matt Jones used after the time of his arrival.

"Did anything seem unusual about the sugar?"

"Only that it was new."

That confused me. "New from the store?"

"No, new from the sugar bag. Yesterday I was about to put the sugar bowl away, and I noticed there were cigarette ashes on the sugar. So I poured all the sugar out and got new, and by the time I was through, Dorothy arrived. She was switching shifts with Sherrie. And we were laughing so, over how Sherrie got ashes in the sugar. Sherrie's the only one of us who smokes, and she's supposed to do it outdoors. And she doesn't even use sugar. None of us do. We're all on diets. The thin and the fat. We all use those artificial things. So how did Sherrie get ashes in the sugar? I guess we got silly, and we laughed so loud your father called and asked why. Oh dear, I'm rambling again!"

I figured Lily and Dorothy didn't like Sherrie. So they enjoyed her goof.

Lily sat up straight, as if that would prevent rambling. "That's how I knew it was about quarter of three when I changed the sugar in the bowl."

I wrote *Sugar bowl* 2:45 P.M. as if the sugar bowl were a person. You see, there's a little directory in the Wizard with room for a person's name and a few other facts. Handy because it alphabetizes everything so you can find it when you need to. I decided to put an *S* in front of everything to do with suspects so they'd all come up together, but sugar bowl had an *S* built in. I mean, the Wizard is really handy. There's a schedule section where I can put in any appointment, even months away, but when I turn the Wizard on, it homes onto today's date and whatever needs to be done. Then it has another section for notes, another section that tells what time it is all over the world, and a pocket calculator. So far I've never needed to know what time it is in London, but who knows?

"Would anyone have had a chance to add poison to the herb tea mix, and if so, when?"

Lily leaned forward in her gray waiting-room chair and almost overflowed out of it. "Beginning Saturday morning, that mix was sitting right out on the kitchen table in a glass canning jar with a screw top and a card on it from me to your father. Which was foolish, because his eyes are not good enough to read it. But I like to put cards on gifts. It's like Christmas."

"So someone could easily have put poison in the tea?"

"But we keep the back door locked." She was crushing the fingers of her left hand in her right hand. I wanted to say Stop! but I didn't want to interrupt her. "Except the key was misplaced for a while yesterday after Mary Sernan's kids were running around. We don't actually use that key. It's extra. The door latches when it's closed. But I noticed it was gone and that worried me," she said, "but we found it lying on the floor this morning."

"Who came by yesterday or today?" I asked.

She was off again, talking sixty miles a minute. "Mary and the kids came Saturday morning about eleven. Your cousin Eltha came by this morning. And then she left when Mr. Jones came, and then just as those men finished lunch — but before I brought in the tea and cookies — the man came with the book."

Now there was a surprise. "A man with a book?"

"I don't remember his name. He hardly stayed a minute. We were right there with him and he never went near the kitchen."

"But what did he look like?" And was he, I wondered, the man whose voice was on my answering machine?

"He looked too young to have a white beard."

I wrote: *S. white beard: at Pop's, just after Sunday dinner* as a directory entry, tapping it out on the tiny keyboard across from the tiny screen. Then I pushed ENTER. That's essential to the process. If I didn't push ENTER, what I tapped in was lost.

I told myself that Pop would be glad if this present he gave me helped to find who poisoned him. He'd been so pleased with himself.

"I've found you a portable mind," he'd said. "just what we all need in our old age."

Well, thanks a heap! I could use a portable memory. But I had no intentions of being old yet. I'm a practically new bride. How can I be old?

"If a pretty young girl had that white hair I'd say it was dyed platinum blond. But he was a man." Lily was still talking about White Beard. "And right after he left, I took your father and Mr. Jones the tea, and they drank it and got sick." She began to cry again.

I leaned over and hugged her, though my arm hardly fit around her. I am always amazed how much there *is* of her, how much there is to be in balance, because Lily is extremely graceful on her feet. She even sits in a chair with a kind of balanced poise. She hugs back without overhugging.

"What else do you remember about the man with the white beard?"

"Nothing, except that I liked him."

"Was there anything worrying my father today?" I asked.

"He worries about money," she said. "He's so afraid he won't have enough to stay at home until he dies. So afraid he'll be put in a nursing home. It preys on his mind. I don't know why it scares him so, when I'm sure you're taking care of his affairs. But it does."

I let that pass. I could hear somebody being paged in the distance, but it wasn't me. At least

Pop seemed to have put aside his last terror: that sometimes there were burglars on the roof trying to get in and kill him. Fear of death disguised? Most of the time Pop is rational. But now and then, when he's under some stress or has a ministroke — Dr. Spicewood isn't sure exactly what — Pop becomes paranoid. And lately this fear was focused on money.

"I know," I said to Lily. "Sometimes he's afraid that the banks are going to fail, like they did in the Great Depression, and take what little savings he thinks he has, and then what would become of him?"

I sighed. "But that doesn't prevent him from *also* talking about how great it is that he's smart enough to be rich."

Lily still had tears in her eyes, but she laughed. "He is one every-day surprise." She pulled a tissue out of a big battered black pocketbook and wiped her eyes.

"But everybody likes your father, because he's never, never dull." Lily began to tear the tissue in her lap. "There must have been an accident, but I can't think how. Who would want to kill that dear man? Who would want to kill his friend?" Her eyes were wide and blue like a baby's again.

I still held the Wizard in my hand. Complete with the gold letters on the front with my telephone number and REWARD. It reminded me of Sherrie, who helped Pop get it for me. Sherrie who wasn't supposed to smoke in the house and still spilled ashes in the sugar. How exactly like her.

Sherrie was Pop's favorite sitter.

Not mine. She treated other women like adversaries. And had a layer of phony sweetness on top of that. I'd come to suspect that when it suited her, she told lies — though I hadn't been able to pin her down to one.

But Pop would never let her go. I even suspected he liked the added drama of my dislike for Sherrie. He also liked to be made much of, and she had a real talent for that. And he liked to look at her. Every day she came to work dressed like she was going to a party. Pop thought that was wonderful. And he paid the sitter bills.

I clicked off my portable mind and slipped it in my pocketbook, thinking how glad I was that big, motherly Lily was in the intensive care waiting room with me, and not Sherrie. A thought to tempt fate, because I looked up and there was Sherrie, swinging toward us through the waiting room.

Sherrie never wasted an entrance, even when she probably didn't know a soul present except Lily and me. She stood quite still in front of us, one hip jutting out, dressed in a pair of black satin toreador pants, a lime-green tank top without benefit of bra, and dangly jet earrings. Her red heels were so high they were like stilts. Those were her working clothes. Heads turned to stare.

"Hi," she said like a challenge. "I went to your father's house at three for my shift. Nobody was there. I finally found your little note by the door." She directed the note complaint at Lily.

"Good Lord, honey," Lily said, "I was so upset I couldn't stop to look for paper. I just took what I had at hand and scribbled a note and stuck it up with tape. I'm glad you found it."

"I found the doctor and talked to him," Sherrie said, allowing her long dark lashes to dip briefly as if she wanted to be modest about her effect on doctors. "He told me all about what happened."

"Only family members can see Pop," I said. "You don't have to stay."

"Oh, but I want to!" Her eyes went wide with guile. "I'll keep you company." She moved Ted's coat and took over the chair next to me.

Did Sherrie hope to get paid for her shift even though Pop was in the hospital? Or did she just hope to learn more about what happened from Lily and me? She crossed her legs languidly.

"Perhaps the doctor told you," I said, "that Pop began having these awful stomach pains. That was right after he drank the herb tea that Lily brought him." Goodness, I'd said that in a way that sounded terrible.

Sherrie's well-plucked eyebrows climbed slowly. That red, red mouth stayed shut.

81

"Lily brought the tea the day before Pop drank it," I reminded her. "Right, Lily? And it stayed there on the table. On your shift, did anybody have a chance to come in the kitchen when they could have touched the tea without your seeing them do it?" That seemed most unlikely since she had been there from 11 P.M. to 7 A.M., but I might as well ask and be sure.

"Of course not," she said.

"And was the sugar on the table in the kitchen the whole time, too? On your shift, did anyone have a chance to put anything in that?"

"No, not at all," she said, pleased with herself, as if that lack of opportunity was due to her innate superiority. "I had a toothache and never drifted off for even one minute. I watched MTV and read a book, and your father slept through the whole shift. So I sat in the kitchen right by that tea, not to mention the sugar bowl, from eleven to seven."

"Thank you," I said. But she didn't inspire thanks.

"So you believe someone tried to poison your father," Sherrie said, with interest. There it was again. I had taken it for granted that he was deliberately poisoned.

I wished Pop could see how pleased Sherrie looked. How her brown eyes sparkled. I thought: She's one of those women who loves a crisis, loves that kind of excitement. Because the calm excitement of a happy relationship, or even a beautiful day, is more than she could ever absorb. Because she's a bitch. O.K., I was prejudiced against her. I admit it.

I realized I'd be pleased to death if the police discovered it was Sherrie who had tried to poison Pop.

Where was Mustache? I hoped his questions would make her nervous.

Poison was a woman's tool for murder. I'd read that somewhere. Men were more likely to use guns or knives or their fists.

And so, I thought, the sleeping-pill killer was more likely to be a woman too. Because sleeping pills were even less violent than poison. And yet Watt had discovered there was a young man on the scene before almost every one of the killings that he thought were related.

Maybe they were a team. The young man and a faceless woman. He was the bait. She killed. And suppose she was the one after Pop. Suppose she was Sherrie. Oh, come on! I told myself. That's much too farfetched. And didn't fit serial killer scenario, not at all.

"When did you move to Asheville?" I realized I'd never asked her that. She'd been with us three months. That would rule out any wild possibility of her being involved in what happened in Winston-Salem two months ago.

"Oh," she said, "I come and go. In the sitter business you can do that. I've even spent the winter in Miami. It's fun to move around."

I was about to try to pin her down more, when Mustache strode into the waiting room.

"I came as fast as I could," he said.

I introduced him to the two sitters. Sherrie blinked in surprise, then smiled sweetly. Lily stopped playing with the tissue in her hands and froze. I should have told them he was coming. Why hadn't I? Did I want to see how they reacted? Or did I just forget?

Mustache stopped in front of the three of us. "I'm sorry to see you again so soon, on official business," he said to me. "At least I'm glad to hear that your father is probably going to be all right."

"Thank goodness," I said. "We're waiting to see him. At least, I am. Lily was with Pop when he got sick. Sherrie would have been on duty now. They're waiting to see how he seems when I go in."

Mustache said he'd been able to get permission to talk to us in an empty office. I asked him to tell a nurse in intensive care where we'd be, in case I was needed for any reason, or when Ted showed up looking for us. Then the four of us trooped off. I took along Ted's coat.

Actually, we passed Ted talking in a phone booth, and Mustache told him where we were going and that he expected him to join us. Ted winked at me and I knew what he meant. He meant he was with me in spirit until he got there in the flesh.

As soon as Mustache shut the door to the small room where he took us, Lily turned to him with a huge sigh. "I'm the one," she said.

84

"I'm the one who made the herb tea that he was drinking when he was taken so sick."

"So please come right in here and tell me more about it." Mustache gestured at an inner door. I realized we were in a double room, some kind of an office with a desk and several chairs, and an inner sanctum. He waved Sherrie and me to a couple of chairs along one wall of the outer room.

Sherrie said nothing. She just gave Mustache a long, slow, appraising How-sexy-are-you? glance, like she was Carmen and Mustache was Don José and that he was making a big mistake not to talk to her first.

As soon as he shut the inner door with a click, Sherrie turned to me and said, "Lily is a fool. She trusts everybody."

Sherrie annoyed me, so I said, "And you trust nobody."

"I'll live longer," she replied. I assumed she meant it as a figure of speech.

"This is no time," I said, "to joke about living and dying." We sat straight and stiff. The chairs in this room were small and angular. Not designed for anyone to sit in for any length of time. I wanted to say if she kept trying to look seductive in one of these chairs, she might get a crick in her back.

But then it occurred to me that if Pop confided his guilty secrets to anybody, it would be to Sherrie. He'd think of her as a fellow conspirator. And in a way he would be right. Her first loyalty would be to him. Never to me. But since he had been poisoned in some unknown way, I thought she might be willing to tell me a little more than she otherwise might.

"You know Pop likes to have his secrets," I began. "And since I know that they make him feel more in control of his own life, I try not to interfere."

She eyed me with a poker face, arms folded over her chest, legs crossed, and said nothing. Outside the door I heard one of those cranky hospital carts roll past, complete with footsteps. A heavy, flat-footed person was pushing the cart. It clanked off into the distance.

"Has he done anything that you know of that might put him in danger?"

"What would make you think I would know?" she asked.

She tightened the arms that hugged each other so that the fingers of each hand were hard against her biceps. I wondered if those perfect long red nails were artificial. Above her over-curled head was a picture of an old-fashioned doctor by a child's bedside. A picture of trust.

Sherrie was not involved in trust. I was sure of that. She felt we were playing some other game. And she resented my asking her to show her cards.

"Lily may have done something to put him in danger," she cooed. Then waited. She wanted to force me to ask, "What?" before she told me more.

All right, I wasn't into games. "What?"

"She takes in foster children. She'd love any brat that came along." I suddenly wondered if in some strange way Sherrie was jealous of Lily. That she could see, but not quite admit to herself, that love made Lily's life richer than hers was.

"She's been doing it for years. Not so much lately since she's working for the sitter service. But she says the kids come back and see her. Even when they've been in prison or something. One of them came to meet her when we changed shifts, about a week ago. He had on a black motorcycle jacket. I could see it cost him. And he had a scar right from the corner of his eye down to the side of his throat, and a tattoo of a snake on the back of his right hand. Now, if she brings that kind of people to your father's back door, what do you expect?"

I laughed. "A man with a scar and a snake tattoo sticks out like a sore thumb. I'm scared of the kind of people who don't stick out."

I hadn't been impressed with Sherrie's boyfriend either when I saw her with him in a downtown bistro. He looked too sure of himself, and had small feet. His legs were crossed and one foot stuck out. I have never trusted men with small feet.

Unfortunately, I also didn't quite trust my own father.

"Pop has a drawer, as I'm sure you've noticed, Sherrie, which he keeps locked, and he wears the key on a chain around his neck."

"Of course," she said sweetly. "He's always saying how he has to have some secret place of his own."

What he actually said was that he was getting so helpless with his damn arthritis that he couldn't even go to the bathroom by himself, and, by God, he was going to have one private corner of his life and we could lump it if we didn't like it.

"I respect his need for secrecy," I said, "but if anything is ever in that drawer that could draw trouble to him and he should tell you about it, I hope you'll warn me to have it out with him."

As soon as I said that, I felt it didn't sound right, but I couldn't think of a way to say it that did sound right. How do you deal in a dignified way with a smart, experienced white-haired man who sometimes acts with all the recklessness of a two-year-old?

Sherrie laughed. "You think he trusts me more than you? Maybe he's like me. Maybe he doesn't trust anybody."

Right then, Ted came in the door.

Immediately Sherrie relaxed and smiled. She had pulled in her claws in his honor.

"I called the sitter service and Anna, and Cousin Gloria in Madison County," Ted reported, "and also Arabella next door." Arabella is Pop's nearest neighbor, a widow whose favorite things in the world are Pop and her three horses. Ted sat down in the seat on the other side of me. "Here's your coat," I said. "We brought it along."

Right then there was a knock on the door and a nurse stuck her head in. This one had fuzzy yellow hair. "Peaches Dann?" she said, like it was a pressing question. The desk must have told her where I was.

"Me," I said, scared to death she was there because Pop was worse. Ted sat up straighter too. I could see he had the same fear.

"Your father woke up and was demanding to see you," she said, voice rising. Like it was my fault. "When we told him you were with the police, he began demanding to see them. Very loudly. There are a lot of sick people in our ICU, and I can't get your father to be quiet. And I don't want to medicate him in case what he wants to tell the police is important." She puckered her face like she might cry and glared at me like why didn't I do something. Quick!

Oh, brother! What next?

CHAPTER 7

SUNDAY, LATE AFTERNOON

Well, you wouldn't believe what Pop wanted to see the police so bad for! It was his damned private drawer. There he lay, with tubes in his arms and bags of solution dripping into the tubes. Nurses hovered nearby. In a way, Pop was responsible for a man being poisoned, though I was sure he wouldn't look at it that way. But at least he wasn't impersonating death anymore. His head was still flat on the pillow, but he grabbed me with his eyes. "Where are the police?" he demanded. I told him about Mustache.

"Of *course* someone is trying to poison me," he said. "The police will have to search my house again. Whoever it was will have left traces. So even though I keep my own special drawer locked, I know the police will have to search there. I need to make your friend with the mustache promise he won't tell anybody what's in my drawer. That's my business." He smiled until his whole face crinkled. I could almost have felt glad that he had a secret that pleased him so much if I hadn't been so annoyed.

At least this overriding interest seemed to

have turned Pop two shades pinker. He was no longer even pretending to be feeble. "Go get your friend with the mustache," he ordered in the tone of Ghengis Khan.

Luckily, Mustache had just finished talking to Sherrie when I arrived with Pop's summons.

Sherrie came out smiling like she'd put one over. What did she think she'd pulled? Or was the smarty look just for my benefit?

Anyway, Mustache came with me, and on the way to the Intensive Care Unit I told him what my father wanted. He laughed. "At least," he said, "your father hasn't reached the stage where he hides things without telling anybody and then forgets where they are and panics." We stopped and let a gurney with patient and drip bottles roll past. "My wife had to search my mother's house for a week," he went on, "before she found my grandmother's engagement ring pinned in the hem of a curtain."

Well, things could always be worse, and as the old saying goes, at any moment they would probably get worse. Mustache had checked and said Matt Jones was still alive, but just barely.

First, he talked to Pop alone, or as alone as you can get in an ICU. I waited just inside the door by the little sink where each visitor has to wash his hands. Earnest conversation in Pop's corner. No fireworks.

Then Mustache and I went back into the little room the hospital had lent us for police interrogation. I told him Watt's theory of a serial killer and that I hadn't told Pop yet. I was waiting for the right private moment. "But," I said, "that theory doesn't match this poisoning." I told him all I'd learned from Lily and Sherrie, even though they must have told him too. "And that doesn't match the sleeping-pill cases either," I said. "Nothing fits. But, let's face it, we sure seem to be a family where the worst can happen any which way."

"I hope," he said, "that you won't take any chances. Leave this to us."

I said I would certainly be careful, only I had no way of knowing what or who to be careful of.

"I've already secured your father's house, and we'll run a thorough search tomorrow morning," Mustache said. "Maybe we'll find some trace of the perpetrator. You don't need to be there," he added in that tone that told me they didn't want me in the way. O.K.

Then, of course, Mustache talked to Ted. Later, we compared notes and discovered we'd told him about the same things, except that Ted, who has an eye for those things, filled in more details.

Meanwhile, the time for another short visit with Pop had arrived. He was so revived by a little police contact, we decided that after this visit we could stop worrying so much about him and go home and collapse. He was still all hooked up to IV tubes, but he was cheerful. "I'm going to be fine," he said. "I'll show that bastard. Don't just sit around here. Go find that skunk who did this to me. Not to mention my friend Matt Jones. Matt says he thinks we are both descended from Governor Zeb Vance. Matt's a very interesting man. So go find out who gave us both poison."

And I thought to myself: So The absent-minded detective rides again on a wild bronco, and everything seems absolutely out of control. This is too much. And, right at the moment, the nurse with the fuzzy yellow hair came over and said she'd like to see us for a moment before we left. She had something for us.

It was Mary's shiny red pocketbook. She'd left it in the emergency room, and they traced it to Pop. And Mary wasn't even the family forgetter. But then again, being upset is not necessarily the greatest for the memory cells.

Ted said we'd drop the pocketbook off at her house on the way home. In fact, he took custody of it. "You're not to be trusted," he teased, "with a pocketbook that doesn't have a strap."

We drove right over to Mary's. Her car wasn't in the driveway. Lights were on in her house, warm oblongs in the dark building with its peaked roof against a silver-gray sky. The sky was dusk, not dark. Mary often left the lights on if she thought it would be dark before she got back. She hated to go into an unlighted house.

A large black car drove off from down the block as we approached.

An unfamiliar gray Volvo was parked in front of Mary's house. I glanced at the license plate, but it was muddy, and I couldn't make out the number in the fading light.

A man in a dark suit was on Mary's front porch, ringing the doorbell. His back was to the street, and evidently he didn't see us. Because when the doorbell brought no response, he put his face up to the glass panel to the right of the door and looked inside.

"What's he doing that for?" I asked out loud, prickling with alarm.

"He acts like there's a peep show inside," Ted said. "But he doesn't act like he cares who sees him watching. That's odd."

Ted drove on past the Volvo, and as soon as he was around a curve out of sight, he backed around in a driveway and drove back with his lights turned off. We parked on the other side of the road from Mary's house, down the road a way. The man was still staring in the narrow glass panel, his face pressed up to the glass. "He's still at it," I said. "Do you think it's safe to park here? Suppose he sees us."

"I can take off in a minute," Ted assured me.

Finally, the man backed off from the glass panel, but then he put his face to the glass on the other side of the door — the lion side, I call it, because on that side a cement statue of a lion sits next to the foot of the steps.

"What on earth is he watching?" Ted wondered aloud.

"And who on earth," I asked, "can he be? And how dangerous is he?"

CHAPTER 8

SUNDAY EVENING

Mary's Peeping Tom continued to ignore us as we sat there in Ted's Toyota watching his strange actions. Finally he finished peering in the glass panel by her front door. He turned around and walked down the front steps past the lion, then around to the unlit side of the house. Mary's house is on a curve in the road with the nearest neighbors round the bend. No lights showed but those from Mary's windows. The sky was dark gray-blue.

I was suddenly sure who this strange man was: one of Mary's unexpected boyfriends that she'd picked up God-knows-where. I shivered. I couldn't see him too well, but he certainly didn't look like your ordinary burglar. He had black hair and dead white skin, luminous in the dusk. He walked determinedly, like a young man. But he had on a two-piece, old-fashioned dark suit. Something Pop might have worn to a family funeral. Something Ted would only have worn if he starred in a play about Dracula on the prowl. And this man's hair, in the black triangle of a widow's peak, was Dracula to the nines. I was glad I didn't believe in vampires.

Not quite. I hugged myself. I was cold. Tired too. This had been a hard day.

I could see that even if Son of Dracula stood on tiptoe he couldn't look in the side windows. He wasn't tall enough. Mary's house is built into a slope, and in the back the cellar is largely above ground and the first-floor windows are above eye level.

He went calmly over to the small prefab shed where Mary kept her garden tools. It's off to the side of the house. He leaned down like he'd dropped something. Then he stood up and unlocked the padlock on the door. Hey wait, where on earth did he get a key? Did he steal it? Did he know where Mary hid it? He disappeared into the shed and came out with a ladder. He carried the ladder over to a side window, not bothering to look around and see if anybody was watching, walking calmly, not appearing to be nervous. I whispered, "Good grief, Ted, suppose he's crazy."

Dracula Jr. put the ladder up to the side of the house, climbed up and stood quite still, staring into the lighted window for a long time. Black against the light. He made no attempt to open the window. Just stared. What did he see in that house? My imagination began to go wild. There were bodies, one in the living room where he looked first, maybe in a pool of blood in front of the big gold-leaf mirror Mary's mother gave her. Maybe a body in the dining area, which he could see from this window. He was trying to memorize all the clues around the bodies without entering the house and becoming a suspect. He was not a burglar; he was a detective.

No. Detectives try to look unnoticeable. They do not dress like Dracula. They do not stand against the light.

But suppose something had happened to Mary and the kids? Were they inside the house, in trouble of some sort? And something was happening to make him stare. But what? And why?

"Should we do something?" I asked Ted. I meant, What should we do? Ted was perfectly still, watching the man as steadily as the man was looking into Mary's window.

"Look," Ted said, "I think we should wait and find out what on earth is going on."

Dracula Jr. climbed down the ladder, took it down from the dining-area window, and disappeared with it around in back of the house. "Shouldn't we go call the police?" I asked. But then I said, "No, you're right. We need to find out what he's up to."

"But we could get his license number," Ted said. "I'll go look."

He grabbed a handful of tissues from the box that lived in the car, reached up and turned off the overhead light switch, then slipped quietly out of the door on his side, making just a few small clicks as he opened and shut the door. He hurried to the man's parked car, past a few bushes along the road, and just as he stood in back of the car wiping the dried mud off the license plate, Dracula Jr. came back around the house. I wanted to scream, Watch out! But that would have been the worst thing I could do. I clenched my fists and held my breath. And Dracula Jr. didn't even glance at his car to see if it was safe from license-plate snoops. He didn't glance at our car, loitering down the road.

With his back to the road, he put the ladder away in the shed just as Ted reappeared by our car and slipped in. "It's a letter plate," Ted whispered. "It says MEMORIA."

"Sounds almost like a funeral wreath," I murmured. "In Memoriam."

I pulled out my Wizard and my penlight, turned the tiny light on, wrote *Memoria* under Notes, and added the time from my watch: 7:30. I pushed ENTER.

Dracula closed the shed door with a squeak and started walking toward our car. Not toward his. Right toward us. My heart began to knock. Suppose he had a gun under that suit? Why would you wear a jacket to case a house, if it wasn't to hide something in? Well, it was a little chilly, but still —

He walked along as calmly as if he were on his way to church.

Ted rolled the car window down and said "Hi." When in doubt, be disarming.

I studied that pale face and shock of jet black

hair that came to a widow's peak over his forehead. Surprisingly, his eyes were lively. Brown and percolating above his straight Roman nose. Close up, he did not look like a maniac. At least not at first glance.

Ted said, "What can we do for you?"

"How do you do," he said, very formal. "I'm Mary's friend, Loy Haven. You must be Ted and Peaches. She said you had a Toyota." He showed no sign of surprise to find us parked there with the lights off. Perhaps he expected us to keep an eye on Mary. Perhaps he expected us to be as eccentric as he was. Odd.

And why on earth would Mary have been talking to this man about Ted's car?

"I'm fixing a surprise for Mary," he said. He stood very straight in his black suit. "It's to win an argument we've been having." He had a listen-to-me-because-I-know voice like Paul Harvey on the radio. "I had to finish before Mary got home," he went on, "but now I'm all set. But there's something I've been wanting to talk to you about. Come have supper with me. My treat. We'll go to Fine Friends Restaurant. I know that you've met Mary there, so you know where it is. I'll meet you there shortly."

I would have liked to go home to a good night's sleep. But plainly what I needed to do was ask this man questions.

I accepted the invitation for us both.

"That's the strangest man I ever met," Ted said as soon as Dracula Jr. was out of earshot.

SENECA FALLS LIBRARY
31 FALL STREET
SENECA FALLS, NEW YORK 13148

"You realize he's the one that wrote that book about walks near Asheville that appeared at Pop's from nowhere. I think we need to find out as much as we can about Loy Haven." He turned on the motor, and I could see him frowning in the faint light from the dashboard. "And why has Mary told him so much about us?"

"But before we go," I said, "let's look in the front windows just to be sure." I didn't know what I wanted to be sure of. But Loy Haven had looked in those windows like there must be something truly sensational inside. Ted parked in front of the house, and we walked past the stone lion guarding the steps, and up onto the small porch. Since there were two glass panels, one for Ted on the right of the door and one for me on the left, we stared together. And there was Mary's living room just exactly like always. Red couch with coffee table in front, and all the little china knickknacks that she'd trained her kids not to touch. The two china birds faced each other on the coffee table. A china cat lurked in a nook on the bookshelf. Mary's living room had always struck me as full of small artificial friends. But I'd hate to have to dust it. Nothing that I could see was even out of place.

"Why our friend even bothered to look in the side windows, I can't imagine," Ted said. "You can see on through into the dining area from the front. And what's to stare at?"

We tramped back out to the car, which sat

MYNDERSE LIBRARY
31 FALL STREET
SENECA FALLS, NEW YORK 13148

alone in the dark street. To tell the truth, I was disappointed. All that staring should have been *at* something. And I was also worried. Mary has this knack for falling for the wrong men. And they've hurt her Her ex-husband said she was a featherbrain and left her. Her brother's partner plied her with champagne and pot and turned out to be a crook. What now for our gentle Mary who loved small children and bright colors and jokes — and the wrong men?

"When we get to Fine Friends, I'll call the hospital and be sure everything is still O.K. with Pop," I said. "I don't want to be where they can't find us if we're needed. But if a mad-man is after Mary, well, who knows how he fits into what? If he stole Mary's shed key, maybe he stole Pop's backdoor key and copied it and put it back. And if he's crazy, maybe he poisoned Pop. God knows why, but we better find out."

You can imagine how disappointed we were to go in the sparkling cut-glass paneled door of the Fine Friends and discover that Dracula Jr. was not even there. And never did show up. We were so hungry and tired that we went right in to one of the tables in a nook near the door and ordered deep-dish pizza and watched the tropical fish in a tank. I really kept expecting our friend to arrive or call. I'd had the feeling that he truly wanted to talk. Whether he was crazy or not. And I sure wanted to know how he would explain himself.

CHAPTER 9

MONDAY MORNING, OCTOBER 5

When I woke up, there was sunshine coming in the window. It lit up the stained glass cardinal from my former life — when Roger and I ran the craft shop. That was a good life. And, after his death, how lucky I'd been to find Ted! Ted who even insists I keep my former name, Peaches Dann, just because he says it would make a better pen name than Peaches Holleran.

Ted lay asleep, breathing easily under our double-wedding-ring quilt. Made by Bessie Justice of Reem's Creek. My life changes but my taste doesn't. And I thought how Ted even breathes like a good man, so slow and even. And then my eye fell on the alarm clock on Ted's side of the bed.

Good grief, nine-thirty. I'd missed my morning writing time. And I felt like I should have been up already, combating evil. Though I wasn't sure exactly where to start. Ted rolled over and opened one eye as if he felt my eyes on him. He sat up and said, "I guess after yesterday we needed sleep." He stretched lazily and grinned. I scooted across the bed and gave him a good-morning kiss. And felt comforted.

There was evil out there but somebody loved me. Somebody who stood with me against the evil. I scooted back over to my side of the bed, swung my feet over the side, and put them my furry slippers.

I must think positive. It seemed like all the strange discoveries — from Watt's list to digitoxin poisoning — were weaving a pattern around us. Like the pattern on the double-wedding-ring quilt, but ugly. I couldn't figure it out.

"I'll make coffee," Ted said. He threw on some clothes and went off to the kitchen. I washed and put on a turtleneck and one of those nice denim skirts that just wraps around and fastens with one button. A little tight. Had I gained weight? Maybe the skirt shrank. I made up my face. At my age, a little extra care pays off. Never mind, the lines at the corners of my eyes are kind lines, not mean and hard. Who was it who said that after forty you have the face you deserve? A masochist.

The phone rang and I picked up the extension by the bed. "This is Lieutenant Wilson." I didn't like the formality of the voice. An announcement voice. "I thought I should let you know that Matt Jones died last night."

"I'm sorry about that," I said, "though I hardly knew him." But he must have been valuable to someone, I thought, like Pop is valuable to me. Outrageous as he is. I hesitated. "So now you're investigating murder."

Mustache said: "I'll be talking to you later."

I put down the phone. I saw Matt Jones in his black hat, with his gun, in the graveyard. If he hadn't met me, would he still be alive? He'd made me feel in danger then. Did his death mean danger to us now?

Not nice to start the day with news of death, but the rich aroma of strong coffee from the kitchen bucked me up. And when I got there, Ted had orange juice and English muffins and coffee on the table by the window. God bless him. I told him the bad news.

"I figured you needed a little pampering today," he said. "But I didn't know the half of it. This will throw your father into a tizzy. Well, I'd better go get the paper and see if Pop and Matt Jones are in it. But I suspect Matt Jones died too late for their deadline."

I sipped my coffee and used the phone on the kitchen table to call and check on Pop, who was problem number one. Thank God, he must be alive since I'd had no news to the contrary.

I always feel like the phone is talking to me with those little beeps. Saying, "So, O.K.," then, "I'm glad to help."

And the call did help. Pop was doing well, and I gathered from the nurse's tone of voice that he was driving her crazy — unfortunate for her, but a good sign. He was receiving some kind of medical attention, so I couldn't talk to him. I was just as glad not to have to tell him about Matt Jones yet. After he heard, he'd be more afraid.

I drank my orange juice and pondered. Problem number two was Mary's burglar. I needed to call Mary and tell her about Dracula Jr. peeping in her windows and see what she had to say. I'd tried to call the night before, but one of the kids must have left the phone off the hook.

Ted hurried back in with the paper, sat down, and began to riffle through it. "I don't see a story about Pop, or Jones," he said, and then: "Oh, look at this! About the man we saw at Mary's!" He lay the paper flat, leaned forward, and read aloud:

"A car-truck accident on Lakeview Road last night about 8 P.M. injured Aloysius Haven and John Helms. Haven told police he didn't see Helms's pickup truck as he turned into Osborn Road. Haven, an assistant history professor at the University of North Carolina at Asheville, was taken to Memorial Mission Hospital, where he is listed in good condition. Helms was treated for minor injuries and released. Haven was cited for 'improper movement of a motor vehicle.'"

"No wonder he stood us up," I said.

I dialed Mary's number, to find out more about her burglar professor, but after seven rings I had to conclude she was out.

The phone rang as soon as I hung up. When it rings, it's not so friendly. It's more demanding: *Bringgg bringgg bringgg:* Answer me now! But it usually brings facts, and we sure needed more facts.

It was Anna. Since she wasn't supposed to be at Pop's house this morning, could she come see us instead? She was in town, giving her sister a ride to the doctor. Could she come see us shortly? "Of course," I said.

As I let her in the door a few minutes later, Anna put her arms around me. I could tell by the way she trembled how upset she was. "Sometimes he thought somebody was out to get him," she said, "but I never believed it." I led her to the big comfortable chair not far from the door, the one with the India print cover. I sat down near her in the rocking chair by the fireplace. I knew who she meant by *him.*

I said, "I didn't believe anybody was out to get my father, either." Because Pop put that fear in such strange ways and only on bad days.

"Come have a cup of coffee," I suggested. "We both need it." Under her country suntan, she looked pale.

We sat down together at the kitchen table, Anna frowning like she wasn't sure where to begin. She had a long thin face like a horse, and hair pulled into a bun on top of her head. Her eyes were trusting but not naive. She had that I'm-in-charge-of-my-life dignity that country people often have, and wonderful bits of Elizabethan English in her speech, like people from our back coves often do. Ted brought her a cup of coffee, for which she thanked him, and offered her juice and English muffins, to which she shook her head no. Then Ted said he had to make some phone calls in the office. I took that to mean he thought she would open up more for me alone. I'd known Anna since my daughter, Eve, was a baby, so he was probably right.

She reached across the table and took my hand. "The police came to see me this morning," she said. "They asked me questions. I don't remember all."

"That's uncomfortable," I said. "But you don't have anything to hide."

"No," she agreed, "but I wanted to tell you-uns about something odd that happened on Saturday — the day before . . ." Tears came to her eyes, but she swallowed and went on, "the day before your father took sick. Your cousin Mary came by Saturday morning. Maybe ten-thirty, maybe eleven. That part wasn't strange. And the kids were with her. They brought your father candy they made." She let go of my hand and wrung her hands together as if the kids were upsetting. My lemon-yellow kitchen, which is meant to be cheerful, made Anna look sick-yellow.

"After those kids came, I couldn't find the key to the back door that hangs on the board by the door. I have my own key, so it didn't matter." Her voice quivered like it did matter. "But I didn't like that key disappearing.

107

Sunday morning I went to your father's house and Lily said she stepped on the key and found it that way. She said it must've fallen farther from the key-board than I thought it could've, and that I'd not stopped to think it could be knocked so far away. A lot she knows.

"I'd looked all over. Lily told me exactly where she found it. And I'd looked there twice. And I think somebody took that key and then put it back to make it look like it fell on the floor. Somebody got in the house."

A shiver went through me. But Sherrie swore she was in the kitchen on her shift. Which would be in sight of the back door. Did she tell the truth? I'd have to talk to Dorothy about her shift from three in the afternoon to eleven at night. Could there be other traps in Pop's house besides digitoxin? I prayed to God the police would find them if there were. "We'll have to throw out any open food that's in the house," I said. "I take it that you told the police what you've told me."

She said she had. "But you're closer to your father and his friends," she said. "You have more chance to find out who chose to poison."

"Exactly what time were you at the house on Saturday and Sunday?" I asked.

"Why, nine to one like always on Saturday, and nine to about twelve-thirty on Sunday. I was out of the kitchen mostly on Saturday, cleaning, doing laundry. But I was in the kitchen on Sunday. Lily or I were in that kitchen all the time. Nobody but us touched any food or drink on Sunday."

"Did anything else odd happen?" I pressed her, "especially after the tea that Lily brought arrived on the kitchen table on Saturday morning and before Pop was taken sick?"

She stared at her hands, rubbing her long bony fingers together. Finally she said, "Lily got a phone call that upset her on Sunday morning. She said her husband tripped over the cat and sprained his ankle. But one of Lily's former foster kids is now a nurse. She's visiting, and she fixed it up."

Sherrie said the foster children were dangerous. A helpful trained nurse sure didn't sound like a threat.

I kept hoping that Anna would say something more telling. And Anna frowned, as if she was searching for the fact that would explain it all. It didn't come.

Finally she stood up. "I have to go back for my sister," she said.

And I couldn't believe Anna had anything to do with poison. Pop had told me he was leaving five thousand dollars to Anna in his will. Not much. Did it seem like a lot to Anna? She had a farm with a mortgage, and kids who always needed money. But I didn't believe she'd poison Pop hoping for five thousand dollars. And there was no possible way she could be involved in far-off serial murders, was there? I gave her a hug, thanked her for coming, and walked with her to the door. I watched her trudge out to her old Ford and take off.

I came back to find Ted holding out the phone. "It's Lieutenant Wilson," he said. "For you."

My heart beat faster. Mustache calling a second time. He must have found something important in Pop's house.

"I have some good news," he said. "I could tell you were upset about your father's secret drawer. You thought there might be something in that drawer that could get your father in some trouble, right?"

"Knowing Pop, I sure did." Yes. Everything swirled around Pop.

He laughed. "I certainly won't break your father's confidence about what's in it," he said. "But I want you to rest assured. So I called you as soon as we found out. There is nothing in his secret spot that could hurt anybody. Nothing whatsoever."

I thanked him. I asked if there were any other clues to show what happened to poor Matt Jones and to Pop. To that, he sighed. "If anyone entered the house who didn't have a reason to be there," he said, "they were careful not to leave any clues that we can trace, at least so far." He paused. "I imagine your father's housekeeper will tell you that your father's back-door key was missing part of Saturday and found Sunday morning." Check.

I thanked him and replaced the phone. Out

the window a robin was on the birdbath. The cat was nowhere in sight. I was glad of that.

The phone rang again. One of those days. It was Mary. Good. I'd been trying to get her.

"How's Pop?" she asked. I told her his friend Matt had died.

"I'm glad it wasn't somebody I know," she said, with a shudder in her voice. She also said she was going over to the hospital, and could the kids stick their heads in and say Hi to Pop? I told her to call the ICU and ask. Maybe they'd even move him out of there. He seemed to be recovering.

And then I told her about the man in the black suit who looked in all her windows the night before. The man who had the key to the shed with the ladder in it.

She burst out laughing. Was this the day when everybody laughed? "He was named Loy Haven, right? He's the one who wrote that booklet about walks you showed me." Check.

"Yes," I said, "and he said he wanted to talk to me. What on earth is this all about?"

"Loy teaches medieval history," she said, as if any fool could see that explained it. "And he's lonesome, so we're friends. Actually, he's shy. He tries to shock people so they won't notice."

"And so?" I asked.

"And he's fascinated by medieval memory systems. They had these complicated systems where you filed things in your brain like it had an index."

"Like an index?" I said, amazed.

"He thinks we should learn more from history than just what happened. He thinks we ought to use the systems they had that worked. So Loy and I made two bets."

"Two bets about memory?"

"Yes," she said. "The first was that he could look inside my house and then tell me everything that's in it, in order, frontwards or backwards. Loy has a one-track mind, and I'll admit that he's eccentric. But he isn't dangerous."

"And you think he was casing your house last night in order to surprise you by remembering everything that's in it?"

"Yes," she said. "Frontwards and backwards. I'm sure he was."

"But did you give him the key to the shed with the ladder in it?"

Her voice became defensive. "No, I didn't do that. But maybe I told him that I keep the key under a flat rock by the shed door. He would have remembered."

"He looked creepy climbing that ladder in that strange black suit."

She laughed again. "He thinks we're too informal in this modern age," she said. "He's a character. But he's nice to me. And to the kids."

"He was in an automobile accident last night," I said. I should have told her that first. But my curiosity got the best of me. "There's a story in today's paper."

Ted handed me the *Citizen-Times* and I read the story to her.

"Good grief," she said. "I have two people to visit in the hospital in one day."

"And what was the second bet he made with you?" I asked.

"Oh," she said, "he bet that he could teach you to remember absolutely anything. I figured that would be the acid test."

After I hung up I realized that I'd forgotten to tell her I had her pocketbook.

I was standing by the phone wondering if this Dracula Jr. really was capable of miracles in the memory department, when Ted came over, holding out the booklet *Quiet Walks Near Asheville*. He held the booklet in a piece of cloth, open to a page near the back. There was a piece of torn paper stuck into the spine. "Look at this," he said.

"But what am I looking for?" I asked.

"Look closely at this torn piece of paper, which I just came across while leafing through the back."

The paper was yellowed and fragile and appeared to have been torn out of an old book, and one line was underlined. It said: *I throw myself on the mercy of the Lord.*

I gasped. "I remember! The two phony suicide notes said that!"

"Yes, exactly," Ted agreed. He sat down at the table as if he needed a firm base to think from. I sat down too.

"Watt told us the notes were found next to victims," he said, "who'd evidently been parted from their assets and then forced to take sleeping pills. The killer seemed to have made his victims write the notes almost in the same words. And look here. This piece of paper is not just stuck carelessly in this book. It's held in place by two small pieces of Scotch tape."

"But this booklet with the suicide-note words was at Pop's house," I said, shivering, "and we don't know how it got there. Except that Mary took this Dracula Jr. to meet Pop. But she says he didn't give Pop a booklet. And if he had, he wouldn't have left incriminating evidence in it! Taped in! Unless," I said, "he has some crazy need to leave things in books."

Ted took the booklet back, *mercy of the Lord* and all. "I had suspected that somebody left the booklet at Pop's for us, since we go exploring and Pop doesn't. And that they'd left it with the corner turned down at the part about the graveyard walk, since I'm interested in old tombstones." He ran his fingers through his hair as if he hoped that would stimulate his brains. "But now I wonder. Is it possible that the words from the old book were left for us on purpose too?" He stared down at the booklet as if it could tell him what happened. "No," he said, "that doesn't make sense."

Then he raised his head and looked me straight in the eye. "But, for better or worse, there is one conclusion we can draw from all

114

this. There must be a connection between the serial killer and your father's circle of helpers, relatives, and friends."

I shivered. "Or between the killer and someone that you or I or Mary or some cousin has brought by the house. That leaves us with an awful lot of choices." I made myself think ahead. "But I know where I want us to start asking questions. Because I'm so curious. I'm for Mary's burglar."

CHAPTER 10

LATE MONDAY MORNING

We went into the office where we write, and Ted put the *Walks* booklet carefully into a small box. "We may have obliterated the fingerprints on it before ours," he said, "but we may not have." He called Mustache, who said he'd send someone right over to get it and talk to us later.

Then Ted took the big calendar down from the wall and laid it flat on his desk. "Before we talk to Mary's professor," he said, "we ought to talk to Dorothy, since she was the three-to-eleven sitter the evening before Pop and Matt Jones were poisoned. We've talked to Lily and Sherrie, who worked the other shifts. So if we talk to Dorothy, we may get a handle on the times when the back door and the tea and the sugar were not right under somebody's nose. We'll see the poisoner's window of opportunity."

I agreed, and called Dorothy, but she was out.

I hung up and immediately the phone shrilled. There on the line was Mary's "shy" friend, Dracula Jr. himself. The very one I was so curious about. A brisk voice with a hint of a

116

British accent said, "This is Loy Haven, who never arrived at the Fine Friends restaurant last night. I want to apologize." He certainly didn't sound like a serial killer.

"I was in an automobile accident right after I saw you," he explained, "and spent the night in the hospital. By the time I had a chance to call, you had left the restaurant." He said that just as cheerfully as if he'd said he was sorry the phone was out of order. I told him we'd read about it in the paper. "But now that I'm home," he added pleasantly, "I hope that we can get together. It will be a pleasure to meet a fellow memory buff."

"When can *we* come?" I asked. I did not care to visit a madman alone.

"Why, any time in the next hour or so would be perfectly suitable," he replied. "I'm on crutches and a little unsteady today, so I'm staying home from classes. I truly look forward to meeting you."

One part of me was flattered silly. One part of me was wary.

I put Ted on the phone to get directions. Turned out Loy's house was just a little way off Lakeshore Drive. Not far. Even I could get there without getting lost.

Shortly thereafter a patrolman came by to pick up the booklet. We were free to go.

"Let's take two cars because I have to go on from there to keep an appointment with a student, and then I have a class," Ted said. But as we were both getting into our cars, he said, "Damn, I forgot my briefcase."

He went back in to get it and I started on. He drives faster than I do anyway, so I figured he'd catch up. When that didn't happen, I thought, Ha! He should follow my system and leave the briefcase at the door where he'd have to trip over it. He must have mislaid the case and had to search.

Anyway, I arrived first. Dracula Jr. lived in a house that was both formal and small. Made of flat fieldstone. There's lots of fieldstone used for building in these mountains. But his house was unusual, like a square mini-fortress, with small windows and a large dark wood door complete with shining brass knocker. Maybe that's what he and Mary had in common — they both liked to shine brass. There were boxwood bushes on each side of the front door, and unlike our boxwood hedge, which mostly sprawls, his bushes were clipped absolutely square, just like his house.

Well, heck, I thought, I might as well go on in. How dangerous can a man on crutches be? Besides, if anything happened to me, he'd know that Ted would know that he was the cause. Right?

He answered my knock so fast, he must have been standing by the door. He hung on his crutches and beamed as broadly as if he didn't have a bandage on one side of his forehead and a cast on one leg: "Welcome."

Ted would be coming in a minute, I explained. All Loy Haven said was, "I'm so glad you could come. We can compare notes on memory systems!" He still had his Transylvania hair-do, that slicked-back black hair with the widow's peak, but no black suit. But he had such lively eyes. He wore a brown tweed jacket with suede elbow patches and a tan shirt. Very professorial. I almost rescinded his nickname but not quite. He was still pale. Maybe sunshine gave him hives.

"I've been looking forward to meeting you ever since I heard about your book," he cried. "I don't meet many kindred spirits."

He stood so close, I felt as if he were invading my air space. "Let's sit down and talk," I suggested.

He leaned back on his crutches as if shocked. "Oh, no," he said. "I want to show you how my resurrected memory system works. I want to show you the real inspiration of my memory bins." His eyes positively glowed.

Perhaps I looked as crowded as I felt. He shrugged and deflated. "We can sit down if you want to," he said more calmly. "I get carried away." He leaned on the crutch pad under his arm and ran his hand over his forehead. Pointed white hand near pointed black widow's peak, half covered by white bandage. "I may need to explain some things to you first."

He waved me into an overstuffed chair and carefully lowered himself into another one opposite, leaning the crutches against the chair arm. "You know, my real interest is in the medieval period."

I could have guessed if Mary hadn't told me. Why else would he have a huge photograph of a stone gargoyle on one wall, a piece of tapestry with a unicorn on it on another wall, and a piece of illuminated manuscript with letters twined in colored vines near the front door. Even right by my chair was a low table with a book on it, where I couldn't miss it. *The Book of Memory: A Study in Medieval Culture* by Mary Carruthers. It was almost as if Dracula Jr. had overdone the medieval thing, as if he were playing a part.

"We need to take advantage of the knowledge from the past," he said. "And I have been experimenting with medieval memory systems like those of Albertus Magnus and Hugh of St. Victor and Thomas Bradwardine and Peter of Ravenna." He said that as if I must know and absolutely love those four men, whoever they were.

I wondered if this man wore his black suit, when he did, to balance his galloping enthusiasm. His eyes felt hot, looking into mine. I looked down at my hands, but then I looked back up. His intensity made me feel I might miss something if I didn't pay close attention.

And I *am* interested in how to remember. I have to be.

"I don't know their memory systems," I said.

"Mostly I've stuck to what works for me."

"I suppose you do know about Simonides?" he said, suddenly becoming more formal. Like this was a quiz.

"He was the ancient Greek who thought of using parts of a house to remember parts of a speech." I'd read about that.

"But I hope you know the whole story," he cried. "Imagine, just by sheer chance Simonides was called out of a banquet to get a message. And by sheer chance the roof collapsed while he was gone, and all his friends were so badly maimed that no one could even recognize the bodies. Their faces were all staved in, bodies mangled and covered in blood." He said that like he was visualizing the scene with relish, leaning forward in his chair, eyes flashing. Like the gore thrilled him to the core. "And how Simonides rose to that occasion! How clever he was to figure out how to tell who was who just by letting his mind go round the table, by visualizing, in order, where each one sat." He nodded approval. "And then he realized he'd hit on the perfect memory system: remembering things by place." Dracula Jr. shook his head in wonder.

"And what a boon for Greek orators," he cried. "Because a roof fell in. We underestimate the beneficial side effects of what we call catastrophe."

I wished Ted would come. The roof looked sound, but Dracula Jr. was making me nervous.

Talk about ambivalent. I didn't want to miss a word he said, but I didn't feel really safe with him either.

"Only after Simonides," he went on, "did an orator know that if he attached each idea to a specific place in a house, he could keep his ideas in order and remember them exactly as he wanted to."

The unicorn in the tapestry behind him pointed its horn right at the bandage near Dracula Jr.'s left ear.

"But Simonides was an ancient Greek," I said, "and you are interested in medieval things like unicorns."

"Ah, yes," he said, "but in the Middle Ages, scholars revered memory so much that they used Simonides' system and every other system they could lay their hands on. They improved on the classic systems. They indexed their memories the way we index books or maps. And they did it with numbers and letters and little bins."

That sounded a heck of a lot more complicated than a string on the finger, but then I'm always game to learn.

"Come, I'll show you," he urged. "So what I'm saying will make sense."

He carefully pushed himself up, and I handed him the crutches. He waved me back to the front door, opened it, and asked me to come outside. We stood in chilly wind. Bracing. Still no sign of Ted. No car in sight, though I couldn't see too far down the winding street.

"Now," he said, "if each part of the house is numbered, so that each idea associated with it may be pulled up on demand at any time, we have an index of the mind, right? The front door is the first place."

I shivered in the wind. "And you remember the number of each part of your house, instantly, on demand?" I asked. "I'm not good at numbers. I have to use tricks to remember a telephone number from the time I look in the book till the time I get to the phone."

"I can remember a series of memory places in my house and a number of other, bigger buildings, including the courthouse and the civic center." He held up his head like he'd won a prize. But then his brown eyes turned from proud to soft. "If you have trouble with numbering, we'll work on that first." So he was a professional teacher. So now I was his pupil.

"Just for practice," he said, "I'll get you to use the same system of unusual images to remember the numbers that we'll use to remember the things and ideas that we put in the bins. That's not exactly the medieval way, but we have to adapt historical systems to fit us."

Bins again. If I waited, the thing would come clear.

He pointed to the large dark-wood front door. He rapped the brass door knocker. "Now, here is the front door," he said. I could see that.

"I'm sure you can remember that the front

door is where we start. Place Number One. That makes sense. But I want you to keep in mind the brass door knocker. I use it in images. So just think about it this way. If you were twenty-*one* and you showed up at this door stark naked and said, 'I'm all yours, Loy,' you'd be likely to get knocked up." He leered. The nerve of the man! He was a professor, for gosh sakes. And Mary said he was shy! She said he hid it by shocking people. Well, I was damned if I would look shocked. My mouth probably dropped open anyway.

"So next to the door you see an image of yourself pregnant and going into labor. You'll remember the knocker as part of Place Number *One*."

"I would hardly expect anybody as intellectual as you to use the phrase 'knocked up,'" I said with all my dignity.

He smiled. "That amazed you," he said. "That's what we aim at in each image you see. That's what's typically medieval." He leaned on his crutches and put his cold hand on my shoulder.

"What is marvelous impresses us and is retained in the memory, Albertus Magnus said. And furthermore," Loy added, as I began to shiver, "Thomas Bradwardine, who was chaplain to King Edward the Third and also Archbishop of Canterbury, said that the best memory images should be wondrous, intense, and extreme." If Loy got that fired up in a classroom, he must be a good teacher — unless of course his female students complained about verbal harassment.

"Bradwardine had an image to help remember the signs of the zodiac," he said, "where a white ram with golden horns stood on its hind feet and was kicked by a red bull with swollen testicles. The ram was bleeding wildly, and next to him a pair of twins were ripped from the uterus of . . ."

"I get the idea," I said, "and it's cold out here." Perhaps my taste was different from King Edward the Third's.

"Oh, I'm sorry," he said. "I get carried away. Come into the foyer."

By foyer he seemed to mean that part of the living room by the front door. He waved at the wall to the right of the door, where a large picture frame held an arrangement of sketches of medieval abbeys.

"Now this is Place Number Two," he said. "It's not as large as some systems recommend, but this is a small house and it works fine for me." So he was a use-what-you-have man. I did approve of that.

"I glued all these sketches into this collage," he said. 'Therefore you might try to see an image of me as a huge living bottle of glue with a removable cap, and glue oozing out the top, and remember *two glue*."

An unattractive thought, but I *am* good at remembering rhymes, and his hair did look glued down. He still seemed a little crazy. Never antagonize the insane. Especially when you're home with them alone and . . . Good Lord, what was that thing he was picking up?

Beyond the glue picture was a bookcase, and from a space between the books he was picking up a battle-axe. I kid you not. A real baltle-axe? Or left from some college theatrical event? I hoped.

"This axe . . ." he said with relish, holding the crutches with his armpits, and waving the axe, "this axe would have been used during the Crusades for cutting down Saracens and by Charlemagne's men in the battle at Roncesvalles."

I stepped back involuntarily. He lifted the axe a little unsteadily, as if he were going to bring it down on my head.

Then he laughed. "Now you must come up with some image connected with the fact that this axe is in Place Number Three."

Actually my mind went blank.

"I've been suggesting images so you'd get the idea," he said. "But one thing the medieval memory experts stressed was that each person must make his own personal associations to remember by. Each person must have his own individual mental index bins and put his own individual memory images in them." He raised the axe high. Just to inspire me? Or because he enjoyed scaring innocent females half to death?

"Tree," I yelled. "I'd rather have you use that on a tree. Not on me!"

"Very good," he said in the kind of encouraging voice he might have used for a class. "And *tree* sounds almost like *three*. Just add an *H*. Now, if you remember me with an axe trying to decide whether to chop you or a tree, that's a good image. An image is easier to bring to mind if there's violent action in it. As I say, Bradwardine wrote about that."

Ted, where are you? I asked myself. Loy couldn't be the serial killer, could he? Because he would certainly kill with a broadaxe at least. Not with quiet old sleeping pills. But his relish for violence made me very uneasy, I'll tell you that.

"Now," he said, "this old-fashioned oak door leads to the bedroom. It's Place Number Four. What image can you think of to fix that in your mind?"

I'm old enough so I don't expect young college professors to make passes at me. Mature men, yes. But this Loy was almost a kid compared to me. And yet I didn't like him edging me toward the bedroom. Not after the knocked-up bit, or the state of the bull's testicles recommended by the Archbishop of Canterbury.

"Just say the first strong image that comes to your mind related to a bedroom door," he ordered.

"*Four*-poster bed," I said. He winked.

"Bradwardine would approve of that. And if you think of action to go with it, even better, my dear. And visualize the bed and the action with the door."

In spite of myself, I saw someone peeking through the keyhole at the action in the bed. Brad whatever-his-name-was had me in his sway.

Dracula Jr. opened Number Four into his bedroom. A black suit, probably the one he had on the night before, was hanging on a mahogany stand. The open closet door revealed assorted, mostly black, shirts. He was taking me in his bedroom. And why wasn't I objecting? Was I fascinated like a rabbit caught in the headlights of a car? Or was I just so durn amazed that I had to hear what on earth he would say next? Curiosity killed the cat. My grandmother used to say that.

Suppose I was taking my time here and Ted was in an accident. Accidents happen. Ted is careful, I told myself, even if he does drive fast.

A large, bushy philodendron plant sat on the stone windowsill. Practically filled it. The thing looked like somebody gave it vitamin pills. The long tendrils were trained around the window, in place of curtains. Like vines curling round the letters in an illuminated manuscript.

"This is Place Five —" He waved at the window. "How will you remember that?"

"Well, like I say, I like rhymes and that plant certainly is thriving, so *five thrive*," I said.

He shook his head, bandage and all. I'd flunked. "*Thrive* would be easy to forget because it's so normal," he said. "Think of this as a man-eating plant. Then you'll wish it didn't thrive. Then you'll remember."

I wished he wouldn't look so pleased with himself.

"Now," he said, "the bed is Place Number Six."

I gave up resisting the method. "*Six sex,*" I said.

He beamed. He didn't have to say it: A-plus. "And be sure to have a good sharp image to go with that." I saw him with Mary in bed. She might never have been there. Never mind. Mary got me into this.

"Some medieval monasteries had to have rules that the monks must not remember by sexual images," he said. "Because they are so effective, and the monks had so many texts to remember." Did he have to keep leering?

"Now, you see that overstuffed chair?" he asked. "Sit down in it. It's heavenly comfortable. And it's Place Number Seven."

"*Seven heaven,*" I said.

"But make that more dramatic," he said. "You could picture God in it complete with long white beard."

Personally, I didn't picture God with a long white beard. But this was Loy's memory device.

"I understand what you're doing," I said, interested in spite of myself. "But after I have the whole house numbered and dramatized so I can remember each number, what do I do then?"

He sat down in a straight chair catercornered to mine and propped his crutches against the stand with the suit on it. "Why, then, after the house is numbered, I'll tell you what I can do," he said. "I can remember any sequence of ideas — in a class lecture, for example — or any list of objects, as in all of the things in your cousin Mary's house. I can remember them frontwards or backwards, or even remember which is the third in the list or the tenth or whatever I want to recall. I am in control of my thoughts."

I couldn't exactly see how God in an armchair, or a broadaxe raised to bean me, or the image that came to me of Loy in bed with Mary, whether she actually ever was or not — I couldn't quite see how any of those images would make the system work.

"O.K.," he said, "let's try remembering what's in Mary's house. The first thing I saw through the window was the china cat on the bookshelf on the far side of the room. Now, my first memory space or bin is the front door. How would you make a dramatic memory image against that door?"

I hesitated.

"What I made myself," he said, "was an image of the china cat, hanging by its paws from the shining brass door knocker of Place

130

Number One. Like the cats in those posters that say 'Hang In There.' If the cat fell, it would break. Think of the crash. I bet you could remember that."

So that's why he kept his door knocker shined up. To help with images.

"Next," he said, "came several red books between two plain bookends. How would you remember those?"

I looked at his glued-down black hair. "The Two place was the picture with glue."

He nodded encouragement. "See your image in that place."

"In front of that collage I'll picture the red books with glue spilled all over. And since glue won't show too much, I'll stick some chicken feathers in the glue. Like the books were glued and feathered. I once saw a picture of a man who had been tarred and feathered, and it upset me so much maybe I'll remember the red books."

"You're getting the idea," he said. "And you'll remember they are in the Two place. Now, next in Mary's house was a rather large sign stuck in the bookshelf. It said 'Think Positive.' Now, it's always easier to remember something concrete than something abstract. What can you think of that is concrete that would mean 'Think Positive' to you?"

Think positive would actually mean I was thinking out the questions I needed to ask this man. That he was not distracting me from the reason why I was here. I was tempted to tell him that. And suddenly I thought: Is this all a show to divert me? Like a mask for him to hide behind? I haven't learned anything about this man himself. And I've been here over half an hour. And where is Ted?

But I knew I needed to change the subject tactfully, to find the right moment, keep him in a helpful mood.

"How about a large wooden 'plus' sign for 'Think Positive'?" I asked.

"Good start!" Was his smile artificial?

"And Place Three," I said, "is by the broadaxe which could cut down a *tree* instead of me, and *tree* is *three* without the *H*."

"So how do you make an image with action?" he demanded.

"Why, in front of the broadaxe," I said, "I see a man cutting down a plus sign with an axe. Or, if he cuts it down, does that mean 'Think Negative'?"

"That question can help you to remember," he said. "The more ideas you cluster around a memory, the easier it is to bring that memory back."

I could get so interested that I stopped suspecting Loy. Was that what he was aiming at? Pathological killers can act almost like normal people, but they don't have normal feelings. I read that somewhere. Could that be what he had to hide?

On the other hand, a pill-killer wouldn't keep

132

a broadaxe in the living room. Would he?

"Say, that memory by shock is really interesting," I said, hoping my fears didn't show. "I've looked at modern memory books, and they suggest you try to remember by using images, surprise, and action. But they don't suggest shock. How long a list can you remember when you shock yourself?"

"I don't know," he said. "I've never hit the limit. When I need to, I just make more memory bins. You see, each space I can stick a memory image in is a bin. Hugh of St. Victor calls memory a line of bins in a numbered grid. And many medieval scholars could remember the grid without further aid. What marvelous trained memories they had!" He was getting carried away again. Or trying harder to divert me. But he stopped and sighed. "I'm not that good. Personally I find it helpful to attach my numbers to a place in the older way. I have several buildings I use, several with numbers and one with the bins marked by the letters of the alphabet."

I certainly wasn't ready for a mental grid all numbered and remembered neat. Just thinking of it made me feel a little dizzy. "So what else was in Mary's house?" I asked. Maybe in a little bit I could ease the subject around from Mary's house to how long he'd lived in Asheville, and if he'd been off somewhere else in the last couple of years. Like, down east where he could murder people.

He shut his eyes a moment. Seeing things inside his head? "Books. The rest of Mary's top shelf was full of books," he said. "I couldn't read the titles from across the room."

So we kept at placing Mary's things, and I kept wishing Ted would come, until we got to Number Six: Two china dancing mice. Well, that was easy to associate with the sixth-place bed: *six sex*. My friend Lula uses the word *dancing* to mean have sex. I was wondering how to work in the mice when the doorbell rang. Good. That must be Ted. He'd get us tactfully back on the right trail. And if necessary, two people can deal with trouble better than one, right?

I followed Loy, who began thump thump thumping on his crutches, back past points six, five, four, three, and two into the living room to answer door one. There stood Ted with no signs of an accident. Plaid shirt not even rumpled. Good. In fact as soon as he was inside, he explained he was late because he'd had to cope with a flat tire.

"Well, we've been fine," I said, "and our friend here will explain to you how he remembers long lists and speeches, all because a roof fell in."

Ted is good at remembering numbers. Opposites attract. And he really seemed interested. So Loy just showed him: door one, picture two, axe three, bedroom door four, philodendron five, bed six, chair seven. Then while I sat down in chair seven, and Ted sat down in the chair across from it, Loy sat on the end of the bed and told Ted exactly the image we'd made up to represent each item in Mary's house so far and how we "saw" each image at a numbered place.

We hadn't used chair seven yet. So, to try the system, Ted made up an image for the next thing on Mary's shelf, which Loy said was a red mug.

Ted said he'd remember it in spot number seven instead of me. "My wife is always writing, so what I see in that chair," Ted said, "is a face with writing on the cheeks and the forehead, and the sides of the nose. I read the writing and it's a *read* mug."

Loy clapped his hands so hard, he almost slipped off the end of the bed. "Puns are great memory aids," he cried. "Albertus Magnus loved them!"

"But doesn't it take you forever to think of all that stuff?" Ted asked.

"At first it did." Loy raised his head, proud again. "But now I know my bins so thoroughly by heart, and I've had so much practice that I can do it very fast." He positively preened. "I can recall hundreds of objects to show other people how well the system works." Compared to Ted with his gray-streaked hair, Loy looked so young. He dressed so old, I hadn't thought about that. The serial killer was described as young.

"Well, this is fascinating," Ted said. "Could you remember things in real time, though? Could you remember everything you did on Saturday?"

"Oh, that doesn't require any system." Loy laughed. He rattled off the things he'd done from jogging with five neighborhood dogs before breakfast to working on an article about medieval puns to spending the evening in the library. Except for the dogs, he'd been more or less alone all day. No alibi. But maybe Mary was right. Maybe he was just shy and lonely.

"Well, I'm impressed with your memory system," I said. "I bet you win your first bet with Mary. What came next on her shelf after the red mug?"

He blinked. Surprised at the switchback to that subject? "Next," he said, "was a small, cheap-looking, imitation crystal ball." How odd. Had I seen that in Mary's room? Maybe it was new. Was Mary into future-reading now, the way Pop had suddenly been lately? Sherrie read the Tarot for him almost every day. I suspected she used that to manipulate him somehow. But I wasn't sure how. And that made me uneasy. My mind was wandering.

Next thing, I heard Ted saying, "And how long have you lived here?" God bless Ted. I'd been diverted. I'd strayed again from the reason why we were at this Loy's house: to find out as much as we could about him.

"Just since college opened in late August," he

replied. "I was lucky to find a house to rent so quickly, and the last tenant even left some furniture."

"And before that?" Ted asked.

He said he'd been down in Durham doing some research in the Duke library for about a year, and working on his book. He was writing a whole book on medieval puns. "And before that," he said, "I was abroad. I was backpacking around Europe studying medieval sites, like the cathedral at Chartres. I did that for two years after I finished at Cambridge."

Very impressive — but, I wondered, wasn't backpacking around Europe vague enough so that he could have been doing something entirely different, and who would know? For instance, my cousin Jason got a fake passport while draft-dodging during the Vietnam war, and went where he pleased.

"I have learned to understand how medieval people thought," Loy said firmly, as if he was afraid we doubted him. "Do you know that they believed you needed a well-developed memory to get to heaven? They believed all the saints had super-memories. Because *memoria* — that's Latin for memory — helped you to know what was moral and right. Why, Thomas Aquinas said —"

Ted headed him off at the pass. "And you got back to this country a year ago?"

"A year ago in July," he said.

Durham put him in shooting distance, so to

speak, of the couple who died in Winston. If he was smart enough to lead a double life. Unfortunately, I figured he was. And smart enough to pick a method of murder that would seem untypical of him. Also, I was sure he could act any part.

"I believe my cousin Mary introduced you to my father," I said, trying to make my remark sound offhand.

"Yes," he said. "What an interesting man! Mary tells me he's been reading the life of Albertus Magnus."

"That was nice of you to give him that booklet you wrote about interesting walks."

He raised his head sharply and stared at me. "But I didn't!" he protested. "I thought of sending him one, but I felt that might be a tactless gift to a man in a wheelchair."

I had to admit it was rather farfetched to think that he left the book at Pop's on the off chance that we'd go to the graveyard and start the Matt Jones train of events. Farfetched to think that was somehow related to a string of serial killings. But life can be very strange. And Loy certainly was.

I didn't like to suspect Loy. He was the only person I knew who was a true one hundred percent memory buff. The only person I knew who seemed to consider me his valued colleague in that field. I suspected he was just eccentric enough so he'd have trouble being close to anyone. Interesting as he was, he might still put off a woman who wanted a relationship. But he wouldn't kill. It's true that if he stole money from elderly people and stashed it away, he could easily remember the numbers of his Swiss bank accounts. He wouldn't need a written clue.

But I hoped Loy was interested in the treasures of the mind — that he wouldn't kill for plain old money.

I kind of liked Loy. If he wasn't a homicidal maniac, he might be husband material. He was smart and had an interesting job. (And Mary picked such odd ducks, she didn't leave much for a matchmaker to work with, did she?) Maybe Mary could make him laugh and relax. Maybe what he needed most in the world was to be able to laugh at himself.

And if I couldn't be sure whether he was a killer or a possible husband for my cousin, how on earth would I ever sort things out?

CHAPTER
11

LATE LUNCH, MONDAY

Just as we were leaving, Dracula Jr.'s phone rang. "I hope it's not the college," he said. "I hope they're not asking me to advise another club. I have to do what they ask, you know, in order to get tenure." He clenched his fists, like what-an-ordeal. "I advise the History Club," he said, as the phone kept ringing, "and that's enough. And I take an active part in the college chapter of the Society for Creative Anachronism."

The what? Too late to ask. He'd picked up the phone and waved goodbye.

We hesitated outside his stone fort, standing between the two square-clipped boxwoods, adjusting to the ordinary world — at least that's what I was doing. The cold wind had died down and we were quite warm in the sunshine.

"Good Lord," I said to Ted, "how do you suppose he'd act if he wasn't trying to get a permanent contracts." I wrote "Soc. Creati. Anach." in my notebook, hoping I'd remember later what it meant.

Ted winked. "At least we can be sure that nobody sleeps in his classes."

A car meandered by on the road in front of

the house. A white-haired man kept looking this way and that out the windows. Lost, evidently. I felt for him.

"And I will never forget seven of Loy's memory places." I had to admit that. "Or how to make an image with enough red-hot shock value to stick in my mind.

"And I need to do that with his real name, and not keep calling him Dracula Jr.," I said. "Or I'll forget and say it to his face." Right now I remembered his name was Loy. But I needed to *keep on* remembering. Well, you could add a *P* and get ploy, and maybe this whole business of trying to shock people was a ploy, a clever trick to hide what he was really like. Loy, the master of the ploy. But Albertus Magnus would have preferred something sexier and more concrete.

"Look," Ted said, "I do have to go on and get to this meeting, and then my class. Then later this afternoon we can figure out what to do next. Try Dorothy again when you get a chance.

"I'll call and make an appointment for us to go to the *Asheville Citizen-Times* right away," he added, "and work it out so we can case some other area papers like the *Mountaineer* in Waynesville and the *Times-News* in Hendersonville and the *Watauga Democrat*, if we need to."

"And I'll return Mary's red pocketbook, which we never managed to return last night," I said.

"Be careful," he said wryly. "The people you suspect the least can be killers."

"No problem," I said. "I suspect everybody. I'm even working at suspecting you, which is hard because we were out of town together when somebody tried to poison Pop."

He kissed me. "And besides," I said, "it's very suspicious how you keep trying to worm your way into my affections."

We got in our cars and Ted took off with only a small squeal of tires.

I drove back over to Merrimon Avenue, stopped in the shopping center, where there's room for the tailgate market in the summertime, and ordered a gyro sandwich at Ike's International. Then I went to the phone booth just inside the door and called Dorothy. I caught her. To be exact, I woke her up. She yawned. "Sorry, I was napping." And then she asked about Pop. At least I had good news there.

Dorothy had been with us over a year. I had no reason to distrust her. But my motto had to be, as Ted said, "Distrust everybody." Dorothy was extremely pious. Her latest bumper sticker said "Trust in the Lord." But she used to be married to a racing driver, so she had hidden depths. Now she was married to a nice young traveling paper-products salesman.

"I'm sorry to bother you," I said. "But answer me a few questions real quick and I'll let you go back to sleep. Tell me exactly what

142

happened on your shift on Saturday." I poised my pencil above my notebook, ready.

I heard her yawn, but then she started right in: "I got there about ten of three because I was changing shifts with Sherrie, and Lily was laughing about how Sherrie wasn't supposed to smoke in the house, so how did she get ashes in the sugar." She yawned again. "I don't think Lily likes Sherrie."

"And then what happened?"

"I sat in the living room with your father. He asked me to play him some musical tapes: some Irish fiddle music and some mountain folk songs and some of the music that was popular when he was young. And then I brought him some soup for supper and —"

I interrupted. "Did you hear any sounds from the kitchen during that time?"

"No, and everything looked perfectly normal when I went out to the kitchen to make the soup. Then, after your father ate, I took the dishes out and everything still looked normal."

"What time did you get the soup?" I asked, pencil poised to write that down.

Silence. She wasn't sure. "It must have been around seven, and I took the dishes back around seven-thirty. He listened to one more tape, and then I took him in and got him ready for bed, and he went to sleep around eight-thiry, I think."

Very early for Pop, but he gets bored with

Dorothy. That's why her normal shift is in the wee hours.

"Then I sat and sewed in the living room, where I could hear if he was restless, until about nine-thirty. Then I went in the kitchen, which still looked normal, and watched television until Sherrie arrived."

I thanked her, hung up, and put my notebook away. Someone could easily have slipped into the kitchen while Dorothy was playing some rousing music for Pop.

When I got back to the table, my sandwich was waiting. I was hungry and glad that a gyro sandwich is pretty hefty — half sandwich, half salad.

I stared up at a travel poster of Istanbul as I chewed. No chance of missing the fact that Ike was Turkish. He even had a harem costume framed in a glass case just at the front of the restaurant. And I got to thinking how Asheville has somebody from everywhere. While I ate my sandwich, I shut out death and thought about that. How unusual it is in a mountain town of only maybe fifty thousand, where some of the people from nearby coves are descended from original settlers. Some of them, even our Anna, use Elizabethan turns of phrase. Like *you-uns* instead of *you-all*. But all sorts of people are drawn here. Some are just tourists. Other people come through and then just announce that Asheville is so beautiful, here in the bowl of the mountains, they are going to quit their jobs back wherever they came from and find whatever job they can in Asheville and stay. I'm not sure I'd have the nerve to do that.

It will be hard, I thought, with a little jolt of reality, to spot a wandering killer among so many newcomers in a town like this. That's for sure.

To cheer myself up, I reached in my shoulder bag and pulled out a printout of a chapter of the book I'm working on. It was a new idea, not even in the outline yet. The outline keeps growing. But if I work on the book a little every day, no matter what, I'll finish it no matter who gets murdered. I read over what I'd done so far on the newborn chapter as I drank my coffee.

No-No's for the Absent-Minded

A how-to-avoid-catastrophe list, almost all from personal experience. I've left a blank space to add the no-no's you've learned the hard way. Embarrassments (Is it by coincidence that this word says "bare ass" in the middle?):

— As you eat a large meal, do not unbutton the single button that holds on a wraparound skirt, swearing to yourself that you'll be sure to rebutton it before you stand up. Especially do not do this unless you have good-looking legs and wear good-looking underpants. I guess the masculine version is not to unzip your pants, for the same reason. The result is not as dramatic. Pants slip down slowly. Wrap skirts fall off.

That reminded me how tight my skirt was getting as I lit into my gyro sandwich. I could certainly unbutton the button safely with a be-careful reminder right in my hands. So I did.

— *Do not set the custard pie in the chair for any reason, however briefly, no matter how full the table is.*

I had baklava, never custard pie, at Ike's.

— *Do not put the outfit you're going to wear to the wedding on top of the car while you arrange your stuff inside. It may make a lovely kite when you take off, but after that truck runs over your dress or suit, the pleats or crease just won't set right. The best you can do is use the tire tracks on the back for a conversation piece. And things can get worse. My friend Charles somehow didn't see the kite effect and never saw his new suit again. Some homeless hitchhiker probably enjoyed it, but is that really the best way to give to charity?*

And never put anything on the hood of your car to avoid putting it on the roof, unless you are ready to get out and chase it through lanes of traffic when your start-up speed blows it away. Papers are particularly infuriating and can also make you look like an absolute fool. The wind created by passing cars blows them around in circles and out of reach just when you thought they were at your fingertips. I may never get

My mind drifted away from the no-no's. Back to that poison. I was beginning to get some idea when the poison must have been put in either the tea or the sugar. It must have been on Dorothy's shift. If she and Lily and Sherrie and Anna were telling the truth. And if one of them didn't do it.

As I ate my baklava, I began to feel we were going to be lucky. We were going to figure this out before Pop was hurt any more, or anyone else was hurt. Things were going well. We were doing a good job. I hadn't goofed up in some time, which was a good omen.

I asked the waitress to hurry and bring my bill. I began to look forward to returning Mary's pocketbook. I might find out something crucial from Mary. I stood up and my skirt fell off!

And, good grief, I had on the bikini underpants that Mary gave me as a joke. I pulled that skirt back up so fast, the three kids at the next table didn't even have time to start laughing. I walked over to the cash register with all the dignity of the Queen of England. I paid and departed.

Out in my car, I pulled out my chapter again and wrote myself a note on the bottom: "Always follow your own advice."

CHAPTER 12

LATER THAT AFTERNOON

The stone lion by Mary's front steps wore a red ribbon around its neck, the latest decoration by the kids. I knocked, waited a second, then peered in the glass panel by the door. There in the middle of the living-room rug was Unhairy Harry on all fours with both kids on top of him. He appeared to be arguing with them, telling them to get off, but with a grin.

Sometimes, I thought, Harry didn't act any older than they did! They seemed to think it was all a joke. But then Marcia, old enough at four not to be entirely silly, saw me and waved, jumped off Harry and came to the door. She opened it wide, giggled, and said, "Aunt Peaches, we're playing horsie." Then she ran back and hit Harry on his blue lean rump and called, "Giddy-up, horsie," and she and Andy, who is only two, burst into shrieks of laughter.

"I think it's time for your horse to have some oats and a rest." I said, and they both jumped off with cries of glee and ran in the kitchen. By the time they got back with two cookies, Harry was standing up over by the bookcase against the wall. The red mug was next to his pale

148

blond hair. Blond as the kids. And next to the mug was the phony crystal ball.

"I think it's time for you to go play with the magic horsie." He leaned down and whispered to the kids like a fellow conspirator. "Remember how we said that if you build a circle of magic rocks in the back yard, he'll fly right into it?" He raised his voice to normal. "And you can take some oats for him. He won't even mind if you eat them yourself."

The kids both nodded vigorously, and he led them by the hand through the small kitchen to the back door, which led into their fenced-in play-yard. I came along too. I looked out the window. Sure enough, there was a pile of small rocks in one corner of the yard, and the kids began to arrange them in a circle.

Harry shook his head. "What imaginations they have."

"And you too," I said.

"They love me to tell them stories. I used to love stories too. My mother used to read me stories."

Harry stopped by the refrigerator. Magnets were all over it, each with a picture or a motto. A rainbow was above Harry's shoulder, a shining sun by his elbow.

"I like to see happy kids," he said. "I wasn't a very happy kid. I think sometimes I like kids more than adults. Their eyes are so open." His eyes were wide, as if he were acting his words out. "They see so much. Every kid is

149

almost a poet. I like that."

"I wish you'd let me see some of your poetry."

He shook his head. "Not now. I'm trying new forms. I'm not sure I have them right yet."

Now, that surprised me. I wouldn't have thought he was the type to stick to forms.

He half turned and picked up a "Think Positive" magnet from the refrigerator and stared at it — Mary's favorite motto? — and hefted it in his hand. "Kids are ready to see what's good. And Mary is almost like a kid. Even though she's a lot smarter than she lets folks think."

He put the motto back on the fridge, next to a smile-face. Then he became practical. "She'll be back in a little while. Would you like to have a cup of tea and some oat cookies and wait for her? Because these really are oat cookies." He pointed to a heaped plate on the counter. "The kids are right about that. We made them this morning out of oatmeal and raisins."

I did not hand him Mary's red pocketbook and leave. Because this was a great informal chance to find out all about him. About where he'd lived before. And whether he'd ever trained to be a pharmacist, and useful stuff like that. I said oatmeal cookies were my favorite kind.

"So where did you live before Asheville?" I asked.

"Fairfax, California," he said, beginning to run water into the red enamel kettle and raising

150

his mellow poet's voice above the water. "I stayed with a friend there, who is also a poet. We did a lot of readings in cafes. Marin County is my second favorite place after Asheville. Different but great." He turned on the gas burner and set the kettle on it.

"And how did you happen to come here?" I asked, doing my part and getting two bright red pottery cups and saucers down from the cabinet by the fridge.

"Oh," he said, "I grew up near here. Over the line in Tennessee." He pulled tea bags out of a canister shaped like a teddy bear with a red bow tie, and put one bag in each cup. "I left after my mother and father died, and the old woman I used to caretake for. She left me enough money to go to college. For which I'll always be grateful. She was a poet herself. Just for her own pleasure. She understood." He poured the boiling water into the cups and handed me mine. He picked up the plate of cookies, then led the way past my favorite of Mary's signs: "Dinner Will Be Served at the Sound of the Smoke Alarm," and waved me to a chair by the small dining room table just outside the kitchen. He put the cookies on the table by a sugar bowl in the shape of a cat and sat across from me.

"And you went to college in California?"

"No," he said, "Guilford College in Greensboro. That was about ten years ago." He put a spoon of sugar in his tea.

151

He must be older than he looked. The dimple by his mouth was what made him seem so young. And the length of his eyelashes.

"And then after college you went to California?"

"No," he said. "Next I went to live on a commune in Oregon. A friend at Guilford knew about it. But some of the members took too many drugs and didn't do much work, so I moved to Aspen, Colorado. I worked in a motel there and did some readings in cafes. I like being a rolling stone," he added. "I won't stay here forever. Though I may take a course at the college next term." He munched a cookie. "This place reminds me of where I grew up; the view of the mountains does." He took a swig of tea. "I think I write better poetry when I feel at home. Then my poetry goes back and resolves things from my youth."

I had to work not to laugh. Imagine Harry at only thirty talking about his "youth" like it was long gone.

"You can be a rolling stone if you live simply and take any job that comes along," he continued. "For instance, I'm working three nights a week in an all-night convenience store." He took a long sip of his tea. "I'm glad you came here while Mary is out," he said. "I have something I want to talk to you about. I'm worried about Mary."

He smiled as if he never worried about anybody or anything, but he went on to explain.

"Mary is so lonely," he said, "and so unsure of herself. She tries so hard to act bright and busy, but really she has no confidence. She doesn't like herself. And I like her so much, I feel bad about that. I gather she had a terrible time as a kid."

My heart sank. "Her father was an alcoholic," I told him. "He died. Her mother was a workaholic." The bright colors and the bright sayings all around us suddenly depressed me. "I suppose you know Mary's mother was murdered?"

He nodded yes, ducking his head at the same time. Bowing to horror? "My father was an alcoholic too," he said sadly. "My mother killed herself. I know what it's like to have nobody there behind you. To be all alone and hurt too. But maybe it makes me a better poet."

So even Mary's friends were sad for her. I'd wanted to believe that Mary was feeling better about life. That all her new friends — like Harry, for instance — were a good sign. That her loneliness was behind her.

"We were there sometimes when Mary was little," I said. "We tried to help. I used to read her Dr. Seuss when she was a kid. But I don't think we knew how bad it was back then." I glanced out the window. The kids were still happily making their circle.

"And maybe that's why she admires you so much," he said, leaning forward earnestly across the table. "She wants to be like you. She talks all the time about what her cousin Peaches is doing."

"Me?" I gasped. "I spend half my time getting around my drawbacks! What a thing to want. And yet I have been lucky." I did have what poor Mary wanted: Love. I sipped my hot tea and thought about that.

"Why, two of the men she's going out with got to know Mary just because she's related to Peaches Dann, the woman who's writing the memory-book. They'd heard about your talk at the library last month on memory systems. That's what Mary told me." He said that with a pout. Was he jealous that Mary went out with other men? As a wandering poet, he could hardly hope for any permanent relationship.

"You mean Loy Haven, for one?"

"Oh, he's not so bad." Harry bit into his cookie, like he could have happily bitten Loy, but he continued to smile, even while he chewed. "That Loy has a one-track mind, and he's eccentric, Mary tells me. But he doesn't do any harm that I know of.

"The other one is named Donald McElvey. He has temper fits, and he drinks too much."

My heart sank even further.

"Mary is scared of him. But he's so sure he knows all the answers that she likes being scared of him, I think." Harry stared into his teacup like he wished he could read the leaves. "She's really attracted to him, I think." He said this with a groan. "He puts her down and puts the kids down. She calls the way he acts 'artistic temperament.' " He shook his head in disagreement; "He's painting her portrait. She says artists can't help having a fiery temperament. But she went out with him once and came back with bruises. There's one on her cheek right now — you look."

Maybe that was jealous exaggeration. I hoped to God it was. But why hadn't she introduced this artist to us? And it fit. Even back in high school she had a boyfriend who went out of town the night of the prom and stood her up. He went on a fishing trip, as I remember. He liked fish better than Mary. Then Andrew married Mary with her bright colors, and got mad because he couldn't make her into a monotone. "A lawyer's wife needs to have dignity," he said. Then her brother's partner Ben played up to her, and he turned out to be a common thief with delusions of elegance. And now this artist with the temper. Mary needed somebody to love her a lot, not one of those jerks. I felt angry.

"But what does Donald who drinks have to do with me?" I demanded.

"Oh, he's got some idea that art is memory condensed and distilled. Something he wants to talk about. I don't know. He's a nut. But he impresses Mary." He took another cookie. No wonder he had baby fat. "Those guys are just the symptoms," he went on, "that Mary needs to feel good about herself, and not go looking

155

for guys that are impressed with her cousin. Or want a free model. Mary is a nice girl. I care about her." He looked down at his hands as he said that, as if he was embarrassed to let me see emotion in his eyes.

"What should I do?" I asked. "What are you doing?" I was ashamed that Harry the rolling stone poet was more aware of my own cousin's problems than I was. And where did he fit in? I wondered. Why did he hang around and see more of the kids than of Mary?

"I hope Mary knows enough to be careful of a man who hits her," he said. "And I hope this artist fellow will move on. But somebody evidently tried to poison your father," he said. "That's serious. We need to all of us watch this fellow in particular. Because we don't really know anything about him."

He handed me a slip of paper with the artist's name and address written on it. "Go see him," he said. Say, he'd thought about this, to have the address handy.

I stuffed the name in my pocketbook. Then suddenly he laughed. "Of course, you don't know anything about me, either. But it's O.K. with me if you watch me too. You remind me of my mother." He laughed. "And *she* always kept an eye on me."

I did not decline his offer.

"There's something strange about this Donald," he said. "Something phony. Maybe you could try to meet him as soon as possible and see what you think."

I thought that all of Mary's friends, including Harry, could have hidden pasts. And Mary took her friends to meet Pop. And somebody somehow put digitoxin in the herb tea that Pop and his visitor drank. So I had reason to meet this Donald. And besides, I was curious.

I finished my cookie, admiring the buttery brown-sugar flavor, and drank a swig of tea.

And suddenly, like a thousand-volt electric shock, it came to me what I was doing. I was eating and drinking alone with a possible suspect. I just plain forgot to be suspicious of what I put in my mouth. My stomach spasmed with a sudden cramp. But since I stayed alive, I realized the pain was from old-fashioned fear.

CHAPTER 13

THAT EVENING

I should have put that slip of paper with the name of Mary's artist boyfriend in the side pocket of my pocketbook, where I could find it. But I was so busy wondering what to do about Mary's trouble that I just stuffed it into the pocketbook jungle.

So that evening, as I sat at my kitchen table with Ted, I had to upend my pocketbook and sort through the drugstore bill I meant to put with my tax stuff and the green invitation to the program I didn't go to two weeks ago and the folded note from a friend thanking me for a funny poem I wrote for her birthday; the Swiss Army knife and the compass and the roll of quarters and the half a pack of chewing gum; my good luck shell and the folded rain hat and the mini-flashlight — and all the other hopes and intentions and mementos that float around with me. Also my dogeared book-idea notebook and my little black Wizard that Pop gave me. And, of course, I looked through my wallet with my change purse and all my credit cards. No paper with name.

"Durn," I said. "I should have put it in my bra."

Ted was at the refrigerator getting out a bottle of white wine. He raised both eyebrows. "Did you say *bra?*"

"Oh, sure," I said. "It's a good place to put small important papers or money to keep separate or whatever. That way, it's quick to hand."

He laughed. "Secrets of womanhood."

"Sure," I said. "I have a section in my book about how handy it can be for things you don't want to lose in the pocketbook jungle. Of course," I added, "it's a sexist idea because a man couldn't keep papers in his jockstrap, for instance. Unless he was a spy or something. But, then, clothes are sexist. Men's tend to have more pockets in them. I don't know why." But back to my search.

I scrabbled down in the bottom of the zipped side pocket of my purse, where my lipstick and my eye shadow and a pencil and my computer-disk duplicate live. No paper. But the second time I looked, I stopped to read that thank-you note even though I knew what it said: "It's fun to be your friend." What could be nicer. And as I unfolded that note, out fell the paper I was looking for, caught inside.

Ted raised his wineglass in a toast. "To practice. I think finding something in that pocketbook of yours is good practice for solving a very difficult mystery." He was right.

"Donald McElvey is the artist's name!" I

held up the slip of paper triumphantly. I'd already told Ted what Harry said about this artist with the temper. And, of course, Mary's boyfriends, being young men, were all suspect.

I'd also told Ted what Harry told me about himself — about living in Greensboro ten years ago and then Oregon and Aspen, and being a rolling stone. But this Donald should be the next boyfriend on the agenda.

"Donald," I considered. "Now, how shall I remember that? If he's an informal artist, the first name will be enough."

"I'll remember the last name," Ted offered.

"I'll put it in my Wizard," I said

I took out my little black Wizard, opened it like a notebook, pushed the ON button and the date came up on the small screen. Across from the screen a row of buttons said: CAL, SKED, TEL, MEMO, CALC. I pushed TEL, which meant name, address, and telephone number, and I entered Donald McElvey, and his address. Except, of course, what I actually put was *S. McElvey, Donald* so it would come up as part of my suspect list. Then I pushed ENTER. All the suspects are under *S*.

"But for quick reference," I said, "I still need to remember 'Donald' off the top of my head. Let's see. If he has a temper, he probably throws things. I'll picture him throwing a painting at me so I have to duck. That's it. Donald Duck."

"Properly violent," Ted said, raising his glass

of wine to me again.

"If Mary took this Donald Duck by to see Pop, Pop didn't mention it." I sipped my own cool dry wine and considered. "But then, Pop doesn't mention a lot of things. We'd better find out all we can about him."

We were sitting at the kitchen table, waiting for the timer to go off. That would mean to turn off the "oven-fried" potato strips that would add such a nice crunchy accent to the chicken casserole with green peppers and onions which was keeping warm on a flame-tamer, ready to go.

"But we can't go see this man tomorrow morning," Ted said, fingering his wineglass. We were enjoying a bottle of white Burgundy, one of two that I'd given Ted for his birthday a few weeks back. We'd enjoyed one bottle on that occasion and saved one.

"As soon as possible," he said, "we have a date to go to the *Citizen-Times* library and look through back newspaper files to find out anything we can about sleeping-pill suicides in the last two years, and about young men who have come to town and opened businesses. I think that's a priority even before tracking down this Donald."

"And at the same time," I said, "we could look through the bound volumes of back papers for the last several months to see if we spot anything that seems like it could be in any way related to our serial killer or to what happened to Pop or Matt Jones."

Ted disagreed. "No, that's too unfocused. We don't have time."

"But possibly interesting," I argued. "Maybe even something innocuous-seeming, like a wedding or graduation story, would make a little bell ring."

And then I laughed. "Billy Sharp will receive his Ph.D. for field research into the psychology of the elderly in relation to financial fraud. He also has a degree in pharmacology from State U."

"Or," Ted said: "The bride is employed as a teacher at Jones School. The groom has been employed as a serial killer in North and South Carolina for the past two years."

A bell began to ding. What? Oh, yes! The timer for the potatoes. We both began to laugh. "Too bad," I said, "that it wasn't the little bell in my head that meant I had the answer."

The doorbell rang. "There it is," Ted said.

We were so curious as to who would arrive unheralded at dinnertime that we both went to the door.

There in the doorway stood Silva Allen. Decidedly wet. "Oh," we both said in chorus, "it's started raining."

Silva used to sit with Pop all the time, but now she substituted when one of the regulars couldn't make it. And occasionally, if she was on a job near Pop's house, Silva would poke her head in and bring Pop some small present.

Her hair was bleached blond and straight and short, now shiny wet. The sky had really been dumping. Her face was heavily lined between the eyes, but she was jauntily dressed in pants and a fringy Western blouse. "I've been thinking about you all," she cried out, "because we were together the last time." By the last time, she meant when my aunt Nancy was killed. Silva had even been a suspect, but was totally cleared. Flash of lightning, boom of thunder. She winced. "I don't want to talk about that, but may I come in?" she asked. We'd both been so startled, we'd forgotten our manners. I welcomed her.

"I heard from Anna that you were working to figure out who gave your father and his friend digitoxin," she said. "My mother takes digitoxin. A lot of people do." Another streak of lightning, crash, bang. "I was so sorry your father was sick."

I slipped back in the kitchen and turned off the oven. We took Silva in the living room. The curtains were open. We only close them if we sit in there with the lights on.

"I could get you a dry bathrobe," I offered.

She shook her head. "I'm not that wet. I just had to run from the car." Crash, bang. The lights went out.

She leaned forward toward me in the semidarkness. "I saw something," she said breathlessly, "but it may have been nothing. I don't know."

163

There were candles in the kitchen-table drawer, but I didn't want to leave until I heard what Silva had seen.

"I saw a man standing near your father's back door Saturday morning," said her voice from the gloom. "About ten-thirty. I had a job down the road and I was driving by, and at one point I got a glimpse through some trees at just the right angle to see him." *Ker-ash.* That one was close. Lightning lit her eager face for just a second.

"What was he doing?" I asked.

"Just standing there. I didn't think anything of it. But I called Anna this afternoon and she said that although I saw very little, I should tell you."

"What did he look like?" Ted demanded. Her face was momentarily bright again.

"He had on a stocking cap, pulled down low, and jeans and a black turtleneck shirt. He was sort of medium-tall, not really fat or thin."

"Did you see his face?"

"No, his back was turned."

"What color was his hair?"

"All I could make out was the cap. The hair must have been short if it didn't show around the cap. All I got was a glimpse from the back and then I drove on, because I didn't expect that it mattered at all. I only knew later." That's all she could tell us.

I knew one reason Silva had come by instead of phoning was that she wanted to know the whole story. And in a way she was an old friend. She'd been the sitter for the 11 P.M. to 7 A.M. shift for a while a few months back.

We told her what we knew.

Almost immediately she said she had to leave. Obviously she hadn't come to linger. Not even until she had time to dry out. She said she had a substitute job down the road. She hugged us goodbye, rather wetly, and promised to keep her eyes and ears open for anything further that might help.

I offered her an umbrella, but by the time she was ready to leave the rain had largely stopped. The thunder was faint in the distance.

"So," I said to Ted as Silva's white car disappeared around a curve, "what does it mean? I have to admit that I'm superstitious enough to believe that anybody who can blow in with a thunderstorm and take it away when they leave should be listened to. Boy, was she in a hurry."

"The only new thing we know," he said, "is that one person was in the yard on Saturday that nobody knew about." One last, lingering thunderbolt shook the house.

We were still standing at the open door smelling the rain-washed air when a dark car I didn't recognize stopped at the end of the front walk. We recognized the man who got out. "Lieutenant Wilson," Ted said. And I said, "Mustache."

"I wanted to talk to you in person about that booklet with the note in it," he said. "And I wanted you to know that tests do show that digitoxin was in the sugar bowl from which your father and Matt Jones put sugar in their tea. We suspected it. Now we know that was the source."

We invited him inside. The lights had come back on and he sat down in the wing chair by the fireplace. I sat in the Woody rocker and Ted sat on the green-striped couch. I held the star-pattern red-and-green patchwork pillow in my lap. And I thought, this is a comfortable, reassuring room. A room of pretty things. Not a room to talk about murder in.

"I want to go back over your experience with the reporter down east," Mustache said gravely. "I'd also like you to tell me in detail exactly where you found this booklet about walks near Asheville. Even the smallest detail might help. I have a feeling that this is going to turn out to be a very complicated case. There may be an outsider involved. But I believe there is at least one insider involved in this, too."

And I thought, good grief, are we all going to be suspects?

CHAPTER 14

TUESDAY, OCTOBER 6

Famous folks and how they remember. That was my project early Tuesday morning. My before-the-day-starts writing time. I could tell about Loy's medieval hero, Albertus Magnus, who taught St. Thomas Aquinas. He taught a saint, but his memory system depended at least in part on shock, which Loy, also known as Dracula Jr., was getting me to try.

So far, so good. Some of the famous dead made their memory stuff easy to find. Ted had suggested Marcel Proust, who wrote whole novels about remembering in sensual ways, such as sucking a certain kind of cookie familiar in childhood and bringing back times past with the taste.

And I had always imagined that the hand Napoleon Bonaparte kept hidden in the front of his shirt clutched the list of things he had to keep in mind that day.

Live celebrities had their words on memory quoted in print, which was helpful. Like George Burns, at ninety-five, explaining that he had an easy way to hide his trouble with names. He just called everybody Kid.

Or Erma Bombeck, who said that it's hard to be nostalgic when you can't remember anything. Her trick is to make you laugh.

Whenever I go to a talk by a famous person I run up afterwards and ask them for their memory system. For example, I asked John Le Carre, who I figured must have great ways to remember when he plots all those spy novels. He said in real life he just relaxes and forgets everything.

I looked at my clock above my desk. Nine o'clock. My chapter still needed more work. But my book time was up; my snooping time had arrived. And besides, Ted had made coffee which smelled great.

We went out with our morning coffee onto our stone terrace. The terrace is at the side of the house so we can see the woods behind and the road in front.

It was one of those unusually warm fall days when the sunshine and the colorful red and yellow fall leaves combined to pull us outside. The kind of day when staying in the house, even an old square-cut log house like ours, felt like treason. The Chinese chestnut tree at the end of the terrace seemed to be leaning toward us to make contact. The boxwood hedge along the long side of the terrace was shining green in the sunshine. Rain-washed and sunlit.

Wonderful. And I figured we needed to revive ourselves before we went to the hospital to get Pop. The doctor had called to say this was the day they were letting him out. Maybe just to get him out of their hair. And maybe because they knew he had people to look after him around the clock. For better or for worse, his old feisty spirit was back. And in case it turned out to be worse, Ted and I could use a little time to feel good first.

We'd come out to enjoy the beauty, but we also brought two legal pads to jot down notes. We sat down across from each other at the glass-topped table.

Ted also had the newspaper in hand. "Here's a story about Matt Jones's death," he said. "It doesn't tell much. No mention of poison. No mention of Pop. Says his neighbors called him the Old Hermit. Kept to himself and appointed himself the guardian of the graveyard. His grandmother Bertha Morgan, who raised him, was buried there." He handed me the story.

"How strange," I said as I read, "and we didn't even specially notice Bertha Morgan's stone." I sipped my coffee and pondered his death. "I'd like us to write down every possible connection between all the things that are happening. Maybe there aren't many. But there are some. I have a hunch we need to do that."

"I never ignore hunches," Ted said, "especially yours. In fact, I wonder if you don't need a whole chapter in that book of yours about hunches."

I saw what he meant. I've mentioned hunches in my book, but only as an aside. When you have a lousy memory, you get good at listening to hunches as an alternative. The way the blind can be good at music. I pulled out my book-writing notebook and wrote that down.

Ted poised his pencil above his yellow pad. "Young men," he said.

"Yes," I said. "There was a young man who had befriended each old person who was robbed and killed in the stories in Millie's world memory. Well, we can't complain about not having young men to choose from. Mary's boyfriends, as we've said before, are all young men, and she brings some of them to meet Pop."

I waved away a yellowjacket buzzing around my head. It wasn't helping. "And Sherrie," I said, "who is my unfavorite sitter, says that Lily, who is my favorite sitter, took in foster children who are now young men and come to visit her a lot. And I have to be unbiased and say that Lily came to work for Pop just when all this stuff began to happen. But then, Sherrie's boyfriend with the small feet, whom I don't like, is a young man, and Dorothy, who sits at night, has a young husband."

Ted jotted all that down. "What else?"

"Pills," I said.

"Yes," he said. "The serial killer killed with sleeping pills." He turned to a new page of the yellow pad.

"And Pop was almost killed with digitoxin, and digitoxin comes in pills. And somebody must have ground up pills into the sugar bowl." The bug came zooming back. I decided the best tack was to ignore him.

"And poison is said to be a woman's kind of weapon," I said. "I don't know how that fits in."

"How about money?" Ted suggested. "The serial killer ought to have a lot of money, even if most of it is stashed away in secret bank accounts. He's apparently stolen a lot of money from his victims. He must have some desire to enjoy it. But the only suspect we have so far who shows any signs of enjoying money is Loy. The rent on his house must cost a pretty penny."

"Maybe the killer lives in Monte Carlo," I said, bitterly, "and jets in for an occasional kill. If so, we'll never find him." I got up, took a section of the paper Ted had been reading, rolled it up, and killed my bug. At least I was rid of that problem.

A breeze stirred the mellow red and gold leaves in the woods beyond our hedge. I folded my arms. It was almost chilly.

Ted tapped his yellow pad with his pencil. He said, "I've mulled this over a lot and I can't prove a thing, but I think the person who tried to kill Pop and killed Matt Jones —" He stopped.

"Don't stop there," I cried. Under the table, he touched my foot with his. Well, maybe kicked is more like it.

And when I looked around to check why my nice husband was kicking me, I saw the man with the beard coming toward us across the lawn.

Suddenly I remembered him. He was the one I once met briefly when he was taking Mary out to some concert. The nice one who made her nervous.

Even now, as he walked toward us, he glowed with geniality. I felt as if he must have come down to do us a favor or bring us a present. His face was roundish, and he was a little bit plump, but it suited him. It went with his smile and his twinkly eyes. He was young, about thirty. Which was what made his hair and beard so striking. They were dead-white. My mother had a friend whose hair was prematurely white. On her it looked good. On our smiling friend it was dramatic. He wore khaki workpants and a red shirt, and the white beard, though it wasn't long, stood out against the red.

White Beard! Of course! He'd come to Pop's house the day my father was poisoned. He must be the very one Lily had described. I was glad she'd had him in sight every minute. I couldn't bear to think this charming man, who seemed so glad to see us, was a poisoner. And besides, nobody down east would have been able to forget what he looked like. How long does it take to grow a beard?

He walked across the terrace and stood in front of us. "Good morning," he said, "I'm

Sandy Lyon. We met, Mrs. Holleran, at your cousin Mary's. And I left a message about a book on your answering machine." I noticed he had a blue book under his arm. Was that the one? Question: Why do so many books about memory have blue covers?

"Won't you sit down," Ted and I said, almost in unison. I tried not to sound too eager. But now we wouldn't have to go find him and interview him. He'd volunteered.

Sandy Lyon. I'd need to make a note of that. "I don't suppose you are related to a friend of ours named Millie Lyon?" I asked. He said no. Too bad. That would have been almost enough to help me remember his name. But as it was I had to take steps. Lyon. Lion. What was violent and remarkable related to Lion? (You see, Albertus Magnus, I'm trying.) Well, of course, jaws or teeth, but nothing came to me about teeth. Well, how about claws? A lion could sure draw blood with those. I visualized gory claws. Oh yes! Sandy Claws: Santa Claus. Wonderful! Because Sandy Lyon looked like Santa Claus. The young Santa. Before his father turned over all the responsibility of Christmas to him and he began to have smile lines. How appropriate!

Santa Claus sank into the chair next to me and breathed deeply. His belly rose and fell. I admit it did not shake like a bowlful of jelly. "What a lovely place this is," he said, "and the air smells good." He sniffed it as if he'd come to an air-tasting. "But I didn't come to talk

173

about that." He turned to me, and put his hand over mine. I had the impression he wanted to hug me but felt he didn't know me well enough yet. "I came to tell you how sorry I am about your father who I gather is quite ill. I visited your father briefly the very day that he became so sick. I liked him tremendously. I hope you won't be insulted if I say I found him to be a true original."

I liked this Santa Claus. He smiled at me so warmly, and there were friendly crinkles at the corners of his eyes. "How did you happen to know my father?" I asked.

"Mary had talked about him," Sandy said. "She told me he liked to read biographies. So do I. Biographies and music and your cousin Mary are among my favorite things." He said Mary's name with something close to reverence.

"But how did you happen to go *visit* Peaches' father?" Ted asked.

"Mary mentioned that he was also interested in Indians." When Sandy said her name he almost sang. "She said he had a collection of arrowheads he picked up as a kid. After I read a new biography of the great Cherokee chief Sequoya, I was sure your father would enjoy it. So I took the liberty of dropping the book off. Then, later I found out that shortly after I left, your father and his friend were poisoned." He leaned forward intensely. "Mary must have been horrified. Is she all right?"

174

That, of course, was what he really wanted to find out. He blushed as he asked. So why didn't he just call up and ask her? I suspected I knew. Men just naturally fell for Mary. I think it had to do with her doe-eyes. Always had. And she rationed time for the ones she was sure she would never be serious about. She went out with them once a month or once every six weeks. Period. And wouldn't talk on the phone with them much more than that. To remind them, she said, that they were just friends. Sandy was one of those.

"Poison is scary," I said. "And we still don't know where it came from."

"After I heard," he said, "I tried to think if I had seen anything unusual while I was at your father's house. But the trouble is that if you haven't been to a place before, you don't know what's unusual, do you?"

Ted kept right to the point and asked him where he came from and how he happened to come to Asheville and when.

"I came to teach music in the high school," he said. "I'm new this year. I'm off today because it's a teachers' work day with no music connection. You have wonderful music in Asheville," he enthused. "It's amazing for a city of this size to have its own symphony.

"Before I came to Asheville," he continued, "I used to teach music in the Durham schools." Bingo. He'd been down east at the time of the killings there.

He leaned over and covered my hand with his again. His hand was warm and dry. A sturdy hand. The kind you might like to hold on to in time of stress. "I've brought a book that I thought might be useful to you," he said.

It simply amazed me how everybody wanted to help me with my memory book. It was kind of nice.

He handed over *Supermemory: The Revolution*.

"There are parts that seem a little extreme to me," he said. "I find it hard to believe that we can remember what happened to us before birth. But the part about using music to tune up the mind and improve the memory strikes me as making sense. I'd be interested to know what you think." He colored again. He was embarrassed to be devious, I thought. What he really wanted was to keep in touch with me because I was close to Mary, since he couldn't see her often. He must have it bad, poor thing.

To test the theory, I said, "Mary has a great memory for jokes."

He lit up, until I almost felt the need for dark glasses. "She's always so much fun! I worry about her, though," he said. Him too?

"I hope you're all being careful," he said. "Are the police getting any closer to finding out where the poison came from, do you think?"

"We're doing everything we can to find out what happened," Ted said. "Even aside from what the police are doing."

"Well, let me know if I can be helpful in any way," he offered.

Then he hesitated, as if making a decision. "I'm inviting some friends to a musical evening at my cabin," he said. "Very simple, but a few friends and I will play some Bach in my clearing in the woods. I think you might enjoy it." He waited for a reaction.

"That sounds lovely," I said. I figured he wanted us to come so that Mary would be more likely to do likewise, and that was fine with me.

"When will this be?" Ted asked.

"Sunday, October twenty-fifth. Perhaps by then . . ."

"God willing," I said, "our lives will be more normal by then."

"Let me tell you how to get there."

It seemed a long time until the twenty-fifth, but I got out my Wizard, put the date in the schedule, and then pushed MEMO to copy in his directions. I felt much more high-tech and efficient than I used to with a plain old pencil. Downright pleased with myself.

"Do you know where the Vance Birthplace is?" he asked.

I said I had a friend who lived out Reem's Creek Road beyond it, and he seemed pleased that he could start the directions from there. "At the end of Reem's Creek, go over a bridge and bear left," he said. "Then go up Maney Branch Road, which may be unmarked, until

177

the pavement ends and the road is gravel. At the top of the ridge, when you can see in both directions, turn left onto Nonesuch Road. That may not be marked either. There's a bunch of kids who have been stealing signs. Take the first left, then the first right, then the first left. The cabin is down a long drive."

I tapped all that onto my little keyboard.

"Look, a helicopter," Ted remarked. I could hear it. And I saw it in the distance. We were not exactly on a helicopter route.

"The narcs use those," Sandy said. "Looking for marijuana."

"No problem," I said. "There's not a bit in our garden. Nothing but late lettuce and kale."

"That's more likely to be the hospital's helicopter-ambulance," Ted said, gazing skyward. "I think it's too late in the fall for marijuana, but then I'm not an expert."

I turned off the Wizard and tucked it away. "We look forward to your musical evening," I told Sandy.

He got up to leave and clasped Ted's hand. This time he gave in to his impulse and gave me a little hug. It was really for Mary — I understood that. "Good luck to you," I said.

He walked back across the lawn and waved once before he got in his big, black, old-fashioned car with the polished chrome.

"Did you notice his car?" Ted asked. "You know that's a classic Rolls-Royce, don't you?

What is a high-school music teacher doing with a classic Rolls-Royce?"

We watched the car glide away with hardly a sound.

"So what chance has he got with Mary?" Ted asked.

"None," I said. "But I like him better than any of the other men she's gone out with, Rolls or no. He seems steady and kind. Funny, old Peaches-the-Absent-Minded-Matchmaker would probably pick the two men Mary likes least, Santa Claus Sandy and Unhairy Harry. No, not Harry. I don't think he's in any position to take on a wife, or wants the responsibility. As far as I can make out, he only owns three shirts, though he's always clean. I guess Sandy and Harry arc both people-people, but different. Harry needs people to like him. I think it thrills him that Mary's kids just worship him. Sandy needs to love, I suspect, more than he needs to be loved."

I poured myself some more of Ted's good coffee from the pot. "Instant off-the-cuff psychology," I said. "Just for you." I reached over and took Ted's hand. "I am very lucky," I told him, "to love a kind man who is also fun."

"And I," he said, "am lucky to love a woman who is never dull, and almost always a surprise."

"That's the only truly bad thing about us snooping," I said. "If anything happened to you, I couldn't bear it. If I thought you were in danger, I'd give it up quick and let the police do it all."

"Don't worry," he assured me. "I take care of myself. See that you do the same."

"What were you saying when Sandy Lyon appeared?" I asked.

"Oh," he said, "I was just saying that I've thought about this a lot and I can't prove a thing, but I think the person who tried to kill Pop and killed Matt Jones is —" He stopped again.

"Yes, go on."

He kicked me again. He was in a rut. Santa-Sandy did not appear on cue, however.

Ted wrote "hedge" on his yellow pad. My heart began to beat hard. Was someone hiding behind the hedge and listening to us? "I think the person who gave Pop digitoxin is crazy," Ted said. What had he originally meant to say? Before the hedge moved, or he saw a speck of color or heard a twig crunch. Or whatever.

The hairs on my arms stood on end. Anyone could easily get behind the hedge. If they walked in back of the house through the back garden, they would have discovered what we were talking about before we saw them.

Ted got up casually and walked toward the boxwood. "Let's think about this and continue later," he said. A truck rumbled by on the street. Ted walked slowly. I figured he was trying not to alert whoever was there. I sat still and kept my eyes glued to the hedge. A minute later Ted came back around it, saying, "if anyone was here, they're gone." I hurried over to join him. I looked to see if our footprints showed. No. The grass did not show prints. The hedge is right near the edge of the woods, a quick escape route. Last night's rain had sounded dramatic, but it hadn't lasted very long. Under the trees, the ground was hardly wet. "An Indian could track someone on this kind of turf," Ted said. "I can't. And that rumbling truck would have covered the sound of running, perhaps. But most likely all I saw was a branch moving in the wind." Still, we looked through the near woods, smelling leaf mold, brushing aside the red and yellow branches. If the leaves had fallen we could have seen farther. But they clung cheerfully to the young trees. The leaves underfoot were from last year.

"Maybe we should have waited," Ted said doubtfully.

We sat back down at the table. "Did I hear you start to say you knew the killer?" If only he did! If only he had a strong hunch.

"No," he sighed. He ran his hand through his hair and it stuck out at even odder angles than usual. Two frown lines appeared between his eyes.

"Yes?" I encouraged.

He sighed again. "I was only about to say I was sure the person who tried to kill Pop was mistaken if he thought your father could be made to leave him money." He shook his head and smiled ruefully. "He'd have to have Pop at gunpoint to get him to do that. Or use some really clever trick."

"Pop can be devilishly persuasive, I'll say that. He might make someone think that he was going to leave them money. But they wouldn't get a penny just by bumping him off. No matter what he told them." Pop looks after his own comfort. He also holds on to every dime. If there was a way Pop could be immortal, and never let go, he'd be for that.

I did not say that last out loud. I didn't think there was anybody near enough to hear, but I didn't want to take even a long-shot chance. I wouldn't want the killer to start an immortality scam. It might work.

With Pop about to be loose again at home, God only knew what he'd get mixed up in.

CHAPTER 15

LATE TUESDAY AFTERNOON

"You don't need to worry about me," Pop said, waving his hand at his house, white against the green mountain. We drove into the circular drive, past the boulder my mother had set off with a flower bed, and beyond to the back door. "The family will rally round me. You'll see."

I noticed there were two cars in the parking space off the driveway, not counting Sherrie's Honda.

The white Ford had a doll seated on each side of the back window, one a Raggedy Ann, the other Raggedy Andy. A sticker on the window said "Dolls Teach Love." That car belonged to my cousin Gloria from Madison County, who ran a doll hospital.

The second car was a pink Honda. I knew that belonged to cousin Eltha. She wore gentle colors like pink and always looked so sweet and mild that it was hard to believe she had been charged with shooting her husband. She was acquitted on grounds of self-defense. Pop just loved her.

We'd taken along Pop's folding wheelchair, and we rolled him in the back way because there are steps in front. Sherrie said Cousin Gloria and Cousin Eltha were waiting in the living room so we wouldn't have a traffic jam in the kitchen. Trust Sherrie, she wore a red satin blouse and a black satin miniskirt to welcome Pop home.

Our cousins came forward, beaming pleasure to see Pop: slender Eltha and plump Gloria. I'm always relieved to see that smile on Gloria's broad mouth, a twinkle in her baby blue eyes. She and Pop love or hate each other by turns. She can have as mean a tongue as I've ever heard, or be a dear.

"Did you bring me an angel food cake or a devil's-food cake?" Pop asked. Gloria's specialty is one or the other. She leaned over and hugged Pop. "Thank God you were spared," she told him. "What would we do without you?"

Cousin Eltha is prettier than Gloria as well as thinner. She has the air of a delicate young girl, even with a gray streak in her brown hair. Pop has always had a special affection for her, maybe because she is as un-dull as he is. Even the jury had to have felt her charm when it found her not guilty. She did admit to killing her husband. Pop reached out for her to hug him too.

Then he took Cousin Gloria's hand in his and said, "That was a beautiful card you dropped off, asking what you could do to help." So, of course, he'd gotten word back that what he wanted was a harem in attendance.

"I'm afraid you're going to get worn out, Pop," I warned, and then realized that wasn't very tactful in front of his two current favorite cousins.

And he naturally wanted to tell them all the details of his adventure, with a few exaggerations and embellishments.

"You go on and take a nap, Harwood," Cousin Gloria said to him. "We'll answer the phone and the door and have a nice visit with Peaches and Ted and be here when you wake up."

Pop did look grateful. He was pale and tired. Sherrie rolled his wheelchair into his room to put him down for a nap.

Then Cousin Eltha announced she'd take a turn answering the phone, and out of habit we all sat down at Pop's favorite round mahogany table. Eltha sat back near the bookshelf with all Pop's biographies, Harry Truman near one side of her head. Suddenly I noticed something that had never sunk in before. The subjects were all men. Not a single biography of a woman. Only Pop's role models. And on the bookshelf near Harry Truman was Sherrie's pack of Tarot cards. Pop, at eighty-three, had his mind on role models, and now lately, on readings of the future. Courtesy of Sherrie. Which meant he still had dreams? I didn't know what it meant. It made me nervous.

The phone kept ringing and Eltha kept

picking it up and saying that yes, Pop did want company, but not perhaps until tomorrow and to please call first. I didn't know when he'd had a chance to tell her that, but it was obviously what he would want, so I didn't stop her. He'd want to milk every drop of drama out of the attempt on his life and the death of his new friend. He'd want a big hug from every relative we had. Which was plenty. As the richest, most successful member of the family, as well as the most outrageous, he kept track of all his cousins and they kept track of him. He still went to family reunions over in Madison County, and every few weeks some cousin or other would bring him a cake she'd baked.

If Mom looked down from heaven, she would have been amused and pleased. Mom who had arranged this graceful room with antique furniture and flowered linen drapes. She'd even arranged the garden full of roses outside the big sliding glass doors. She'd arranged for Pop to have a phone in front of him on his favorite table, and the books he liked best within reach in back.

Now his phone brought word of all the cousins who cared. Not to mention the ones who were just plain curious. But between phone calls, Ted and I had a chance to tell Gloria and Eltha all about the poisoning from our point of view, which was fine because it still left Pop lots to tell from his viewpoint. We didn't tell about the serial-killer angle, of course. That was not a family affair."

"Now about this Matt Jones," Gloria said. "If your father thought he was a cousin, it's strange I never heard of him."

"He might be from the odd branch of the family that moved to Buncombe County," Eltha suggested, folding her hands and acting prim. She evidently didn't think that shooting her husband was odd.

"It's sad that one of our kin came to see Harwood and was poisoned," Gloria said politely. Then she and Eltha left the subject of Matt Jones. Where did I think the poison came from? they wanted to know.

I said I had no idea, but someone had evidently been able to get hold of heart medicine. And digitoxin was poison to those who didn't need it.

That inspired them, gave them a chance to talk over every person they knew who took digitoxin, from Cousin Georgianna's mother to their preacher's wife. Pop hardly slept long enough to let them exhaust the subject.

Out he came shortly, wheeled by Sherrie. He couldn't bear to miss anything. He was pale, but made up for it with a bright red flannel shirt. He rolled his chair up to the table next to Eltha, and said, "You keep getting prettier." Then he turned to Gloria. "You both do." What did he want?

"Now what I need is a bodyguard," he told them with his charming, helpless-flavored smile. "I've sent out word to the whole family. I need somebody with police experience, somebody I can absolutely trust."

My mouth dropped open. He'd never mentioned that to me or Ted.

"I want Peaches and Ted to keep their minds entirely on finding out who tried to kill me," he said self-importantly. "I want them to find out who killed a guest in my house. The rest of our wonderful family will have to help see that I'm safe while they do."

Cousin Gloria immediately swelled up with pride. "Why, Harwood, I know just the person to be a guard — Cousin Troy's boy Ed, who went to work for the FBI and then got so homesick he came back to work for Sheriff Mander in Madison County. The sheriff believes in family. Why, it's the very mothers of the boys who have been in his jail that helped elect him, as you know. He's as good as he can be to those boys and good to the mothers, too. And I'm just sure he'll give Troy's son a leave of absence to come look after you."

We could stand as much help as we could get, looking after Pop.

Then two things happened at once. Pop called Sherrie and told her that he needed to go to the bathroom. "Sorry to leave ladies," he said. "But I'll be back soon."

At the sane time I heard somebody knocking on the back door. Ted said he'd go, but I said, "Look, it's probably a cousin with a

188

cake." So we both went.

Actually, it was a cousin with a big pot of chicken soup. Georgianna. She came from the more affluent side of the family. Her brother was a very successful lawyer. Her grandfather had been a judge. Her ex-husband was a doctor, and she was assistant librarian in Marshall. She was also the family expert on genealogy. Ancestors were her thing. She wore fine librarian-type glasses, steel-rimmed. But she always looked more like a potter or a weaver, somehow, in full skirts and ethnic blouses. Today's blouse was Mexican with orange and red flowers.

She put the big pot down on the kitchen table, gave both Ted and me a hug and told me, "I'm so relieved that your father is better. He's my fair-haired boy. You know that. Now, this soup is for your father, but I have something for you, too. It's in the car." She rushed out and came back in a minute with a blue and white book.

"This is a book about memory," she said. And I could see the gold letters said *Memory's Voice*. She handed it to me and I looked at the smaller, red subtitle: *Deciphering the Mind-Brain Code*. By Daniel Alkon, M.D., it said. I hadn't even had a chance to read Sandy Lyon's book about music and memory and such yet. I hoped I'd have a chance to do that as life got calmer. But I said thanks.

"One of the college professors gave this to

the library," Georgianna explained, adjusting her glasses on her nose, "and I just leafed through it to find out if it might be a book to help you. And this is some interesting book." She patted it like it was a friend. She had long hands with knots at the finger joints. Keeping-track-of-things hands.

She lowered her voice and leaned closer. "Why, this book helped me know why my brother Jim always picks bitches."

"It . . . what?" I said, amazed. I figured I must have heard her wrong.

Ted was nodding like he understood."

"Why, this book will be good for you as a writer *and* as a detective," she said. "It tells how a person's brain picture, or memory of himself, can make him be a victim." She nodded, as if she felt I needed encouragement to believe that. "I may not have explained that exactly right, but that's the general idea." She adjusted her glasses again and sighed. "And, you know, so many nice women like Jim," she said. "He could marry one of those in a minute. But he always picks women who make trouble for all of us, the whole family. He picks bitches."

Now, I've got to admit that sparked my interest — her brother Jim, the lawyer, had been married three times, and each wife had made off with everything he had at the time. Since he was a very successful lawyer, that was plenty. The first one kept the family heirloom jewelry from his mother's side, and the second one got

190

a farm that had been in the family for generations, and the third one — I forget what she got.

But what on earth did that have to do with memory? I mean, I've known other people like him, who always seem to pick somebody destructive to be close to. Even when they seem too smart to act that way.

Because of memory? How could that be? That would be a heck of a lot worse than losing your car keys.

"Of course, this book has a lot of technical stuff about synapses and neurons." She directed that to Ted. "But it connects that stuff to the tragic story of a young woman who was doomed by destructive memories." If Geargianna liked to read about doomed women, no wonder she needed cheerful orange and red poppies on her blouse to perk her up.

Not exactly light escape reading to distract me from a serial killer or someone trying to poison Pop.

I thanked her for the book, which she then said she'd checked out of the library for me for three weeks. Great. After I'd read the book I'd have to return it to the library. And she grinned at me like I should be grateful.

"This book," she said, "could even tell you how your ancestors affect your memory."

What? Georgianna was into ancestors, all right. But I must have heard that wrong. I didn't get a chance to ask.

"Peaches, where are you?" Pop yelled. "Who are you monopolizing in the kitchen?"

Ted grinned and winked.

Pop ought to be resting, but knowing Pop, bragging about adventure might be better for his health. And what could I do with him, anyway?

And you know what they say: Where does a five-hundred-pound gorilla sit?

Any place he wants to! That was Pop.

CHAPTER 16

WEDNESDAY MORNING, OCTOBER 7

We pushed open the *Citizen-Times'* front door and found ourselves in the lobby with a map of Western North Carolina inlaid on the floor. The day's front page was framed on one wall. "Citizens Manned," a headline blared. The elevator and stairs were to our left.

Here we were, armed with the needed permission from the executive editor to do our research in the paper's library, and ready to go.

We went up in the elevator with two young girls. The one with the big fuzzy sweater was saying, "So I told him, get lost."

We got out on the second floor and threaded our way through the cluttered desks in the newsroom. Ted waved to a couple of friends but didn't stop. He'd already asked several of the reporters what they might know about suspicious deaths or odd young investment counselors who were new in town. They hadn't been much help. Ted had said he wasn't surprised. "If you don't know a thing is significant, you don't bother to remember it. I don't myself. You remember the things you know will matter." He'd said he hoped that we'd do better in the files.

The library was small and oblong with a gray rug on the floor and wood-paneled walls, and so full of metal files, cardboard boxes of manila envelopes, and shelves of stacked newspapers and books that there was just room to move around. The librarian — Ted introduced her as Holly something — got up from her desk near a window and came over to welcome us. She was cheerfully dressed in a bright blue skirt and sweater and a pair of imaginative earrings made out of a string of semiprecious stones. She seemed really pleased to see Ted, whom she already knew because she'd spoken to his journalism class, and seemed glad to meet me.

She pointed this way and that, and told us that the files contained clippings going all the way back to the late 1930s. There were editions on microfilm back to the 1870s.

But we would hardly need that unless we needed to find out about our serial killer's ancestors. Which I figured was about as unlikely as you could get.

Ted explained that we needed to look at the file on suicides that had occurred within the last two years, and also the file on new businesses in case the person we were looking for had just started one. We might need other files to follow up what we found there. He said we might also like to look through the back bound volumes of the paper. I saw those over in an extra-tall shelf. They looked like books for a giant. An elegant giant. They had black spines with gold lettering.

About the new-businesses file, Holly shook her head, earrings bouncing. New-business stories were filed under the name of each business or under the names of individuals. There was no file where all the businesses were together.

But suicides were a different matter. She led us to a file cabinet in the back of the room and opened one of the narrow horizontal drawers where the clippings were kept in manila envelopes. She handed us an envelope and explained that it contained suicides for 1991 to the present.

We took the clippings over to a small table with two chairs, near the bound volumes. We both took notes on our impressions. And we compared thoughts as we went along.

"Shooting and jumping seem to be the preferred ways of death in this file," I said after I'd looked through about ten clippings. "Sleeping pills are not."

Ted grimaced and shook his head as if he wanted to say no to both. "Maybe the jumpers are not positive they want to die," he suggested. "Some of them survive. The attempted suicides seem to be in this file too."

He had in hand a story headed "Masonic Temple Jumper in Fair Condition."

"But some certainly succeed, if you want to call it that," I said. "Here's a story about a man who jumped from the Smoky Mountain Bridge in a purple jogging suit. He fell ninety-five feet. And that was that. Perhaps we just have a bunch-up of jumpings."

And sure enough, I found only one more and that wasn't local. A strange story about a woman who was raped and thrown off a bridge twenty years ago, and escaped death by a fluke, and then last year she had come back to the bridge and either jumped or fell. I shivered. Horrors in the mind can last for twenty years and then be fatal.

Suicide is hard for me to understand. Because I know how it is for me if I'm waiting in line for something. As soon as I get impatient and get out of the line, the line speeds up and I can see that I would have got what I wanted quick if I'd just stayed. If I killed myself, I'd win the lottery the next day. The whole idea of suicide is so final. That's what gives me the shivers. It says no to grace and luck and hope.

"Around here people seem to shoot themselves most of all," Ted said bitterly. He does not believe in having guns around the house. Most of our neighbors do. Ted gets in arguments with men who wear National Rifle Association caps. So far he's survived.

We sure did have shooting stories: *Parkway Suicide Shot Self*; *Sheriff Convicted of Embezzlement Shot Self*; *Man Shoots Lover, Then Self*; and more. One man even apparently tried to kill himself by wrecking his car, and had a gun along for insurance so he could shoot himself if the wreck failed. It did and he did. Job complete.

But no deaths from sleeping pills. Of course, if the serial killer were only just hiding our way, there'd be no hint of one of his murders-masked-as-suicides in the file. We were looking just to be sure.

All we found were the lengths to which people would go to kill themselves, like the man in jail who hung himself by his shoelaces. A terrible record of what seemed to me like insanity and human desperation.

"Look at this!" Ted said suddenly.

It was a story reminiscent of Greek tragedy. A woman was convicted of killing her sons when her husband got custody of the children. Shades of Medea. Her defense was that she was on a kind of tranquilizer that seemed to have flipped some people into strange behavior. But she was convicted. And then she killed herself.

She used another tranquilizer to do that. Something called amitriptyline. She managed to take three times the toxic dose.

Now, that was close to sleeping pills. But the story wasn't local. The AP carried it from Kansas City.

"Yes," I said sadly, "prescription drugs can be used to kill."

Only one hopeful story in the bunch: About a hot-line for teens to call if they felt suicidal. I was sad to think that so many teens feel suicidal that a hotline is needed.

We put the suicide envelope back in its drawer.

"I suppose the police sometimes come by and use your files," I said to Holly, who had come over to see what we needed next.

She said they never had. The people who wanted material from the files were often the relatives in criminal cases.

"The relatives of the victim?" Ted asked. We stood in the corridor between the wall files and a bank of drawers down the center of the room.

"Yes," she said, "and also the relatives of the accused. Often they live out of town and they want copies of all the stories. We'll send them, for a price. Of course," she added, "a long time ago we let almost anybody do research in this library. But now, like many other newspapers, we don't. Too many outsiders get in the way of our own people."

As if to illustrate how busy the library was, two young reporters came in and began to look through the files.

"In fact," Ted said, "when it comes to the bound volumes, the two of us could look through them in more comfort, and take up less of your space, if we went to the public library, couldn't we?"

"That's what we recommend to people," Holly admitted.

So we thanked her for her help and walked over to Pack Memorial Library, right next to the huge Asheville Civic Center, where a sign said there'd be wrestling tonight.

The library was full of space and light. Window walls everywhere. After all that suicide stuff, space and light were just what I needed.

We found the recent newspapers on shelves against the back window wall. The gal at the information desk had sent us there for the most recent two months. Microfilm picked up the issues earlier than that. No giant books of papers at the library. They stored their news in more compact form.

We leafed through recent copies of the *Citizen-Times*. Especially business news. Nothing seemed to fit our search. A regional motor freight company had opened a center in Asheville. A new home-health-care company would serve four counties. But no ads for investment counselors who said what Watt's serial killer said twice: "You'll be delighted at our results."

"Phooey," I said.

"But don't get discouraged," Ted said. "Next we'll try the out-of-town papers: Hendersonville, Brevard, Marshall, Boone, and such. But on community newspapers like those, I think I'll just call up and talk to someone on the staff and see if they've heard anything would help us with our problem. On those small-town papers, the staff will know about any new business person in town, even someone as unremarkable as an investment counselor. They'd be likely to know about local suicides too. I have a few more *Citizens* to look through, and then I'll do that."

"And I'd better go call and check on Pop," I said. "When I talked to Lily this moming, she said he had nightmares last night and stayed awake a lot. I'll just call to make sure that he's O.K."

"Good," Ted said. "I'll keep my fingers crossed that he's feeling better." Then he grinned. "And if he is, don't let him talk you into doing anything wild. We have enough on our hands."

CHAPTER 17

IMMEDIATELY AFTERWARD

I left Ted scanning papers and went to the pay phones in the library corridor. Even the corridor was alight with window walls. A nice library. On one phone, a man in a three-piece suit was checking something in a notebook. "Order number three fifty-six," he said with the air of someone enmeshed in a two-hour call. I waited briefly for a teenager draped with book bags to get off the other phone, and then called Pop.

He sounded petulant: "Peaches, your cousin Mary is trying to reach you." That was an accusation. "She is upset. Little Marcia had a fall." Then his voice got louder, like a TV commercial. "I hope you will deal with this immediately, I mean right away, so she won't call back and bother me. I have all I can do today without that."

"Yes, Your Majesty," I said "And don't you think you could act like a kindly uncle instead of an old grouch? I thought you were the head of the family. And I'm the absent-minded detective, right?" I was pretty sharp with him even though I knew he'd had trouble sleeping. Heck, so had I. I'd lain awake trying to make poison and sleeping pills and everything else fit together. No luck. "You want me to solve who tried to kill you right away, quick even before the police can, and now you want me to tend to everything else too." Silence on the line. The man at the next phone stared at me like he couldn't believe his ears. I'd been annoyed. I'd been indiscreet. I remembered once my father said the good Lord took care of fools, drunks, the United States of America, and me. I hoped the good Lord was still at it. I called Mary.

"I'm stuck." Her voice cracked like she might cry. "Andy is throwing up. He may have the flu. And I have to take Marcia to the doctor." Pause, like she was fighting off panic. "Marcia fell and did something to her wrist. I have ice on it. The doctor says to bring her in to get it X-rayed. It could be broken."

Oh, dear, I thought, I don't want to spend the afternoon baby-sitting at Mary's. And maybe catching flu. I'm supposed to be the dashing detective, right? And yet I wanted to help.

"All the people who would be willing to stay with Andy can't," she wailed. Good grief, if Mary, of all people, was wailing, things were bad.

"I'll be there as quick as I can," I said.

I explained the situation to Ted, still busy with papers, and was at Mary's in ten minutes.

She stood at the open front door with a man I didn't know. But I knew what he did. He was

202

dressed like an artist in a cartoon. He wore a beret over long hair, and a wildly flowing big shirt that gave the feeling of a smock. There were assorted paint spots on his pants. Obviously he must be the artist that Harry didn't like. Busy playing himself.

"You mustn't take on so," he was saying to Mary. "These things happen."

"I have to hurry," Mary apologized. "The kids are calling. See you soon."

As the artist turned around to come down the steps, he said, "You'll spoil them!" and then, seeing me, "Oh, hello. Are you Mary's cousin Peaches? You have an interesting face. I'd like to paint you some time. I'm Donald McElvey." He pronounced it *Mack´-ul-vee*. He had an interesting face too. Snappy eyes and a selfish down-at-one-corner mouth.

Mary waved at me and hurried inside. I told Donald that I was glad to meet him. True. I wanted to size him up. I wished I had longer. Then I followed Mary.

She vanished into the downstage bedroom, where Andy was calling "Mommie, Mommie, Mommie." Marcia was on the living-room couch with a plastic Ziploc bag of ice held to her wrist and a worried pout. She had on a yellow shirt, with mud on it, denim pants, and red sneakers with a hole in one toe and no socks. She must have been making mud pies when disaster hit.

"Shall I quick put a clean shirt on Marcia?" I

called to Mary. From the bedroom I heard the unmistakable sound of gagging. "Or will you just take her to the doctor as is?"

"Thanks," she said in a distracted tone. I took that to mean clean her up.

Marcia said, "I can wear my pink shirt with the teddy bear on it and the teddy-bear socks." She liked any excuse to wear those.

Well, I figured, she might as well get whatever fun she could out of whatever she did to her wrist.

I ran upstairs to her room with the animal-party wallpaper and found the shirt right away in her closet. Luckily it was a button-down-the-front one that would be easy to slip on. In the sock drawer I found one teddy-bear sock one red sock, one yellow sock, and one blue sock.

The rest must be in the laundry. I found clean pants and a pair of blue sneakers with no hole. I ran back downstairs and began to change Marcia's clothes, feet last.

"I want my teddy-bear socks," she whimpered, as I started to put the shoes on her bare feet.

Mary appeared, and said "I suppose all you found were odd ones. I think socks run away. But only one from each pair. There's a high divorce rate among socks."

"I want my teddy-bear socks." Marcia began to cry.

"I'll look for your socks while the doctor makes you feel better," I said. "O.K?"

Mary looked in the mirror, reached in her pocketbook, got out a comb and quickly combed her hair, which certainly needed it. She was frazzled from everything happening at once.

"I started to write a chapter in my *Memory* book on motherhood," I said. "But I haven't been a young mother for a long time. I'm sure it's changed." I smoothed Marcia's hair.

"You should write a chapter on socks," Mary said. "Write about how you remember where all the left socks are. I'd like to read that." She picked up Marcia and rushed out the door with her.

I went in to check on Andy. He was pale, but he seemed to have quieted down. I put my hand on his forehead, and it didn't feel as if he had a fever. "I'll sit right here," I said, "and you close your eyes." He was asleep almost before I finished the sentence. Too bad Mary wasn't still there to appreciate the silence.

I smiled to myself. Poor Mary had been having a bad day. She needed cheering. Now, it so happened that the existing fragment of my chapter on motherhood was about socks. I had saved it with my manuscript, wondering if I could rewrite some of it for a chapter on the vagaries of clothes.

I thought Mary would be amused by the sock bit when things got better. I went out to the trunk of my car, where I kept a copy of my manuscript in case my house burned down, and I pulled out the bits and fragments from the saved-to-rewrite folder.

I extracted what I wanted and propped the pages up on Mary's pillow, in the room upstairs where she'd taken to sleeping to be near the kids since her husband left. She could read about socks after the kids were asleep.

Actually I rather liked what I'd written, though I certainly never expected that leaving those pages on Mary's bed would have such a crucial effect as it did.

Motherhood and Socks

Precisely when you need them most, like when you're getting the kids all dressed up for a party, socks like to demonstrate that they have a mind of their own. Your knitted chums stay determinedly unmatched. If two socks are the same color, you can bet it's a practical joke and there's a hole in one of them.

But I can tell you how to outwit socks and end up with no more than one odd sock per kid. Honest.

Pick a color that goes with everything, like maybe white or blue. Get your kid socks in his own color and no other. Then he or she will always have socks that match until you get down to one last one.

Got more than one kid? Repeat the process — with another color.

But the kids will complain, you say. They'll say their friends all have lots of different socks and their mothers keep them matched.

My daughter, Eve, did complain. But luckily I'd heard the story about the cookie-making grandmother. Where I heard it, I have no idea, but I'm grateful to whoever it was that told me.

It's about the living-on-Social-Security grandma whose opposite number had lots of money and took the grandkid out and bought her fancy clothes. So the granddaughter arrived for a visit and said, "When are you going to take me shopping like Grandma Holt does?"

And our heroine said, "Grandma Holt is your shopping grandma. I'm your cookie-making-grandma." And the kid went happily into the kitchen with her to make cookies.

And what, you may ask, does that have to do with matching socks?

When Eve complained, I got her a few pairs of socks in assorted colors. I put her in charge of keeping them matched. In about a week she gave up and said even more pitifully than before: "Other mothers give their kids two socks that match every day for school. Why can't you?"

If this happens to you, do not get guilty. Get same-color socks.

Then pick out something you do extra well that your kid likes. Then you say, "Those others are sock-sorting mothers. I'm a story-telling mother" or whatever. You have then begun to teach the kid the very valuable lesson that life is likely to be a trade-off, and she needs to learn how to make the best trades she can.

Then you tell yourself that teaching character is more useful than remembering where you left the lost socks.

The doorbell rang, and tore me from my own words. I ran to answer it before the ringing woke up Andy.

Dracula Jr., otherwise known as Loy Haven, was at the door, wearing black again, though this time it was an informal turtleneck. I liked him better in black. He fit my original expectations better. He fit his nickname.

"Oh, hello," he said. "I was just going to leave off something for your husband with Mary. But since you're here, that's even better."

I was sure he could afford stamps, so I figured it was another case of an excuse to see Mary more. No luck this time.

"Your husband asked me about that little booklet I wrote, *Quiet Walks Near Asheville,*" he said. "This is the new, expanded edition, just off the press. I thought be might like to have one. He told me he's interested in old cemeteries, and I've added another walk that goes near one of those."

I thanked him and said that I, too, was grateful to him because the shock system of memory did seem to be helping me with names. "Only problem," I said, "is that I'm scared I'll come right out and call someone by his shock-cue name by mistake."

208

He smiled, and I had the distinct impression he hoped to be around to watch when it happened. Ghoul. But such a friendly, helpful ghoul.

He departed, and I put the new booklet on the edge of the bookcase near the front door. I realized I was sleepy myself. Andrew was in the four-poster in the downstairs guest bedroom. I didn't dare go too far away lest he should call. I slipped onto the bed near him as quietly as I could. Then I caught up on the sleep I'd missed while fretting in the night.

When I woke up, I gradually became aware of sounds like a party in the next room. And Andy was gone. I jumped up to see where he was and what was going on. I peered out into the living room, and there he sat, at the dining room table down at the end of the room, with Mary and Marcia. And there was Ted, who grinned at me like he knew a nice secret. Andy waved as if he'd never been sick at all.

I called, "Hi. I'm just going to comb my hair." And Mary called back, "We have ice cream."

I went in the bathroom and splashed water on my face. A wave of laughter came from the next room. I took a towel off the ceramic hook shaped like a goose's head — one of Mary's animal friends — and rubbed my face dry. When I took the towel from my eyes, Ted was in the doorway. He must have finished his research and come by to see how Marcia was. His eyes shone.

He came into the bathroom and stood close to me, facing me, vibrating with excitement. "We may have a lead," he whispered. "I talked to my friend Rachel Rivers-Coffey, publisher of the *Watauga Democrat* up in Boone. She knows of a possible suspect."

I caught my breath. "God willing!"

"She says they've had trouble with fraud in Boone. So the girl in the classifieds department has been told to watch out for ads that might be come-ons."

"And they found one?" I caught hold of both his hands and squeezed. "Did they?"

"A man came in with an ad last week for some off-beat-sounding counseling. The paper turned down the ad, but they have the man's address and phone number. And the wording of the ad said something about being delighted."

"Maybe this is a break!" My heart beat faster. Oh, what a relief it would be to have some solid clue. I still thought Matt Jones was killed by mistake. The attempt had been on Pop's life.

"So I think we should go visit Rachel, and then this man," Ted said. "But we must keep quiet about this. Lieutenant Wilson does think that there's an outsider mixed up in this, but he also thinks that whoever it is may have an inside accomplice. We have to be very careful." He let go of my hands and kissed me on the nose. "So please watch out."

"Exactly what did the ad say?" I was dying to know more.

But before he could answer me, Mary was calling, "Ted, Peaches, why are you hiding back there? What are you conniving at? Come have some ice cream!"

And Marcia shouted, "I scream, you scream, we all scream for ice cream!"

"Wait until we're alone," I whispered to Ted, "so you don't have to whisper, and you can tell me all the details." I knew Mary. In one minute she'd come drag us to the table. Better to come of our own accord. I'd just have to stand the suspense.

Mary and the kids had their mind on chocolate ice cream, not on murder suspects. I could tell it was chocolate as soon as I looked at Andy — he had it smeared all over his chin. And each of the kids had a bowl of it. Right-handed little Marcia, with a blue cast on her right arm, was valiantly eating with her left hand. A huge teddy bear sat in a chair beside her. Not one I'd ever seen before. Then, in the next chair, was Mary, looking tired after her medical day. She waved us over. Said she hoped I'd had a good nap. I sat down next to Marcia, and Ted went around and sat down next to Andy, who was on Mary's far side. Andy and Ted are great pals.

"Welcome," Mary said, "Marcia's wrist is not badly broken. She has a pretty blue cast, so we're celebrating. And Pop outdid himself and sent Sherrie out to get Marcia a teddy

211

bear, which she dropped off." She waved at the almost-life-sized beast.

I could just picture femme fatale Sherrie buying a teddy bear. Never mind. This was His Majesty at his best. Maybe I should bawl my father out more often.

"Have some chocolate, with chocolate sauce." Mary waved the ice cream serving spoon at me and pointed to a pitcher dripping sauce into its saucer. "We're being wicked today," she said, "and having this instead of supper. Andy is O.K. I guess he was just upset.

"Have a nice big dish," she invited. "That's one thing they told us at the women's seminar last Saturday. Sometimes you have to coddle yourself."

Before I could say a word, the doorbell rang. Mary jumped up and went to the door. And there stood Silva, this time without benefit of thunderstorm. Her bleached blond hair frizzed around her face. Not just dry, but too dry. Why had she come? Mary brought her over to the rest of us.

"Hello," I said. "Good to see you again."

Silva was tense, the worry lines deep between her eyes. But she was naturally nervous at the best of times.

"Your father called the service and asked me to come for a shift here," she said to me. "What can I do to help?" she asked Mary.

Wow. Pop was outdoing himself in spades. Of course he was sending a message to me, too:

Stick to the case.

Mary said, "Won't you have some ice cream? We brought home a gallon, to cheer Marcia up."

"I haven't come to eat, I've come to work," Silva said. But she pulled up a chair and sat down next to me. "I've come to take the place of one of you people who's all tired out."

"Silva was at the self-help seminar with me," Mary told us, still holding out the ice cream spoon ready to serve. "Boy, you really hung in there," she said to Silva. "You need some ice cream, then you can work. And you need some too, Peaches."

"How long did the workshop last?" I asked.

"From 3:30 in the afternoon till 8:30 at night, with something to do every minute." Mary served a dish and placed it in front of Silva whether she wanted it or not. "And then some of us went out for coffee afterwards to unwind."

"Just a little ice cream for me so soon before supper," I warned as she began to heap a bowl. Ted wouldn't take the big bowl either.

"Thank you, but give me a rain check," he begged. And Mary said, "Oh, I know what you like, Ted. I keep it just for you! I have an open container in the refrigerator." She jumped up from the table and went into the kitchen. That small galley of a kitchen is just beyond the end of the dining room table. So I could see Mary open the refrigerator, knocking a rainbow magnet on the floor. She brought out one of those round containers of frozen juice concentrate. She buys the big size and just takes out as much of the sherbetlike concentrate as she needs each time. I knew what it was: limeade. I don't know what it is about limeade that Ted likes so much. Maybe the tartness. The very thing the kids don't like. Ted's limeade is always still there in Mary's fridge because she and the kids don't drink it.

Silva said O.K., she'd have some limeade too. "I'm really thirsty," she said, frowning. One of her hands fiddled nervously with the fingers of the other in her lap. "I had ham for lunch," she explained. Strange how even after we'd been through so much together, I didn't feel I knew Silva well. She was one of those people who doesn't confide in anyone unless they have to. Today, even her clothes didn't confide. She wore a plain blue shirt and a denim skirt. And yet I knew she wasn't plain and simple. She was angry at the world because her only son had killed himself, but at the same time, she was ready to be helpful to anybody in need or pain. Hence her work for the sitter service. I did learn that much when my aunt Nancy died. There's nothing like solving a mystery to learn about the people around you. But there was still a lot about Silva I didn't know.

Andy turned to her and giggled. "You have vanilla hair and chocolate eyes," he said.

Mary mixed the limeade up in a pitcher and took out two oversized hand-blown green glasses and put some ice in the glasses. Her

214

mother had probably brought her those the time she went to Mexico. Mary likes things to look pretty. She was also generous whether you liked it or not. She filled those glasses full.

She sat one in front of Ted and another in front of Silva. She put a dish with twice the ice cream I wanted in front of me.

Just as Ted raised his limeade to his lips, I said, "Our friend Drac— I mean, Loy — was here. He left you a new, expanded edition of his booklet about walks near Asheville. He's added another walk near a cemetery."

"Where is it?" Ted asked.

"The walk?"

"No. The booklet."

"Right over on the edge of the bookcase," I said. "Next to the red mug."

Ted put his glass of limeade down. "I'll get it." So, O.K., some people get excited about collecting stamps. Ted gets excited about collecting inscriptions from tombstones. And thank God he does.

I saw Silva raising her glass as if she were toasting Marcia. I saw her taking long swallows like she really was too thirsty to sip.

Ted brought back his pamphlet. This edition was quite nice, on slick paper with a full-color front.

I was just poking at my ice cream and looking across at the pamphlet when Silva said, "I feel dizzy." Her voice went high with fright. Her face was damp with perspiration. She said,

"I'm going to be sick!" She stood up, unsteady on her feet. She started toward the bathroom.

I looked at her glass, empty. My stomach flipped over.

"Stick your finger down your throat," I cried out. Because, after Pop's adventure, I knew that whatever you ate or drank before you felt funny was safer out of your system quick. She was already staggering toward the bathroom. I jumped up to go with her.

Mary had one arm around each child. "I need to stay with the kids," she said. "You go and see what . . . whether . . . I hope to God it's not . . ."

"Stay," I called to her as I followed Silva. "We'll cope." I could see Ted already at the phone. I knew he must be calling for help. Better to be safe than sorry.

I caught up with Silva, who was standing by the toilet, staring down at it. She was breathing fast. "I feel so dizzy," she said. "Everything looks yellow." Then she began to throw up.

That was the best thing she could do, I was sure. I put my arms around her and steadied her. And she was also doing what Lily said about Pop, sweating like a pig. I was wet just from holding her. Her blond hair was wet and plastered to the back of her neck.

Ted appeared in the doorway. "The ambulance is coming," he said. He wet a washcloth and handed it to me.

"Would you feel better if I wiped your face?"

I asked gently. She nodded.

Then, since she had had the dry heaves, I persuaded her to drink some water and then spit it out. She was still gray and trembly and wet, but for a moment she stopped heaving. And in the distance I heard the ambulance siren. "Help is coming," I told her.

Ted went to the front door, and in a moment two men in uniform rushed into the bathroom, and I was so glad to put Silva into their expert hands I could have cried.

"You're going to be all right," I told her. I prayed that was true.

And I rushed out into the guest room, where Ted had withdrawn to make room. I threw my arms around Ted. I was so relieved to feel him warm and healthy and alive, I almost couldn't stand it.

"Somebody meant to kill you," I gasped. "You're the one who drinks limeade. Somebody who knew that tried to kill you, and I hope to God they didn't succeed in killing Silva."

He held me tight. But what could he say?

"Someone is afraid of you, Ted," I said, keeping my head tight against the comfort of his shoulder. "But if he is, why doesn't the skunk just leave and go off somewhere else? Why not? But something about this place draws him. Keeps him here. Unless he's just crazy. But thanks to good luck, at least for today, you're safe."

CHAPTER 18

EARLY THURSDAY MORNING, OCTOBER 8

At two o'clock in the morning the phone rang. I sat up in bed and looked across at Ted's digital alarm clock. Two-oh-three, to be exact. Ted sat up, too, and switched on his bedside light. He reached over next to the pile of books that live on his bedside table and grabbed the phone. Nobody calls us at such an hour just for fun. "Hello?" he said, as if it were a question.

And I thought: Silva is dead! They've called to tell us.

We'd asked to be told of any change.

Then I hoped it was just the police with some other question. But they'd grilled us all within an inch of our lives earlier in the evening. And they wouldn't call at such an hour without a good reason.

Ted pulled the quilt up round him. He sleeps in the buff and the house was chilly. The light from the lamp showed the roundness of his muscles above the patchwork quilt, also the goose bumps.

"Oh, hello, Watt," he said. "Well, yes, I was asleep, but what's the news? Thanks for returning my call. There's been another poisoning, and that's why I said call back no matter how late." Then the light made his frown into dark lines, but he said, "Good thinking." And then, "Good God, that's a whole other aspect." He looked across at me and mouthed: "Connections."

I let out my breath, relieved. No death report.

"I mean," Ted said into the phone, "that we've felt all along that there should be some connection between the person who tried to poison Peaches' father with digitoxin and the serial killer. And now there's been another poisoning that looks similar to Matt Jones's." He filled Watt in on what had happened to poor Silva when she drank the limeade. "She had symptoms like the other two."

Of course I knew Ted had been on the phone to Watt back at the world memory base down east several times, telling him about Pop and Matt Jones. And evidently he'd called him right after the ambulance took Silva, and left a message. That would have been his only chance. The police arrived at the scene right after that. Now Watt was calling back. God bless him.

I was dying of curiosity and Ted could see that. "Let me just tell Peaches what you said." He put his hand over the phone. "Watt does have news. He's just back from out of town. He went to see the investigators he'd talked to about these sleeping-pill cases. He asked if any other pills were involved in any way. And sure enough, in the Winston case, other pills, including digitoxin, had simply vanished at the time of death." I shivered. My hunch was right. Connection. "And there's something else that I'll tell you about in a minute," he said.

While he held the phone to his ear and talked on, I sat and thought about that. Other pills, not only digitoxin, had disappeared. We had us an amateur pharmacist — who had misjudged the dose to kill Pop. But then, Pop in his way is pretty tough. And this damn poisoner had tried to kill Ted, and it was touch and go whether poor Silva would die in his place.

I shivered and pulled the quilt closer around me. How many medicines were poison and had a minimal taste? And maybe a delayed reaction? Hard to spot. Perhaps the police could search the houses of all suspects. Maybe they had and hadn't told us. Mustache was more standoffish since he'd mentioned that my cousin Mary and I were the only two with any real motive for killing Pop. And I told him I didn't believe it was Mary.

But if the killer was smart — and he must be if he had killed a number of times without being caught — he wouldn't have those pills lying around his house. Where would he put them? If I was the killer, I'd bury the whole cache somewhere in a sealed plastic bag.

Ted hung up. "This may be important," he said. "In several cases the person who was later found dead from an overdose of sleeping pills was rushed to the hospital earlier with an over-dose of something else."

"So the serial killer's method may fit!" I sat bolt upright. I didn't know whether I was more relieved that this made sense, so we might be able to figure it out, or scared that we were in the early stages of a killing pattern.

"The earlier overdose was as much as a month before the sleeping-pill killing," Ted said. "But in each case this was dismissed as an accident because it was an overdose of something the person normally took. And the problem was," he went on, "that in the cases that were assumed to be suicides, nobody checked for missing medicines. Only in the case that was considered a possible murder. There, the investigators discovered that although the medicine bottles were still in the medicine cabinet after the victim died, not a one had more than two pills in it. And only the fact that that was true of every single prescription made anyone suspicious.

"But in checking back," Ted continued, "Watt found that there was one family that noticed the same thing and thought it was odd. That was a presumed suicide. They were sad because they figured their mother must have been planning suicide for long enough to use up her pills and not buy more."

"So in only two cases," I said, "does anyone know more or less for sure what kind of pills have disappeared."

"So far, all that Walt can tell us is that digitoxin and tranquilizers and sleeping pills have been taken from what appear to be murder victims."

"And maybe the digitoxin was used here," I said. "Because in one way Pop, and maybe Matt Jones and Silva, don't fit the earlier cases. Pop didn't get an overdose of his own medicine. He got somebody else's."

"We better call the police," I said. But Ted said he'd asked Watt to do that so they'd get the benefit of his deductions first-hand.

"We better sleep on this," Ted said. "Because now more than ever we need to be on our toes tomorrow."

And we were both so exhausted that we managed to drift off.

I sat up out of a sound sleep because the telephone was ringing so loudly. Again? But the real telephone on Ted's bedside table wasn't ringing. I must have been dreaming.

I felt like something or someone wanted to reach me. I felt scared and wide-awake. Maybe just some part of myself felt a danger and wanted the rest of me to pay attention. I've had these telephone dreams before. And usually, afterwards, something I've forgotten has made trouble if I haven't found it out. Like the time I forgot to put gas in the car before I went to a wild part of Madison County and it began to get dark. Thank God the sheriff's deputy happened by. Or the time I forgot my flashlight when I had to cross a narrow plank bridge in the dark.

I strained to think what I could have left unthought-of, unlocked, turned on (as in the stove) or — or what? But wouldn't Ted have noticed?

Ted lay next to me, breathing deeply. The rest of the room pulsed with darkness. Except for Ted's breathing, the house was quiet.

I crept out of bed, not bothering to put on slippers. The house was chilly but not unpleasant. I pulled my bathrobe off the chair as I passed. Ted slept on. He needed that sleep, especially after being woken up at 2 A.M. He would be driving to Boone. I could sleep on the way. I went in the kitchen and checked the gas stove. All the burners were turned off. I checked the windows and the doors. They were all locked. I racked my brain. I heard that phone ring again in my mind. Much shriller than a real phone. We were about to set out on a trip, perhaps a dangerous trip, to Boone. If the ring was a warning, it must have to do with that.

I went in our office and turned on the light on my desk. The shadows in the corners heightened my spooky feeling. The wood-paneled walls magnify shadows. The knots in the wood became unfriendly eyes watching. In real life, someone was watching us and we didn't know who. Maybe even that helicopter we saw the other day. Maybe someone in the helicopter was watching us. And he was looking in the windows tonight. I closed the curtains. With woods in back of us we don't usually bother. I turned on more lights quickly, the ceiling light, the one over Ted's desk.

I went back over to my desk, which is nearest the door, and picked up the house copy of my manuscript from next to the printer. (It's nice to have it in two places. After all, my car could be in an accident. And I'd never remember how to say what I'd written just right.) I shuffled through to the chapter on how not to get lost.

Couldn't hurt me to review it. And reading what I've written always calms me down. I get interested.

Chapter 17
You Really Can Get There From Here

There are people who can always remember which is their right hand and which is their left, even without looking for the finger with the ring on it. They know instinctively which is east or west, even when the sun is not conveniently rising or setting in one of the same. These people never get distracted and never miss road signs. And when someone rattles off directions at a mile a minute, these people manage to hear and remember every word. When they go to a new place, they recognize all the landmarks on the way back. This chapter is obviously not for them.

Oh, how I wished *I* was one of them! I'd written this chapter with the idea that getting lost was inconvenient. But now it could conceivably be a danger to life and limb! Was that what my dream meant?

This chapter is for people like my friend Bob, who tells me he keeps his sanity by remembering to enjoy where he is even when it's not where he meant to be. Once, in Washington, he set out to tour the White House and somehow found himself at the zoo instead. "So," he said, "I saw the giant panda eating bamboo, instead of maybe glimpsing the President in the distance. The giant panda was worth seeing, too, and much more likely to sit still for inspection." He says he's seen lots of marvelous sights that he'd never have come anywhere near if he hadn't been completely off the track.

Boy, was I full of optimism when I wrote that.

And look at Columbus. He'd never have found the New World if he hadn't been trying to find a shortcut to somewhere else. He would never have been famous if he hadn't been lost.

And *we* could get famous. Headline: "Couple Found Murdered at End of Dead-end Road." I looked at the closed curtains. Suppose somebody was out there beyond them *right now.*

Waiting to follow us whenever we left. Maybe my dream was warning me to watch out for that.

But perhaps you are in a hurry. You have an appointment. Or you have to get to a convention at least on the same day that it starts.

The first rule is this: Start early. Do not let yourself be talked out of it. "You're crazy to give yourself a whole hour to get there," says a well-meaning friend. "It won't take even half an hour," he says.

As I turned the page, my elbow hit the phone on my desk, an innocuous black phone. But I started. The phone seemed to crouch, waiting to pounce. But if the phone was warning me, it was my friend, right? And starting too late was not likely to be the problem with this trip, was it?

Do not be seduced. The well-meaning friend is not the one who will find himself at the town landfill when he's supposed to be at an interview for a dream job or a party in his honor. Arriving early is rarely a problem. Take a book to read or stationery on which to write some thank-you notes, or in my case, a chapter to work on.

Oh, this chapter was so cheerful. Not for fugitives from injustice. But I read on.

The second rule is to get good directions. And get the kind of directions right for you. A map helps. For some people that's enough. I need landmarks if possible. "Go down Main Street until see the large red movie theater on your left. Turn right into Cascade Heights Road. The house will be the fourth on the left, the one with the wooden flamingo in the front yard. If you come to a stone building with a tower on top and a taxidermist on the ground floor, you've gone too far." That kind of thing. Write it down, of course.

I should tell Ted that we both needed to go over our route in case anything happened to either of us. Horrible thought. But better to be safe than sorry. An atlas and a box of maps were over on his desk. He loves maps. I find them confusing to follow.

I need detailed, concrete directions, if possible, because I'm prone to Peaches' Curse, which works like this: If I'm in a small town, the local teenagers will have decided to twist or hide all the street signs for a lark just before I arrive. Or a wayward kudzu vine will have covered the sign I need.

That would definitely not be good if Ted and I were chased and looking for the fastest road.

If I'm in a city looking for the marker that

227

shows where Route 40 goes off, a large moving van will be stalled in front of the sign. On a thruway, if there's going to be an accident or anything to distract my attention, it's going to be right near the point where I should have remembered to look for a "turn here" sign.

I'd read newspaper stories about people who were shot by car thieves who didn't even have a reason to want to shoot them in particular. Whereas . . .

So, anyway, there I am lost. I need help. Now here comes the tricky part. It's very important to know who to ask directions from, beginning of course with "Where am I now?" Otherwise you can get so hopelessly lost you may never be seen again.

I'd written that as a joke.

After extensive experience in this matter, and entirely missing the hog-hollerin' in Spivey's Corner and the King Tut exhibit in Charlotte and God knows what else, I have a list of people to ask in reverse order. In other words the top half of the list includes all the people to avoid if possible. Because who not to ask is even more important than who to ask.

This, I figured, was the most valuable part of the chapter. In fact I admired this part so much

228

that I forgot to be scared as I read.

Who Not to Ask

(1) Cheap labor. Once there were filling stations where grown-up men worked and sold maps, and could tell almost anybody how to get almost anywhere. Now you are just as likely to find a convenience store that sells fill-it-yourself gas out front and hires teenagers who have never been out of the neighborhood to work the cash register. They will cheerfully give you terrible directions. If given the choice between asking one of these or a five-year-old child, you might take a chance on one of these. Once or twice I have been helped out beautifully. More often I have ended up at the wrong end of the county.

(2) Motel clerks. Why do these clerks, however polite, so rarely know how to get to less-known spots in their own city or well-known spots in any other city? Shouldn't directions-giving be part of their job training? I've even been given a printed map by a motel clerk, who then said, "But keep asking along the way. A lot of street names have changed since we printed this." Yeah, yeah.

(3) Whoever you bump into. Intelligent-looking bystanders or store clerks in stores sometimes know the way. Usually they don't. Sometimes they won't admit they don't. They just make the whole thing up. Especially dangerous after dark.

I began to shiver again. I heard a house-settling noise, or was it someone sneaking down the hallway? Stop that! I said to my imagination.

And Who to Ask

(4) Delivery-truck drivers and taxi drivers. Mostly they know the way, however difficult, especially within a city. You come across a few these days that don't know enough English to explain. Learn Spanish and Swahili, and taxi drivers are your best city bet. Make them give you landmarks.

But tiny Boone is not a city.

(5) Delivery fleet dispatchers. These boys even know exactly how long it should take to get there. The easiest to find are in the kinds of pizza restaurants that guarantee delivery within a certain number of minutes. Often available in small towns as well as cities. If being lost has made you ravenous, you can kill two birds with one stone.

(6) Old-timers. In the country, look for them maybe sitting on a small store porch, watching the world go by. They practice looking stupid so you won't know how much smarter than you they think they are. Be extremely polite. You do not want to be the butt of their sense of humor. My cousin Mabel, who went to Vermont, says they have a favorite expression up there. If you

look uppity and a place is hard to get to, they just say: "You can't get there from here." Continue to be polite no matter what. After old-timers laugh, they'll help. They'll talk slow enough so you can get it all down. And even tell you the next good place to ask directions.

My eye fell on a knife on the edge of the bookcase. Only a paper knife, but it made me think. In the mountains, good old boys carry hunting knives. But certainly our enemy was not a good old boy. He didn't operate like one.

One last and most important warning. Beware all those who say, "You can't miss it." They are the most dangerous kind. Be warned that your explainer knows the way so well that he considers it an absolute cinch, so he is likely to leave out steps that he thinks are completely obvious. Like whether you take Route 70 East or West. Like you have to be in the left lane well ahead of time because the turn sign comes up so suddenly. Whoops, lost again on a larger thruway with no place to turn around for miles.

With these rules in mind, I never get lost permanently, or else I wouldn't be here, right?

Let's face it, this chapter was not for serious problems. Just the usual. And this was not even a usual hour. The round schoolhouse-type clock over my desk said 4:30.

But I had an ugly hunch that even for the

usual way of getting lost, this chapter was incomplete. Something important was missing from my words. Something I had particular trouble with. But I couldn't think what. Well, if I discovered it along the way, I could improve the book. I wanted it to be a good book, but I admit I didn't want to die for it.

Oh, come on, I told myself. You're jittery because of poor Silva. Just remember: Nerves don't help. Finding facts does.

Why, maybe the real phone had rung and stopped just as I woke up. At four in the morning? I patted the real phone on my desk and said, "I promise to be very careful."

CHAPTER 19

LATER THURSDAY MORNING

"I admit I'm glad we're going to visit the paper in Boone first," Ted said, standing in the kitchen by the refrigerator. I was leaning on the kitchen table, yawning. Four hours sleep is not much.

"Why?" I asked. "Boone is the farthest one away."

"Exactly," he said. "No one will expect us to go there. The police seem tough with us for now. Maybe we can slip out of here without being noticed by whoever it is who evidently wants to kill me and Pop." He scowled and pushed his glasses tight against his nose in the way he does when he feels threatened. It's as if he feels he has to have his glasses at the best angle so he can see as well as possible to defend himself. "I can't say I like knowing I'm probably the one who is supposed to be dead."

"No! Me neither!" I went over and gave him a big hug. He smelled good, of soap and after-shave and just essential Ted-ness.

"But Silva isn't dead yet," I said, praying that was true. She'd looked so gone I was expecting it, though. I had to admit that.

God knows I was sorry Silva had drunk

233

poison that surely was intended for Ted. But I was so grateful he'd been saved.

So now we'd be super-careful with what we ate and drank. Breakfast would be boiled eggs and crackers. The crackers had been sealed in plastic. We'd opened a new bag of beans to make coffee and a new can of milk to use for cream. Maybe I was being silly, but those precautions made me feel a little safer.

I went over to the hanging cabinet, got down two mugs and poured us each some coffee from the electric pot. It smelled delicious.

"I can't help thinking about that mug that Silva gave Pop last Christmas," I told Ted as I handed him his. "And how it said *'I intend to live forever'* in big, bold type. And Pop's still alive, for now if not forever, and Silva —" I felt myself choking up.

"Come sit down," Ted said firmly, and took my arm and led the way to the table.

"I know," I said, as I settled myself in my chair, "the only thing we can do for Silva right now is to find out who poisoned her. And that could help us find who poisoned Pop, too."

I told myself to think positive à la Mary, or at least act positive. "Thank goodness Pop's squared away so we can leave as soon as we eat breakfast," I said. We were lucky that Pop had managed to hire cousin Troy's boy on leave from the Madison County Sheriff's Department. Some kind of cousinly arm-twisting got that done fast. Pop would have the police looking in, plus a million cousins. What could go wrong?

Out the kitchen window, beyond the birdbath, the trees shimmered. Trembly like I felt, positive thoughts and all. My nightmare hung in the back of my mind.

Ted cracked his eggs into a cup. "This is a pretty spartan way to eat," he said. "I wonder if it's really necessary. I sure would like some jam."

I got up and got a new jar from the cupboard. When I came back, my coffee cup had vanished. Oh, dear — one of those days. When my hands do things and the rest of me doesn't remember my hands are there. A day full of mysteries. But not the right kind. I went back to the cupboard and eventually found my cup and saucer in a corner.

I started to take jam, and then realizing we didn't have napkins, I went to get some. When I came back, the jam had vanished. I must have moved it somewhere. Ted already had some. Well, what the heck, I didn't need jam. I would sit still and be very calm. That always helps.

I doodled two flowers on the pad I keep by the phone. Ted went to get a map to look at while we figured what to do. I doodle when I'm nervous.

"I called the paper," Ted said, "and talked to Rachel again. She says to come by the *Watauga Democrat* at about two o'clock."

Ted was still studying the map, but talking

about the pre-map part of our trip. "We'll wind about through some of those twisty roads here in the Beaver Lake section," Ted said, "to make sure nobody is following us."

God willing, I thought, remembering the warning phone that rang in the night. I didn't tell Ted about that He had enough to worry about. My hand was still doodling. I must *not* be nervous. I must be calm.

"Then we'll take off," he said. "We'll talk to Rachel; then we can do any skulking we need to around Boone, have supper, and maybe leave Boone around seven. We'll be home by bedtime at the latest."

The phone rang — but not as loudly as the phone in my dream — and so did the doorbell. I started. Come on, this was ridiculous. I must pull myself together. I picked up the phone on the kitchen table. It was Mag, still devastated because Silva had been poisoned in her house. Even Mary was off balance. "I don't know if they suspect me," she said, "but they certainly suspect it's somebody I know. I can't drop all my friends. But suppose it is one of my friends? What am I going to do? Suppose somebody tries to kill me and the kids?" She paused. "And, oh yes, thank you for the sock stuff."

I suggested she go over and stay with Pop and his bodyguard. But to keep the kids as quiet as she could. Pop can get impatient.

Ted came back from the front door. He said somebody wanted to save his soul, but he told them not today. That happens here in the mountains. Some folks take your soul seriously and are certain you won't save it without outside help. But suppose this was a ploy related to the murders?

I looked at the clock. Good grief, eleven o'clock already. I'd woken up early, as usual, but worked on the no-no's chapter and lost track of the time. Ted had slept late after our night adventures.

But I felt we ought to leave by eleven-thirty to be sure of being in Boone by two. Because my dream said I shouldn't start late, right?

I half-ran over to the sink with the breakfast dishes, carrying the plates, cups and saucers, and also the "cream" pitcher, hooked by one stray finger through the handle. I can't tell a lie, it was what my mother would have called a lazy man's load: too much at a time. Somehow, that finger delegated to the pitcher wouldn't hold it straight. Cream spilled on the floor. I put the dishes in the sink, grabbed a paper towel, and hurried back. I guess I didn't see one arm of the spill. Instead I stepped in it, and began to slip wildly.

Ted caught me. "Whoops!" he said. "This looks like the Marx Brothers Syndrome."

"You've been reading my manuscript!" I was pleased he liked to peek.

"Sit down a minute," he said. "You need to relax, or who knows what you'll do." He disappeared for a minute and retuned. "Read that out loud," he commanded, in exactly the tone he might have used to say, "Take this medicine now!" He handed me a page of my own prose So, O.K., I read it:

The Marx Brothers Syndrome

You know the Marx Brothers Syndrome is in effect when the things you forget all spring booby traps. The MBS is likely to roar into action when you are under pressure to do things just right.

"Well, at least right enough so we don't get killed," I said. "Forget that and keep reading," he said sternly.

The MBS is related to the Very Bad Day Complex, but different. For example, you have on a white skirt to go to church but you tell yourself you can carefully put a frozen Sunday dessert in the big chest freezer in the garage without getting dirt on your skirt. The key to the freezer sticks. You forget the skirt as you struggle with the key and suddenly your only clean skirt has a great big stain. You are so upset you trip over the dog.

"In that case I could stay home," I said crossly. "But today we mustn't stay home." "Read," Ted ordered.

Or suppose you're all dressed up to go to a

party, with your hair all beautifully curled. Someone calls that the water in the sink won't go on. The faucet is stuck. You put on an apron. You're getting hip. But as you work with your left hand to loosen the faucet, you have the dish sprayer in your right hand. You forget the sprayer. Suddenly the faucet works. Whoosh! No makeup. No hairdo. And whoever is watching will laugh. They can't help it.

That's part of the Marx Brothers Syndrome.

"Now, what I like best is your cure," Ted said, as he walked over and inspected the window to be sure it was locked.

"You take three deep breaths," I said sheepishly, "and then imagine exactly how it would have looked with the Marx Brothers doing what you just did. O.K., you're right. I should do that. Except first — no, forget 'except.' Getting rid of the Marx Brothers Syndrome comes first."

So I envisioned Groucho Marx slipping in milk and falling flat, and Harpo tripping over him. And Chico falling over both. I laughed. I felt better.

I got busy and packed enough stuff so we could be gone several days, which also worked off nerves. In nothing flat, we were ready to go.

I started to throw my bag in the back of the car. There was a heap of dry-cleaning-to-go — mine and Ted's — and the couch throw. I left it in the back to remind me to take it, and put my suitcase in the trunk. We were going in my Volvo. It's more comfortable for trips. But Ted drove. He hates to be a passenger.

We wound past Beaver Lake on Lakeview Drive, and since there seemed no sign of anybody following us, we came back onto Merrimon Avenue and found our way from there to Interstate 40 eastbound. Then, after we passed the little town of Black Mountain, we began descending Old Fort Mountain, steep rock wall on one side, spectacular view on the other. The red and yellow leaves were lively in the distance. We went down in order to go back up. That's the mountains.

I dozed off and woke up thinking out loud. "Mary is right to be afraid the killer is one of her friends," I said, and shivered. "Or else how did digitoxin get in the limeade concentrate in her refrigerator? Of course, the police are looking into that." But then somehow I found myself thinking about Mary, more than about the killer. Puzzling about my cousin. "I've known Mary almost from the day they brought her home from the hospital in a pink receiving blanket my mother knit," I told Ted. "Ma loved babies, and after me she couldn't have any more. She loved Mary." I felt sad remembering baby Mary.

On the steep downward slope in front of us, a truck's brakes were beginning to smoke.

"But I don't really know Mary," I went on. "I don't know why she picks friends who're so strange. We still don't know much about the artist-boyfriend that Harry says is strangest," I said, as Ted zipped round a curve.

"But Mary has always had man trouble, which is odd because Mary has her choice of nice men. But even back in high school she went steady with that kid who ran off and stood her up. And then she still went out with him afterwards! Later, when that stinker got busted for dealing drugs, I was pleased to hear it. He deserved to get busted for being mean to Mary. That's what I thought." An idea hit me. "Hey, maybe he was into drugs when he told the fish story. But he was good-looking. And charm! He could talk the birds out of the trees. That's what Uncle Horace said, and he didn't like him either." I watched the road roll by and puzzled about Mary.

The cassette deck played *Brigadoon*. I guess the sign of real comfort with somebody is that you don't have to talk. The landscape got flatter. We passed a lot of trees and a couple of signs for potteries. The road had long straight stretches. Still no sign of anybody following. That was good.

"Mary was born just six years after my Eve," I said, still trying to sort Mary out. "Eve used to play with her like a baby doll. Give Mary her bottle. Sing her songs. Mary was a good baby. She never cried. She wasn't allowed to cry."

Ted gave me his that-isn't-logical glance. "How could a baby not be allowed to cry?"

"Aunt Nancy used a method she said the Indians used in times of danger." I was embarrassed to tell him about it. I hadn't liked it. "I saw it once. Mary started to cry. She was about six months old. And her mother gave her a hard spank and then pinched her nose shut so she had to breathe through her mouth and couldn't cry."

Ted turned from the road and looked at me, amazed.

"I wasn't happy about it," I said, "but nobody could tell Aunt Nancy what to do, short of calling the police. And the baby seemed to be healthy and even happy when we played with her." Ted was still staring at me like I had two heads, but I went on: "And for better or worse, that nose-pinch stuff worked. Mary was a quiet baby and she became a quiet kid."

"So you call her the Smile Girl," Ted said dryly.

"She was cute. Aunt Nancy dressed her like a doll, a Victorian doll, with lots of ruffles. People stopped on the street and said how cute she was, and she'd smile and show her dimple."

"Look at that stone house," Ted said. "Wonderful stone work." It's not that he's not listening to what I say when he breaks in like that. He just doesn't want me to miss anything. The house was nice, all made of flat stones in a crazy-quilt design.

"And Mary is still cute," I said, "with bright colors and that perky turned-up nose. But speaking of stone, it's like she's behind a stone wall. It's like you can see her and be with her but you can't really reach her." I sighed. "Maybe I *should* have called the police. But they would have taken one look at Aunt Nancy and known she couldn't have done anything wrong. Nancy affected people that way. Even me. And I never worried too much about Mary. It was her brother Albert who acted like he hurt. I always tried to be nice to Albert. But Mary could take care of herself. She even took care of her father in a way. From the time she was a little kid. If he was acting funny, she'd distract you. Horace didn't show his liquor often, not back then. But if she saw you looking at him in a strange way, she'd say, 'Hey, look at me,' and sing a song or stand on her head or whatever." We rode along in silence while I thought about that.

"There's Woody's Chair Shop," I said as we passed through a built-up area. "That's where they made the rocker by our fireplace." The rocker goes back to my first husband, Roger. So Ted didn't know all about it. "It's kind of nice when you drive through the mountains and see all the places where pretty things are made by hand," I said. "I like to sit in our chair and know where it came from and who made it. It's like good wishes from the makers flow to me. We're in touch. And why can't I be really in touch with my own first cousins?" I felt another stab of sadness. "We were raised close."

When I'm thinking aloud, Ted lets me ramble. He's a good listener. But if he thinks I'm off the track he catches me up. One advantage of out-loud.

"Mary was raised in Connecticut," he said. "You lived in North Carolina."

"But every summer we spent vacations together. Roger and I lived near Pop and Mom, and Nancy and Horace would come stay here in the mountains near us. It was like Aunt Nancy was afraid to be alone with a kid for too long. And, after a while, Aunt Nancy was getting a one-month vacation. They spent one-twelfth of the year with us. The least-rushed twelfth. Sometimes we went places together, like Myrtle Beach. And sometimes Mary and her family came for Christmas too. My mother worried about the kids. 'With Nancy working all the time,' she said, 'and Horace . . .' Well, we knew about Uncle Horace."

Ted and I passed a small graveyard. "I guess I feel like you can lose somebody while they are still alive," I said. "If you can't reach them. If they can't hear you. I'm afraid of that for Mary."

I sighed. "I don't know why Mary is so much on my mind. Not just Mary *now,* but even Mary *as a kid.*"

"It's been my experience," Ted said, "that if something is on your mind there is a reason. Just wait a while. We'll find the reason."

We began to pass stacks of flat stones, a stone

company, on the left. Then another. With Ted driving, I didn't have to worry about getting lost. Just to prove we were on track, a sign appeared: "Linville, Blowing Rock, Boone." And then banks of shiny rhododendron leaves. Beautiful. Then a sign by the road warned us of wild curves. It looked like a curvy snake with an arrowhead at the end. Boy if you had to drive fast on that road you'd take your life in your hands. Even Ted drove slowly.

White lines drifted across the windshield. "Is that snow?" I asked, amazed. "We never have snow this early."

The road ended at another road and Ted turned left. Fog thickened the snow. Cars turned into fuzzy headlights. We turned right and began to snake up a twisty hill, back up the mountain. The fog came and went as we climbed. The left side of the road was a steep drop-off. The white stuff was sticking and piling up fast now. There was no rail at the side of the road. If we skidded, there was nothing to stop us going over. And no place to turn. Ted needed all his concentration to drive. His whole attention was on the slippery road.

And then, by good fortune, we came to a parking lot by the road near a gate with a big sign: GRANDFATHER MOUNTAIN. A gatehouse-type building with light showing through the windows stood on the far side of the lot.

Ted swerved into the lot and stopped. He said he'd go in and ask about weather conditions. He came back with a grin and said the rangers inside were all eating barbecue that one of them had just brought from Boone. And the barbecue-fetcher said the lower road to Boone was completely clear. No snow at all down that way.

We turned in the slushy parking lot. Boy, was I grateful as we crept back down that slippery road that we didn't pass a single car, which meant that we weren't being followed. If someone were following you on this slippery road, they could force you off and over the side in a heartbeat. I went off the side of a mountain road once and survived. Once was about all my luck could stand.

When we got down on the lower, flatter and longer road to Boone, there was not one snowflake. Signs touted attractions. Antique shops, trout fishing, heated gem mine. Oh, come on: *Heated* gem mine!

Maybe it was a good omen. The rest of the trip was painless.

Boone is a relaxed town with low buildings and lots of craft shops and fast-food restaurants. It's a college town and a tourist town. Ted found the *Watauga Democrat* office in a block of small shops, looking almost like a small shop itself.

His friend Rachel welcomed us and took us into her office for a chat. A cheerful office with two big desks and a big mirror to reflect light. "There's something about these mountains that attracts free souls, especially in the spring," Rachel said. "But the same thing, whatever it is, seems to attract con men, and sometimes it's hard to tell right away which is which."

Well, at least it wasn't spring. Not spring — and not that February eleventh death-date that kept turning up on computer printouts.

"Last year," she said, "some men showed up, for instance, and offered to resurface driveways cheap. And then they demanded too much money for a lousy job. The sheriff asked us to warn readers. But then again, three men arrived in town and announced that Jesus had told them to have faith — that if they wandered preaching the gospel, somebody would always feed them and help them to survive. And they appeared to be on the level."

"And recently someone tried to place a suspicious ad?"

"If you're looking for ads placed by advisers who might be in a position to defraud the elderly, take a look at this." She handed Ted a sheet of paper with a small typed item in the middle. Ted took it and read it out loud.

"Adviser will help you: Trained counselor will guide you in dealing with the future. Psychic readings. You'll be delighted. Reasonable rates." And a phone number.

Ted held on tight to the piece of paper. "Now this is a possibility, although it's not like the earlier ones," he said. "Before, it was a financial adviser. Now it's a psychic adviser. The person

247

we're looking for tends to use the same words over again. In one of his ads he said, 'You'll be pleased with our results,' and in another, 'You'll be delighted with our results.' This is not quite the same, but there is a similarity: 'You'll be delighted.' Now, that is worth looking into."

"The classified gal took this but told him she'd have to check on whether the ad fit our guidelines. So we have his name and address."

Ted made the call to the adviser, a William Hill, who said he could see us at seven o'clock. I was disappointed at having to wait, but Ted was almost pleased. He asked if we could look through the newspaper files just to check if any other story might shed light on the kind of fraud we were researching, and Rachel said, sure, except the only files were bound volumes. We looked through them with interest, and I decided I might like to live in Boone, where the college was always sponsoring interesting talks. Ted had a lovely time as he always does looking through newspapers. But we didn't find anything else that seemed suspicious.

We all had a bite to eat at a restaurant down the street. To our surprise, one of the rangers from Grandfather Mountain was at the next table.

"Snow still bad?" we asked him. He laughed. Every bit had melted away. So we decided that after we talked to the adviser, we'd go back by the short road — the upper road that had been too slushy to use when we came.

The man we sought lived and worked in a trailer park at the edge of town, in a real trailer, a white one. The kind on wheels ready to go. Now, that would be handy for a serial killer, to be ready to roll. An old rusty, red Mercedes was parked by the trailer. I don't usually pay much attention to the make of cars, but this one was such an interesting old car that I noticed it. Ted said it was a diesel.

A man of about fifty opened the door of the white trailer. One of those people who strike you instantly as so sensitive that you must watch out not to crush them. His skin was as fine as a baby's, with many crinkly lines around his wide blue eyes. He stood curled in on himself like a rhododendron leaf on a cold day. Shoulders rounded, head slightly bent. A smile kind of jerked at the edge of his mouth, as if it wanted to come, but all the time his eyes were wary, like he'd smiled once and been burnt. Good grief, he looked like he was the one who needed advice.

He said he was William Hill, and how did we do?

Ted introduced us and explained that he was researching a magazine article about alternative advisers and he'd like a counseling session to see how that worked and then he'd like to interview Mr. Hill about his own experience.

Immediately the smile burst through, as if this man would just love for Ted to ask him questions. Now, that was odd.

William Hill. What could I associate with his name? Will Kill was close. Good Lord. I felt the hair on my neck stand on end. What a name for a suspect Loy Haven would approve. But this man looked like the last man in the world who would ever kill a fly. Was that a front?

He led us inside to a small table with benches on both sides, and we all sat down. Behind him was a shelf of books. Quite a variety, from *Principles of Psychoanalysis* to *The Tarot Made Easy* to the *I Ching*. In the middle of the table was a small, cheap-looking crystal ball — plastic, actually, I imagined. It looked like one of those paperweight things with snow inside that you shake and then the snow falls around a church or a snowman. Except there was nothing inside. Why, it was like the one that had suddenly appeared on Mary's shelf. I felt a jolt of adrenaline.

"You might like to know," he said, turning his voice low and dignified like a preacher, "that I have a degree in psychiatric social work from NYU." Then he talked faster, as if he had to persuade us before we got up and walked out. "I spent five years working in a drug treatment center in New York City. Most of the people I counseled went back to drugs." He turned hurt eyes fast to me and then to Ted. "I couldn't take it any longer. There was so much pain out there and I could hardly make a dent. And so often when they came in I just *knew* who wasn't going to make it. I burned out."

He was convincing. I felt like I had to offer him comfort. To do something to lessen his pain.

And how did this fit with a phony crystal ball?

"I had to have a respite," he said, eyeing each of us like we'd said he didn't. "And I had to have some means of livelihood." He waved his long thin hands around like he meant the beat-up trailer ate money. "So I've been traveling and doing this. I'm good at it, actually." He smiled shyly. "I stop a few months here, a few months there. I think I do as much good as I did in drug treatment. And it doesn't make me feel so bad. I give hope."

I translated that to mean he told people what they wanted to hear. Well, there's certainly a good market for that.

"Most people are more impressed by the crystal ball than the degree. But you look like the degree type," he said to Ted. "And I can tell you have a problem."

"As a psychiatric social worker, you keep things to yourself?" Ted asked.

"Even as a crystal-ball reader I keep secrets," he said. And he curled even further in on himself as if Ted's question hurt.

"O.K.," Ted said. "Somebody tried to kill me."

That got the man's attention. He opened his eyes wide. He opened his mouth. "Seriously?

They tried to kill you? I thought I'd gotten away from that kind of thing when I left New York."

But why would he admit such surprise if he was selling himself as psychic?

"People come to me with all sorts of problems," he told Ted. "Sometimes it's all in their minds. With you I can tell it's real."

He held his long thin hands over the little plastic globe as if he were warming them. "Just let me try my crystal ball and see what happens."

Then he shut his eyes, not looking at the ball at all, and slipped into a kind of sonorous voice like a TV evangelist. "You are in danger," he intoned.

Did he think that would help us?

"There is a black cloud over you. You must watch in back of yourself at all times. If you survive for a week, you will be all right." Then he said, "You have great inner strength. You *will* be all right." But he said that in a different voice, like it came from him and not from the crystal ball. Then turning to me, he said, "And you never let go of hope, so you have good luck."

Now, that got to me. I wanted to believe it.

Ted, who never hesitates to ask questions, asked where Will Kill Hill came from.

"Most recently from Asheville," our psychiatric-socialworker, crystal-ball reader said.

I was careful not to look startled. "I was

252

there up until about a week ago," he said. "It's a lovely place, but I get restless. Lots of people there are interested in knowing their future. I didn't even have to advertise, I got so much business by word of mouth." He rambled on about Asheville, and we let him. Ramblers often drift something useful. Ted was staring at the bookcase. He always says you can know a man by his books and pictures. Suddenly, I heard this Will Kill say ". . . this medieval get together." What?

"Medieval?" I said. My ears perked up.

"Given by the local chapter of the Society for Creative Anachronism," he said.

Loy Haven, alias Dracula Jr., had told us he belonged to the Society for Creative Anachronism. An anachronism was anything out of its proper time. This Will Kill looked too sensitive for any time I ever heard of. And what if this strange man knew Mary's friend Loy? Did strange characters attract each other?

"I play the part of a medieval seer," he said. "We all have roles, you know. That's mine. I went to this party they were giving. Wherever I go I try to find the local chapter. To find kindred spirits. And I get business that way. People who want private readings."

"Did you meet a man named Loy Haven who teaches medieval history?" I asked

"Perhaps," he said. "Does he hang around with a girl who cracks jokes?"

"A brown-haired girl?" I asked. "Who always

wears bright colors?"

"The red she wore was not authentic," he said. "Her date said so. Bright red dye was not available to any but the wealthiest before the Victorian era when they invented aniline dyes."

"And you gave her a reading?" I asked. That would be how Mary acquired a plastic crystal ball. And why it was sitting on her shelf next to the red mug.

"My readings are always confidential," he said in such a defensive voice that I knew he had.

"She's a cousin," I said.

"Were you able to help her?" Ted asked. His eyes were focused sharp now, like he'd caught a glimpse of something important.

"That," Will Kill said, "is private between a client and myself."

I had a sinking feeling. Pop just loved any kind of psychic reading. So Mary probably took this strange man to see Pop. I just knew it. I was furious. That's all we needed — some crystal-ball reader to egg Pop on. Or maybe to poison him.

And why didn't the sitter tell me? It would have been Sherrie, of course. Sherrie didn't tell me anything. And, furthermore, she believed in all that stuff. She read the Tarot cards for Pop, and he just ate it up. But much as I'd like to, I probably couldn't blame Sherrie for introducing Pop to this strange man. This Will Kill. Mary had probably done that. Mary whom I did not understand. Perhaps she didn't understand herself. So she went to a man who said he had a crystal ball. Who gave her one! Or sold it to her, more likely. I bet that's why it was sitting on her shelf.

Ted kept asking questions, about where this Will Kill was on Saturday afternoon and evening (poison-in-sugar time), for example. Had he been in Asheville then? Will Kill said no, that last Saturday he was home in Boone reading a book and he went to bed early.

And when Ted asked him where he came from before Asheville, he claimed to have been out West, wandering around in his trailer. That would be hard to check.

As a parting gesture, William Hill tried to sell Ted his own private crystal ball for only thirty-five dollars, but Ted said that personally he believed more in logic. And this Will gave up easy. He did not strike me as determined enough to be a suspect. But he might be sneaky enough to play laid-back.

CHAPTER 20

THURSDAY EVENING

By the time we set out for home it was dark. There was only a sliver of moon. Ted drove and I drowsed off, but woke up again almost immediately to hear him saying he needed a cup of coffee as we pulled into a McDonald's with its golden M in the sky. He drove toward a well-lighted space near the sign.

"Look," he said, "what's that lying on the ground there, right where we're headed? Somebody's sweater, I bet. I'd better not run over it."

"Right," I said. "It may belong to a sweater-dropper like me." That's the problem with a one-track mind that can even forget a hand. It can *easily* forget a sweater over an arm. That's one reason I put name tapes with my telephone number on all my sweaters.

Ted opened the car door on his side and leaned out to look, unfastening his safety belt at the same time. He is always in a hurry. And, whango! the buckle on his shoulder strap bounced up and hit him in the side of the head.

"Are you all right?" I cried out. He gave me a dirty look. "What do you think?" he asked, straightening up and rubbing his head. His glasses were gone. Ted has not had practice in goofing up. He really hates it. "Damn, I've dropped my glasses," he complained. "The damned buckle knocked them off." He leaned out and looked around. "There they are," he said with relief. Then he stepped out and there was an ugly *crunch*. "Damn!" he said, even louder. I did not ask if he was all right.

"The lens fell out," he groaned. "It wasn't with the frames. I've stepped on the lens." He sounded like the end of the world had come. He leaned over and picked up the glasses and the broken lens, then he sat back down in the car and held out his hand for me to see. The lens was in three pieces. He put the pieces in an envelope he found in the glove compartment and put the glasses on. One eye stared out bare, the other from behind glass. I heard giggling. Three little blond girls and their mother had come out of the building.

"I could drive with one eye shut," he said. Then, "No, damn it, I couldn't — not safely. Not on that road." If there's one thing Ted can't bear it's to be helpless in any way. When he had flu he was impossible."

"And there's no way I can fix these myself." He sagged and bristled all at once like a sick porcupine. I suddenly felt like giggling myself. Not wise.

"What do you want to do?" I asked. "Do you want to go back and spend the night in Boone? Or do you want me to drive?"

I could see him weighing that like the choice between being hung and shot. His lips were pressed together in an unhappy line.

"I know you hate to be in a car where somebody else is driving, but we can manage," I said. I didn't add that I hate to drive on a strange road in the dark.

I noticed that a car had parked way over at the edge of the parking lot. I didn't register what make, but I probably noticed subconsciously that it was not a rusty red Mercedes like Will Kill's. I thought: what an odd place to park. He'll have to walk a long way for his hamburger. Also he (or it could have been a she) seemed to be reading a map or something in a bad light, holding it up in front of his face.

"Let's go on," Ted said firmly. "Forget the coffee. You drive. I can navigate. I can do that pretty well with one eye shut."

I was still half aware of that car at the edge of the parking lot. Maybe he's lost, I thought with sympathy, and trying to figure out the way. I didn't mention it to Ted. He was so upset about his glasses, he didn't notice. I got out and walked to his side of the car. I picked up the sweater that had caused all the trouble and draped it over a shrub for someone to find. Meanwhile Ted slipped over from the driver's seat, and I got in behind the wheel.

"You," I said as cheerfully as possible, "are in charge of seeing that we don't get lost."

After we passed beyond the last few lights of

Boone, nothing pierced the dark but our head-lights pointing downhill. They picked out trees and not much else along the side of the road.

Actually there wasn't much place to get lost. The road snaked downhill without choices. It's the direction-choices that get me. Besides, Ted was there to make them if necessary.

After about fifteen minutes, I became aware of a gleam of light behind us. Then it vanished. In a minute it appeared again then vanished. And suddenly that car in the parking lot came up like a slide show in my mind.

"We're being followed," I said. Panic struck me. Stop that, I told myself.

"Other cars use this road," Ted said. "Someone may be in back of us by sheer chance." I told him about the car in the Mc-Donald's lot. "There was something odd about that car," I said. "The way the person hid his face." And yet it hadn't seemed so odd at the time.

"Look," he said, "so much has gone wrong that you're just feeling anything could happen."

The lights behind us came around the next curve, clear and closer. "He's going to pass," Ted said. "Then you'll know we're not being followed."

But he didn't pass. As we came to the next curve, the car speeded up and I knew somehow that it was going to ram me off the side of the road. No, I was wrong. And why should it? It was just nervy. And besides we were passing through woods on both sides. "He's going to wait," I said. "That's what I feel. Silly or not. I feel he's going to wait and ram us off the side of the road when we get to that part beyond Grandfather Mountain where the road drops off on one side." I tried to laugh as I said that, to show I knew I was being foolish. The car was following uncomfortably close.

"If we come to a side road, turn off and see if he follows," Ted suggested.

I speeded up some just to make the distance between me and the car a little greater. The other driver let me do that, but he kept me in sight. He had his bright headlights on, blasting my rearview mirror with light.

"You're going too fast." Ted said. "Easy does it." Imagine Ted telling anybody they were going too fast.

I slowed down a little. Our follower stayed the same distance back. Thank goodness for that. I glanced at the gas tank. Nearly full. We'd topped up as we left Boone. If we crashed off the side of the mountain, we could explode in a great big fireball. I was sweating. But that wouldn't make me wet enough so I wouldn't burn. Oh, how I wished I didn't have a good imagination.

"O.K.," said Ted. "I think that's a road off to the right. Watch carefully and turn in if it is."

There was a space in the trees, and as I got close, I could see Ted was right. Our car strained at the turn and kind of lurched into the road. I sped in but not so fast that I didn't see the other car begin to turn, too.

"O.K, turn again if you find a place," Ted said. "Then we'll know for sure whether he's following us. If he is, go as fast as you can and we'll try to turn off when we're out of sight around a curve, into a driveway or something, and cut our lights. We may lose him that way. He'll go on and we can double back."

Oh, how I wished Ted were driving instead of me. He's great at maneuvering. I'm not. We came almost immediately to another turn. "Slow a little," Ted said. "You don't want to lose traction as you turn. Then speed up as fast as you can."

And then I went so fast, I scared myself to death. At each curve I expected to go off the road, but even though the car hitched and bucked and swayed, somehow it held. Another road turned off of the one we were on. I screeched onto that. Maybe our chaser wouldn't see I'd turned. Maybe he was deaf. No houses now. I was on a deserted dirt road with no place to hide. The damn road would probably end and he could corner me.

"There's a house and a driveway up ahead," Ted said. "Turn in and see if you can drive around in back of the house. Slow down so the tires won't screech. Maybe there's a lawn there. Cut your lights as soon as you can."

I swung in, and though the driveway ended, there was grass where I could drive in back of the house. I cut the lights and the motor. My heart was beating so hard, I couldn't hear if the car behind was following. He wasn't going to try so hard to follow us unless he had an underhanded reason. I was sure he was the killer. I just knew it. "There go his lights," Ted said. "I think that worked." I leaned back in the seat, weak and shaking. "We'd better knock on the back door and call for help," I said. "Maybe the sheriff can trap whoever it is on the road. There is a law against stalking, isn't there?"

We got out and ran to the door. We banged and waited. No answer. No lights. "This is a summer cabin," Ted said, "and this is October."

"There's nobody here," I whispered. All I could see through a small window in the top of the door was blackness. "And if the road peters out, he'll know where we are if this is the only house along here."

We jumped back in the car and I tried to turn around without lights. The small bit of moon was not enough to see by easily. I saw car lights coming back down the road. They turned into what must be a driveway further along. He was exploring each driveway.

I switched on my lights and shot out of ours to get as much of a head start as I could before he could turn back around.

"When you get to the main road," Ted said, "turn back toward Boone. That may confuse him, and at least we won't have to go over that part of the road with the steep drop-off. He doesn't act like he has a gun." Even Ted was scared now. Sure that the driver of the other car was a bad guy. "If he was going to shoot us, I think he would have done it already. On the stretch of road without houses."

Back to lurching around curves. Ted could actually remember where we'd turned each time. I was completely disoriented. "Good!" he said. "Here's the main road." I drove out and turned — toward Boone, I thought. Toward Boone, I was sure.

"No, no!" he cried. "The other way." But it was too late. "Don't try to turn back now," he gasped out. "There isn't time. Maybe we'll find a house this way with lights. Maybe before he gets in seeing distance we can find some place to turn off and hide again."

I hadn't seen one when we were coming up the mountain in the snow. But then we'd only come partway up this road before we had to turn back.

The quicker we found a place to hide, the better, I figured — and expert speed driver I'm not.

"Is that a place?" Ted asked. Up ahead I saw what looked like an old road into the woods. I managed to slow down enough to turn in. Even as I turned, though, I saw *his* lights come round a curve. Damn, he'd probably seen me. Yes, he turned in, too. Delighted no doubt to see us dead-ended. In front of us, the trees suddenly thinned out on both sides. On an impulse I turned sideways into the woods and then jammed on the brakes. *He* came hurtling on, not turning quite so fast. There was a crash and a bump, and the car vanished downwards. The bottom of my stomach went down with it. How on earth had I known enough to turn? Just on a hunch that the road didn't look right ahead.

"Back up," Ted said. "We need to get the law here fast. We don't know if he's hurt or crawling out of that car with gun in hand. He didn't shoot us on the deserted road, but that doesn't prove he doesn't have a gun or a knife."

"Wait," I said as we got to the main road. "Let's mark the spot." I threw a white sweater that was in the back seat onto the side of the road by the turn-in.

We drove on back toward Boone and stopped at the first lighted building, a small cabin by the road. An elderly man came to the door. A television was blaring in back of him. I pointed toward the phone and he nodded.

I called the sheriff while Ted managed — partly by shouting, partly by arm-waving — to ask the old man to explain where we were. Then Ted took over the phone and explained to the gal who'd answered the emergency line exactly where to find us.

He also gave her the telephone number where we were. He hung up and said we'd been ordered to stay put, and somebody would get to us fast.

We managed to shout loud enough to explain we were waiting for help. The old man nodded and invited us to watch some wrestling with him. We watched a couple of bouts that starred the Hangman in a black hood, and Beautiful Bill with long blond hair, which his opponent pulled. I sat on the edge of my seat, waiting for the deputies.

When they came, they wanted me to stay with the old man, but Ted and I pointed out that with a killer maybe loose in the woods and plainly somebody who had it in for us, I'd be safer with the deputies.

We led the deputies back to the spot still clearly marked by my sweater, not knowing what to expect. We'd heard our follower's car go off an edge and make a crashing noise. But I'd gathered from the sound of the crash that the car didn't fall a long way off a steep cliff.

The driver could have been killed, or merely knocked out, or merely stunned and now gone.

He could now be hiding somewhere near us in the woods. There were two deputies, a tall one with pitcher ears and a small one with a big nose. They said we ought to wait in our car, but Ted made a good case again that we'd be safer with them.

By the light of their big, heavy-duty flashlights, we found a path down to the place where the other car was lodged. The place was a drop-off which people had used for a dump. But the weight of the car had carried it beyond the trash area. It lay among ferns that were bright green in the flashlight beams. With light reflecting from the windows, I couldn't see if there was a body inside. Dead or alive. This could be the man who tried to kill Pop and Ted and succeeded in poisoning Silva and Matt Jones. Who else could it be?

We had to stand a good way back from the wrecked car with Deputy Big-Ears. Big-Nose down below looked inside. "Nobody here," he called.

Boy, what a disappointment.

He stood among ferns, lit yellow-green by the flashlights, and bits of flat rock, and leaned into the car, looking around. "There's a big old hunting knife here," he called. He held it up, and the blade winked in Big Ears' flashlight beam. Nose lowered his trophy and examined it in the beam of his own light. The blade gleamed.

"It's got initials," Nose called to Ears. "Initials on the handle: R.B.K. Looks kind of old."

Did we know any R.B.K.? Ears wanted to know. Silently I began to go over the people I knew. Not a one had those initials. Ted said the same.

"We don't even know for sure whether the driver was a man or a woman," Ted said. "We never got a single good look at whoever it was who had a knife marked R.B.K."

"No," I agreed, "and he or she is still out there, somewhere in the night, loose."

CHAPTER 21

LATER THAT NIGHT

By the time we told Deputy Big-Ears everything we could about being followed, it was so late my knees were weak. I was so exhausted I thought my brain screen would go black before my head hit the pillow.

We found a serviceable-seeming motel on Route 221, down the mountain and not quite to the intersection with I-40, and managed to wake up the Indian gentleman who was in charge. He gave us our room key, and we found a clean, simple room, put the safety chain on the door, and got right into bed.

Then the reruns of our chase began in my head and I couldn't cut them off. Which would have been O.K. if I'd seen any revelations. This was strictly repeats. Slamming around curves in my mind. Seeing the gleam of that knife and puzzling over those initials: R.B.K. I did not know an R.B.K.

So, O.K., I'd made myself think about something else. Ted had to wind down, too, and was reading a book. With all the excitement, he'd actually remembered to bring the one that Cousin Georgianna gave us. But then he yawned and fell asleep before long. I didn't want to wake him up, so I took my notebook for jotting notes on *How to Survive Without a Memory* and went in the bathroom. It was an old-fashioned bathroom with little white octagonal tiles on the floor, and a real enamel bathtub instead of plastic, but stained green beneath the tap from dripping water. The light was low-watt but it would do. I put the top of the toilet down, sat on it, and thought about the art of not getting lost while driving a car.

I'd written a whole chapter on that. But then, when the chips were down, none of it had saved me from turning the opposite way from the way I meant to turn. None of it headed me the right way in the dark with nothing but wall-to-wall trees for scenery. Was that what my telephone-dream had been warning me of?

So my chapter wasn't finished. Come to think of it, I hadn't included anything about turning into an unfamiliar place on an unfamiliar stretch of road, even in the daytime. Not even about turning into a garden-variety fast-food stop, and remembering which way to turn when I came out. Lots of times I'd gone several miles the wrong way before I discovered I should have gone right instead of left.

There must be some trick to help in this situation. Of course, in the daytime there was the obvious one of memorizing landmarks, or even writing them down. *Turn in the direction of the traffic light.*

And if you lost the piece of paper you wrote that on, or forgot the image you were using to remember — like a picture of yourself, in your mind, real thin because you were eating *light* — well, in the daytime you could ask somebody: Which way to Winston-Salem? Or whatever. And if you were lucky, they would tell you right. And if they told you wrong, you could then ask somebody else. Or you might be near enough to find a road sign.

But not on a deserted road at night. And, in fact, even in the daytime when you had directions, you could go wrong. One time I was coming out of the driveway of the Carolina Inn in Chapel Hill and I asked directions how to get somewhere or other and a real reliable college-professor type told me, "Go left, then left again, then just go straight until you get to it." That sounded so easy. Downright foolproof. But the street in front of the Carolina Inn is a one-way street, left as I drove out. Did he include that in the two lefts? Or did he include that in the given, because you couldn't go any other way, and did his directions start at the first road that turned off the one-way road? Life is full of these choices that don't occur to me until the person I've asked is gone.

But never mind that. What do you do when you are confronted with: (1) no one to ask, and (2) no obvious landmarks?

In my mind's eye I pictured driving into

a dark road and then immediately doing a U-turn to come out. A U-turn is easy. It's the time and distraction between the turn in and the turn out that makes a problem. Then I forget which way is which.

So I thought about the basic, unadorned U-turn. How would where I went in be related to how I came out?

And suddenly the answer came to me, and it was so simple that I couldn't imagine how I'd let all these things — landmarks I couldn't quite remember, and people who made up directions and all the rest — confuse me all these years. I started writing quick, before the answer could get away:

If you are driving along and turn right *into a road or parking lot, then no matter how you turn or twist inside that place, when you later want to keep going the same way, you turn* right *— the same way — when you come out.*

And your right hand was the one without the wedding ring. Or the one with whatever ring it was your pleasure to mark it with. What I had to remember was simply *right, right.*

Then flushed with inspiration, I drew a picture of how it would work if you turned left:

If you turn left *into a parking lot or road and meander around, to keep going the same way, you'd turn* left *as you come back to your route.*

270

Why, if I had known the *right-right, left-left* rule and remembered that I'd turned right as I went into that first turn off the main road as I came down the mountain from Boone, I'd have known that if I turned right when I came out, I'd be continuing the same way. And I didn't want to go the same way.

Half the human race probably know *right-right* in their bones. I have uncooperative bones. But some other people have uncooperative bones, too. Now I had a rule for us all.

And to keep in mind whether I'd turned right or left to begin with, I could put some marker on the left or right side of the windshield shelf, or I could cross the fingers on the appropriate hand as I drove along on a chase.

And what would I do if I had to weave in and out of many curvy roads on a night chase? And had no chance to write down a few rights and lefts? Well, if I was lucky I'd have Ted along. That was his area of expertise. If I was unlucky, then the only rule I knew was simply not to panic. With a clear head, even catastrophes can come out fine, I told myself.

I closed my notebook. I'd better get some sleep. I was going to need a clear head.

CHAPTER 22

FRIDAY, OCTOBER 9

As soon as I woke up, my eyes went to the safety chain on the motel door. I was glad it was there. Comforting like the coffee Ted was making in the little electric pot the motel put in our room.

God knows where the man — or maybe woman — who escaped into the dark might be. I hoped he was not still following us. Who on earth could he be? The poisoner? The serial killer? A dangerous stranger? Or someone we thought we knew well? Had I dreamed that the sheriff's deputy had radioed in the license number and discovered our follower was driving a stolen car? Stolen in Asheville. No, that was real. But all of last night felt unreal.

We'd slept late after our wild night. Through a crack in the motel curtains, I saw sunshine. The clock-radio on the table between the beds said 9:30 in glowing red numbers.

Ted handed me my cup of coffee. I took a sip, then sat on the edge of my bed and dialed Pop's number. Time to check. Lily answered. "I am so glad to hear your voice," she cried. "Your father is frantic to talk to you." I could hear him growling in the background. Then she said, "Just a minute, he wants me to wheel him into his own room so he can talk with the door shut." Her voice sounded guarded, as if she were picking her words not to upset him more.

Oh, dear, I thought, he's having one of his bad days. I drank a little more soothing coffee. So what was he frantic about today?

"Where are you?" Pop demanded loudly. "As soon as you went off and left me here alone, I was robbed."

He was about as alone as a rock star on stage. With a bodyguard, sitters round the clock, Mary and the kids, umpteen cousins bringing cakes, and the police sticking their heads in.

All I could actually see was the black motel phone, practically an antique; the table, my coffee, the buff motel wall, the rumpled bed across from the one I was sitting on. But, more demanding than these, I could see Pop's face before me, drooping with self-pity. Bloodhound mode.

"We're off doing exactly what you asked us to do," I said tartly. "What do you mean, robbed?" Ted, who was standing by the other bed buttoning his shirt, raised his eyebrows when he heard "robbed."

"Someone I trust, someone in this house, has come into my room and robbed me of a five-thousand-dollar gold coin!" Pop said.

So it was a really bad day.

"We put all of your coin collection in the bank, Pop," I said, trying to sound reasonable.

"Don't you remember? After somebody broke into the house, you let me do that."

"Oh, those were small potatoes," he said scornfully. 'This is from my new collection. And if you don't believe I have a new collection, I'll give you the name of the coin dealer. He is a fine man who's helping me find what I need. In fact he just got me this coin. I had it out, looking at it, and now it's gone."

"And where do you keep this coin collection?" I asked cagily. If it was real, I certainly needed to know where it was.

Long pause. Naturally, he didn't want to tell me. But he wanted me to believe it was real. Finally he said, "I keep it in a locked drawer." Long pause. "In the drawer in my bedside table."

Instead of Pop's hound-dog face, I saw that table. It was really a small bureau. One of the antiques from Ma's mama. Mahogany with a marble top and a long drawer with nothing to protect it but an old-fashioned key. Pop kept the key on a chain around his neck ever since he'd announced that was his private drawer. It was about as safe for coins as the piggy bank I had as a kid. Anyone could open it with a paper clip. I almost said, Oh, come on, Pop. That's ridiculous.

I had never looked in that locked drawer, out of respect for Pop, who had asked me not to. But Mustache had looked in it. Which was one reason I felt free not to insist. And now free to

274

doubt what Pop said. Mustache had laughed and said there was nothing in that drawer to worry about.

"O.K., Pop," I said. "I'll call the dealer, and call you back." That seemed the simplest and quickest way to calm him down. I hoped the coin shop opened before ten.

I dialed. Busy signal. In a little bit I dialed again. I got a cheerful voice. It belonged to Bill Wright, Wright's Coin & Stamp Shop, he said. And what could he do for me today?

"I'm Harwood Smith's daughter." I wondered if he would inform me he couldn't discuss a client's business. But before I could say another word, he told me Pop had just called and said to tell me anything I wanted to know. Well. That was progress. On the other hand, it began to seem there might really be a coin. Which would complicate life.

"My father says he lost a five-thousand-dollar coin —" I began.

"Forty-seven hundred," he corrected. "I was terribly upset to hear it. It was a 1907 twenty-dollar high-relief Roman-numeral Augustus Saint-Gaudens gold piece."

Well, it certainly had an impressive title.

"At least," he sighed, "it wasn't uncirculated Saint-Gaudens. It wasn't quite in mint condition. If it had been, it would have been worth fifty-five hundred. I finally got hold of it for him on Wednesday. Part of a collection. I'm shocked to hear he may have lost it or had it stolen." His voice went low with what sounded like real grief.

"And you delivered the coin?" I asked. I liked his voice. It was friendly. But, say, if this man frequented our house, maybe I had a whole new suspect. But why hadn't I ever seen him?

"Oh, I don't deliver." He sounded shocked.

"But my father is in a wheelchair and he rarely gets out," I explained. "And on top of that, he's been sick. Did you use a special courier?"

"Of course," he said. "Your father's friend, Miss Sherrie. She actually came with an armed guard this time. She explained the guard is her boyfriend." He chuckled at that. "She's always the go-between. Your father almost never calls me. Miss Sherrie tells me he has spells of thinking that the phone is bugged." My heart constricted. Sherrie hadn't told me about that. Pop had been in worse shape than I realized.

"Do you have a record of what he's bought and sold?" I asked. "I'd like to get a list and check the rest of the collection. My father is rather elderly and sometimes he gets mixed up." And then on a hunch I said, "Could you give me the price of the last four coins you sold him before the Saint-Gaudens gold piece?"

I heard a rustling of papers; then Mr. Wright said "He bought an 1854 three-dollar gold piece for twelve hundred dollars, a 1937-D three-leg buffalo nickel in mint condition for fourteen hundred twenty-five — that's a good buy. And a 1798 draped-bust silver dollar for eight hundred forty-five. Also a pretty little Liberty-seated twenty-cent piece for only six hundred fifty dollars." I repeated all that out loud as I wrote it down.

Ted was sitting on the bed now, paying full attention, frowning. His antennae almost quivered.

I thanked Mr. Wright and said I'd be by to get the complete list as soon as possible.

"All right," I said to Ted, angrily, "I'm going to apply the acid test now. I'm going to call Pop back and ask him how much he paid for these coins. Pop told me he paid three hundred dollars more for the Saint-Gaudens gold piece than Mr. Wright said he paid. If Pop gives me higher prices for the last four coins he bought before that, I smell a fish. And if that's the case, we better go deal with the coin problem first thing." Damn Sherrie. Was she a thief as well as a flirt? And if so, what else?

"You think Pop will remember prices?" Ted asked doubtfully.

"Oh, when it comes to money, he keeps records," I said. "He'll have it all in a ledger book."

I dialed the number reluctantly, suspecting that I was about to dive into a can of worms. Pop picked up the phone himself and sounded triumphant, even before I told him what I'd found out. "I told you so," he cried. "Of course I have a coin collection. Did you think I dreamed that? Listen, coins can be a damn good investment. If the banks fail, I'll be O.K."

"But the coins are so expensive!" I said. "What did you pay for the last four you bought, for instance?"

"None of your damn business," he said.

"If I'm going to help you, it *is* my business," I said firmly. "If you're going to keep them there at your house, and not even in a safe at that, then I have to raise your household insurance and add a rider to cover the coins."

He fell for that, or maybe he really meant to tell me all along. He gave me four prices, pronouncing them slowly so I was sure he was reading off some list. Each price was just a few hundred dollars higher than the price the dealer mentioned. Was that how Sherrie managed to buy all those fancy, sexy clothes?

I never did like that woman with her party dresses on the job. And now a boyfriend who was an armed guard? Were Ted and I the only people in the world without guards? I thought the only people who needed them were rock stars and the head honchos in the Mafia.

"We'll be home today, Pop," I said. "Now, you sit tight and don't worry."

"At least," Pop said, "I was robbed before the 1933 ten-dollar gold piece came. There are only eight of those in the whole world, and it's worth forty-five thousand." He sounded dreamy, not alarmed. He must have it wrong this time. How could there be only eight in the world? Especially if the coin was made as recently as 1933. He had something wrong, but, by God, he had ordered a forty-five-thousand-dollar coin to keep in his bedside table! And if that wasn't there yet, the coins that were there must be worth plenty!

"Don't worry, I'll stay right in this room," Pop said. "I'll say I feel sick and sit right next to this drawer until you get here." That might not be such a safe thing to do, either, especially if the thief was an insider, somebody in the house "protecting" Pop. But I knew I couldn't talk him out of it.

The flowers in the picture on the motel wall simpered down at me. Magnolias. They were everything-is-always-going-to-be-all-right flowers.

I hated them. I could have taken the frame off the wall and thrown it on the floor. Hard. And stamped on it. Because the truth is that almost everything in the world has to be got around or fixed. And that is most particularly true of my father, the rare-coin magnate.

CHAPTER 23

NOON

The leaves were warm autumn colors on both sides of the four-lane as we drove along toward the mountains. But I was thinking of the trees that were black in last night's darkness, not the ones that glowed in the morning sun.

Those initials on the knife that had glimmered in the darkness still puzzled me: RBK. Ted and I talked about that. Did they belong to the person who stole a car in Asheville and followed us? Nobody in Asheville had known where we were. Or so we thought. "It's as if somebody in Asheville can hear what we say in our house," I said, hugging myself for warmth, "and obviously the person who stole that coin has the run of Pop's place, even with a bodyguard on duty."

"Listen," Ted said, as he overtook a pickup truck full of hounds, "we'll keep trying to find out how someone knew where we were. But there's no point in speculating on what happened to Pop's coin until we get to his house and find out what really went on."

"But I can't help wondering."

"There's something else," he said, "that you

might like to wonder about. Something that might actually get us further right now." He wove around a big red truck lumbering up a hill.

His voice was low, in that I've-worried-about-this-a-lot tone. "In every spare minute, I've been reading that book your cousin Georgianna wanted us to read," he said. "The one called *Memory's Voice: Deciphering the Mind-Brain Code*. I finished it before you woke up this morning."

Ted could read when I'd be so bushed I couldn't put one word in front of the other. And he read so fast, I couldn't believe it. And then he remembered what he read. Wonderful. We passed a waterfall coursing down the mountain side of the road. Ted thought as fast as that water fell.

"This guy Daniel Alkon who wrote the book wanted to know why some people make the same self-destructive mistake over and over, and he studied the brains of snails," Ted said.

I admit this sounded crazy to me. Crazy that with a killer loose, and Pop maybe robbed, we should worry about the brains of snails.

But Ted sat straight and determined behind the wheel. He was headed somewhere in his mind as well as on the road. Ted who was in charge of logic.

"This Danid Alkon discovered that a kind of sea snail could learn to connect two things: light, and turbulence in the snail's tank. The snail could remember that when a light shone, there was going to be water swishing around."

"But how on earth," I asked, "could anyone know what a snail remembered?" Yes. A crazy morning. We passed a car pulling a trailer with a name on the side: "Wild Nostalgia No. 2."

"Because," Ted said, "the snail *showed* it had learned by contracting the foot muscle that held it to the side of the tank."

"Sign language?" I must have sounded cynical.

"No," he said, "it contracted the muscle when a light flashed. That showed it had learned that turbulent water usually accompanied the light and would knock it loose if it didn't hold on."

O.K., I could see that, but it sure seemed a long way from the things we were trying to sort out: from a Saint-Whoever-it-was gold coin to digitoxin or fatal sleeping pills.

"But the foot contraction wasn't the important part, just the first step," Ted explained earnestly. "Alkon was able to show that infinitesimal parts of the snail's brain-wiring actually changed. The memory that two things were connected was actually written in the wiring of its brain."

I tried to digest that. Maybe any memory problem was not enough wire in my brain. I almost laughed. I tried to think where I'd heard about two things connected like that. Somewhere before. Yes. With dogs. There was this

282

man, Pavlov. And he rang a bell just before he gave dogs meat. And after a while their mouths watered at the sound of the bell even when there wasn't any meat. Bell and meat were connected. "Like Pavlov's dogs." I said.

"In a way." Ted nodded. "But a snail's wiring is much simpler than a dog's. And the parts of it are bigger. So Alkon was able to actually find the spot where the change was written. He could stick the tiniest possible electrodes into that spot and hear a difference after a snail learned about the light. There were more electrical signals."

"He could *hear* the snail learning that two things went together? *Hear* changes in the brain?" Well, I'll tell you, it's hard for me just to believe that pictures go through the air and make television, even though I see it every day. Now Ted wanted me to believe this man could *hear* learning.

"Now, what Alkon figures is that in a much more complicated way, when a person is taught by life that two things go together — say, love and cruelty — that is actually written in the brain too." He whizzed around a red sports car with two teenagers in it. When he's excited, he forgets to even glance at the speedometer. Well, I was in a hurry to get home too.

"Long before psychiatrists, there were wise men who said you had to know yourself to live life well," Ted continued, waving one hand. At least the other hand stayed on the wheel. "But in this book, Alkon is saying more than that. He's saying you can have a memory that something hurtful has to go with something that you need, like love. If, say, to get your father's love, you had to put up with beatings too." He frowned as if to say, Here comes the bad part. "And that memory can be written in your brain in a way that can't be easily changed."

I was confused. "What does that have to do with knowing yourself?"

"If you can't bring that memory out and look at it," Ted said, "which is a kind of knowing yourself, and then somehow have new experiences that teach you that the old memory is wrong" — he took a breath — "new experiences that write a better memory in your brain — then you're stuck with mistakes that are etched in your head and you don't even know it."

"And this Alkon learned all that from a snail?" I was incredulous.

Ted honked at a car that was weaving up the hill. "Well, it's complicated. That was only the beginning, and you ought to read the book." He passed the weaving car, which was driven by a wizened old man in overalls and a black felt hat. A well-aged mountain farmer, like Matt Jones.

Ted turned and looked me in the eye. I was glad the road was straight for a stretch. "But I've known enough people who made the same dumb-seeming mistake over and over, even when they had good advice about why not to . . ." He groped for the right words.

"I get it!" I said. "You mean, like Mary always falling for men who put her down or even men who are crooks. Falling for the wrong men. It's like she's programmed to do that, in some way."

But, I thought to myself, why do we keep coming back to Mary when we need to find a killer? If there's one thing I'm sure Mary is not, it's a serial killer. I *know* she hasn't had a chance to be in the places where people were killed. And aside from that, she wouldn't want to hurt Pop or Ted. I was absolutely sure of that.

"We've seen that the new people who have come into Pop's life lately are mostly Mary's boyfriends," said Ted, actually slowing down around a sharp curve. "And intuitively you keep worrying about what Mary's like — what makes her pick the wrong men." He smiled at me like I was some kind of naive genius. "You have to admit that if she's true to pattern, the man she picks to trust and love the most will be the killer."

I could actually feel the hair on the back of my neck stand on end. "Oh, I'm sure that's not true," I cried out. I said it extra loud in order to keep it from being true. I wanted to yell, *No!* I wanted to go out of the absent-minded-detective business right then. I wanted to cry.

But there was a terrible dark logic in what Ted said. And furthermore, it felt right. Maybe there were things about Mary's father that I didn't know.

I cried out: "Kind, good men have cared for Mary." But what rushed into my mind were the high-school-prom stinker and the boy who wrecked her car and vanished in college, and her dreary husband and her brother's partner the crook.

I stopped and puzzled. I had to see this Mary thing through. I made myself speak slowly. "But she's not attracted to the nice ones, you're right about that."

"So maybe," Ted said, "she remembers from life with her father that love has to come from men you can't count on."

"But Uncle Horace wasn't cruel, I don't think," I said. "He was a nice guy. He drank, but he was utterly charming. How could she learn to link rottenness and love? He did spend all Aunt Nancy's money on the horses, but he wasn't exactly a crook, and certainly not a killer."

Wait, I told myself. Be honest. "But Mary has always liked stinkers and crooks. I admit that. I think they bring out her motherly instinct."

And I thought how bleak it must be to always seek love from men who couldn't really give it. I reached over and touched Ted. "I'm glad I'm attracted to you," I said.

He growled like a mean wolf and then laughed.

"And there's something else," I said, startled again at what I realized. "Why did Cousin Georgianna give us this Alkon book? Sure, it's about memory, but there are lots of books about that. They explain it in different ways. Why did she give us this one, which says that remembering can help make someone repeat and repeat what does them in?"

"She said her brother was like that," Ted reminded me. "He picked bitches to marry, and they hurt the whole family."

"So she probably gave me this book to read because she believes somebody else in the family is doing that now. Mary or somebody else. Or Mary *and* somebody else. Maybe," I said, "when we get to Pop's, Georgianna will be there. And we can ask her exactly what she's trying to tell us. That would help. And then we'll go to see Mary's boyfriend, the artist, the one that Harry says is so destructive. But first we have to find out about the coins. We're going to be busy."

"And if we live through the next week watching out for what's in back of us, we'll be all right. That's what the crystal ball said." Ted the cynic laughed. "It doesn't require a great deal of imagination to figure that out. But I have to hand it to William Hill and his crystal ball — he was sure right about how we needed to watch what was behind us last night."

"And today too," I said. "We need to be alert, with eyes in back of our heads." I glanced in the rearview mirror. Only a pickup full of pumpkins in sight. Our trouble would lie ahead.

CHAPTER 24

AFTERNOON

"We'd better hurry to Pop's," I said to Ted, as we grabbed some takeout food at Taco Bell. "To find out about Sherrie and the gold coins." That thought cheered me up. "If she took money from Pop, and maybe even stole a coin, isn't she our best candidate for the killer?" I knew I was prejudiced. "Or at least for killer's assistant? I know Watt thinks the killer is a man, but behind every good man there's likely to be a smart woman, right?"

Ted turned off Tunnel Road into Town Mountain. He shook his head no. "If Sherrie were the kind of woman who killed old people with sleeping pills after she robbed them blind, even if she did it as part of a team, I don't think she'd be so foolish as to steal a few hundred dollars here and there," he said. "Mary's mean artist-friend is a better bet. But, of course, we have to look into what happened to Pop's Saint-Gaudens gold piece, too, or your father will call the governor and the FBI."

Lily came to Pop's front door as soon as she heard us drive in. She had dark circles under her eyes — dark circles in that normally cheerful plump face. I thought of a panda with indigestion.

"Thank God you're here," she said as we came inside and shut the door. Under her breath, she added, "Your father is in a terrible state." She stared around as if looking for an answer. "He's called up Sherrie to come, though it's not her shift. I couldn't stop him. He says he has to question her. He's in a wild state."

Pop was sitting right there at his table, not eight feet from the door, glowering. Next to him sat a young man with a square jaw, slightly hooked nose, right-angle ears, and wow-look-at-me muscles. The muscles bulged under his khaki shirt as if he'd taken steroids and lifted weights. He had to be the bodyguard.

Pop did not stop to introduce him. "It's about time you got here!" he growled. His hand was right by the telephone. I hoped he hadn't already called the governor, or at least the mayor. The little mahogany Chinese God of happiness on the bookshelf behind him would certainly disown this grump.

"Hello," I said to Muscles. "You must be Pop's new bodyguard. I understand you're our cousin."

He nodded. "Ed Morgan."

"Ed has a big gun," Pop said. "Right there strapped to his side. But it didn't stop somebody from stealing my coin."

Muscles blushed.

I kissed Pop, and then Ted sat down next to the bodyguard with the big gun and I sat down on Pop's other side.

The doorbell rang. Lily opened it. I expected Sherrie, but there was Harry in jeans, T-shirt, and running shoes, eyes downcast. He hesitated on the small Persian rug right in front of the door, as if he was sure we weren't going to be glad to see him. As if we might not invite him onto the larger rug that covered most of the floor. I sensed he must have had some sort of run-in with Pop. That wouldn't be hard.

Harry would be perked up to know that we were seriously considering not only Sherrie, but also Donald the artist as a suspect. Just as he suggested. But I didn't tell him anything. Harry certainly wasn't Mary's sexiest and favorite boyfriend. I figured she ranked him just one step above Sandy Lyon, which was pretty low. But any boyfriend of Mary's was suspect.

"Good morning," Harry said, turning first to Ted and then to me. "I've just been over having breakfast with Mary and the kids."

What? Had he spent the night? Was I wrong about how she rated him? He smiled hesitantly at Pop. "Your father said she'd been here with him long enough. So he asked me to stay with Mary and the kids today to be sure they were all right."

Aha. Harry had stood up for Mary when Pop was annoyed. That was it.

Pop let out a low whistle. "Those kids wear

me one-hundred-percent out! Right, Ed? And nobody has been poisoned or even had an attempt on his life in two days, so I asked them to go home."

"Won't you come in and sit down?" I asked Harry. Perhaps that way I'd get the rest of the story.

But Harry didn't join us. "Mary and I left the children's suitcases," he said. "We were all so busy keeping them quiet we walked right off without their clothes." He walked over to two red and plaid suitcases sitting to the right of the front door.

"So you left Mary and the kids alone?" I asked, surprised.

"No," he said. "The police came around to ask her some more questions. They said they'd be there until I got back." He picked up the suitcases as if he were about to leave.

Did the police questioning Mary mean a new development? I crossed my fingers.

The doorbell rang again, right behind Harry, and he started. He set down the suitcases and opened the door. It was Sherrie. She hadn't toned herself down to look sweet and innocent, I'll say that. She had on a black satin dress with a short, short skirt and purple eye shadow.

Pop beamed. "You look gorgeous!" he cried. "Come over here."

She sauntered over. Harry came over, too, like a flower following the sun. Was he as hoodwinked as Pop? Even Muscles eyed her hotly.

292

Pop took her hand in his and smiled up at her. "Have a seat here by me." She smiled back.

Now, wait a cotton-pickin' minute! That's not the way to start interrogating a suspect. And besides, I had to move over a seat for her to sit by Pop. But I did it in order to hear what would come next. Harry sat down next to me.

Pop ignored us all and plunged right in. "Sherrie, my new gold coin is missing from my collection. And you're the only one who knew where I keep my coins until I had to tell Peaches this morning."

Sherrie smiled at him as if she was on the point of laughing. Her mouth jerked at the corner. "Are you accusing me of being a thief?"

Muscles squirmed as if he were embarrassed. Pop was the one who should have been embarrassed, about the way he was doing this.

"You did go off and leave me yesterday afternoon, Sherrie, and get a substitute because you said it was your birthday, and you didn't like to work on your birthday." Pop's voice lowered mournfully. He had been deserted.

"Friends took me out to dinner," Sherrie said briskly. "We were at the Market Place until about nine o'clock." Trust Sherrie to end up at the most prestigious restaurant in town with somebody else paying.

But what on earth was Pop getting at? Sherrie would have had a better chance to steal the coin if instead of going out, she'd been on duty, wouldn't she?

293

"I called the police," he said, "and they searched everybody in the house. I told them I was quite sure this was related to Matt Jones's murder, so they had to come." He leaned back in his chair.

"But you stopped by before that," he told Sherrie. "You said it was to see if I was all right with the new substitute sitter. After you left, I found that the coin was gone. You were gone when the police came. You had the perfect chance." He shook his index finger at her triumphantly, like she was a naughty girl and he was clever enough to know it. She smiled, as if to say, So what?

"And then after nine o'clock you could take that coin to some fence out of town, or find some other way to get it off your hands." He sounded so pleased with himself. I bet the old fool had never mentioned that to the police.

A voice next to me spoke out. "But after Sherrie left her other friends, she was with me," Harry said. I was startled. With Harry? I had almost forgotten he was still there. And they were so different, Sherrie and Harry. He seemed to own only one jacket, and that was denim. He wore sandals or running shoes. He did not pretend to be rich. I couldn't even imagine her wanting him for a friend. What could she get out of him? But then, Harry seemed to like women he didn't have a chance with. Perhaps they inspired his poems. I could never get him to read me one, so I didn't know.

In fact, the last time I asked, he said he was in a new experimental period and I'd have to wait. Ah, the young.

"Sherrie and I had a bet," he said. "The winner had to take the loser to *Last of the Mohicans*. We wanted to see the scenes filmed around here. And that was the last night it was going to be playing in Asheville for a while. I won. Sherrie is a good sport, even on her birthday." He smiled at her. This was Be-Nice-to-Sherrie Day.

Sherrie smiled at him, then glared at Pop. "You've always trusted me," she said, "and you're smart about people. You were absolutely right to trust your intuition about me. So who talked you into changing your mind?"

She meant me, of course, though she ignored me. Not that Pop needs any encouragement to change his mind when he wants to.

"Pop," I said, "ask everybody to stay right where they are. I'm going to look at the scene of the crime."

"The police have already looked," Pop said. "You're wasting your time. Your nice friend with the mustache was away because his mother died, but I liked the people who came."

But Sherrie's eyes shone with anger. "I'm willing to wait. I didn't steal any coin."

Pop fished up his key from inside his red-checked shirt, took it from around his neck, and hand it to me. I went in his room and opened the drawer in the little chest by his bed.

The coins were all laid out in little clear plastic cases in trays, blinking in the light from the window. Ted had come with me. "Be sure to get the sales records Sherrie gave your father," he said, "to compare with what the dealer told you." They were neatly folded on one side of the drawer.

I looked at the coins, and tried to count them, to see if there were the same number as were listed on the records. There were some empty plastic cases, which suggested some were missing. Meanwhile, Ted got down on his hands and knees and looked under all the furniture, under Pop's spool bed and the high-boy and the big comfortable wing chair and the table by it. "Coins roll," he said, "and Pop undoubtedly had the gold coin out of its case." He peered under the bureau with the lion-claw feet. "Pop drops things. Sometimes he doesn't notice he's dropped something." He unmade the bed, throwing off the star patchwork quilt that Cousin Gloria had made for Pop. He shook out all the covers, then put the bed back together. "He looks at the coins while he's lying in bed, right?" Ted scratched his head. "And he always keeps the door open while he takes his rest, doesn't he?"

"Yes," I said, "he likes to be able to call out and have someone come running. But I don't think a coin could roll far enough to go out in the hall."

I was still looking in the coin drawer. "Some

coins are missing, I think. And the funny thing is they're not terribly valuable ones like the Saint-Gaudens. Just sillier Kennedy half-dollars. It says here he had a set of six for seventy-five dollars."

Ted came over and looked with me. "Very odd," he said "But I'm not finding either fifty-cent pieces or gold coins so far."

One thing about Ted, he doesn't give up until he's explored every possibility, even the way-out ones. "This house is settled, so it tips," he said. "You told me that. So a coin might roll a long way."

Good grief, I had told him that and it stuck in his mind and got lost in mine. The tilt isn't enough to notice except when I spill something; then I have to mop it up before it follows gravity. But I hadn't spilled anything here in a while.

I put Pop's purchase records under my arm, locked the coin drawer with the ineffective little key, and followed Ted down the hall. He went all the way to the end. A long way. I would never have looked that far. He came to a heating vent in the floor. A grille, possibly not even from the present heating system. But still sitting there in the corner. He asked if I had my Swiss army knife in my pocketbook, and of course I did, and the pocketbook over my shoulder. He flipped out the screwdriver, un-screwed the grille over the vent, reached down, and pulled out three dusty quarters, two pennies, and a gold coin. He held his hand out flat so I could see them. Or at least as flat as Ted's hand gets. It's rounded under the fingers and under the thumb. A strong healthy hand. And in the center the gold coin flashed, with a woman in a loose robe on it. I looked close. She had a torch in one hand and a branch of a tree in the other. Her hair was long and windblown. Her dress was windblown too. Sloppier than the woman on a dime.

I was amazed to think Ted found Pop's coin but that the police had missed it. But the police didn't know Pop had a trick floor.

Ted shined the quarters on his pants. "Nothing special among them," he said. "You can't win 'em all."

Ted carried the coins back into the living room and showed them to Pop and cousin-bodyguard Ed and Harry, and, of course, Sherrie.

"Why, that's wonderful," Pop said. His mournful hound looked lifted. "I'm glad Peaches married you, Ted." He reached over and patted Sherrie's hand as if to say he'd had faith in her all among.

"And never mind the half-dollars," he said. "The police told me they were gone. They were a long-term investment. I may not be here long-term." He beamed at Sherrie. "I may have left those out on my table myself. They may have gotten mixed in with my change." He wanted everything to be just lovely.

And by my side, Harry had burst into a huge grin. He leaned across me toward Sherrie. "I knew you'd never steal," he said.

Ha-ha. Did he cheer himself up with Sexy Sherrie after being turned into a baby-sitter by Smile-Girl Mary? Was he one of Sherrie's buttered-up men? It seemed more likely somehow that she'd admire Muscles.

Harry jumped up from the table, and enthusiastically shook Miss Black Satin's hand, the one that Pop was not patting. Oh, really! I could hardly bear to watch Harry and Pop making such fools of themselves. Even Muscles kept ogling. But Harry was actually saying goodbye. He particularly smiled at me. "My mother had a dress like that," he said, indicating my flowered cotton. "It looks nice on you." He picked up the suitcases sitting near the door and trotted out in his running shoes.

Nice try to put me in a better humor. Did my annoyance with Be-Nice-to-Sherrie Day show that much? I turned to Sherrie, doing a slow burn but controlling my temper. There was an important way Sherrie could help me. She could answer a question more mysterious even than why she'd been stealing from Pop. So I attacked that question first.

"How long have you known that the coin collection was in that drawer by Pop's bed?" I asked her. What I wanted to find out, of course, was how it was that the coin invoices went back almost six months. Pop acted as if the coins had been in that drawer all along, but Mustache had told me on Monday, just four days ago, that there was nothing in that drawer for me to worry about. Yet thousands of dollars in coins lying around my father's house was a booby trap. Something odd was going on.

"I've known about his collection since I began to work here about three months ago," Sherrie said. "Why?"

"I began to buy some really nice coins right after Sherrie came here to work," Pop said.

"And the coins have been there ever since?" Ted asked.

Pop and Sherrie both frowned and looked confused. "Of course," Pop said. "Why?"

But I certainly wasn't ready to let Sherrie know why. Not until we knew more about what was happening.

"We know that something very strange has been going on about those coins," I said.

Cousin Ed shifted in his chair and his gun clanked. He didn't really need to know quite how outrageous Pop can be.

"I may say some things that will embarrass you and Sherrie," I said to Pop. "Do you want Cousin Ed to go out of the room?"

"Certainly not!" Pop crowed. "You can't embarrass me."

Sherrie began to blink, but she took her cue from Pop. "I have nothing to hide!"

I looked her straight in those blinking eyes. "It's not that simple to fool everybody," I said. I pulled out the purchase records. "You served as courier for Pop and helped him buy and sell coins, right?" I asked.

"Yes," she said belligerently "but he made all the decisions about what to buy. I did what he said."

Pop nodded.

"But you didn't want to talk to the dealer over the phone," I said to Pop. Talk about changing his mind. He'd talked to me about the coins over the phone, but by then he believed a thief knew where they were, anyway.

"You can never tell when the phone might be bugged," he said defensively. "I am a very rich man. That's why Cousin Ed is here to protect me."

"And you're a foolish man," I said, provoked, "to keep a lot of money around the house."

He leaned back, lips pursed in rejection of that word "foolish." Near his ear, the speak-no-evil, hear-no-evil, see-no-evil monkeys make me feel like he needed a fourth: Think-no-evil-even-if-it's-right-in-front-of-your-damn-nose.

"So Sherrie did all the dealing for you and brought you the coins and the records?"

He nodded. "That seemed like the best way."

"It was the best way to tempt her to cheat," I said. "Mr. Wright gave me the prices of the last four coins she bought for you. The prices were all lower than the ones on these signed invoices that she brought to you. Now, since he freely gave me the true price, I assume Wright wasn't the one who was cheating."

Sherrie turned on me. "But how would I have gotten hold of these signed invoices?" she demanded.

"I don't know how you got hold of a blank invoice," I said, "but obviously you copied it and typed in the descriptions of the coins and the doctored amounts. I assume you traced the signature."

"And you must have used cash," Ted said. I could tell by the way his voice hit a higher note that he was really shocked at all that loose cash. "I suppose Pop gave you cash to pay, so we wouldn't find out what was going on."

"How much did she raise the price?" Pop asked. I regret to say that he seemed to be staring at Sherrie half-amused and half-admiring. Dividing his eyes between her and the gold coin now on the table in front of him.

I read him the list of fake and true prices. I reached over and picked up the coin Ted had found. "For example," I said, "you paid five thousand dollars for this coin. But Sherrie only paid forty-seven hundred."

He turned to her, eyes wide in amazement. "By God," he said, "you've been stealing several hundred dollars a month."

"And spending it to look good for you," she said, holding her head high, mascaraed eyes defiant.

I didn't doubt she'd spent that much or more on clothes.

At last, I thought, he'll have to realize what a fool he's been. He'll have to realize this gussied-up tart may need to look good for him in order to milk him for a lot more money than a few hundred dollars a month.

"Turn around," he said to Sherrie. She had the nerve to get up and revolve slowly like a model in a fashion show, satin undulating as she moved.

He beamed. "A few hundred dollars a month," he said dreamily. "And I say it's been worth it."

"You're not going to do anything about this?" Ted was shocked.

Pop would never give anyone a nickel. He could, as they say, squeeze a penny until Abraham Lincoln yelled Help. But here he was, pleased at being defrauded. I did not understand my father.

"I will pay you to manage this coin account," he said to Sherrie, "and to go on lighting up an old man's life. We will consider what you have taken as retroactive salary. I should have paid you sooner."

I was so horrified, I couldn't think of a word to say especially not in front of Sherrie and Muscles. I'd actually thought Pop was having more good days lately. That his mind was sharper than it had been for a while. That he was less bothered by irrational fears. But the fears were still there: of the telephone being tapped, for example. And the rational fear of real things — like huge amounts of money right by his bed, and a woman who wanted to defraud him — was not to be counted on.

"I'll put these coins in the bank for you," I said coldly. "After all, more people know where they are now. Which makes having a lot of money right here in your room even more dangerous."

"I'll get Sherrie to do it," he said with that mulish gleam in his eye. "I promised the police I'd do it," he said in a hurt tone, "but I wanted you and Ted to see my coin collection first. Sherrie and I need to get a joint safety deposit box."

And did he intend to give Sherrie forty-five thousand dollars *cash* to pay for the fancy gold coin he said he'd ordered? He probably hadn't even thought ahead to that.

By God, he deserved to be robbed blind! And end up as broke as he feared. That was my first thought. Then I pictured him in my kitchen demanding service and having no money to pay sitters. I certainly didn't deserve that. I was very lucky that someone as occasionally impossible as Pop was self-sufficient. Could hire his own sitters. And what could I do to protect him?

I stood up. "It was nice to meet you, Cousin Ed," I said, "and good luck." I could see the "good luck" confused him. But imagine Pop hiring someone to protect him and then hiring the one person who admitted cheating him to manage his money. How could you look after someone like that?

I needed to get out of there and confer with Ted, that's what. I needed some logic so I wouldn't be washed away in the flood of unreason. My head ached. I needed an aspirin.

Ted and I were out of the house before I realized I'd been so upset that I hadn't even asked Pop whether he'd had dealings with the man with the crystal ball.

But then, it might be better to begin by asking Mary whether she'd introduced Pop and the Boone seer, as I was almost sure she had. I'd do that later.

As soon as I felt sane.

CHAPTER 25

LATER THAT AFTERNOON

We met Mustache as we drove down Town Mountain Road. He beeped his horn once and pulled over in one of the few straight stretches. Ted took it that he wanted us to stop, and pulled over too. We all got out. It was a nice day even to stand on the edge of the road, among the trees, gently nippy with leaves circling down all around and sunshine showing through the branches.

"I was on my way to your father's," he told us. "But, maybe, you all could come back to police headquarters with me. I'd like to get you to fill me in on some things before I talk to your father," he said to me, kindly not adding that Pop was sometimes confused.

Of course we told him right away about finding the missing coin. Then we followed him down the mountain and parked near the police station with the old-fashioned red-brick front. Properly impressive. We followed Mustache up the steps in front of the building and then up another flight of steps inside. He took us into a small office on the second floor. He sat on one side of a big, slightly battered desk. We sat in chairs on the other side.

"Before we start," he said, "you may not know yet that Silva Allen died just two hours ago. She never recovered from her heart attack brought on by an overdose of digitoxin."

I felt a sharp pang of sorrow, but I wasn't surprised. I'd been afraid she wouldn't pull through.

"So we're evidently dealing with two murders," Mustache said.

And one was probably meant to be Pop, and the other was meant to be Ted. And someone evidently meant to kill both Ted and me last night. I crossed my arms and hugged myself.

"I just got back to town," Mustache said. "But someone from the Sheriff's Department in Boone talked to me this morning. And, by the way, I've had word that the car that apparently chased you-all last night was stolen from a schoolteacher on Lakeview Road. He was foolish enough to leave the car keys in it. I'd appreciate a report on last night from your point of view."

First I told him I was sorry to hear his mother had died. Then, of course, we filled him in.

But we weren't much help when he asked why we thought somebody might want to push us off the side of the mountain. "Maybe we know too much," I said. "But if so, what is it we know?"

"The initials on that knife may mean something, but we still can't imagine who RBK could be," Ted told him.

Mustache shook his head as if he was baffled too. "Your father is sure the theft of his coin is related to the poisoning at his house," he said rather dryly. "I've doubted that, but I've read the report about the investigation of the coin theft, and I talked to the men who went out to the house. And there's one odd point. Apparently your father insists that his coin collection has always been in the drawer of that chest by his bed?"

"Yes," I said, "and Sherrie, who helps him with the coin collection, says the same thing."

He tapped a pencil against his teeth. He shook his head. "Last Monday, when we searched the house, that drawer was empty except for a photograph of a baby in a diaper and another of a pretty woman who looked a little like you," he said firmly.

"Probably me as a baby and my mother," I said. "That's *all?*"

He nodded. "But the coins were in the drawer, just as he said they'd been all along, when my men investigated the theft of the gold coin."

And then I had a wild thought. "Suppose," I said, "somebody poisoned Pop in order to get him out of the house so they could steal those coins at leisure. And they took them Sunday night." I considered that. "In that case, Matt Jones was just unlucky."

Mustache and Ted both waited for me to

think this out. "It would be easy for someone with a copy of the door key to steal the coins while Pop was in the hospital," I said. "But why would the thief then put the coins back? And he must have done it before Pop got back home on Tuesday. Because Pop would check. And if they'd been gone, Pop would have yelled so loud you could hear him downtown."

"I think I know." Ted leaned forward eagerly. "The thief saw the invoice for the forty-five-thousand-dollar coin on order. He saw that when he took everything home and had time to study it. And since the coins were on trays, he could easily put them all back in the drawer as if they hadn't been touched. and wait to steal an extra forty-five thousand dollars."

Mustache sat and thought about that.

"And since Pop didn't get home from the hospital until Tuesday, the house was empty Monday night," Ted said, "and the thief could have taken his time getting the coins back just right. A simple passkey would open and shut Pop's drawer. A paper clip would probably do it."

Mustache rocked back and forth in his chair. "I can't think of a better explanation," he said. "But if that's right, the person who took the coins must know he can get in and steal them again at any time. It must be someone with easy access to your father's house," he said to me.

"I don't like to say this," he added, "but your

cousin Mary has easy access to the house, so she could have stolen the coins, and meant to steal them again. And on the other hand, if by any chance she meant to kill your father, and merely misjudged the amount of poison needed, she does have a motive. He told me he's left her well provided for in his will. Could she be working with the person who poisoned the sugar and followed you down the mountain?"

I went cold as ice. "Mary would never —" I began. "I don't believe it."

And yet Mary certainly could have poisoned the limeade she gave to Ted and Silva. But why to them?

"Do you think there's any chance she's being blackmailed, or has any other large hidden expense?" Mustache asked. But what on earth would anyone blackmail Mary for? Bad puns?

"There's something you don't know yet that's connected with those coins," Ted told Mustache. Then he explained about Sherrie and the faked invoices. And when he finished telling about how Pop said it was worth it, Mustache shook his head in disbelief. "Always a surprise with your father," he said. "At least he knows what he likes!"

The surprise made him laugh. But Mustache had to know by now that laughing at Pop was at your own risk.

"It's good to see your father well again," he said. "Though now we know that his overdose of digitoxin was not entirely foreign to the killer's method. Your friend Watt Jenks called me and told me how he believes the killer or killers he's been looking into somehow gave their victims overdoses of medication that sent them to the hospital. So I'm in touch with my opposite numbers down his way."

"But, of course," I said, "Pop didn't get an overdose of his own medication. So that wasn't exactly the same. But he did go to the hospital, just like the others did a few weeks before their sleeping-pill deaths. We have to be very sure it doesn't get that far with Pop."

That seemed to impress him. "Perhaps this perpetrator is like Charles Manson and his group," he said. "They liked to wander around inside people's houses at night, just to get a sense of power."

"I remember," Ted said, "back in the sixties. They'd sneak inside when the victims were at home asleep, and wander around. Then they'd kill on a different occasion. Perhaps our man likes to search the house by himself, with the victims in the hospital."

"But theft hasn't been part of his method in the past," Mustache said, "even if giving an overdose of medication has.

"Be very careful what you eat and drink," he warned us, "and leave the investigating to us, please."

Then he seemed to relax. I had the feeling that the serious part of the interview was over.

"I see you still have that pocketbook that contains everything you might ever want in an emergency," he observed. "The pocketbook that hangs on your shoulder."

"And goes with everything," I said. "Yes, I rarely used to leave it anywhere, but the last time I did, back after Aunt Nancy was killed, *I* was nearly killed as a result. So now I'm a fanatic. If you ever see this pocketbook anywhere without me, you'll know I've been kidnapped or worse."

"Put a note in it like they do in bottles in the ocean" — he laughed — "so I can come and save you. Oh, and by the way," he added, "I have two snippets for your book. I have two different mnemonics for the names of the planets in the order of their distance from the sun."

He pulled a piece of paper out of his pocket. "Here are the catch words for the planets: *Man very early made jars serving up new potatoes. Or My very educated morther just served us nine pancakes.*"

"Mercury, Venus," I said, "but then what begins with an E?"

"Earth," Ted said. "You'd be in a pickle without that."

"Mars, Jupiter, Saturn," I said. "And I'm not sure of the rest. Funny thing, this makes three mnemonics that folks have given note to remember the planets, but nobody ever told me the names of the planets I have to remember. Fortunately there is one thing, if only one, we can be pretty sure of. The killer is not from Mars."

Mustache walked us to the door and said, "Take care of yourselves."

Ted and I walked down the stairs of the police station in silence. Ted started the car and finally, as the motor purred, I spoke. "The next thing we need to do is go see Mary. I know she's not in with the killer. What on earth could she have to do with those sleeping-pill deaths down east?"

And yet as we drove toward Mary's house full of cute china animals and small jokes — the house with the phony crystal ball on the shelf, the house where Silva drank poison — my gut said watch out. I had this ugly feeling that Mary was at the exact center of whatever was threatening us all.

CHAPTER 26

LATER THAT AFTERNOON

We stopped at a phone booth on Merrimon Avenue to call Mary. She said we were welcome to come on over unless we minded a traffic jam — a human one, that is. She said Harry was there because Pop had asked Harry to stay with her. Loy was there because he'd come by to check out her costume. He was taking her to a banquet of the Society for Creative Anachronism — "You know, they act out medieval things." The costume she borrowed for the last get-together hadn't been up to Loy's standards.

Ah, I thought — a chance to ask her questions about who she met at the last meeting.

"What kind of costume now?" I asked. She said she was going to be a Saxon maiden. Loy was going as a knight. "He has this broadaxe," she said.

"I'll be glad to get out of this century," she said with feeling. "But this is not really a good time for Loy to be here because Donald is due to come work on my portrait. This is my fourth sitting. It really is coming along. But Donald is always late, so it'll be O.K., I think."

Bingo. Mary with top suspects. Her boyfriends. Including Donald the artist, who Harry said was the meanest. Donald who was impatient with the kids. Only Sandy Santa Claus Lyon wouldn't be there. The guy with the teacher's salary and the Rolls-Royce.

What would we find in the house where poor Silva drank her death and Ted was almost poisoned? I reached out and touched Ted's hand as we drove along. I told myself that lightning never strikes twice in the same place. But I knew that wasn't true.

We arrived to hear shouting. "You can't even live real life boy. Don't you go dragging my girl off to such foolishness."

Someone had left the front door open. We walked in. Mary's artist, complete with beret, was standing in the middle of her living room next to a portable easel. Not far from his left hand stood a chair with a bottle and a glass of whiskey on it. He was the shouter. Dressed up again in a big flowing shirt like an artist in a cartoon.

But Mary was queen of the costume department. She had on a long earth-brown dress with tight sleeves and, over that, a big-sleeved sky-blue dress with brown embroidery. Flattering. It showed off Mary's sky-blue eyes.

She was standing down at the dining end of the room, looking properly anachronistic next to an electric lamp, and with one hand on a modern dining-room chair. Loy stood next to her with his hands on his hips, feet apart. He

315

was wearing what he so often did: black. Just a turtleneck shirt and black jeans, but with his dark widow's-peak it still added up to a Dracula outfit. Harry and the children were in the doorway to the kitchen. Like that was their refuge. Out of costume. Harry still had on his jeans, his T-shirt, and his running shoes.

"Mary doesn't need an army of weirdos hanging around," the artist said. His face was flushed. He didn't quite slur his words, but I could tell he had been drinking. "And I need quiet while I paint her and I certainly don't need her to be dressed up like the knight's lady. Hey, all that stuff is gone, thank God. Now, you get out of here," he said to Loy.

I was immediately on Loy's side. Loy was at least sober. I wondered how he'd deal with this right-now reality.

Mary was frozen in her medieval-maid dress, holding tight to her chair, obviously not knowing what to do next. She looked pretty in her long-ago dress, except there really was a shadow of a bruise on her cheek, like Harry had said. She was half smiling. Mona Lisa, of course. Was she medieval? No. Later than medieval. The smile was not part of the costume.

Maybe Mary liked having men fight over her. I wouldn't like that, but I had a bond I could count on. Somebody I mattered to, who mattered to me for the long haul. God willing. Right by my side. Maybe if you weren't sure you would ever have that, a nice raucous fight over your charms would be great for the morale.

And what should Ted and I do? To begin with, we stopped where we were, just inside Mary's front door, to be sure we knew what was going on. They were all so enmeshed in their own tensions, I don't think they even saw us. To our left was the front bedroom with the door open and a tumble of rich-looking dresses on the bed. Just beyond the door, the bookcase. And, yes, the small crystal ball was still there on the shelf — symbol of what Mary wanted to know, glimmering next to the "Think" sign.

"Mary has a right to have any friends she chooses, Donald," Loy was saying up ahead. He seemed coldly sure of himself, head high. And either he hadn't noticed us, or wanted to get something settled before he even nodded. "Mary doesn't need to be bullied and told what she can and can't do." He took two steps toward the artist as if this Donald, with the paintbrush in his hand, were some misbehaving student in one of Loy's classes. "Perhaps you need to get out of here until you can behave like a gentleman," he said.

"A gentleman!" the artist cried. "God knows I don't want to be a gentleman!" He reached for the glass and took a long swig of whiskey. "I want to be a real man with my feet in the mud." I noticed for the first time that he was barefoot. Some Birkenstock sandals were on the floor in the doorway to the bedroom. He evidently took them off when he came in the front door.

I had a trick to remember this Donald — now, what was it? I hadn't used it in a while. Something to do with a cartoon. Maybe Duck? That was it! If he was violent like Harry said, he might throw things. I pictured him throwing a picture right at my head. Then I'd have to duck. Donald Duck. A few repetitions would make it stick.

What surprised me most about this Donald Duck — repeat, Donald Duck — was that he wasn't young. He wasn't old either. Maybe about forty. But old enough to wear shoes. Older than Mary's ex. Andrew may have been as pompous as Methuselah, but he was only twenty-seven years old when he left Mary.

And maybe Mary liked that about this Donald. That he was the opposite of Andrew. Except, according to Harry, both Donald and, apparently, Andrew put her down. But then, Harry was jealous. He was staring at Donald with open hostility burning in his eyes.

"Mary doesn't want to be a lady," Donald said. "She wants to be a plain damn woman. And she doesn't want a gentleman. She wants a man who's good in bed." He hiccuped.

Mary said, "Look, I'll have on my clothes for the portrait in a minute. And this dress for the banquet is just lovely, Loy." She gave him a glowing smile. She acted as if no one had raised his voice. "Maybe you wouldn't mind taking the kids outdoors, Harry," she said. "You don't know how I appreciate the way you've made us feel safe."

"By God," the artist said, "any fool who wants to feel safe is missing half of life. Live it to the edge, I say. Be gloriously happy or shoot yourself. Be a roaring success or a crashing failure. Not some namby-pamby in between."

Mary beamed at him. "Never be afraid," she said, "of anything but boredom. Better to be dead than in a rut." Somehow I knew from the singsong note in her voice that she was quoting him. He'd said that before.

Donald bounced on the balls of his bare feet while he talked, like he was just spoiling for a fist fight. He had thick wrists and hair on the back of his chunky fingers. I didn't like his hands.

I also didn't like the way Harry meekly took the children outdoors. Somebody ought to stand up to this boor. But then, of course, someone ought to get the children out of the way before mayhem burst forth.

With Mary's collection of china animals and glass objects even the crystal ball on the edge of the bookcase, this was not a room for anybody to go berserk in.

"I will see you later," Loy said to Mary, ignoring the artist. "And I'm glad to see *you* here," he said to us in a voice heavy with significance, recognizing us for the first time with his eyes. I wasn't sure what he was trying to get across. Probably asking us not to leave Mary alone with this barefoot middle-aged bohemian who seemed so sure he was good in bed.

We were still standing near the door. Ted winked at Loy. Then Ted stepped forward, held out his hand to Donald, and said, "I can see you are a true artist who doesn't let convention stand in his way."

Yes, I thought. A clever way to put it. Because that's the way this Donald must see himself. And how does Mary see him? As someone ready to take charge? Someone as volatile as her father? Somebody who can hit her now and then because he's just a natural man?

Donald continued to bounce on his toes. He seemed impatient to start painting.

"I'll be back in a minute," Mary said, raising her long skirts off the floor to stride quickly into the bedroom and change. She shut the door behind her.

"You strike me as a man who knows what he thinks," Ted said to Donald. I knew by the way Ted cocked his head that he thought he was being clever. "Who do you think put the digitoxin in the limeade in the refrigerator here on Wednesday?" Ah. He was trying a sudden attack.

Donald raised his head quickly and stared at Ted. "God knows," he said firmly. "I don't."

"I need to know," Ted said, "because that person was probably trying to kill me. I'm usually the only one around here who drinks limeade. But another young woman did, right here in this room, and she's dead."

"So, good for you," this Donald said contemptuously. "You're alive." Then he shrugged. "Harry had the best chance. He's around here a lot. We all had a chance. But who the hell would want to kill you?"

He said it like Ted was not worth the price of the poison.

I wanted to walk over and hit the man. I was shaking.

But Ted just went calmly on with his questions. "Where are you from?" he asked.

"Wherever I please," the artist said. "Wherever I like the light. I've been here in Asheville about a month. I already have pictures at the Blue Spiral Gallery. I like it here. But when I don't, I'll leave."

And good riddance.

"And where were you before this?"

"None of your goddamned business!" he said.

"Perhaps you'll admit it is my business where you were last night," Ted said. Oh, it's wonderful the way Ted doesn't lose his cool. "Last night somebody followed us, and I think they intended to force us off the side of the mountain, except their car got wrecked first."

"So who was in the car?" Now Donald seemed casually interested.

"The car was wrecked, but the driver got away. It was a stolen car. Were you the driver? Where were you?"

"I still say it's none of your business." A huge

grin spread over his face. "I never tell where I sleep at night on the grounds that it may tend to incriminate me." He tossed off the rest of his glass of whiskey and roared with laughter.

Mary, who was just opening the bedroom door, laughed too. I wondered if she'd heard what he said.

Mary had come back in blue jeans and a red- and black-checked shirt. Of course. This was to be an informal portrait of a "plain damn woman." Her cheeks were pink. Her eyes sparkled. She liked this man. He was not dull.

I hated Donald. But even though Watt had said the killer liked to play parts, it seemed to me that Donald would stick out like a sore thumb. Didn't a serial killer have to be a little bit subtle to do his job and get away?

Ted must have felt he'd discovered something. He was writing in a small spiral notebook.

Donald Duck ignored us and arranged Mary in a small gold- and green-striped armchair. A rather elegant chair she must have inherited from her elegant mother. Plain black- and red-check shirt against satin stripes. For some reason, the effect was great. It was like a statement about Mary: "There is more than one side to this woman." And in that context, Mary's smiling, straightforward face said, This woman doesn't know herself.

I had to admit he had an eye, this artist. Not a kind eye. I went around and looked at what he'd done. Oh dear, one of those painters who expresses feeling, not likeness. I could hardly tell that the swirls of reds and blacks were Mary. I couldn't tell if it was good art. For his sake I hoped he was talented. His "artistic" temperament needed some good quality to balance it.

I ignored him and turned to Mary. "I met a friend of yours in Boone, Mary," I said. "William Hill."

I waited for her to make some comment.

"I don't want to talk about that," she said finally. "And it's none of your business." She was taking conversation lessons from Donald Duck.

"He said he sold you a crystal ball," I prompted.

Donald Duck broke into a great throaty laugh. "Damn it, Mary, you want to live in the past *and* the future. You want the Middle Ages and 2001!" he wheezed between roars. He bent over laughing. Still grinning, he straightened up, reached with one hand for the bottle of whiskey, refilled his glass, and took a long swig.

"I love you, Mary," he cried, throwing out his arms as if he were going to hug the air. "You're absolutely crazy!" I hoped the paint on the brush in his hand wouldn't splatter.

Mary preened with pleasure.

And I decided I'd better stop asking about Will Kill and come back to see Mary later. No point in letting this unpleasant man learn even more about our business.

He took another long swig, and turned to me. "You know, we may be related," he said. He bounced on his toes in such a pleased way that I figured he knew I'd hate that.

"My mother came from up here somewhere. Her name was Jones. Mary says this Jones guy who died was related to you in some way."

"My father says so," I said. It was not my idea to rush out and claim kin. I hadn't liked Matt Jones. And there were certainly enough Joneses in the world, maybe a few million, and plenty here in the mountains, so that even if I had to be related to Matt, I didn't have to claim Donald.

I remembered something I'd heard Pop's next-door neighbor Arabella Horton say. She went around dropping quotes, and frequently quoted Mark Twain. She said Pop was the only person she knew who didn't fit what Twain said: "God gave you your relatives; thank goodness you can pick your friends." Unlike Pop, I saw no reason to pick all my relatives for my friends. And I did thank God for the choice.

"I don't know that I want kin who are always mixed up in crime," Donald said. "I have all the trouble I can handle, all by myself."

"And what do you mean by that?" I asked.

Donald hiccuped.

CHAPTER 27

THAT EVENING

We left Mary's house hungry and were pleased to head for home. "After we get something to eat," I said, "let's go over your who-could-have-done-what-and-when list and update it."

I knew that Ted, who is good at that sort of thing, had been laying out a big chart on a piece of poster board. He'd put in the times from my notes in my little black Wizard, and from his notes, and he'd also made a few phone calls in spare moments to fill in spaces.

"We could brainstorm while you throw together some pasta," he said. "Get some of that good sauce out of the freezer."

"I have some canned chili I can heat," I said. "Let's just eat out of cans until this is solved."

He opened his mouth as if to protest, and then closed it. "I guess you're right," he said.

He went off and got the great big white chart from the office and spread it out on the kitchen table. "Let's begin," he said, "with when digitoxin could have been put in the sugar. We're lucky we can be pretty sure when that was: between about three in the afternoon and about nine-thirty at night on Saturday the third." He put his finger on that area of the chart. "That was the day before your father and Matt Jones drank tea and had to be rushed to the emergency room. It was the day the backdoor key disappeared in the morning, and at about two-thirty Lily found some cigarette ashes in the sugar bowl."

"Which she assumed Sherrie had carelessly dropped onto the sugar, since she smokes so much," I added, opening the chili can and dumping the contents into a pot. "But Sherrie hadn't been there since the day before."

"So Lily says she threw the sugar out and put new sugar in the bowl at about quarter of three Saturday." Ted was tracing the line that said "Lily" across the calendar. "And Lily and Dorothy both agree they laughed about Sherrie and her cigarettes when Dorothy arrived at three. You remember Dorothy came from three to eleven that day."

I was glad he wrote it down so I didn't have to remember. I reached into the vegetable drawer of the refrigerator and got out the lettuce: romaine, Ted's favorite, and some curly endive.

"Then, beginning at about three, Dorothy said she sat at the living-room table with your father, until he went to bed early at eight-thirty. And after he was asleep, she said she sat in the living room and sewed for an hour."

"For which," I said, "read *dozed off.* She isn't supposed to sleep on her shift but the other sitters say she often does."

"So after the sugar bowl was refilled and left on the kitchen counter at about three," Ted went on, "nobody was in the kitchen, except briefly, to get the sandwich Anna left for Pop, until about nine-thirty. During that time anyone with a backdoor key could have come in and put the digitoxin in the sugar. After that, there was no good opportunity for anyone to do it except for the sitter on duty.

"Dorothy said that about nine-thirty she went in the kitchen and watched a favorite TV program and sewed some more," Ted continued. "She was in the kitchen from nine-thirty until eleven, when Sherrie arrived."

"Then Sherrie says she sat at the kitchen table and first watched MTV and then read a book during her shift," I said. "Very quiet shift, Sherrie reported. Pop slept through."

"Then, at seven in the morning," Ted said, "Lily arrived. She says that since Pop slept late that morning, she was in the kitchen right near the sugar until Anna arrived at nine-thirty."

"To help out, even though it was Sunday," I added, "because Matt Jones was coming to lunch. So somebody was in the kitchen all morning."

"At eleven-thirty, Cousin Eltha came by for a visit with Pop," Ted said, pointing at the time. "Then at noon Matt Jones arrived and Eltha left, and I gather that's about when Anna left."

"And Lily says she left Pop and Matt Jones

alone," I said, "which meant she was in the kitchen until Sandy Lyon rang the doorbell right after Pop and Matt ate. Then, I gather, she went back in the kitchen and fixed the tea."

"Therefore," Ted said, "three to nine-thirty was sugar-poisoning time unless Dorothy or Sherrie or Lily or Anna did it while on duty. The earlier evidence suggests a young man is involved, but it's possible that Dorothy or Sherrie or Lily or Anna was his accomplice. The sitters would have been foolish to do it on their own shifts, but one of them may have been foolish."

I was impressed. "You're wonderful at making charts like that, Ted," I said.

"But some things we can't know," he said. "We have no way of finding out when the digitoxin was put in the limeade. The container had been sitting in Mary's freezer compartment unsealed for several weeks since the last time she made some for me."

I looked down at the lettuce between my fingers. I wished we weren't discussing digitoxin while I fixed dinner. I washed the lettuce within an inch of its life.

"Now, the other time when we need to know a suspect's whereabouts," Ted said, "is between about eleven-thirty Thursday morning — I can hardly believe that was only yesterday, when we left Asheville for Boone — and twelve-thirty last night. If the person who followed us down the mountain — and then wrecked his car and vanished — also followed us at a distance when we went to Boone, he had to have left when we did. If that person had some unusual way of determining where we went, so that he didn't have to follow, he'd still have had to be in Boone, two hours away from Asheville, at about seven o'clock when we started back. And, in fact, the person who followed us was in a lucky accident, at about eight o'clock."

"Lucky accident for us, not for him." I laughed.

"That means he couldn't possibly have gotten back to Asheville before about eleven-thirty that night. And if he was unable to hitch-hike because of all the deputies out looking for him, where would he have got hold of a car at all? I've checked. There is no report of a stolen car in that area that night. Just one stolen in Asheville earlier and wrecked near Boone. So it would have been difficult for anyone to get back to Asheville even by the next morning."

"But possible, if only barely," I said, spinning the lettuce dry and putting it in the refrigerator.

"So," Ted reasoned, "someone would have to have been away from Asheville from eleven-thirty that morning, at the latest, to eleven-thirty that night, at the earliest. Probably considerably longer than that. Now, let's place our suspects," he said crisply, turning to another page in his notebook and taking out the pen that is always clipped to his shirt pocket. "Tell me if you think of anyone I've left out." He turned to a neat list. "First let's look at Mary's boyfriends: There's Donald McElvey."

"And he won't say where he was and when, and doesn't care if that makes us mad," I pointed out. "He's probably Mary's favorite, which according to your theory, makes him the number one suspect."

Ted nodded. "Then there's Loy Haven, your Dracula Jr. He said that last Saturday he was home working on a scholarly article about medieval puns."

I could believe that.

"He says he was in the library Thursday evening at the time we were chased, but the librarian isn't sure if she talked to him that day or the day before. I asked her." Ted underlined Loy's name. "He taught at Duke for a while, which puts him in striking distance of the serial killings."

Still, I hoped the killer wasn't Loy. I like to see colorful people flourish.

"Loy seems connected to us in all sorts of strange ways," I said. "He took Mary to a medieval party where she met our Boone fortuneteller, William Hill, who read a crystal ball for Mary and probably for Pop when Hill was in Asheville. And the man says he was living in Asheville as recently as a week ago, but he was apparently in Boone at the time the car was stolen in Asheville, and at the time the sugar was doctored.

"But somebody followed us back from Boone and probably meant to force us off the side of the mountain. And nobody knew we were in Boone" I said. "Except Rachel and the *Watauga Democrat* and this William Hill."

"But the car that followed us wasn't Hill's old rusty Mercedes," Ted said.

"Then there's Harry," Ted said. "He seems innocuous and helpful. But that could be a front."

"He'd be O.K. at not drawing attention," I said as I peeked in the oven to see if the chili was burbling. "And that must be one talent necessary to a serial killer. But Harry was babysitting Mary's kids at the time the digitoxin must have been put in the sugar. And Mary told me that she came home to find that although the kids were pretty sleepy, they were still up listening to Harry read them a book at nine-thirty. It's a point of pride with the kids, she said. As long as anybody will read to them they'll stay awake." I took the chili out of the oven and put it on a trivet on the counter.

"And even later that night, he was working in the Jiffy Shop food store," Ted said. Oh, Ted's great at tracking down these details. "His shift was eleven to seven, but he went in before eleven to let a friend go home early."

"Yesterday, didn't Harry say he was with Sherrie at nine, watching *Last of the Mohicans*?"

"Yes," Ted said. "So at the time of the chase last night, Sherrie and Harry say they were together in Asheville two hours away from Boone." He frowned. "If they were lying to protect each other, Sherrie would still have had an alibi for the time of the chase because she was at her own birthday party part of the time. If, on the other hand Harry was chasing us, he'd have had a heck of a time stepping out of a wrecked car and making it back to Asheville in time for Pop to call him at six-thirty this morning when the kids woke Pop up. Still, Sherrie is certainly a suspect," Ted continued. "She has an alibi for chasing us down the mountain, but two people could be involved in this. And obviously she could have put the digitoxin in the sugar during her shift."

"And I don't like Sherrie, as is well known," I said.

"We've left out one boyfriend," Ted said. "Sandy Lyon. Who owns a Rolls-Royce on a teacher's salary."

"And has invited us to a musical evening at his cabin in the woods. He's so nice that Mary doesn't find him sexy." I sighed. "So according to your theory, he's a lousy suspect. I hope it's not Sandy."

"But he was one of the last people to be in the room with Pop and Matt Jones before they were poisoned," Ted pointed out. "Also, he used to work in Durham. So he could have been on the scene of the sleeping-pill murders.

"We've ignored one obvious suspect," Ted added. "Mary."

I made myself think about that. "She could easily have stolen the key," I said gloomily.

Ted glanced at the chart. "She was at some kind of a women's self-help workshop on Saturday from noon until eight-thirty in the evening, while Harry baby-sat. She had coffee with a couple of the women in the workshop afterwards. Perhaps the coffee didn't take long and she could have slipped by Pop's and poisoned the sugar on the way home."

"But she was with her kids when we had our Boone adventure," I cried out. "She told me so. I hate this," I said. "I don't know why I ever wanted to solve a crime — except, of course, to stay alive."

"We'd better stop and revive ourselves with food," Ted said, removing his chart from the table. He set the table while I poured us each a cold can of Coke. I put the salad out and served the chili, and said, "Boy, this is what I need." And we both fell to and ate.

As I ate the last bite, I yawned.

"We did stay up late last night." Ted yawned too.

I sketched two closed eyes on the pad by the telephone. "Hey, somebody has been in this house while we were gone," I cried out.

"What makes you say that?" Ted's salad fork stopped in midair.

"I tend to doodle on this pad while we talk. I know I did yesterday. And now the pad is blank."

"You threw the doodle in the trash," he suggested.

We looked in the trash. No doodle.

"What did you write on the pad?" he asked.

I wasn't sure, so we did that old rubbing-a-pencil-across-the-pad trick, to highlight the impression left by the writing that had been on the missing page.

And there, overlaid by my two closed eyes, but still plain as could be, was "BOONE" with the two *O*s made to look like eyes, and the eyes looking at "2:00 *Watauga Democrat*."

I groaned. "Good Lord, I need to wear mittens on very bad days, so I'll notice if I write!"

"But you ought to be able to write on the telephone pad in your own house!" Ted said angrily. "If someone read that, someone has broken in here." His eyes darted around the kitchen. "We'd better look around and see if anything important is missing."

We even looked in the drawers of the little mahogany bedside chest that Ma's mother left me. I keep my favorite costume jewelry there. Nothing missing.

Our house is not a good one to rob. Our nicest things all hang on the wall in plain sight. But not many thieves are looking for Cherokee baskets or antique quilts.

Still, I could tell that someone had been through my bureau drawers, though I couldn't prove it.

I began to look in the folder of the stuff we'd brought back from our trip to the cemetery. A big folder behind the bedroom door. "Hey," I said, "the gravestone rubbings are missing!"

"Oh, come on," Ted said. "Who would want those?" But he came over and looked in the folder.

"See? They're gone," I said. "Even the rubbing of the little marker that someone made by pouring cement into a hole in the ground. I can't quite remember what it said. But it was for Baby Klonk, which sounds like hitting somebody over the head."

I kept looking around, hoping I'd just absent-mindedly moved the rubbings. Ted went to examine the doors and windows for signs of forced entry. "If someone came into this house, they must have had a key," he said. "Someone is good at stealing keys."

"Why should anybody bother to steal those rubbings?" I asked. "Even if something written on one should give us a clue to goodness knows what? We can go back to the cemetery and do them again if we want to. Poor Mr. Jones won't even be there to shoot us."

"I have a list of the rubbings with my notes in my desk," Ted said. We hurried to the office and he opened the top drawer and pulled out a folder. "Here's the list:

Peggy Albert 1855 to 1905. Beloved Wife of John Albert.

Martha Jones, Much-loved Wife of Arthur

Jones, Ezekiel Brown, Lawrence Carpenter. 1851 to 1930.

Mary Lou Jones Klonk 1942 to 1977. Wife of William Klonk.

Baby Klonk, Daughter of William and Mary Lou Klonk, 1975 to 1976.

Robert Bourk Klonk 1920 to 1972. Beloved Father of William Klonk.

Herbert Long 1912 to 1989, Greater Love Hath No Man Than This, That He Gave His Life For a Friend.

"That's all," he said. "They don't sound like anybody would have any reason to steal them."

We didn't have long to stand around and wonder about that. The phone rang. It was Sherrie. She was sick, or so she said. Could we stay with Pop until either the service could get someone else there or Dorothy arrived at eleven?

I looked at the clock: 8:05 P.M. "Is Pop still awake?" I asked. "Wide-awake," she said. "He had a nap."

I said that I, at least, would come right over. But when I explained to Ted, he said he'd come too. This was a time for sticking together. "And besides," he said, "we need to ask Pop some more questions."

But first we called the police to report our break-in, told them our emergency situation, and that we'd be back as soon as we could, certainly by eleven. I figured whoever broke in got what he wanted. He had no reason to come right back.

We found Pop complaining loudly that Sherrie wouldn't talk to him. And wouldn't bring him a dish of ice cream. She was sitting in the kitchen, leaning her head flat against the table. When she sat up, her color was terrible, a kind of light blue, which almost matched her blue chiffon blouse. And I guess it shows my prejudice against the woman that it never even occurred to me anyone had poisoned her. I didn't even ask her if the world looked yellow. Giving Sherrie poison would be like taking sand to the desert or hauling water to the ocean. I guess I had faith nobody would do any of those things. She even insisted she could drive home. And maybe I shouldn't have let her drive — but I did.

I took Pop a dish of chocolate ice cream, which I got out of a container sealed in plastic that hadn't been opened yet. And since Ted and I hadn't had dessert, I brought some for us too.

Pop seemed overjoyed to see us.

"I heard you had your fortune told, Pop." Ted jumped right in. "Are you going to win the lottery?"

"I have to find out some more about my ancestors," he said, savoring a spoon of ice cream.

I figured the ancestor bit was to divert us, and wondered why he wanted to do that. "We met a man named William Hill who said he read a crystal ball and told the future," I said.

"That was fun," Pop said. "Of course I don't entirely believe that stuff, and I refused to buy a crystal ball. It was plastic."

"There are people like your cousin Julia who sometimes just know things," Ted said. "I called her once out of a clear blue sky and she picked up the phone and said, 'Hello, Ted.'"

"Well, I hope this man knew a little bit. He said something would happen that would be a terrible shock to my system. He said my relatives would help me find answers and then I'd be all right. And then I went to the hospital. That was a shock, all right!"

"It wouldn't be hard to figure out that relatives would be mixed up in anything that happened to you, Pop," I said. "You always say that if you look carefully enough you can find out how we are related to almost anybody in Western North Carolina."

Pop frowned. "But now I remember something else that man said. He said I'd get help from relatives who were alive" — he paused and looked at me like I was exhibit one — "and," he emphasized, *relatives who are dead.*"

That kind of got me. I thought of the gravestone rubbings. From the graveyard that Pop's new-claimed relative Matt Jones had been guarding. Nobody has a gravestone until he's dead. Well, almost nobody except surviving spouses. If all the strange things that were happening were tied up together, then that little

338

graveyard, with recent stones — and the stones from the nineteenth century — was related to two murders last week. Could that be?

"That crystal-ball man said that what was going to happen might hurt my relatives a lot more than it hurt me. And Matt Jones was hurt worse. He's dead. So you watch out." Pop pushed his empty ice cream dish back.

"Oh, great," I said. "I'll wear a bulletproof vest." Not that that would help with poison or sleeping pills.

"This afternoon I was reminded of what that crystal-ball man said," Pop told us. "The icemaker broke and ice spewed out all over the kitchen floor. Sherrie wheeled me in to see it. Then we called for help."

"You called Ace Appliance?" I asked.

"No," he said triumphantly, "I did something better than that. I called Cousin Georgianna, because she knows our family genealogy."

"You what?"

"The ice reminded me of that crystal ball," Pop said. "We turned the icemaker off. You can see about that. And Georgianna knows all about my relatives who are gone. Now you're alive and you're trying to help me. But to figure things out, this crystal-ball reader said I need the help of relatives who are dead. So I asked Georgianna to come right over. She'll be here any minute."

"Now?" I was amazed. "It's quarter of nine at night."

"Sherrie said the ice was an omen, to pay attention to the crystal ball. So I told Cousin Georgianna this was an emergency. And this was the soonest she could come."

I almost laughed. And Pop said he didn't believe in crystal balls. But by a happy coincidence, Cousin Georgianna was just the one we wanted to talk to. To ask her what she was trying to tell us when she gave us that book about memory and making mistakes. So, never mind why things happen, as long as they work out.

"Can I ask her a question first?" I asked. "Once Georgianna gets started on ancestors, there's no pulling her back."

"Certainly," Pop said. "Be my guest. After all, figuring out how to help me is likely to be hard on you because you are my relative."

I tactfully kept my mouth shut.

CHAPTER 28

ANCESTORS

Cousin Georgianna carried a huge accordion file. She was wearing a red blouse with a high neck and flowing sleeves that might have been worn by an old-time Russian Cossack. She probably liked those full ethnic blouses because she was so darn flat-chasted. But I half expected her to start playing the balalaika or doing a sword dance. Instead, she put the file down on the table next to Pop and asked, "Now, Harwood, what do you want to know?"

"Sit down." Pop pointed to the chair on his right hand. "I need help from my dead relatives," he said. His hands were in front of him, fingertips tented. His lips were pursed. Eyes demanding. "And you know more about them than anybody else alive!"

Georgianna is used to Pop being outrageous, so she just sat down and waited for further explanation. As always, she looked gloomy in a friendly sort of way. Like somebody who was glad that if she couldn't win, at least you might.

"Ted and I need to ask you something too, Georgianna," I said quickly, leaning forward in front of Pop so I could look her straight in the eyes. "Something relating to the book you lent us. Pop says we can ask first before you and he get lost in genealogy."

By the way Pop glared at me, I knew he'd forgotten his offer, but Ted jumped right in before we could be one-upped. "We were fascinated by the book on memory, and especially by the part about how unexamined memory can make a person repeat destructive behavior over and over because the wrong memories are written in the brain. And you said that reminded you of your brother."

"We all know about Jim." Pop laughed. "We call him Lady-killer Jim. I hear he has a new girlfriend, but the family teases him so much he's scared to marry her."

"That's progress," said Georgianna. She looked so cheerful, dressed in her red Russian blouse, but she spoke like she expected progress to go backwards.

"So, we wondered why you gave us that particular book — out of all the books on memory — just *now*," Ted said. "We wondered if you thought there were other members of the family with this self-destructive kind of memory and if maybe you felt that was somehow connected to what happened to Pop and Matt Jones."

"Well, I'll be damned," Pop said. "The things you think of, Ted."

"I certainly never thought I was pointing fingers when I gave you the book," Georgianna said, head jerking up like the sword dance was starting, eyes startled.

"We are a fine family," Pop declaimed, "except for one or two I could name who hit the bottle a little hard."

"But I have to admit," Georgianna said, "that something in that book is like the warnings my mother gave me." She squirmed in her chair as if her bottom didn't fit it.

And, next to her, Pop was turning into a storm cloud. He'd arranged for her to come tell him what he wanted to know. And we were wasting his time. That's what he meant by those raised eyebrows.

"The book suggests that just as one person can have destructive memories, families can hand that kind of memory down from one generation to the next. As a kind of tradition." Georgianna said that in a minor key.

"We stick together in our family," Pop said. "That's a good tradition. And if even my dead ancestors can help me, that's really sticking together." He looked from one of us to the other as if he dared us to disagree.

"I remember my mother used to say there was a wild, crazy streak in some of our family." Georgianna sighed. " 'You mustn't do that,' she'd say to me, 'or you'll grow up to be like Grandma Anne.' "

Pop stared at her in wonder. "Why, we've had three preachers and four lawyers, a judge, and me in the family. We've always had good people." His hands twitched, as if he might slap her hands with a ruler.

"My mother related it to drink," Georgianna told Pop. "She told me I must never take a drink. We had it in our blood to go crazy from it."

"Pooh," said Pop. "I was never hurt by a good drink."

Now Georgianna turned first to me and then to Ted, as if Pop were hopeless. "My mother showed me the family records and how William Cutler, who came to this area way back in 1790, had a son Homer who beat his wife to death while he was drunk."

"Your mother made that up," Pop cried. "She wanted to scare you. That's ridiculous."

I had certainly never heard it. But then *my* mother hadn't believed in horror stories to improve the young.

"There are no records of any arrest that I've been able to find," Georgianna admitted. "But back in those days, out in the country, it was hard to tell whether a woman died of a fall or a beating. The children were off with their grandmother when it happened. The story in my family was that Homer Cutler beat his wife to death with a stick of firewood because she let the fire go out." Her eyes grew angry like they did when she talked of her ex-husband. Then she sighed again.

"So he had a crazy streak, but she picked him out and married him," Georgianna said. "I

344

wouldn't want to be like either one of them."

"And what became of the children?" I gasped.

"The grandparents stayed here and raised the children, and their father moved on to Tennessee. And my great-great-grandfather, Morris Cutler, was one of those children."

"And was your great-great-grandfather my ancestor?" Pop asked. "I can never keep us all straight."

"You are descended from his sister."

"But that was a long time ago," I said. I wanted distance.

"But it wasn't the last time in our family that a man got drunk and beat his wife," Georgianna said. "My mother says our family used to believe that was a man's own business. And a wife better figure how to get along with him."

Pop kind of shrugged. "And what does that have to do with us now?"

"Didn't you grow up hearing about the Klonks?" she asked Pop.

"That's a name I've heard," Pop said. "I'm not sure where."

I was about to mention it was on several stones in the old graveyard that Matt Jones had guarded. That in fact we'd just had rubbings with that name on them stolen from us. But she went on fast, in that kind of intense voice that means don't interrupt.

"Back in the 1870s," she said, "right after the War, we'd had so many troubles around here

345

that maybe nobody would have noticed if a man got drunk and beat his wife and then she died. But my great-great-uncle Tom Cutler poured kerosene on his wife Nell and burned her, and the house caught fire and burned down, and he was too drunk to get the baby out."

"I have heard that story," Pop said. He squirmed. I don't guess he liked the story any more than I did. I hated it. It made my skin crawl. I could see Pop also wanted to get Georgianna's attention back on him. But he felt he owed some politeness to Georgianna's burned-up ancestors. They weren't *our* direct ancestors. That relieved me. How terrible for Georgianna to grow up hearing these stories, and being told she had to be careful or the ugliness might burst out in her.

"My great-great-uncle Tom married again," she said. "God knows what kind of woman took him on, and that whole branch of the family are no good. They moved over here to Buncombe County. They're the ones my mother held up most for bad examples. You asked me how we're related to Matt Jones. Well, one of that man's daughters married a Jones. Matt Jones came from that line. The other daughter married a Klonk."

Pop brightened. He could see again how he fit in.

"And it hasn't stopped," she said. "Just some sixteen years ago, a William Klonk — whom I didn't know, but his family is descended from Tom Cutler — was arrested for beating up his wife, Mary Lou, and his kids. The youngest kid died." She grimaced in pain.

I felt sick for her. "But you are only distantly related to those people, Georgianna," I said. "And you're not like that. You never could be. You spend your time finding ways for people to enrich themselves with books. You're kind. Every family has black sheep."

"You've kept track of the whole family, black sheep and all," Ted said. "Most of us work at forgetting our misfits."

"You've come up with only three violent misfits in two hundred years in a big, far-ranging family," I said. Were we a family more prone to violence than most? There was, of course, my aunt Nancy's murder. I didn't want to ponder that.

Pop was listening carefully now. "You're saying our dead relatives could warn us," Pop said. "Watch who you pick to trust."

That's not what I'd heard, but it was what Pop wanted to hear. He sat back in his chair, satisfied.

"Some of those Klonks are in the graveyard where Ted and I took grave rubbings," I said. "And somebody evidently broke into our house and stole the rubbings."

Well, of course Pop had to hear about that, but I could tell that from his point of view the story was lacking in guns, villains on the spot, and melodrama. He even seemed to think that the chase from Boone was mostly in our imagination.

"Peaches and Ted just lost those Klonk family tombstone rubbings," he said to Georgianna. "Peaches can lose anything."

"They're not worth stealing," Georgianna said bitterly. "Most of the Klonks were just white trash." She hated the way our relatives fell short.

And I was annoyed at both Pop and Georgianna for doubting our story.

But after Cousin Georgianna left, I got to thinking I could be grateful to Pop. For whatever reason, he hadn't followed either of the destructive family patterns that Georgianna believed in. He didn't drink and become violent. And he certainly didn't marry someone who mistreated him or me. My mother had had a sharp eye for what wasn't working, and a sense of humor. She never taught me that I was no good and deserved an abusive spouse. Thank God. She taught me that life is a trade-off, and you need to make the best trades possible, and then laugh at whatever still doesn't work.

My mother enjoyed life and loved kids and flowers.

Flowers. A picture flashed into my mind. A book of wildflowers. And my hand opening the book and looking at the flyleaf. And on the flyleaf in an unsteady hand was written, "My book: Mary Lou Klonk." And that was the name on one of the gravestone rubbings stolen from our house. Which said "Deliver Us From Evil." The woman whose husband, William, killed their child. That was shocking enough to remember! I was sure the book was the key to something. I was not sure what. And where had I seen the book? My mind stayed blank about that.

CHAPTER 29

SATURDAY MORNING, OCTOBER 10

First thing in the morning, the police examined our house for signs of a break-in. No sign except that the rubbings were gone. Like Ted, the police concluded that whoever it was used a key.

Then the light dawned. "Oh, good grief," I told Mustache. "I know what happened. The thief got the key out of my stone!"

I led him out into the garden, and there among the real rocks was the imitation rock I ordered from a catalogue way back before I married Ted. The plastic rock opened up like a box. I left an emergency key in it so that I couldn't lock myself out of the house. I always left my stone near a special rosebush at the end of the terrace.

Since I've been following my own advice and putting keys on hooks and pocketbook snaps, I've been so much better about not losing keys that I forgot the rock. *Moral: Reform can be dangerous. Don't forget you reformed.*

And who knew about my emergency rock? I had to admit that Mary did. I had suggested that she get one once when she got locked out in her bathrobe, and her husband, now departed, had a fit.

Good Lord, could Mary have broken in? I asked myself. That didn't make any sense.

As soon as the police left, you can guess where Ted went — right back to the newspaper files to look up the stories of the ancestors and relatives Georgianna told us about, especially William Klonk.

That was not a job that required two people. I stayed home and called Cousin Georgianna at the library in Marshall. I asked her if she had shown me a wildflower book with Mary Lou Klonk's name in it. I was sure it was a clue, but not sure how. She had never seen such a book.

Had I seen it with the kids' books at Mary's? Why would it be there? We weren't directly descended from the Klonks. Their branch of the family had split off in the eighteenth century. We were hardly related at all, except by Pop's standards.

But when I called Mary, she said she'd seen some kind of a flower book and wondered where it came from. "Let me look." Silence for a couple of minutes. "Here it is!" she crowed. "But I can't be sure the name is Klonk."

So I went over to her house to look at the book. She had it out on the dining room table open to the signed page. The page was yellowed with age, and the book somewhat dogeared. Studying the faded signature, we agreed that although it was hard to read, the name probably was Mary Lou Klonk. And when had I seen it? Some time when I read to the kids.

I leafed through the pages. There were lovely color plates of trillium and ironweed and butterfly-weed and more. This book must have been a treasured possession. "Perhaps someone meant to lend it to you," I suggested.

"But who?" She seemed entirely perplexed.

I sat down and told Mary about Cousin Georgianna's terrible family stories. I watched her face every minute for signs that those stories, and specially the Klonk story, meant more to her than ancient history. She seemed about as shocked as I'd been. We agreed Georgianna must have grown up having nightmares.

I told Mary that Ted was at the *Citizen-Times* looking up the original news stories about the more recent Klonk horrors. Mary didn't seem alarmed at that, either. She said it sounded like a good idea.

"And where are you going now?" she asked.

I said home. That's where Ted would bring copies of any stories he found.

All of this Klonk history was available to anyone who looked in the back newspaper files, so I hadn't thought I needed to keep what Ted was doing secret. But when I got home and sat down at the kitchen table with a cup of tea, I wondered if I should have told Mary.

The cat was watching the birds in our bird-bath again, tail twitching. I rapped on the window and she went away to lurk in the bushes.

Maybe I shouldn't have told Mary or Georgianna about that wildflower book. I suddenly had a hunch I should have kept everything I knew or suspected to myself until I had a better idea of why the name Klonk seemed related, somehow, to the murder of Matt Jones and Silva and the attempts to kill Pop and Ted.

But what could I do about an after-the-fact hunch?

I was edgy. I started when the phone rang. Ted's voice was cautious. "Look," he said, "I figure you ought to know this right away, even before I come home. That Klonk baby who was killed in 1976 had an older brother named Henry. And several things came out in the testimony at the time of William Klonk's trial that may be meaningful. William had a traveling job. And while he was gone his wife, Mary Lou, forced the older child, Henry, to take sleeping pills every night so he wouldn't wake up while she entertained her boyfriend."

"Sleeping pills!" I could see that would fit somehow. But how?

"The boy was asleep from the pills when his father came home and beat up the mother and Henry's baby sister and battered the boy," Ted said. "That's what a neighbor testified. The father was drunk. The younger child died. The mother became a vegetable and went into a state institution. We saw her tombstone. She died a year later."

"And somebody broke into our house and

stole a rubbing of her tombstone!" My mind was racing.

"This boy, Henry, was only fifteen at the time of the trial," Ted said, "but a short time later he stole money from a widow he worked for. At the time of the last story I can find, he had vanished."

"And what was the younger child's name?" I asked.

"She didn't have a name. They called her Baby."

I shivered. I saw that primitive poured cement gravestone which said *Baby Klonk 1975-1976*.

"That was the child whose father killed her." I shuddered. "And the brother — who saw that happen — would now be in his early thirties. The brother whose father beat him up, whose mother drugged him with sleeping pills."

And all of Mary's boyfriends could be about that age, even Donald who looked a little older.

And this boy who vanished — had he spent his life turning the tables and making older people, making mother and father figures, take sleeping pills?

"And one other thing," Ted said. "The date when William Klonk beat up his family was February eleventh. That's the date of two of the serial murders down east. Most of them were clustered around that date. But not all."

My brain whirled. This couldn't be a coincidence. Not possibly. The serial killer must be the boy who disappeared. And somehow, in his twisted mind, he felt he'd be safer if he stole the Klonk grave rubbings. And when he did, he discovered we were going to Boone. And then he followed us to kill us somewhere on a lonely stretch of road at night. He had a knife, an old knife. But that wasn't the way the serial killer operated — that's what Mustache had said. I was confused. Thank God, I thought. At least today isn't February 11.

Ted said he was coming home shortly. I was grateful for that. I said I'd call and update Mustache. He would want to talk to both of us.

But I couldn't reach Mustache. I left word that we had some extremely important information for him. "No," I said, "I would not like to leave it with someone else. I would like to talk to him, and I expect to be home until he reaches me. He can come by or call. I will make it a point to be here. Please tell him that."

I sat and pondered February 11. A day for killing. How does a person begin to kill?

I heard a car. Ted must be back with the newspaper stories. That was quick. I went and looked out the front window. No Ted. I looked in the cupboard to reconnoiter lunch. I mustn't brood. Still no Ted . . .

The cat was stalking the birdbath again. A foolish bird actually flew down on the grass. I banged on the window. I heard another car. I kept an ear cocked. The cat stared at me coldly.

She knew her attention span was longer than mine.

The doorbell rang. It wouldn't be Ted — he had a key. I peeked out a front window to see who it was. Sandy Lyon. His elegant Roll-Royce with the shining chrome stood out at the sidewalk. I could see he was whistling. He looked so benign that I wanted to open the door and invite him in to soothe my nerves. No, I told myself, don't open up for anyone until Ted comes. We'll be safer two against one. Our serial killer had had lots of practice. And he was someone people trusted. To the death. Sandy rang again, then wandered off to his car.

I let out a sigh. How awful not to be able to trust anybody, but I mustn't! Distrust was better than a hole in the head, as they say. The doorbell rang again. Oh, come on. Fate was trying to drive me crazy. So if it wasn't Ted with his key, who was it now? I peeked again.

Somebody in a cowboy hat and dark glasses. How odd. I knew all sorts of wild characters, but no sun-shy cowboys. So this seemed sinister, even while it made me want to laugh. But wait. The way he stood, leaning just a tiny bit forward, seemed familiar. Good Lord. It was Harry. Who on earth was he trying to be, and why? I didn't see his car. Harry, who Mary treated like a baby-sitter instead of a boyfriend. Which made him a lousy suspect, according to Ted's theory. Just like Sandy was a lousy suspect because Mary would hardly go out with him at all. Good. Because it was true: Mary trusted the wrong people.

Harry. In my mind I saw him sitting on the red couch at Mary's, reading *Where the Wild Things Are* to Marcia and Andy. Saw their apt pleasure. I went ice cold. Who would you trust more than the one you left your kids with, let your kids get attached to? Who?

I pulled a piece of paper off the pad by the phone and on it I wrote "Harry August is the killer." Did I believe that? My fingers seemed to believe it. Harry said he loved kids because he'd had such an unhappy childhood. A Klonk childhood? But wait — Harry had an alibi: He was baby-sitting the kids during the time the sugar was tampered with. They'd said he was with them the whole time. Though he could easily have doctored the frozen limeade concentrate at Mary's. I stuck the anti-Harry note in my pocketbook. Right at the top where it wouldn't be hard to find. I wasn't sure why I did this. Perhaps so that if anything happened to me, somebody would at least know Harry was the last one in my vicinity.

Could mild, pleasant Harry have some kind of fixation about sleeping pills? And suddenly, I thought: Oh, my God, he gave the kids sleeping pills! So he could leave them long enough to poison the sugar. But if so, why didn't they tell anybody they'd been asleep?

The doorbell had stopped ringing, and I heard a car start up. Ted should be home by now. What was keeping him? I peeked out the window again. There went Sandy's Rolls-Royce, with Sandy driving, and Harry in his cowboy hat and dark glasses in the passenger seat. The whole picture seemed unreal. They *were* leaving. I was for that. But what were they doing together? They'd never been pals. I added another note to my pocketbook. "Sandy Lyon may be part of the killer team."

I wanted to leave and hide somewhere where nobody would ever expect to find me. I had to stay until Ted arrived, and until Mustache called or stopped by. Ted, please hurry!

I got two salad plates ready for lunch with a bed of well-washed lettuce and half a hard-boiled egg each and a few anchovies out of a newly opened tin, and canned marinated artichoke bottoms. I made them extra-luxurious to celebrate Ted's return. But he didn't come. Eleven-thirty. I stashed the salads in the refrigerator. I sat and read some of the book that Sandy had given me earlier. About how music can help the memory. I was nearly at the point of phoning Ted at the paper when I became aware of a whirring, beating noise in the distance. Very odd.

The phone rang. Maybe Ted saying why he was so late. I went cold as soon as I heard the voice. It was trying to disguise itself. Going extra slow like a cassette tape when the battery is giving out. "Go immediately to Sandy Lyon's cabin in the woods," the strange voice said, "if you want to see your husband alive. Go fast. In fact, run, and don't touch that phone after you hang up." Then he gave me directions to get there, but I knew I already had directions. Sandy gave them to me when he invited us to his party. I pulled the Wizard out to check, but I was so unnerved I figured I'd do better to follow the directions just like I'd written them down when I was calm and thinking straight. I put the Wizard in my skirt pocket.

"I have binoculars and can see in your window now," Slow Voice continued. "The helicopter will be following you and watching you the whole way. If you stop, your husband will be killed." The helicopter? Was that the noise I heard? I looked out at the wooded hillside beyond the garden. I couldn't be sure if I saw something gleaming, like binoculars reflecting light.

Perhaps it should have occurred to me that if I went, there would simply be two of us in mortal danger. I didn't think. I *felt*. If Ted was in danger I had to go. I reached for my pocketbook on the table. I stopped, hoping the recovery was fast enough so whoever was watching hadn't noticed. I left the pocketbook and grabbed the car keys off their hook. I left the back door into the garage propped open. If Mustache came to the house instead of calling, he would know an open unlocked door meant that something was wrong. I pushed the button that opens the outer garage door and started to jump in the car. My eye hit the clothes on the back seat — I still hadn't taken them to the cleaners. Without even a conscious plan, I opened the back door of the car, grabbed the clothes and tossed them onto the front seat. I drove out of the garage fast. Too bad we didn't have a phone in the garage. I might have tried to call 911 undetected — I'd have been out of sight. But the only phones were too far away to take a chance.

The droning, throbbing sound continued. I looked up. There was the helicopter! It looked like the one I'd seen before. Which Sandy had said must belong to the narcs. Who on earth *did* it belong to?

The young Klonk must be part of something much bigger than killing for his own twisted reasons. I imagined him heading a drug ring that owned the helicopter. "That's ridiculous," I said out loud. Perhaps he'd stolen so much money he had a helicopter just for his own use. But that was fantastic.

I drove frantically. Not daring to hesitate, much less stop. I drove out Merrimon Avenue past Beaver Lake, where a cheerful couple paddled a canoe as if nothing could be wrong. I drove past Reese's Tire Deal and the pizza place, on and on. So far, I remembered which way to go.

No sign of Sandy and Cowboy Harry in the Rolls. Perhaps they weren't involved. There were small shops an along Merrimon, and then a big Ingles supermarket on the right. I turned off onto Reem's Creek Road, which was smaller and flanked by houses and small farms. There was even a sign for a golf course. Sandy's cabin was out Reems Creek Road. I remembered that. I pulled the Wizard out of any pocket. I'd need it soon.

I kept the gas pedal down. I wanted to get there as fast as possible to be sure Ted was all right. At the same time, I didn't want to get there at all. Because suppose the killer or killers had us both, what then? The helicopter buzzed above me.

The pile of dirty clothes included three sweaters and a light brown jacket. All with name tapes and my phone number on them.

A pad of paper and a pencil lay on the seat next to me. As I drove, I scrawled, "Sandy Lyon's cabin up Paint Fork gap. HELP Police" on three pieces of paper and put one in the pocket of the first sweater. Just before I passed the road into a golf course, and trees hung over the pavement, I dropped the sweater in the road. It was a far-out chance that anyone would find it and look in the pocket. But a far-out chance is better than none. I dropped the brown jacket with another note in front of an old square log house with a sign that said "Vance Birthplace." Beyond this point I wasn't sure if I could remember where to turn. I could still hear the helicopter. I slowed enough so that I could open the Wizard with one hand

and turn it on. I pushed MEMO. The directions should be the only thing under that. The screen came up empty. I've done something wrong, I told myself. Electronics don't forgive. I turned the Wizard off and on again. "Memo?" was all the screen said. I pushed the arrow that was supposed to scroll down the screen. Nothing. I knew what I must have done. When I'd punched in the directions, I'd forgotten to push ENTER. That first helicopter had come over right after Sandy gave me directions, when I should have pushed the button. And diverted me. No ENTER meant no directions. I went cold with panic.

It took all my resolve to follow rule number one: *Never waste energy beating up on yourself for what you forgot. The worse the situanon is, the more you are going to need your energy to figure out what to do instead.*

Had Sandy said something about going over a bridge? Maybe. I kept looking desperately for water, and, lo and behold, a small stone bridge over a creek appeared. God bless it. Then the road forked. Durn. I took a chance that I should go left, and prayed. There were no more forks for a while. That was wonderful, assuming I was going the right way.

I began to climb steeply, and suddenly the road went from hard-top to gravel. Hey, Sandy had mentioned gravel. And hadn't he said something about the top of a hill? I could hear the whomp-whomp of the helicopter but I couldn't see it. I was sweating. After snaky curves where the tires slipped on the gravel, I came to the top. A dirt road went off to the right and another to the left. I had no idea which way to go. I picked the left, where a sign said Nonesuch Road, and was about to turn. Wait. I had one more sweater with a message. It was dark blue and had no pocket. I'd stuck a note up the sleeve. I dropped it out the window and turned.

I thought of my turn-in, turn-out rule. If you turn in left, you turn out left to keep going the same way. I put the Wizard on the left side of the dashboard as a sign. So that if my turn in was wrong, I could at least find my way to turn out back to square one by turning left again. I came to another dirt road off the first one, to the left again. I might as well try it. I turned down two fingers on my left hand. Dead end at a small dump. I turned around and went left when I got back to the first road. I was still going away from the main road. Please let me find the way. Soon there was another road off to the right, and by the grace of God, this one had a sign at the end: LYON.

Off in these woods, the air smelled good. Enjoy it quick, I thought, while you still can. It was colder here. I began to shiver. I was also near the spot where the killer, or whoever, was going to do whatever he had made his plan to do. I knew I shouldn't have come, but I couldn't help it. The trees were thick enough here so that the way was greeny dark. Beautiful, with ferns and moss along the wood road. Beautiful because almost no one came here. There were no discarded gum wrappers or beer cans. Nobody to yell "Help" to, either. I parked well down the little wooded road from the house when I caught the first glimpse of it ahead. If my telephone caller was behind me in a car, his car couldn't pass mine. There'd been a hollow sound to his phone call. He could have used a car phone and then followed me. Walking in would slow him down. If he was in front of me and didn't hear me, I'd have the element of surprise on my side. I doubted the helicopter could see me through the tree tops. And besides, its sound was fainter now. Odd.

Or, of course, there might be two killers here, or more. Harry and Sandy in a car and somebody else in a helicopter? Or maybe Harry and Sandy had only happened by. Maybe it was some totally unknown combination: Sherrie and one of Lily's foster children? Donald and Dorothy? I approached the house, circling as quietly as possible through the woods.

Even from a distance I saw Sandy's antique Rolls parked in front of the rough log cabin. The car gleamed from polishing. No other car was in sight. So O.K., I was no judge of character. I would once have sworn on a stack of Bibles that Sandy was a good man. I wouldn't have been quite so sure of Harry. I felt stupid as well as scared.

I crept around the house. The windows were no help. Their blue curtains were shut. I crept around to the solid red front door up at the far end of the building. The door was open a crack. I stood next to it, listening. All I could hear were the chirps of the insects all around me.

I held my breath, pushed the door inward, and looked inside. Nobody in my line of vision. No sound. The log walls inside the cabin were the same as the walls outside. Thick brown logs with cement chinking between, like neat icing on a many-layered cake. Down the center of the one big room, a row of vertical beams supported a rough floor above. A ladder went up beside the nearest beam into an opening in a loft. Someone could be hiding up there. Or down below. So many things were crowded into that big room. They confused my eyes as I looked around for Ted in the shadows. In the corner across from the door at the same end of the room, two violins and two cellos stood up at attention on a wire stand. A jumble of sheet music was on another stand, and there was a big laundry basket full of small instruments like recorders and rattles and such. Beyond that, a rough couch with big pillows at the back was obviously a bed in disguise. A large table stood in the middle of the room crosswise. On one end, sat a bowl with a spoon in it and, on the other end of the table, a tall wooden drum. Several straight chairs were drawn up to the table. Beyond it, in the far corner of the room, the door of a closet hung open. A tuxedo on a hanger was hooked to the inside of that door. The closet was on one side of a back window. An old black kitchen stove and a refrigerator and a sink were on the other. But no Ted anywhere. Beyond the sink was a closed door. That must have been to a bathroom. No sign of any human being. Someone must be hidden. The Rolls was parked out front. Sandy's money evidently went into his car and his music, not his house. And where was he? The silence scared me.

I tiptoed into the room. A voice in back of me said, "Stand still." Harry stepped out from behind the open front door. He had removed the hat and the glasses and was himself again. I was almost relieved — until I saw the gun in his hand, pointed at me. He took a key out of his pants pocket, locked the door, and put the key back. "Walk straight over there to near the stove," he said.

His voice was mild as ever, but there was a kind of gleam in his eye I didn't like. It was the look my father got when he saw a chance to make a lot of money. No, it was more like the look my cousin Heartbreak Bill got when he spied a gorgeous but naive girl. It was a sort of innocent predator look. Like Harry and Heartbreak Bill were quite sure that, for them, what they were about to take advantage of was perfectly O.K. Life owed it to them.

Harry took my arm and pulled me toward the back of the room. I was so shocked I was calm. He pulled me to the farthest standing beam, not far from the stove. It was a rough beam, really just a tree minus bark and limbs. A very large ball of rough tan twine sat at its base. The loose end of the twine was tied to the beam. "Stand against this post," he ordered. I don't argue with guns. He picked up the ball of twine, and began to walk round and round me, keeping the gun on me all the time. I could see that if I tried to break loose in the brief moments when he was on the far side of the post in his circle, I wouldn't get out the locked door before he had a chance to shoot me. So what could I do? And this was so strange, like a children's game gone wrong. I half expected him to start singing, "Here we go round the mulberry bush" as he went round and round me.

"Where is Ted?" I demanded.

"He's on his way here," Harry said, circling in front of me. "He got a call just like you did shortly after you left. I see the two of you are fools about each other," he added as he circled in back.

I began to feel enmeshed as a fly in a spider web, with many circles of twine around me. He dared to put the gun down, and my struggle didn't free me. He cut the twine from the ball and firmly tied the end. Then he fastened the loose end of the ball of twine around my ankles.

He laughed like a happy boy of fifteen who had just played a practical joke. He looked so innocent in his striped T-shirt — one of his three shirts — and his jeans and running shoes. Unbelievable. I smelled the gas from the stove faintly. Perhaps the pilot light was out.

"Where on earth did you get a helicopter?" I asked.

"None of your business. I get what I need," he said, picking the gun up again. "I've learned how."

So how would you get around a clever man who acted fifteen, who dabbled in murder, got whatever he needed, and had a gun in his hand?

I prayed Ted had left my pocketbook where it was. If he saw it there on the table, he must have suspected something was wrong. But then he *knew* that when he got the phone call. If he read my note that said Harry did it, and Sandy Lyon helped, that wouldn't have kept him from coming to the cabin. Now what could I do?

"Where is Sandy Lyon?" I asked. "His car is here. I saw the two of you drive off from my house together in it. You in your sun-shy cowboy getup." I tried to sound conversational. To get information without stirring him up.

"I like to play parts." He stood in front of me and tested his handiwork. Believe me, it held me tight. "And nobody who saw me drive by would know it was me." He walked over and unlocked the door. He came back and sat down in a chair at the table. Sideways, so he could see me and the door. Waiting for Ted. Not even impatient. A clock on the wall near the music corner said 12:15. It took me half an hour to get here. If Ted came in and got the call shortly after I did, he'd be here soon.

"Sandy's on the floor of the Rolls asleep," Harry said cheerfully. "He kindly gave me a ride because my car broke down near your house. Or so he thought. Then we both had a nice cold cola. And he went to sleep. He will wake up in his car here and find you and Ted gassed to death in his house and he won't know how long he's been asleep or how he got here. It won't look good for him, do you think? A few of your father's coins are in among his things, too. But perhaps he can plead insanity."

Gassed to death? He meant to use the stove! I still smelled the hint of propane. And I thought: He's going to put me to sleep forever with gas instead of sleeping pills. It was all as fantastic as the helicopter. Like a dream No. Nightmare.

"You've been clever," I said. I was angry. "You got the kids to give you an alibi for the time you put digitoxin in Pop's sugar. You gave them sleeping pills, didn't you? Just like your mother used to give you sleeping pills when she wanted you out of the way. But how did you get them not to tell they'd been asleep?"

"You are snoops, you and Ted." He laughed. "You won't leave anything secret." He got up and began to pace around. "Mary told me how

369

Ted was going to find the newspaper story about my father. Mary is a good reporter. She helped me last Saturday too. She talked to Lily on the phone just before she went off to her women's seminar last Saturday, and Lily groused about the ashes in the sugar. So then I saw my chance." He grinned like he'd got an A-plus report. "The police would know the poison was put in after that. All I had to do was have an alibi for after that. And I did, until noon the next day." He nodded. Pleased with himself. Where was Ted?

"My mother taught me about sleeping pills," he said, thumping the tall drum as he paced past it. And for the first time I saw his boyish face twist into bitterness. "She was very clever at first, but she got careless." He came close and looked me directly in the eyes. "You give a kid drugged cocoa and when he falls asleep, you leave." His tone became tough. "You have to be there sitting in the same position when he wakes up, so he thinks he just dozed off. And sometimes he begins to think he's crazy. Because he loses time." He glanced at the clock and then at the door. Undoubtedly reminded that time was passing and that Ted should appear soon. He knew exactly when Ted started.

But he must think there was still a little time. He kept talking, right into my face again. "So my mother had a few safe hours with her horny boyfriends. And then when it was about time for me to wake up, she'd be sitting there, sometimes with the book she'd been reading to me, and as I opened my eyes she'd be on the next page from the one where I'd gone to sleep. 'Oh,' she'd say, 'you drowsed off.' I remember some heavy object had often just fallen when I woke up. That's how she set the waking-up time. You women are very clever," he said, smiling at me again. There was actually admiration in his eyes. A lot of good it did me, caught like a fly.

"I felt a little crazy until she got careless and I figured it all out," he said, pacing again. "And even after she must have known that I knew, she went right on drugging me. And I played along. My father got violent. Even before the last time, when he found a man leaving and almost killed my mother." He paused in his pacing. "I wanted to seem dumb. So he wouldn't blame me for whatever he found out. Maybe my foolish mother actually thought that drugging me would protect us both."

"Now you control who sleeps," I said.

"Yes," he said. "I do." He turned to me, dead serious, and briefly, he was an adult, not a child. Not playing a garne. "At least I did," he said slowly. "I was in control. But as soon as I decided to come here, to the place where I came from, where I grew up, it stopped being easy." He took a deep breath, like he needed sustenance. "I started to feel as stupid as a kid," he said bitterly. "I made blunders. You found me out."

CHAPTER 30

IN THE CABIN

Harry sat at the table, midway between the drum on one end and the bowl with the spoon in it at the other. He sat sideways again so he could talk to me — over beyond the table and tied to the beam — and also keep one eye on the door. So what could I say to take Harry's mind off Ted's arrival? To give my beloved husband the weapon of surprise.

Maybe some subject far from the here and now would help. "You're a poet, Harry," I said. "You took your unhappy childhood and made it into poems. Didn't you? You told me you were even trying new forms now that you were back where you felt at home."

"My poems are deaths," he said, still in that quiet voice that he'd used to read to the kids. "Every one was perfect just like I dreamed when I was a kid. I really was in control."

I shuddered to think of murder as a poem.

"But I began to long to go back home, back to the mountains," he said. "I don't know why, when I was so unhappy here. But the idea got a hold of me. I took the newspaper. I always do research. I know all about the people who will be in my poems. I saw your father's name and I remembered it. And I read what he said about how anybody could be rich if they would just try hard enough and be as smart as he was."

I cringed. Why didn't I somehow keep that story out of the paper?

"And I knew your father had to be my next subject." His eyes narrowed with anger. His hands clenched. "When my father was down, he asked your father to give him a recommendation for a job. Your father wouldn't do it. My father raged about that. So this time, I'd even have revenge!"

But his father was a drunk. He'd said so. And he'd hated his father. He'd all but said that. I knew it wouldn't help me to remind him. My father must have been one of many people who refused to give his father a recommendation. No point in saying that either.

"And so it was a challenge to me to get as much money out of your father as I could. The old fool. With his 'absent-minded detective' for a daughter. I thought it would be fun to steal from your father right under your nose." He grinned. Age fifteen again. But I knew by the way his head was cocked that he was still listening for Ted's car with strained senses, even while he gloated over Pop.

He turned back to me. "I got Sherrie to tell me about your father's coin collection. People tell me things. I don't look dangerous," he said with satisfaction. "But then I was accident-prone," he groaned. "I dropped that *Walks Near Asheville* booklet, with the Klonk grave-yard marked, right under your nose. As if a part of me wanted you to go there. And I left a line that I like to put in my poems right in it."

"The line from the old book," I said.

How eerie, I thought. He forced his victims to include those words about the mercy of the Lord in their suicide notes.

He paced around and twanged a string on a violin. And still he held his head in a listening position. Not as accident-prone as I wanted him to be.

"You underestimated how much poison it would take to kill my father," I said. What would he say to that?

"I gave your father digitoxin to make him so sick he'd have to go to the hospital, not to kill him. I did it so that I could slip in and steal his coins. I'd done something like that before. Making someone sick so I could get in and case the house, and plan the final poem." He came back and sat down at the table. "But these mountains jinxed me. I thought Mary said *your* father took digitoxin. I was wrong. *Her* father used to take it. I was mixed up. So the hospital knew it wasn't an accidental overdose. That was bad luck."

"But you did take the coins," I said. "Then you saw that you could wait a little longer and your haul would include one more coin worth forty-five thousand dollars. So you brought the coins back, and laid them out like they'd been there all along."

"Which added to the challenge." He smiled. He had a dimple. "But, you see" — the smile faded — "I'd lost my touch." He jumped up again, and began to pace back and forth in front of the table. "I still thought I was lucky that Sunday afternoon. I went over to your father's house at four o'clock. After he was in the hospital, but in broad daylight. I was so impatient to get in. It was like a fever. I took the coins then. And suddenly, something simply told me to get out fast. As I drove down Town Mountain Road at about five o'clock, a police car was driving up. I believe they went to your father's house. I believe they just missed me. I thought that was luck."

He stopped and stood perfectly still, listening.

"And then Matt Jones died," I said

"Matt Jones died because of his own greed," he said angrily. "He took six spoons of sugar in his tea." He threw himself back in the chair. He was aiming the gun right at my chest.

"Matt Jones's death attracted too much attention. And then instead of getting out like I would have done in any other place, I stayed and tried to get that extra coin and tried to get Ted out of the way." He said that like someone had cornered him. Like maybe it was my fault. "You said you'd stop looking for the killer if Ted was in danger," he accused. "But you didn't. You're too cocky to leave things to the police. You can't be counted on." He massaged his forehead with the fingers of one hand. "This place where all the memories are. This place messes up my head."

And I could see it now. His thoughts didn't quite fit together right. So close, I could miss the cracks. But the cracks were there.

I was cramped, tied to the post. I was angry. "You didn't need money. You must be filthy rich. After killing so many old people who never did a thing to you. God knows what you've done with their money."

He smiled again, like that was a compliment.

Did I hear a stick crack outdoors? Like someone who was trying to walk quietly had slipped? Harry's head rose to attention.

"How did you steal Pop's key?" I asked, hoping to sidetrack him.

"Little Andy let me in," he said in an affectionate tone. "I got a copy made, then put the key back when I took the coins." All so simple.

"And you took the wildflower book to Mary's house, didn't you?"

"I love those kids," he said. "I wanted to share it with them." He got up, pulled the curtains back, and looked out the window near the closet. The light in the cabin seemed to double. I wanted to scream: "Ted, go away." He wouldn't go away. Any more than I would, if he were in danger.

"You were very clever to know that Sherrie

had something to hide, just like you did," I said. "By giving her a phony alibi, you gave yourself one."

"I have to be clever," he said casually, returning to his seat. "For example, after you led me to wreck that car, I circled back and hid in the back of your car under the laundry. You gave me a ride down the mountain. Then I could hitchhike back to Asheville."

Good grief. I had never thought of that. I kept forgetting to take in the dry cleaning. But if I hadn't forgotten the cleaning, I couldn't have dropped the Help-help sweaters. Dear God, please let someone find one.

"But on that road from Boone," he said, "you stole my last good luck. You stole my grandfather's hunting knife." He was up and pacing again.

"With his initials!" I was thunderstruck. It was the sheriff's deputies, of course, who had the knife.

"R.B.K.," he said dreamily. "Robert Bourk Klonk. He managed. He had a big house. He had money. At least, enough."

"But you don't even enjoy *your* money," I said. Keep him off-base.

"Sometimes I do," he said, picking up a recorder with his free hand and tooting a note. "I play different parts. Sometimes I play a rich man." He went over, pulled back the curtains on the window by the music corner, opened the window, and looked out. The room became daytime-bright.

And Ted was somewhere outside now, I was sure of that. I prayed he wouldn't bumble in like I had.

Harry went over and opened the door a crack. He stood in the place where the door would hide him if it opened. *Watch out, Ted,* I prayed silently.

The door moved slightly. I held my breath. If Ted was looking in as I had, he'd see me there tied up. Like the captain's daughter tied to the mast in the storm. Like Joan of Arc tied to the stake. Like a damn fool who didn't figure out how to avoid getting trapped. The door stopped moving. He'd had the sense to suspect Harry's presence, I figured. Then in a few minutes I saw his face briefly at the music-corner window. My heart jumped into my throat. Harry raised his gun, but the face was gone. "You'd better get in here," he yelled, "or this woman is going to be dead meat." He slipped back into his place behind the door, out of sight.

The door suddenly burst open, and for a minute I thought Ted had managed to knock Harry back against the wall so hard that he was knocked out. He staggered, but he recovered.

"Don't move," Harry said, "or I'll shoot you and then I'll shoot her. If anybody hears, they'll think I'm hunting.

"Come right on over and see your love," Harry said tauntingly. He kept the gun in Ted's back as he hurried toward my Joan of Arc post.

"Thank God you're alive," Ted said. I guessed his thanks might not last long.

Harry ordered him to stand with his back to the post. And since Harry had tied the end of the twine to the post back when he spider-webbed me, all he had to do was keep the gun on us and repeat his round and round.

"One false move and I'll shoot her," he told Ted.

The last time we were nearly killed we were tied up. We were in a horrible rut. It was at least less final than being shot. So far.

"What are you going to do?" Ted asked him.

"I intend to leave you here," he said, winding round and round. "With the doors and windows shut tight and the gas on. I'll get out. These mountains are getting too dangerous. I've come to my senses. Too bad I didn't manage to get your father's money," he said to me sadly. "He's the richest plum I've tried to pick. And I'll really miss Mary and the kids. They're nice kids." He smiled fondly as if he meant that. Some part of his cracked self could love kids. While he killed their relatives.

"I guess I won't need my pocketbook," I said. "I've been so careful not to leave it anywhere, and today I was so upset that I left it on the table in the kitchen."

Harry was still circling.

"I saw it when I got home." Ted's voice came from behind me, but so close. One of his hands touched mine.

Harry laughed. "This is silly talk for your last minutes on earth."

My mind raced. My pocketbook was still there in case Mustache came by.

"Did you lock the door?" I asked. I'd left the door from the kitchen to garage swinging open.

"I rushed out the front door so fast," Ted said, "that I didn't do anything but leave." I could tell he sensed I had a reason for asking.

That meant one chance in a million that Mustache saw the open garage door and then my pocketbook and read the notes in it. And we had the other chance: that somebody would pick up a message sweater. We absolutely had to delay Harry from turning on the gas.

"My father's coins aren't in the bank yet," I told Harry. He stopped and stood in front of me. "I'll tell you how to get hold of them," I said, "and I have signing privileges on my fathers bank account. I'll even sign a big check for you. Then I'll call the bank on that phone and tell them it's O.K. In return, you leave us tied up and maybe drugged but alive, which will give you time to escape and become somebody else."

Because, of course, he would become somebody else. He had been a well-off investment counselor and a poor poet and even briefly a cowboy. But he always remained a half-crazy kid, with the heart scared out of him. Dangerous as a snake.

I knew that after he got the money and the coins he would kill us anyway, but perhaps I could delay him long enough for help to arrive.

"There's one of Pop's checkbooks in the glove compartment of my car," I said. "The compartment is locked. The car keys are in my skirt pocket."

I could see he was torn. I was sure he didn't need the money. It was handy to have, but in fact it obviously meant more to him than buying power: He must get some kind of a tremendous rush when he stole something valuable from the person he knew he was going to kill. Something like that.

Finally he went out to look in the car.

Both of us worked hard at our bonds while he was gone.

But soon I heard Harry storming back. There was, of course, no checkbook. He slammed into the room angrily. "You lied to me," he shouted. "I don't let people lie to me." He was red in the face. I was afraid he was going to shoot me.

Ted waited until he paused for breath, and then he said to me, "You must have left the checkbook in the box in the trunk."

"I can't remember." I tried to sound pitiful, so Harry would calm down.

Harry stared at Ted, then at me. He didn't know whether to believe us. "And how do I get hold of the coins?" he asked. "Tell me that and I can check it and see if I should believe you're on the level about the bank."

The coins were actually in a safe deposit box but, thank God, he didn't know that. If I could get him to go and search, that would be a real reprieve.

"My father had Sherrie bury them out by his pond. I was furious at him, but with Pop, you can't always stop him from acting like a nut."

I could see Harry believed that. It was the sort of thing Pop almost might have done. But Harry wouldn't need me to get the coins. I'd made a tactical mistake.

"If you called the bank," he said sadly, "you'd have some way to alert them. You're trying to trap me, aren't you? You're trying to fool me and put me off," he shouted. He was suddenly out of control. He slapped me hard on both cheeks so that I felt like my neck might snap. Somehow I knew his father used to do that. His father obviously did worse. But Harry stepped back and said, "I'm not a violent person. You just got to me." His face creased with pain as if he were ashamed of himself. So putting us to sleep forever was O.K. — but hitting made him feel like his father and he hated that.

He pulled himself back together. "You're trying to put off death. But I'm in charge." He marched off and closed the windows and locked them. He checked that he hadn't left anything of his in the room, then took a paper towel and used it to keep his fingers from touching the knobs on the stove as he turned on four burners and the oven. Then he walked quickly over to the door, turned around, and said, almost kindly, "You won't feel any pain." Then he became brisker. "But be quiet. If I hear you screaming, I'll come back and shoot you." He shut the door tightly in back of him. I heard the lock turn, and he was gone.

I wondered if I ought to hold my breath. But I couldn't hold it forever.

I was struggling with my bonds, but I couldn't get them loose. I could hear Ted writhing against his. They might be nothing but heavy burlap twine, but they worked.

I heard a car outside. It must be Harry driving away in the Rolls. No, he was going to leave the Rolls. He must be driving away in our car, except it sounded like he was coming closer. I must be getting woozy from the gas. I went on struggling for all I was worth. My wrists were raw. The gas smell was getting stronger.

"He's far enough away so he won't come back," Ted gasped. "Let's yell as loud as we can." We raised the roof.

To my amazement somebody yelled back. And then somebody was battering the door. It was a pretty solid door, but finally I heard it splinter. Ah, sweet music.

I was never in my life so glad to see the police. Mustache rushed over and turned off the gas burners while someone else began opening the windows. Someone undid our bonds and pulled us outdoors. I can't tell you how beautiful the outdoors was. The trees were as green as in a dream. The sky was magic blue. And the air! I gulped it in.

The young man who'd pulled us out looked pleased to see us so alive.

"Sandy Lyon is outside in the back of the Rolls-Royce, and Harry August is on his way to my father's fish pond," I told our savior.

I could see he thought that I was drunk from breathing gas.

CHAPTER
31

MONDAY, OCTOBER 12
SWEET MUSIC OF LOVE, PLAY ON

"You brought the book?" Ted asked as he stopped for a red light.

"Oh, yes. I promised Sandy Lyon I'd return it at lunch." I patted the super-memory book in my lap. "Boy," I said, "there sure are a lot of ways that people try to improve their memories — everything from drinking gingko tea to eating sardines to learning to relax." I flipped through the book. "But Sandy was right. The ways I liked the best were musical ones. Imagine! It says here that you can remember what you learn better, just by listening to baroque music while you learn it."

"That's why I'm so smart," Ted said. "Because I like Vivaldi and Bach." The light changed and he sped forward.

"I wrote down the name of a company it says you can send off to. You can get a tape with subliminal suggestions, the kind so fast you don't even consciously hear them, mixed in with that kind of music."

"I see that you never intend to stop improving your mind."

"My mind could use it," I said. "Harry almost made a complete dead fool out of me."

"And me, Vivaldi and all."

"How amazing," I said, "that I could scared silly by a helicopter that was nothing in the world but the air-ambulance from Mission Hospital. I wonder if any of the other people involved in this case were as gullible as I was and still won't admit it."

Ted passed an old car with three kids and two hounds in the backseat. They were all squirming.

"Since we're off to the ex-suspects' lunch, you can ask them," he said. "But give yourself credit. Harry had an amazingly clever streak mixed in with his craziness. Mustache is pretty sure that it was Harry who called the helicopter on a false alarm to some place on Reem's Creek just to fool you."

"He had crazy good luck mixed with final bad luck," I said. "He never knew himself well enough to escape being twisted by the really bizarre things that froze him when he was a kid. Harry was the monster. Not Dracula Jr. Kind of eerie that Harry chose to swallow his whole supply of the sleeping pills he hated so much. He didn't even try to get out of town. He just gave up. In a way, I guess he died when he was fifteen years old. Or maybe younger." We passed two teenagers coming out of the Weaverville post office, laughing. I was almost able to be sorry for Harry.

"The thing that scared me most," I said, "was when I thought that you might die because I forgot to push the ENTER button on my Wizard." I sighed. This was no time to be negative. We were alive and well. "But the truth is," I went on, "that in life, you're not so likely to be done in because you goof to begin with, as because you give up trying after that. Right?"

"Exactly," Ted said as he drove into the parking place right across from the Four-Cent Cotton Cafe.

Inside, we found most of the ex-suspects and ex-victims. Sandy Lyon was our host. We were the last to arrive.

"I've invited you all out to lunch," he said, "even though it's only a short while since our recent trials, because I am grateful to each of you." We were alone in the intimate little restaurant, which is usually closed on Monday. The chef, who was a friend of Sandy's, had fixed a special assorted-salad lunch just for us.

I suspected we had all come partly because we were so curious as to why Sandy had asked us. Ulterior motive was written all over his face.

"Welcome to our survivors' celebration!" Now that he wasn't weighted down with unrequited love, Sandy seemed to be sprouting a wry sense of humor. But I got a lump in my throat. One of us hadn't survived. Poor Silva would have liked to be here! I never knew Matt Jones, but Silva had become a friend — always nervous, but always kind to Pop.

Our host was not just plain O.K. but absolutely blooming. Ted and I really liked Sandy. We had liked him all along. In fact we were hoping that Mary's sudden interest in him would bear fruit. The same could *not* be said of Donald Duck, glowering in his beret, which he never took off. Say, maybe he was going prematurely bald and trying to hide it! And I had an idea that Loy/Dracula Jr., who was poker-faced and in his black-suit mode for the occasion, was jealous of Sandy.

Pop had been unwilling to miss the event and Sherrie, officially on duty, had wheeled him right up to the end of the table. She wore black chiffon without enough underwear. Come to think of it, I wondered if she owned any underwear except one or two lacy slips. Even when Pop found out that she was the one who had told Harry about the coin collection to begin with, Pop refused to fire her. At least, the coins were now in the bank. Of course, I'd thought that once before.

Mustache had found time to come. Perhaps, since Pop and had been involved with four murders within a year, he thought we needed watching. He'd come right over to me and handed me my sweaters and jacket. "As I told you on the phone," he said, "these were brought in to us by a terrified tourist, a kid hoping for a reward, and a farmer who wanted to know if this was a joke. It would not have been a joke if we'd had to wait for him. They all came in the day after you all were almost gassed to death."

"Which is why it helps to send out several SOSs," I said. "One of them might work."

"And besides," Ted said, "I saw the sweaters, and although I didn't figure I had time to stop, I knew I was going the right way."

"And one of your SOSs *did* work," Mustache said. "It's lucky I knew your ways. As soon as I arrived at your house and found the door open from the garage into the house and your pocketbook sitting there, I remembered what you told me: 'If you ever see this pocketbook without me, you'll know I've been kidnapped or worse.' So I looked in your pocketbook, and there was your note. I took the pocketbook as evidence and sent men to both houses, Harry August's and Sandy Lyon's."

I said, "Thank God," and gave him a hug.

Mustache sat down next to Lily, who, as usual, was looking warm and maternal and frumpy. She patted his hand and said "You did a good job."

We all began to sip wine and munch on rolls.

I was sitting between Loy and Ted. "You see, I'm on time, and it was no effort at all!" I said to Loy. "Your system of shocking images really helps. We had to be here at quarter of one, which is a slightly offbeat time. But I just searched for a medieval thought and remembered they used to draw and quarter criminals."

"For somebody who says she can't remember anything, you come up with the damndest facts," Ted said, breaking his roll.

"Anyway," I said, buttering mine, "I just thought of a quarter of a man who had been drawn and quartered. Quarter of one. Then I couldn't forget."

We were only a few seats down from Sandy and Mary.

Sandy pulled his white beard and shook his head. "It can't be good for you," he said, "to think shocking thoughts all day. But help may be at hand."

Then he stood up, raised his voice, and spoke to all of us. "First," he said, "I'd like to propose a toast to my late aunt Martha, whose kind bequest has made it possible for me to be generous to my friends."

We all drank to that. At least the Rolls-on-teacher's-salary issue was put to rest.

"Next," he said, "I have a little memento for each of you since we've all been through a very difficult time together."

The general curiosity upped several degrees. Our eyes were all on our host. I wondered if the twinkle in his eye was entirely benign.

"For Lily, who spends her whole time trying to nurture us with special treats, and was a suspect because of her goodness I have a box of chocolate-covered cherries, which I understand are her favorite.

"For Sherrie, an item of clothing which can

be exchanged if it is the wrong size. Mary picked it out for me." Sherrie immediately put down her wineglass and opened the package. It was a black-lace bra. Sherrie laughed and said, "I guess every girl should have one." Why, she was getting almost mellow.

And when he wasn't lovesick, Sandy had a downright racy sense of humor.

"For Loy," he said, "this package contains a nice big desk calendar, so he can be sure to remember what century it is."

Loy raised his wineglass in a toast. "And may you remember the decade, even when you're out in your 1930s Rolls-Royce."

"For Donald," Sandy continued, "I have a new green beret. The black one he has is too funereal now that we're all safe."

Donald downed the rest of his glass of wine and snarled, "This is all silly. You're here to tell us Mary's had such a shock she's going to marry you, isn't that right? I give it six months."

I crossed my fingers. Married? Let it be so.

But Sandy wouldn't be ruffled. "Your painting is better than your casual charm, Donald," he said, and picked up another package that was plainly a bottle.

"For Lieutenant Wilson, I have a bottle of champagne to celebrate the fact that he and his men managed to save Ted and Peaches, and incidentally save me from suspicion of murdering them."

Mustache thanked him.

"For Ted and Pop, I have twin bottles of champagne to celebrate the fact that neither one was killed. Good to have you aboard."

Pop said, "Hot dog!"

"Now, next to last, I have a present for the woman who sometimes refers to herself, I'm told, as the Absent-Minded Matchmaker. The world needs matchmakers." Was he really about to make an announcement about himself and Mary? Everybody at the table sat up and listened. Some beamed, like Lily. Loy sagged. Donald Duck glowered.

But Sandy still turned toward me, announcement undelivered, present in hand. "So that you may not have to think shocking thoughts all day in order to remember, this present is for you, Peaches. Also in gratitude for the fact that you and Ted were kind enough to avoid dying in my house. I might never have gotten over that shock."

Ted said the pleasure of not dying in Sandy's house was entirely mutual.

Sandy handed me a square box wrapped in satiny red paper. I opened it up, and inside was a portable cassette player with headphones.

"I've taken the liberty of getting you a tape of the kind of music that's supposed to increase your learning-power," he said. "And I've had it specially programmed with subliminal messages that say you *can* remember. Just listen to this while you're gardening or working around the house or whatever. See if it works."

I was pleased. I told him I had actually been thinking of sending off for a tape like that. And that I was very grateful.

I thought, Wow, what big important presents. What had come over him?

"And this is for Mary," he said, "because when I told her I was going to get Peaches a Walkman she said, 'Gee, I've always wanted one of those.' Her subliminal message says she's going to be very happy." We all leaned forward expecting him to say why.

Mary took the package in red shiny paper like mine, and she beamed.

"Now you may wonder," Sandy said, "why I'm so joyful and grateful to you all. It's because of a happy announcement I have to make." Yes, yes, I thought. Hurry up.

"Last month Mary here told me she'd only go out with me every six weeks because we were going to be friends. She said I was kind but not really her type. Not exciting."

Donald said, "I'll drink to that!" but the waiter hadn't yet refilled his glass, so he didn't.

"Now, friends, you know that almost broke my heart. But after the late excitement that you all so kindly contributed to, she says that what she really wants is a nice, uneventful man. I have the pleasure of announcing we will be married in December, and you are all invited."

We all broke into applause except Donald. I wondered why he stayed, of course he was waiting for that glass of wine.

At that moment our food began arriving, and, as we ate, the rest of us proposed toasts friendlier than Donald's.

I managed to get Mary aside in the ladies room. "I think this is great," I said. "I have to admit I thought you were only attracted to mean men."

She grinned. "They are sexier. But when I saw that I let a killer baby-sit my kids — boy, talk about shock therapy! And Sandy's very good at hugging when you feel shocked."

"I'm glad," I told her. That was an understatement.

"Actually," she said, "that chapter you gave me about socks helped."

I stood there with my mouth open, amazed.

"Yes," she said. "Where you said you have to tell a kid that life is a trade-off, and you simply have to make the best deal you can. My mother never taught me that. She taught me you had to be perfect or forget it. When I had my shock therapy, I realized that when it came to men I wasn't making the best deal I could."

Shock therapy plus sock therapy. Never mind. Something worked!

As soon as we got home I put on my earphones and began to play my tape. "Just sounds like music," I said.

"Of course," Ted said. "That's what subliminal means. You don't consciously hear whatever it is. The sound flashes by too fast."

I noticed what a kind mouth he has. I kissed it. I put my arms around him and felt the solidness of his muscles. I felt his warmth like a drink of whiskey. Maybe the survivors' luncheon had reminded me of how close we'd come to dying. I kissed him again. "We could take a nap, so to speak."

He kissed me. "Yes, we could."

The doorbell rang. Whoever it was, I didn't want to see them.

"I'll go," Ted said. "We won't let them stay." There was lipstick on his cheek. I didn't notice it until his hand was on the doorknob.

There stood Sandy, puffing and pink in the face. "I gave you the wrong tape," he said in alarm. He stared at the lipstick on Ted's cheek. He got pinker. His mouth quivered like he might laugh.

"Don't ask me how I got the packages mixed, but I had a red marker on Mary's and a green marker on yours. And when she took hers out to try it, I saw what a terrible mistake I'd made. I certainly don't want Mary to keep remembering and acting like she used to act!" He handed me a tape with a green label on it. "This is yours. I need the other one for Mary."

He squirmed in that aw-shucks way. Like he was doing something he felt sheepish about.

"What's on Mary's tape?" I asked. I did not hand him the tape I had. "I've been sublimned by this. I have a right to know. Now, 'fess up."

He turned beet-red. But then he laughed. "You promise you won't tell?"

"If there's one thing we're good at," Ted said, "it's not telling."

"I want her to be happy," he said. "There's nothing wrong with that."

"No," I said. "Of course not."

"It says 'Kind men are wildly sexy.' "

We all three of us got the giggles. You might say that Ted and I were too old for the giggles. But who's to say who is too old for what?

The employees of G.K. Hall hope you have enjoyed this Large Print book. All our Large Print titles are designed for easy reading, and all our books are made to last. Other G.K. Hall books are available at your library, through selected bookstores, or directly from us.

For information about titles, please call:

(800) 223-2336

To share your comments, please write:

Publisher
G.K. Hall & Co.
P.O. Box 159
Thorndike, ME 04986